KATHA

Rupa . Co

KATHA PRIZE STORIES - VOLUME 1

'The conception and execution of the *Katha Prize Stories* series surely represents a unique and special moment in Indian publishing history ... What has emerged out of this conscious and well-planned exercise is a fascinatingly supple range of short fiction ... Sure to provide fresh impetus to readers for a deeper engagement with the rich plurality of our own regional literatures.'

— The Economic Times

'. . . an excellent collection . . . the range of craftsmanship and technique is amazing, ranging as they do from surrealism to stream of consciousness and even a bit of magic realism . . .'

— The Hindu

'Readers will effortlessly float through these 185 pages . . .'

— Sunday Chronicle

'There is here an elegance of language . . . and above all there is an intuition about English, an understanding of the charged effect it can produce by its conventions of the wry understatement.'

— The Hindustan Times

'. . . refreshing . . . transcends but does not erase linguistic character.'

— The Times of India

'. . . wonderfully lifelike characters . . . a fine collection of short stories . . .'

— Indian Review of Books

This book was made possible by a grant from ITDC Ltd.

KATHA

PRIZE
STORIES
VOLUME 2

The best short fiction published
during 1989-92 in twelve Indian
languages, chosen by a panel of
distinguished writers and scholars.

Edited by
Geeta Dharmarajan

First published in 1992 by
KATHA
CII/27 Tilak Lane, New Delhi 110 001

Distributed by
RUPA & CO.
15, Bankim Chatterjee Street, Calcutta 700 070
94, South Malaka, Allahabad, 211 001
P.G. Solanki Path, Lamington Road, Bombay 400 007
7/16 Ansari Road, Daryaganj, New Delhi 110 002

Book Design: Designations
Logo Design: Crowquill
Original Cover Design: Taposhi Ghoshal

Typeset in 10 on 13 pt. Garamond by R. Ajith Kumar at Katha.
Laser output by Alphabets, New Delhi.
Made and printed in India at Pauls Press, New Delhi.

ISBN 81-85586-08-x (hardback)
ISBN 81-85586-09-8 (paperback)

CONTENTS

THE NOMINATING EDITORS

The Katha Awards have been
made possible by a grant from
India Tourism Development Corporation Ltd.

PREFACE

It is said that everything that has happened or is to happen has already been told; that with Vyasa's *Mahabharata,* all plots have been exposed. Yet, here are nineteen stories nominated from twelve languages which we believe tell the story as it has not been said before. Quintessentially Indian, each one is wrapped in a certain magic that tries to communicate a culture, the 'codes, beliefs and acts of our daily life,' a way of speaking that belongs to a special little place in the world created by a language called Assamese or Tamil, Gujarati or Oriya — to name only a few of the languages represented here — and yet is shared by all of us who are Indian.

These stories have been chosen by a distinguished panel of people whose knowledge of their own language is respected. Except for the English nominations, which are being published here for the first time, the others were selected out of fiction published in the last three years, 1989 – 1992, making these stories doubly special — this is not the work of one but of many hands. Somewhere an editor of a reputed publishing house or magazine had chosen to publish a story that a writer herself or himself had singled out of all their writings . . . and out of this exercise have come stories whose common claim is only to excellence. Translated specially for this volume, these seventeen stories alongside the two written originally in English receive the Katha Awards for 1992.

For this volume, we have tried to include as many languages as possible though the *Katha Prize Stories* series does not even *try* to be representative. Due to reasons beyond our control, only twelve languages are included here; also, Shri Khushwant Singh's Punjabi nominations and Shri Nrisingh Rajpurohit's Rajasthani, came in too late for inclusion.

As with our last collection, we see this as a book primarily for the Indian reader who wants to read what is being written today in the various languages which she/he cannot read. We could not see italics as the magic device one sometimes wishes for that can give meaning to the word it singles out from the narrative. We have tried to use Indian words as naturally as possible. But we did worry over what and how many words to gloss. We have used the footnote rather than a full-fledged glossary, and this too, grudgingly, only to explain those words which the context does not elucidate, or as in *Kandhas,* where a little more information would make the story more accessible. Also, we have tried not to reduce words to a standardised Hindi pronunciation. Hence, *kumkum* in north Indian languages is *kunku* in Marathi, *kunkuma* in Telugu and *kunkumam* in Tamil and stays so in the English translation.

We have been lucky to find sensitive translators; some of them new-comers to this exciting but exacting craft. And, for the first time also, we have tried team translations. For a whole year we have been hoping to refute the belief that, in India, translating between the languages can only be via English or Hindi. So much is lost in a second generation translation. We wanted to translate our last year's stories directly from their source languages into Tamil; and are yet to succeed. We hope that team translation is the way out!

This has been a learning process all the way, starting with something as irritating and finally so Indian as the dancing tenses, the easy mercury-like movement between the past and the present, to translating Bimal Kar's very clever use of a simple syntax and the definite article to create a certain atmosphere of innocence.

We dared to take on M.T. Vasudevan Nair's story after he had warned us that it was 'highly untranslatable.' The very word 'yakshi' gave our translator many sleepless nights! It couldn't be 'ghost' or 'spirit' for both these words came loaded with certain connotations, undesirable in the context of the story; hence we decided to leave 'yakshi' as yakshi hoping that Yakshi herself would be better able to explain herself than mere translators! Also, the rich, complicated Kerala ethos with its backdrop of the matriarchal family house or taravaadu, the receding feudal set-up and the joint family system that has begun to crack up, and the colloquial words used by Nair added up to make this one of the most difficult stories to translate.

Mohan Parmar's 'Wado' was a story that we had to read many times before it would reveal itself. It speaks obliquely of an extramarital affair, at another man as the double of Khemo, the husband. Its sensitive use of imagery puts it in a class by itself. Bhupen Khakhar's 'Pages from a Diary' was another difficult story to translate. To retain the flavour and casualness of random diary entries, we finally resorted to a conscious use of Indian English. An unsentimental, almost mystical depiction of homosexuality, it represents here one of the two movements responsible for the recent changes taking place in Gujarati — the Gadyaparva movement led by Bharat and Geeta Naik (The other is Parishkrit-varta led by Ajit Thakore, represented here by 'Wado.') In the other languages too, though the level of experimentation does not seem to be as high, there does seem to be a fresh wind blowing, bringing in its wake more publishing outlets for short fiction, more discerning editors, and a spate of new writing. An exciting new time for the short story seems to be just around the corner!

This volume of *Katha Prize Stories* would have been impossible without the warm and continued support of many. First amongst this would be the people who agreed so spontaneously, with such unstinting generosity, to be our Nominating Editors; and ITDC Ltd., without whose grant we could not have given the prize money to our writers and translators. I would also especially like to thank Laura Sykes for editorial help. If there are still too many words and expressions that are not Standard English, they are there in spite of her good advice. My thanks also go out to staff members, past and present. And to those others who have helped so much yet wish to remain anonymous, my thanks are as heartfelt.

A friend I really miss is Rosalind Wilson. She was a Council member, a member of the Katha editorial committee and, above all, a person I knew I could always turn to when help was needed, or advice. On behalf of Katha I would like to dedicate this volume to the memory of Rosalind.

New Delhi, September 1992   Geeta Dharmarajan

M T VASUDEVAN NAIR

•

LITTLE EARTHQUAKES

•

NOMINATED BY SUJATHA DEVI
TRANSLATED BY D KRISHNA AYYAR
AND RAJI SUBRAMANIAM

Listen. I must tell you something. It is really interesting. How fearfully they talk about her, how scared they sound. I don't always understand what they say but . . . even I believe them sometimes.

'She'll pierce you with her damshtra, that fierce canine tooth of hers and grrr . . . she'll suck all your blood in one go. And your bones? She'll chew them up with her giant molars and spit them out.'

And who is this she? Why, it is poor Kunjathaal, the yakshi. They say she comes twice every day: At ucchakkaanam, and once again at midnight. They say, You can see her walking on the upper slope of the parambu.*

Ucchakkaanam is that time of day which begins when Amma lies down in the kitchen for a nap after she's handed out the rice kanji to the servants and ends when Valiamma, my mother's elder sister, gets up to make the afternoon tea. It is called ucchakkaanam in our home. God knows what language that is!

It is at that time that Akkara Mutthashi — the grandmother who has come from the hamlet across the river to live with us in her old age — goes for a stroll in the parambu. She picks leaves and roots. Mutthashi alone knows which are medicinal. Before she dies she must pass on the secret to a little girl in the family, the kutty she likes best. Who else but me!

When Mutthashi became bedridden I started going alone to the parambu, when there was no one around to stop me. Amma and Valiamma say that it must have been then that some evil spirit possessed me. And there is this Thekkukaran Ravunni Nair to fan the flame. 'All this trouble started when this cursed old hag came here,' he says, putting the blame squarely on Mutthashi.

But when I go out I only see this other witch who walks stealthily

---

Except in towns, the pattern in Kerala is one of houses surrounded by groves and woods, ponds and, usually a serpent mound. This area is called *parambu*.

'Little Earthquakes' was first published in Malayalam as *'Cheriya Cheriya Bhookambangal'* in *India Today* (Malayalam), 22 August 1990, Madras.

through the parambu. No one knows about her, but me. She is none other than Valiamma's precious daughter. Sarojini Edathi. People don't know about her 'celestial' lover either, the gandharvan who waits for her on the steps of the Nambudiri's outer pond, fishing with line and tackle.

At ucchakkaanam every day I also see the one who stands at the wooden grille in the western wing of the house, all excited, gesticulating to Nanikutty who wanders into the parambu on the pretext of grazing her goats. It's my brother. If you ask me, Ettan is the one who's possessed. But who'll believe me?

And she who sits drying her hair in the inner courtyard . . . She drives me away as soon as she sees me. She won't let me even peep into the large books filled with photographs of cinema stars that she devours every day. That woman thinks she's something great. She's just three years older than me, and my own sister too. But what's the use? She has no time for me.

One day, at ucchakkaanam, I was taking a stroll in the parambu. And . . . there was someone under the mango tree. At once I knew that this was the yakshi they'd been talking about.

I wanted to run but my feet wouldn't move. I wanted to scream but no sound would come out of me. I closed my eyes tight and chanted 'Arjunan, Phalgunan Arjunanphalgu . . .'

I heard a soft voice.

'Janakikutty.'

It had a strange fondness in it. I liked the way she called me by my full name. Others call me Jatti.

I opened my eyes slowly. Kunjathaal was standing next to me.

You've seen the Athemmar girl, haven't you, she who was married off to that Kunnamkulam boy? Well, Kunjathaal looked exactly like that. A white mundu with the traditional kara and kuri; a white blouse; a white cloth around her shoulder. She had a red spot of chaandu on her forehead. Studs in her ears. A necklace of sovereigns around the neck.

'Why has Janakikutty come alone?' she asked.

I kept quiet.

'Why doesn't Janakikutty's Mutthashi come nowadays?'

I couldn't take my eyes off her mouth as she talked. I told myself that I should not show her that I'm frightened. So I asked her as if I was not at all scared, 'Where is your damshtra?'

The Athemmarkutty burst into laughter. Ah, what pretty teeth! She said, 'The damshtra grows big only when we have a prey. But it scares everyone away. That's why we have no one to play with.'

In the rear slopes of the parambu there is a dilapidated outhouse. A servant used to stay there. Around it is a thicket of palm trees. Yakshi went and sat there, took out betel leaves and nuts from the folds of her mundu, tucked them between her molars and started chewing.

I looked longingly at her. Yakshi glanced at me as she said, 'Small children shouldn't chew betel.'

I collected seven small smooth pebbles. We sat there and played my favourite game, kothengkallu. You should see Yakshi playing! How easily she scooped up four, five stones at each throw. Naturally, it was Kunjathaal who won. That is what Yakshi likes me to call her.

'Tomorrow, Janakikutty, you win.'

She smiled. What if I lose? At least I have someone to play with.

Yakshis are so true to their word. If my edathi says, 'I'll give it to you tomorrow,' it means she's putting me off. She won't give it to me. But yakshis are not like that. And the next day, it was I who won.

Every day at dusk, Mutthashi teaches me to say my prayers. This has started recently, after she heard my mother say, 'At least this much good can come from this good-for-nothing hag.'

I have not seen my real Mutthashi, that is, Amma's and Valiamma's mother. She died years ago. This Akkara Mutthashi is my real Mutthashi's younger sister. Amma and Valiamma, when talking about this Mutthashi, always say, 'It is due to this hag's character that her children didn't look after her. Etta!' Etta is their own language of abuse. And when this Mutthashi was laid up in bed Amma moaned: 'What problems! Now I have to wait on this wretched old hag.'

That evening I told Mutthashi about Yakshi and how I played kothengkallu with her.

'Shhh . . . Don't tell this to anyone,' Mutthashi warned. 'I know these yakshis. None of them will harm you, kutty,' she whispered in my ears.

When we got bored with kothengkallu, Yakshi and I would roam all over the parambu. It was then that I saw Karineeli.* You know that parapoodam* that comes dancing in the Velakali temple festival. And you must have seen Kali who comes to sweep our courtyard and collect the cowdung. Kali looks just like the parapoodam and this Karineeli is a younger version of our Kali. Karineeli wears no blouse; only necklaces made of stones and beads. Her teeth are black. That may be because she chews betel.

Karineeli was standing beneath the kanjira tree. I didn't know who she was. Kunjathaal was angry. She muttered, 'Hmm . . . ! That Karineeli!'

Yakshi and Karineeli stood glaring at each other. I have seen Amma and Valiamma staring at each other like that. This was much more frightening. I feared war. But nothing happened.

'Why does thampuratti* not let me join her game?' Neeli asked.

My friend Kunjathaal grimaced, then nodded her head. 'Okay. Come.'

Karineeli drew a game board on the ground. She brought broken tiles. And the three of us sat there and played vattu.

When I told all this to Mutthashi that evening she patted me and said, 'Nothing wrong with you, kutty. No evil will befall you.'

One day when we were walking through the compound Kunjathaal showed me the brahmarakshas.* It was standing on that dilapidated platform on which we had played kothengkallu. You've seen Kunju Nambudiri who died, haven't you? Imagine Kunju Nambudiri grown

---

There are many other-worldly characters who people Janakikutty's world. *Kunjathaal* and *Athemmar* (page 15) are derivations from the word 'Akathullaval,' or the 'lady inside,' meaning a Nambudiri Brahmin woman. 'Kunju' means kutty or child. While, *brahmarak-shas* is the spirit of a Brahmin, *Karineeli* and *parapoodam* are the spirits of lower caste persons. In temple festivals, a man wearing a dark mask plays the part of parapoodam.

Thampuratti: literally means queen. All upper caste women were addressed thus.

three times as tall. The bramarakshas was exactly like that.

'If we don't go near it, not even for a friendly chat, it won't do us any harm,' Kunjathaal said.

As a matter of fact it did not even look at us. Unlike those other friends of Neeli — Parakutty, Karikutty and Kallaadimutthan who always hid in the thicket and peeped at us. Sometimes they dared to inch towards us but one stare from Kunjathaal would make them scurry back into their holes!

One day, a poisonous thorn pierced my foot. The wound was deep. Neeli got angry and started abusing Kallaadimutthan. 'If the wound turns septic and Kutty suffers . . . I'll . . . You . . .'

Next day there was not even the pain of an ant bite. These people are so true to their word.

I used to sleep with my Mutthashi but now I sleep at the foot of Amma's bed, next to my sister. Edathi doesn't like this. She goes to sleep early, except on those days when Sarojini Edathi joins us. Then they jabber away till Amma comes.

I don't sleep well these nights. It's not a sickness like these people say. The reason is a secret. Shall I tell you why? It is jealousy. Envy of Kunjathaal and Neeli who could wander around and play even at night.

Once I saw them walking through the plantain grove munching something. I went to the window and called out softly. 'Kunjathaal . . . Neeli!' But they didn't hear me at all. What friends!

It was then that my mother woke up and what an earthquake there was! She lit the lamps. Everyone came running. Mutthashi also came, dragging her frail frame, grabbling the walls for support. Amma shrieked, 'We have enough troubles, you old hag! Don't add to them. If you should fall down, collapse . . . Maaranam.'

Paniker was sent for. He was a clever man. He arranged cowries on the floor, studied the indications and told them all about my playing with Kunjathaal and Neeli — at least that's what they told me. But shall I tell you how they were fooled by him? When he said that Thekkanchovva was also with us, these people believed him at once. That's where Paniker made a mistake.

Paniker sent a hundred and one rupees through Ravunni Nair. An offering to the goddess Anakkara Bhagavathy. Good. May Bhagavathy enjoy the gift.

But, believe me, Thekkanchovva has never come to play with us. Or Vadakkanchovva. Even if they come, we shall not ask them to join us. How do we know what kind of people they are?

At times Amma would feel sad. Sometimes she'd be angry. I've heard her mutter so many times, 'What if somebody falls ill? What if somebody dies? The father of my children, what does he care?'

But how can Achhan come here every now and then leaving his job in the tea estate at Valpara. Ettan has been there once. He says if they bring in even one basket of tea leaves that are not tender enough, Achhan rejects the whole lot. Even while processing the leaves Achhan has to be there. If Achhan doesn't supervise these things then complaints will pour in from shopkeepers — 'Is this tea or is it dust?' and the customers will grumble, 'This tea tastes like tamarind water.'

It was when he recruited a woman on the pretext of needing an extra hand on the estate that Achhan lost his head. That is what Amma says. If this urvashi tries any of her tricks on Achhan, I will tell Kunjathaal. If I haven't done so yet it's because when she gets angry her damshtra comes out, and then it won't be this urvashi alone who'll get hurt. Achhan will too.

Even when I'm quiet, Edathi and Sarojini stare at me. I don't like it. When I stare back at them they run away. They are a little afraid of me. Aren't they?

Every day even now I go to Mutthashi after my head-bath. Mutthashi rubs rasnadi powder on my head. So vigorously that it hurts a little. Then she presses her finger, still smelling of the powder, to my nostril. To prevent my catching cold.

My school is about an hour's walk from home. It seems Achhan had written to say that I shouldn't walk down to school. Amma and Edathi seem to have agreed. If I go walking people will see me and what will happen to their prestige then!

If they'd asked me, I could have told them that there is a short cut. How many times have Kunjathaal, Neeli and I walked or run through the western end of our grove to Asari's parambu near the bridge. I don't know why people foist fake diseases on me.

But now they are on the look-out for someone to come and teach me at home. And they have clamped another restriction on me: No going to the parambu, noon or no noon.

I told Kunjathaal when she came near the deserted snake mound that day. So Kunjathaal and Neeli started coming into the house when everyone was asleep, during ucchakkaanam. We'd walk through all the rooms. We'd laugh at the funny postures of those sleeping. One day Ettan, who usually stood at the western window waving to Nanikutty, saw me and came at me with his hand raised. Kunjathaal's damshtra started lengthening dangerously. 'Don't do anything!' I warned her. That's why she held back. Neeli starts spitting when someone makes her angry. And immediately that someone's body breaks out in bubble-like eruptions. If Neeli didn't spit now, it was only because *I* asked her not to.

We would always go to Mutthashi's room and play dice because Mutthashi never minded. Once Amma, or maybe it was Valliamma, saw us moving about in the house. At once . . . another earthquake. And another astrological consultation.

This time they called not one Paniker but a set of two other Panikers. And it was not my horoscope alone that was studied. Everybody brought their horoscopes along. And why not? After all, the Panikers had come from so far away.

Amma wanted to know all about this urvashi who had administered the magic potion to Achhan. Hence the drawing of patterns on the floor, the arranging of cowries and the incantations that went on and on, for practically everyone in the house. And walking up and down, up and down in the southern wing, pricking up her ears to listen to what the Panikers had to say about the prospects of her getting married, was . . . who else but Sarojini Edathi.

It was now decided that they would bring in a renowned sorcerer from Kallaadikottu or some such place. Thekkukaran Ravunni Nair went to meet this mantravadi and came back, having fixed an auspicious date for his visit. I overheard all that he said about that mantravadi.

Immediately I called Kunjathaal. She ought to know what they are going to do, no? A dagger would be made red hot on burning coals; nails would be driven into a log of the kanjira tree. The fire and the heat, the scalding and the piercing would drive the evil spirits away not merely from the humans but from the village itself.

Kunjathaal heard me out and pooh-poohed this with a giggle. So I told Mutthashi. Mutthashi also just laughed.

The Mantravadi came from Kallaadikottu and started the elaborate ritual. A lot of lamps were lit and a round, sacred kolam was drawn on the floor.

In the beginning I was a little scared. When Kunjathaal and Neeli came and stood behind me, I felt better. Then Mutthashi came, dragging her aged frame. She sat down beside me and all my fear vanished.

The man drove nails into the kanjira wood.

I turned around and looked furtively at Kunjathaal. Kunjathaal was in a rage. But Neeli winked at her and grinned.

Then the wood was set on fire.

Oh, what heat! How much smoke! I fell backwards. Kunjathaal held me and I promptly fell fast asleep.

'The evil spirits have all left. Disappeared! Now there will be no trouble whatsoever.' When the Mantravadi said this, I was resting my head on Kunjathaal's lap.

I laughed.

Kunjathaal whispered in my ears, 'Sleep Janakikutty, sleep.' She smelt of sandal paste and new clothes.

Next day Valiachhan, that is Sarojini Edathi's father came. Mine didn't.

Mutthashi sighed. 'Mmm. Just two months leave. Within that time he has to get Sarojinikutty married. Luckily, the bridegroom has been found.'

It was someone called Sankaranarayanan. He worked with Valiach-han.

Kunjathaal and Neeli crept quietly into the house that evening. Everyone believed that the Manthravadi's ritual had banished them from the village.

'Will I be fortunate enough to see Janakikutty's marriage?' Mutthashi asked Kunjathaal. Kunjathaal seemed lost in thought.

Now the other story: When Edathi and I went to bathe, Bhaskaran who fishes there with line and tackle was shouting at Sarojini Edathi. Sarojini Edathi's eyes were filled with tears. When they saw us, they moved away, heads bent.

The wedding would be at the Bhagavati temple; the feast at the house. How I wished Kunjathaal and Neeli and I could wear skirts and blouses of the same colour and style.

After Valiachhan came, the excitement started. People coming and going. Even on the day of the engagement ceremony there were about forty guests. Mutthashi was given Idichu Pizhinja Payasam, a delicacy made with lots of jaggery and coconut milk, besides the usual rice kanji. It was I who took it to her.

Mutthashi wanted to get up and get dressed. 'Even if it gets dark I want to go to the temple to see the wedding,' she said.

'No need,' Amma said brusquely, 'Two people would have to support you. Before she goes to the temple, Sarojini will come and do her namaskaram. You can bless her with rice and flowers.'

That day, Mutthashi fell down on her way to the bathroom.

'Ah, and this person wanted to climb to the hilltop Bhagavathy temple,' they sighed.

They lifted Mutthashi and put her on the cot in her room with Valiamma muttering all the time to Valiachhan, 'This is just what we want, isn't it?'

'A fall at this age, and there's no getting up.' Who else would say this but the all-knowing Ravunni Nair.

That night Mutthashi had high fever and vomiting. A doctor was brought from Padinjarangadi — a doctor with a large dot of sandalpaste on his forehead.

Mutthashi was restless.

I tiptoed into her room.

'Nothing serious. Don't worry,' she said to me.

My friends Kunjathaal and Neeli also came to look Mutthashi up when nobody was around.

Pacing up and down the courtyard Valiachhan cursed and harangued. 'This blasted woman! Sells and squanders everything, drives out her own children and when she has one foot in the grave she has to find this of all places to take refuge in.'

'It's mahodara,' Ravunni Nair said. 'The doctor said we'd better get her into the hospital.'

'Ha! Hospital! Even if it's a common cold, these doctors will say, Get into hospital. Must be getting a commission.'

Every once in a while Valiamma would moan, 'Oh God, what if she dies now . . .'

'Well then, good riddance. She is not our direct Mutthashi.'

'Whether you like it or not, she is the eldest member of the Taravaadu.* What difference does it make whether she is Mutthashi or Mutthashi's sister? If she dies there will be mourning,' Ravunni Nair told Valiachhan. Living as he did in Bombay, Valiachhan was quite ignorant in these matters.

In the midst of all this, Valiamma and Valiachhan went all the way to Thrissur to buy the clothes, utensils, and ornaments for the wedding. Only these Thrissur people know the latest fashions. Edathi wore the new jewels and preened herself before the mirror in the room where all the purchases were displayed for everybody to see.

Taravaadu is a joint family of Kerala, till recently, matriarchal.

I prayed and prayed that Kunjathaal and Neeli would come now. They did come that night . . . just when I was praising the beauty of all the things. Kunjathaal wasn't impressed. After all, she is a yakshi. If she wants she can magic all sorts of beautiful jewels out of thin air. And, as for Neeli, she doesn't want gold either. She is happy with her necklaces of stones that jingle when she walks. 'That's all we are allowed to wear,' Neeli once told me. 'Who said so?' And she merely said, 'That is the rule.'

The medicines prescribed by the doctor had arrived, but Mutthashi had not taken any of them. It was Ettan who found this out. Then Kunjan Vaidyar was brought in to treat Mutthashi.

Guests who came for the marriage would come to Mutthashi's door and peep in. A mother and daughter who'd come from Pattambi said to Mutthashi, 'Why give these people so much trouble? Pray to God to take you away. Aren't these children looking after you as best as they can?'

I was standing at the door when they came out. The mother peered at me. 'Isn't this Kunjukutty Amma's second daughter?'

The woman with them said, 'Hmm.'

'How is she now?'

'She's feeling better, they say.'

I went and sat on the floor near Mutthashi's cot, winnow in hand. With so much to be done for the wedding, I've been given many responsibilities. I have to clean all the lamps in the attic. I have to clean the rice and lentils. One day when I was doing this Kunjathaal and Neeli came in. I didn't talk to them. How could I when I had so much to do?

Since Sarojini Edathi would have to live in Bombay after her marriage, my elder sister is teaching her basic Hindi. It is on me that Sarojini Edathi practices what she learns.

'Jatti, bahar jaao!'

'Jatti, idhar aao!'

I in turn practised this on Kunjathaal and Neeli. What fun!

'Kunjathaal, idhar aao!'

'Neeli, idhar aao!'

While at this one day I heard a sudden call. I turned. Ettan was standing there saying, 'Edee! If you start all this nonsense again, watch out, I will tear you to pieces.'

'What's the matter?' Amma came running. And, seeing me she started muttering: 'Just in case anyone thinks we have money in this house, this cursed girl will see to it that it is exhausted! Go in,' Amma ordered. 'Don't you loiter outside at odd hours.'

I secretly signalled to Kunjathaal — It's all right! — and went in.

Achhan was to come that night. But he didn't. That created a little tremor. Then, there was a letter from him. He had very little leave; he would come on the day of the wedding and go back the same day. An earthquake!

Guests started pouring in. They were received. Jewellery was displayed, sarees and brocades too. Tall tales were exchanged.

Who had the time to see if Mutthashi or I had eaten?

I was mad with rage. That night, when Kunjathaal was on her usual beat, she looked in through the wooden grille in the southern wing of the house. 'Where is your damshtra?' I asked her. 'You'd better suck the blood of all these wretched people.'

'Really? You really want that?'

'Don't kill,' I said. 'Just frighten them.'

She looked as if she was seriously considering my request as she shook out her hair, turned into a yakshi and looked at those who were sleeping. Then she laughed. They were all strangers. Folks who'd come three full days ahead of the marriage.

After Valiachhan came, Sarojini Edathi slept in Amma's room. My bed was shifted out. As if I cared. Let her practice her Hindi with Amma. If I want . . . Hmm-hm, no. I won't do it.

That night, a sound woke me up. People were running all over the place. A real earthquake!

'Quick! Bring that pill of hers that will make her breathe more easily!' someone was ordering.

'May nothing happen before the marriage.' This was Valiamma's prayer.

Mutthashi's condition was critical again.

So much noise and commotion and through it all some slept like logs.

I got up and rushed to Mutthashi's room. When I reached there, Amma saw me. 'Get out! Go back to bed. Who asked you to come here?' she screamed.

Next day — the pandal was up in the courtyard. Alongside the kitchen a long, narrow shed had been erected for the cooks. Huge vessels and ladles were brought from the temple storeroom. Valiamma brought my new skirt and blouse back from the tailor. Not a colour that I liked. But the material was good. Silk.

'We have got all this for you. Do you know why? So that you'll be a good girl and behave. Don't make people say things about you. Understand?' Valiamma stroked my hair.

From now on, I'll not utter a word — that's for sure.

But I kept wondering what new games Kunjathaal and Neeli were playing without me. They were not to be seen around here. But then, looking at all the hustle and bustle, who'd want to come here?

Mutthashi's room reeks of urine. When Mutthashi breathes there is an awful sound. When she sees me she beckons me with her head and I go stand near her. Valiachhan and Ravunni Nair keep peeping in.

When the decoration of the pandal was over, two loudspeakers were mounted and they started playing recorded music. One loudspeaker was turned towards the fields. Another towards the hill. Let my Yakshi too hear the music.

The bridegroom's party was to arrive in two buses and three cars. Ettan was to receive them. They would be taken straight to the temple. The nadaswaram players would be waiting under the banyan tree.

To the cooks Ravunni Nair said, 'They will all be back here by nine-thirty. By ten, the first batch of plantain leaves must be spread out for the feast. Will you be ready?'

The night resounded with the activities of the cooks. Inside, there was no space even to lie down.

It didn't look as if Mutthashi would attend the wedding.
'Touch her feet before you leave. After all, she has the status of a Mutthashi. Also place a new mundu at her feet. Not that it is going to bring any benefit. Still . . .' Amma advised Sarojini Edathi, and Ravunni Nair said with a sarcastic chuckle, 'Yes, shortly new clothes will be needed for the mourning.'

I had planned to wake up early, bathe, wear my new skirt and go show it to Kunjathaal. But when I woke up, Ravunni Nair was shrieking to my mother. 'She has wrecked everything, Kunjukutty Amma!'

Practically everyone was in Mutthashi's room. Valiachhan also came running.

'It's all over. All over!'

'Not a word. Not a soul other than us should know till the feast is over and the bridegroom's party has left. Understand?' When he looked up, it was at me. I was standing near the door. I could see Valiachhan was angry.

Valiamma called me to her. 'Jatti, come here. Let me tell you something,' she said. 'Mutthashi's condition is very bad. You should not go into her room. Go. Have your bath and get ready. Achhan will be here any minute now. Um. Go.'

'Thank God, the child knows nothing.'

'Ravunni . . . keep watch. Don't move an inch. If anyone else comes to know, there will be enough busybodies to say the wedding should be stopped. And they will quote the shastras. I hope you understand?'

I got dressed. Edathi plaited my hair with a beautiful blue ribbon.

Sarojini Edathi's makeup had started around midnight. Four people were needed just to decorate her hair. She was never beautiful. But now, decked up in her loud saree and those glaring ornaments she looked worse.

'What are you waiting for, ladies? Hurry.'

The women started to move.

'Sarojini Edathi, don't you have to go in and do namaskaram to Mutthashi?' I asked.

'Girl! Shut up and go!' Amma said to me. All the anger at Achhan not having come for the wedding was directed at me.

Nobody even paused at Mutthashi's door.

I stood in the corridor, hesitating.

'Edee, what are you hovering around there for? Come fast,' Valiamma scolded me.

I went towards the kitchen, saying I wanted to drink some water. I got out from the rear and ran through the parambu.

The rustle of my new silk skirt was like music. Near the outhouse, Kunjathaal was sitting combing her hair. She was alone. 'Do you know what Sarojini Edathi did?' I burst out. 'She went to the temple without doing namaskaram to Mutthashi.'

Kunjathaal said nothing. I became angry.

'You call yourself a great yakshi. What is the use? Can't you help Mutthashi? She wants to see the wedding.'

Kunjathaal laughed.

'You said you could fly to the top of the pala tree. Is that also a bluff?'

Kunjathaal looked at me.

'Um. I'll come to the wedding too. You bring Mutthashi. Neeli and I will wait at the gate.'

I wasn't sure if she was joking. I hesitated. Kunjathaal said, 'I am serious. I am sure Mutthashi will come. You call her.'

I ran back to the house. When I was entering Mutthashi's room, Ravunni Nair asked 'Why is kutty here?'

'Mutthashi . . .'

'You can't go in. Shouldn't you be at the temple?'

'Mutthashi should come too.'

'Mutthashi is dead, kutty. We are not telling anybody until the feast is over. Kutty should also not tomtom it. Don't go in. You'll get scared . . .'

I turned a deaf ear to him. I leaned on the door. It opened slightly. He looked at me in anger. 'Go in, go in . . . what does it matter to me?' he said.

I went in.

Mutthashi was still. She had covered herself up to her neck. She must be angry and so pretending to be dead. Sometimes when she has had a quarrel with Amma or Valiamma she'd lie thus, without even touching her food. Mutthashi always had such tricks up her sleeve.

Mutthashi shouldn't die without seeing the marriage. I won't allow it.

'Isn't Mutthashi coming? It is I . . .'

Standing at the door, Ravunni Nair gave a sarcastic grin.

Mutthashi opened her eyes. Just as I expected.

'It is time for the muhurtham. Let's go. We have to rush.'

Mutthashi sat up in the bed.

'Do you want to change your mundu?'

Mutthashi shook her mundu to take out the crinkles and wore it again. She draped a sheet over her head. In one quick movement she got off the bed, took my hand and started walking.

Looking triumphantly at Ravunni Nair who still wore his mocking expression, Mutthashi and I stepped out. Kunjathaal and Neeli were at the gate. Hand in hand, the four of us ran. Mutthashi was faster than us. In fact she was pulling us. When we had passed the lane and reached the foot of the banyan tree we could hear the nadaswaram.

We went through the outer courtyard of the temple. It was jammed with people. No one noticed us. We had arrived in time. The bride and bridegroom were about to garland each other.

A beaming Mutthashi sat through the whole wedding. When the ceremony was over all the elder relatives and friends came forward to shower rice and flowers on the bride and bridegroom. Mutthashi looked at me. I scooped up a handful of rice and flowers and gave it to her.

I asked Kunjathaal. 'Do you want some?'

Kunjathaal was looking at the bridegroom. Her eyes spat fire. The damshtra slowly grew longer. And longer.

And when the bridegroom posed, bouquet in hand for a photo with Sarojini Edathi, I noticed Kunjathaal jump towards him. I burst into a loud scream. What happened after that I don't know. Only when I saw Sarojini Edathi with the new Ettan who has become her husband did I feel relieved. So Kunjathaal didn't do any harm. They invited me to go to their house after I got well. 'If you were not feeling well, why did you come running to the temple like this, alone?' they asked.

'Not alone. Mutthashi came with me.'

'Bhagwane. Bhagwane!' Amma began chanting.

'Ask Ravunni Nair. He saw us.'

'My kutty's having one hallucination after another!' Amma moaned.

This has become their habit. They won't accept anything I say. They always invent something of their own.

To show them that I *was* saying the truth I described in detail how Mutthashi had come to the temple to shower rice and flowers on the married couple. All that they did was to look at each other and whisper.

After Sarojini Edathi and her husband's family left, they told everyone that Mutthashi was dead.

I said to myself, So what if she dies now. At least she saw the wedding.

I f she didn't die till the marriage was over, it's because she was an old hag who loved her family,' the maidservants who had came to sweep and clean the house were saying when Ravunni Nair came out of Mutthashi's room, screaming.

I could hear the commotion from where I lay.

'Was it not I who gave her her ceremonial bath? I who laid out the body? But, oh God, what do I see now. Rice and flowers in her hands!'

So! When I said so, they would not believe me.

'Mutthashi's spirit has entered kutty. Heard what she said?'

Nobody has entered or possessed anybody. The four of us did go to the temple. That is a fact.

'Even in death she won't leave us in peace.'

Ravunni Nair began talking of sending for the mannaan to come perform the last rites. 'If we don't, her spirit will hang around us forever.'

I lay there with eyes closed. Kunjathaal and Neeli came into my room. I could sense that from their smell. I didn't speak to them. Frightening people with the damshtra at the wrong time!

'Don't come near me,' I said. 'Hereafter I am not going to play with you. Go away.'

Even through shut eyes I could see them leave, heads bent in shame.

You know that a body has to be cremated only with logs of the mango tree. For Mutthashi, my relatives brought a tiny branch of a mango tree, saying there was a lot of the fuel left over from the wedding and that would serve.

From where I lay, I saw Mutthashi being carried out.

Mutthashi won't go. She'll stay. Isn't that what Ravunni Nair said?

I got up.

I could see the courtyard. Through the wooden grille of the front hall, beyond the cashewnut tree, I could see the funeral pyre. Four or five people lifted Mutthashi, laid her on the pyre and arranged pieces of wood on the sides and over her. The fire was lit.

Oh, how scorched Mutthashi must be feeling . . . Don't . . . Aiyo . . . Don't!

There's smoke all over the place. Nothing can be seen. But look! From out of the smoke, whom do I see coming . . . yes! It is none other than Mutthashi!

Mutthashi will not die. Mutthashi will not leave this house. There's still much to be done. Mutthashi is still to show me what herbs and roots are to be gathered and how the paste is to be made and applied for eruptions, wounds, swellings.

The white cloth with which Mutthashi had covered her body turned into wings. Mutthashi came towards me, flying. Before I could turn my eyes from the courtyard, Mutthashi had landed on my bed. My happiness knew no bounds. I held Mutthashi in a tight embrace.

'You pretended you were dead and made a fool of all these people, no?' I asked.

Mutthashi laughed softly.

Do you know where Mutthashi is, Chechi? Chechi, you are a nurse, no? Then, why are you not wearing the white coat nurses always wear?

Let everyone go. So what? The one who came last has not gone. Do

you know who it is? She sits right behind me, a little girl. She wears my skirt, her hair is cropped short.

Yes, it is Mutthashi.

Chechi, let's play.

Chechi! Why are you running away? Why are you shouting and calling people? Has an earthquake started here too?

Mutthashi? Has Mutthashi also gone?

No, Mutthashi sits on top of the window sill. How did she get there?

Yes. There, holding her hand, helping Mutthashi climb down — Yes that is *them*. So they have also come.

'Silly! You and your irritation. We hadn't gone anywhere,' Kunjathaal whispered in my ear.

Now for kothengkallu and vattu and all my other games, there is a foursome. Mutthashikutty and I are partners. Kunjathaal and Neeli the other team. How well matched we are!

Ah! What more is there to wish for!

GOPINATH MOHANTY

·

SHIKAR

·

NOMINATED BY SACHIDANANDA MOHANTY
TRANSLATED BY SACHIDANANDA MOHANTY
AND SUDHAKAR MARATHE

From the dark pit at the bottom of the hill one by one they rise. The hair on their heads untouched by oil, around their waists only kaupunis. Group after group, so many people! Nearby, beside the hill, barely visible, their village. Over there the women of the village going towards the waterfront. And the herds of cattle and goats returning homeward. Supine on the backs of their buffaloes, feet dangling, the young cowherds are being carried home.

On either side of the path, the sunset lights up fields of tobacco and mustard, jowar and kandula, vegetable patches covered by dense clinging beans and melons on scaffolds. Their handiwork, a miracle. Scattered on single trees like birds nests on delicate branches are their little huts. To ascend each, only a length of bamboo for handgrip. From these they watch their fields, spending the whole night on the machan, blowing on horn and flute; under the banyan, here and there, stone fireplaces and ashes of dead fires; here they must have cooked last night, after cutting the pleasingly rich harvest of their land; they shall do so again.

In all certainty, bonded labourers. Even before the crop ripens, Lambodar of Sunarigad will have claimed one gadisha of the produce of this patch, thirty puti of that one. And after they have struggled through the year, they would find him waiting with the agreement papers — 'Come, measure out my portion, one gadisha plus interest. Don't you remember the provisions, the seed and cattle feed you took? Get on with it, start measuring. Hunh, all told, how much? It must be one gadisha and fifteen puti. After having settled everything, you still owe me fifteen puti. Why are you staring at me like that? Shake the straw well before you take it home. Well, what am I supposed to do? Not claim my lawful share?'

No. They cannot be sharecroppers or landowners. Why else would they be shift cultivators? To provide for at least a couple of years, they take on tigers, the jungle, courts and fines! They banish fear by turning their bodies into tough wood — they swing their axes against the trees,

'Shikar' (Title of the original story) was first published in Oriya in *Sharashjya*, 1992, Cuttack.

making sparks fly; young and old, they all wrestle with the hills in rain or sunshine.

Only yesterday, the land belonged to their forebears . . . This mustard, this kandula, this tobacco, their village surrounded by mango trees clinging to the hillside.

Over there by the tall shady tree, their thatched huts stand facing each other. In rows. Here, all are equal in thought and deed. At the centre of the village is the home of Goddess Jhakiri. Above her is Dharma, and below there is Basumati, mother earth. All men are brothers.

From secret cracks between rocks, from the mud knoll by the side of the pit, from beneath the sal and mahula trees, they peer. It is hard to make out the men from the trees. They puzzle over these light-skinned folk that have come riding in their machine. Who are these people, friend or foe? What are they up to?

The motor car has come to a stop. The two children in it are crying. They must have some badhuli flowers! In the red light of the sunset, bunch after bunch of red badhuli flowers are being plucked. Like Kandha* children, these are also fond of flowers and their father must indulge them. What would they say if these people invited them in, if they said, 'Let's cook dinner together, let's enjoy ourselves. We will share the little wine that is left, perhaps slaughter an old cow. You can then have all that we have: chickens, eggs and bananas. We will light a fire and guard you through the night. At dawn, the whole village will welcome you into our midst. After all, this is your home too . . . For you too are people like us.'

Watch out, they may come running now.

The sun has set long ago. In the west, between two hillocks, the blaze of fire has dimmed. All around, shadows have lengthened. There is no habitation, village, or cattle anywhere, only the jungle, the hills in the east, the burnt out

---

The *Kandhas* are a tribe of the Koraput and Kalahandi regions of Orissa.

hilltop that appears dark, fearsome. Like an unwashed ribbon, the path stretches and is swallowed by darkness.

Stretching a finger towards the base of the hill, Laxminarayana narrates his tale —

This is the place, sir, this nullah called Jhupabai, and beyond, Jhupabai village. Breaking out from the netherworld, through layers of rock, Jhupabai joins Nagabali river, like a calf running after its mother. There is another roundabout way to the village. It is here that men with guns surprised them. The day before, men from ten neighbouring villages had been beaten, had fled for dear life! Having cooked their supper near the mango grove, some were rolling tobacco leaves for a smoke; they had started from home a fortnight before that and their wanderings had given them blisters on their feet. Having heard of their presence here, the gunmen swiftly climbed the mound and began firing at them.

'What? Gunfire?'

Sricharan was surprised. He could not relate gunfire with this peaceful forest and his vision of their primal life. Suddenly, they had entered his consciousness. No effort was required for such meditation, no rigour of asanas or pranayama to picture them as characters in an imaginary novel or to watch them on the white screen from amidst a crowd; very easily, effortlessly, this picture arose before his eyes, touching him like an invisible wind. Like a radio catching a tune from afar, Man's imagination has given body to images of fields and cattle, peasants and labourers. Not through bloodshed, not through gunfire.

Excited, Laxminarayana continued his narration like an eyewitness unfolding a historical account. It seemed as if he had been infected by some barbarism, his ancient bones awakened by some wild bloodthirsty urge —

The firing went on, dhu dha dhu dha dhai dhai dhai. Not the guns to shoot birds with, but vilayati rifles. Each shot could knock out an elephant! So many fell into one pile. The survivors fled for their lives straight towards Jhupabai, which was, as it were, waiting to grab them into its hungry mouth. Breathless, one after another they fell into the nullah like a pack of disoriented wild boar, one after another, many many more than had perished in the actual firing.

Laxminarayana wiped the sweat off his face and continued —

Then the gunmen collected the dead, the crippled, those crying out in agony. They dragged and shoved all of them into the nullah. There was no telltale sign left anywhere. That quite broke the backbone of the villagers, their stubborness. How disobedient they had been! The cheek to refuse to pay tax to the great king and to pay it to the small one instead! As the government's force arrested their leaders, the revolt spread to all the villages. Even women took part, and poured hot water on 'suprent' sahib, who was more feared than even the tiger. But after the firing, the same men chickened out, fell at the feet of the Paika,* carried out unquestioningly all that was asked of them. The land became quiet. But not before this side of the path was laden with many corpses. O, to think of those bitter days . . .

The two children were listening in rapt attention as though it were a fascinating tale from a history book. After all, killing, bloodshed, gunfire — children love to listen to such tales from beyond their ken.

Kuna asked, 'What kind of a battle was this? Our history book says that many many people died when Mohammad Ghori attacked India.' Kuna reads in class six, and has never seen anyone die. 'Tell me, was it *really* a big battle?'

Laxminarayana replied, 'No, it was more like a skirmish.'

'A battle?' asked Mini. 'We have read of so many such battles in our textbooks.' She is in class seven. 'This is nothing! We have read of many! The Mahabharata war. The battle of Panipat. Of Plassey. The Second World War . . .'

Kuna asked, 'Did more people die in those battles?'

Laxminarayana, who had no notion of history, countered: 'Who says so? More died here, in this revolt! To think of the mayhem caused! It was we who showed the gunmen the way to this place. How else would

---

A *paika* was a traditional Oriya warrior. Peasants called for armed duties during strife were also called paikas.

they have found it? The Kandhas were all chased and killed like dogs. Not one escaped.'

Kuna said, 'What happened to them after they died?'

'What do you think?' Laxminarayana said. 'They turned into ghosts!'

Mini exclaimed: 'Ghosts!' and out of fear came to sit close to her father.

Kuna said, 'All lies! Baba told me there is no such thing as ghosts, no Baba? But tell me what happened to the bodies of all those people who died and lay in the nullah? What happened to their bodies?'

'What could happen?' Laxminarayana said, shrugging his shoulders. 'The nullah was crowded with jackals and vultures, but those who came could not eat all the bodies. The stench of rotting flesh spread for miles. In the end, everything but the bones turned into earth. Even the bones, I think, will turn to stone. But who will bother about that? The revolt of the Kandhas was crushed wasn't it?'

Mini said, 'What about the relatives of those who died? Did they cry?'

'They certainly did. Women from many villages still come to Jhupabai, they roll on the ground, pull their hair out, tear at their cheeks and faces with their nails, and howl. Only in the evening do they return home. It is said that one lost her mind, killed herself by jumping into the nullah. But whether they cried or not, that does not matter, I guess. Those who died are gone. You see, for one whole year, there was no cultivation, everyone was terror-stricken. Taking advantage of this, many outsiders came and bought up land, dirt cheap! It was a free-for-all. Land was bought by moneylenders. They gave loans, engaged labourers for wages, paid taxes to the king. Everything became straightforward! Wherever you went, you saw 'decent' people, what you call gentlemen. And these Kandhas, they are after all of a lower order. The gentlemen treated the Kandhas like cattle and grew rich. Look, over there, see what a big house Chakuli Parhi has built.'

'Chakuli? That's for eating! What a funny name!' the children said, giggling.

'Yes, it's accepted in these parts. Chakuli Parhi is a big man, has fifty wives besides his lawful one. He is a tiger of a man! No one can outdo

Chakuli in cunning. At any one time he has so many court cases going on . . .'

Laxminarayana is a veteran chaprasi of this place. He still upholds the decision to crush the revolt of the Kandhas. His ideal is a tiger-like man. Naturally, he respects Chakula Parhi. He sports a manly moustache and never shows his head without the cover of a turban. He takes good care of his clothes. Besides, he is a famous hunter of tigers, deer, peacock and fowl. He finds his meat and also earns his livelihood from hunting. His superior, Sricharan, has come here on transfer, been here for the last two months. Laxminarayana wants to impress and captivate Sricharan with his knowledge, experience, skill and resourcefulness. Both have just been to Kalyansinghpur from Raygada. Sricharan's children had gone along to see the new countryside. They were now on their way home.

The account of the killing of the Kandhas had destroyed Sricharan's peace, and he was unable to pay attention to Laxminarayana. Involuntarily there arose in his mind a deep sadness, anger and grief. He is an outsider. He belongs to the rural areas of Puri district. By train one comes to this place via Khurda, Berhampur, Vijayanagaram, Parvatipur, then Raygada, a distance of 333 miles. But the difference in topography is more striking than the actual distance covered. Huge hills, dense jungle, and more outstanding than these, the Kandhas. But he realised that even they are people like him.

Yes, the same people who love, hate, laugh, and cry, without any ill will towards others, they wish to live in peace too; people who, like cattle, only ask for some comfort, some degree of peace and the pleasure of togetherness. They spend their days the way trees shed leaves, in rain or sunshine. Despite any of their boasts, they are really scared of violence and bloodshed. They sing of moksha and nirvana, but love the bondage of wordly life. Yet they invite the sharp weapons of retribution upon themselves. How often have wild hordes come riding, the Dravidas, the Anaryas, and then the Aryas, fair people after the dark. Crossing hills, streams, rivers and the ocean, close on their heels has come the colonial policy that the victor possesses the land, the vanquished becomes the serf. One cultivates, the other reaps the harvest. Man does not eat the flesh of fellow men. He survives by the proper means of sustenance, his food, his land. And along with victorious arms have come priests of all religions, sprinkling magic waters in ablution, to win the hearts of the vanquished. 'Life is transient,' they explain, 'real peace lies elsewhere. Abjure worldly life and flesh for the sake of the spirit!'

After dusk has come the night. The car is on its way towards Raygada. They who had troubled Sricharan's imagination by beckoning him to stay back, they who had appealed to his common humanity, are no longer present. They are creatures of the imagination. Bullets had felled them long ago. Their bodies have dissolved into this red earth over which this car is moving relentlessly, with Sricharan inside.

The car's headlights cut a narrow road out of the darkness. In the front seat are Laxminarayana and the driver. At the back, Sricharan and his children. Loaded gun in hand, Laxminarayana waits for the kill. He has awakened an excitement in the children by pointing out that the headlights will make the eyes of the animals glow in the dark.

Now and then a glowing eye was visible. It was as if someone had left a burning ember on the road. Invariably it is the eye of a bird.

Suddenly, there appeared a pair of green eyes.

'Tiger!' whispered the driver as he accelerated. Laxminarayana picked up the gun as a jackal crossed the path in flight. Many more eyes later, suddenly a hare stood still, caught in the light, and then it fled, hop-hopping before the pursuing car. 'Watch out! It's going to get run over!' the children cried out. Sricharan touched the driver's back, to slow him down, and the hare escaped into the bushes. And then there appeared a pair of eyes two feet above ground level.

'It's a tiger!' said Laxminarayana.

The vehicle shot forward like a meteor. The creature stood erect, a striped animal . . . not a tiger but a hyena! Next came a big bear, its face turned downward. 'Kill him,' they shouted, 'why didn't you kill him, Baba?' they complained. And Sricharan thought, those that are infantile not only in body but also in spirit, all those selfish irresponsible men, would naturally scream — 'Kill, kill!' Those who watch violence and killings on the television at home, or in the imagined pages of fiction, they would merely know the supremacy of brute force, not the horror of the tragedy. Such slaughter only feeds their egoism. They would not know how to fight and die an untimely death — the American school boy in the Asian battlefield. Even this denizen of the forest, this tiny hare might perish, thought Sricharan. How long would it be spared? Maybe a day would come when there would be no hares left in the forest.

Breaking into his thought once again there came a pair of green eyes, moving slowly towards the left side of the road.

'It's a tiger,' the driver whispered, focussing the light on the animal.

It was indeed a massive tiger. With its mouth open, its whiskers aquiver, it sniffed the air. In the darkness, Laxminarayana trained his gun on the tiger . . .

Then came the shot.

The tiger crashed to the ground, and raising its head, dragged itself to the other side of a rock. The gun roared again. And again. The tiger convulsed, pawed the ground wildly, then lay flat out.

Dead.

The children shouted in unison, 'Let's go.'

Cautioning everyone to wait, Laxminarayana loaded the gun and moving ten steps forward, pumped a bullet straight into the tiger's head. Taking aim, he threw a stone at the creature. There was no sign of life. He said, 'The tiger is dead! You can all come out.'

It was a time for jubilation. Even Sricharan competed with his children in rushing around, crying out their victory.

Dragging the carcass nonchalantly by the tail, Laxminarayana voiced his regret. 'I think we have wasted four bullets. Perhaps one bullet would have done. Only the tiger would have then taken one hour to die.'

'You certainly have an excellent aim; you shot the tiger in the dark,' Sricharan congratulated him. But Laxminarayana and the driver were busy dragging the tiger to the car. Said the driver, 'It's a huge tiger. Laxminarayana is sure to win a prize.'

'It's only a leopard,' Laxminarayana said in apparent disappointment. 'It'll fetch only thirty-five rupees, perhaps less.'

'You'll never get less than thirty-five,' Sricharan reassured him. 'But I am determined to take the skin and send it for tanning.'

The children pestered them with questions about the size and the eating habits of the tiger as they felt the tiger's whiskers, its ears, its tail. Their joy was understandable. After all, they too had had a share in the kill. The question, Who spotted the tiger first? was hotly debated till, annoyed, Sricharan ordered them back into the car.

Everyone felt that he had killed the tiger. Ceremoniously, the carcass was lifted onto the bonnet of the car, clearly a difficult job for the three men, even with the help of ropes. Finally, the body rested on the bonnet, with its face slightly propped forward onto the windshield.

As the engine started, there was a curious meow behind them. Laxminarayana said as if to end all speculation: 'The tiger is already dead.' But Mini was right. Unseen by Sricharan, a tigress with her cubs, smelling the spoor, the blood, had roared in futile rage. By then, of course, both vehicle and men were far away.

As the carcass jiggled on the bonnet, Sricharan thought, it's a good thing the tiger is dead. It must have killed so many men, the world must be a somewhat safer place now. There certainly is reason for killing it. It is a hostile creature, and feasts on men! More reasoning followed. Man kills only out of necessity. After all, has not Krishna explained to Arjuna in the *Bhagwadgita* that slaying one's enemy is one's moral duty?

Perhaps there will be no end to violence. The land has been soaked in blood, the sky has been echoing cries of agony. But age after age, strife and violence seem to go on. And those who lost, the victims, have fallen into the Jhupabai nullah. Sricharan pictured the holocaust of history as if it was something captured on film. Each time he saw the tiger, he saw it as a symbol of exploitation, inequity and callousness in the world, and he rejoiced in the repeated vision of the tiger being killed. The symbol of violence is dead! He does not worry about how it perished, the fact that the tiger is dead, and his own desire has been fulfilled, is enough.

One has to fight relentlessly for peace, and then maybe there will be no more war. Sricharan pictures himself returning from the last battle on earth. Now the world is safe . . . before him he sees the dead body of the tiger.

While thinking of non-violence, unwittingly Sricharan has become a votary of violence. His pride and egoism have already blinded him. For his self-satisfaction he has become a warrior, strutting about on the stage swinging his tin sword vigorously, making the floor shake with his stride.

The car moved on. Laxminarayana shifted between commentary and silence as he tried to satisfy the curiosity of the children. Sricharan now saw only a path before him, and the dark forest, and on the bonnet a dead tiger that would never consume men again.

Soon the car left hilly terrain and moved into the plain interspersed with human habitation, dim lights. In the distance some silhouettes of people. Victory was no victory unless it was broadcast, thought Sricharan. People may not be able to see the tiger in the glare of the powerful headlights. He flashed his torch on the carcass. The children clapped together as the driver slowed down the car. As expected, the people on the road jostled each other, craning their necks to look at the dead tiger. There was surprise, fear, relief. Sricharan smiled in the dark, as if he were receiving their compliments.

By the time they reached their house, it was ten at night. As the car came to a halt, the children leapt out excitedly to call the others.

Laxminarayana got down and unloaded the car, while Sricharan stepped down. Soon there was a commotion, the family and neighbours all gathered in no time, everyone intent on the dead tiger.

— Look at its whiskers! And its tail!

— What huge teeth. He must have crunched men with those fangs.

— We must send its skin for tanning.

— We must not forget to stuff the head. Then it will look like a real tiger!

There was so much comment, such curiosity all around.

The youngest child, a one-and-a-half year old, was half asleep.

Shaking him gently awake, Sricharan's wife brought him near the dead tiger. 'Don't worry, dear. The tiger is dead.'

The little one hesitated, but seeing his brother and sister touching the tiger, he gathered courage to stroke the tiger's skin as he said, 'Oooo, poor thing. The tiger is dead!'

Everyone laughed.

Sricharan was shaken. After the hunt, he had forgotten about the tale of Jhupabai. But now he recalled the bloodied forms of the Kandhas. The mound of corpses . . . And once again their blood streamed out and soaked the earth.

Pensive and remorseful, gaze turned downward, Sricharan turned abruptly and went into his house.

SHYAMAL GANGOPADHYAY

•

THE FIG TREE
STANDS WITNESS

•

NOMINATED BY SARAT KUMAR MUKHOPADHYAY
TRANSLATED BY SHAMPA BANERJEE

Dadamashai passed away when I was a boy. That must be nearly fifty years ago. Today that world is a fairy-tale. The lanes and by-lanes of those days, the conversation, the food . . . all appear hazy now. But one thing still comes clearly to mind. A sister of my mother's had come from Delhi to attend my grandfather's funeral. When I woke up that morning she helped me get ready. I remember this because her fingers were as beautiful and plump as they were hard. It was as if she used fingers of steel to splash water on my face.

This Maashi had two sons, Debesh and Khagesh. And a daughter called Lotika. Lotikadi had just started wearing saris.

The year after Dadamashai's funeral, the same Maashi arrived again with her two sons and daughter to spend the summer with us. With her came her husband, my meshomashai.

Those days mangoes and fish cost nothing at all in our small suburban town and we'd have our fill of these, then sit back and talk. Debeshda had picked up a song from a Hindi film he had seen in Delhi. *Yeh na bataa sakunga mai.* It was the only song he knew. We thought he sang it beautifully; now I know he didn't quite pronounce the words right. The words meant, 'This is something I cannot tell you.' Probably a song sung by the film's heroine.

Next in line was Lotikadi. At that time, Lotikadi was a first year Arts student at Raisina College in Delhi. Handkerchiefs, perfume, powder, soap and kohl were inseparable from her. Those days in the town where we lived, these were still unfamiliar objects. I remember I was only in elementary school then and Debeshda's song and Lotikadi's fragrance kept me in a perpetual trance.

The youngest of the three was Khageshda. He taught me to kill birds with a catapult. Khageshda would prowl around the garden at the back of our house, with a catapult in his hand and an animal rage in his heart. His goal — a squirrel, or a dove's nest.

Maashi was all rosy with high blood pressure. She always wore a

The Fig Tree Stands Witness was first published in Bangla as *'Shakshi Dumur Gach'* in *Bibhab*, Puja Special 1990, Calcutta.

delicately-embroidered blouse from Delhi. But Meshomashai would sit, wearing just a lungi, his feet up in a chair, eating bowls of puffed rice. Maashi nagged him about this in front of all of us and Meshomashai would say, 'I'm a clerk at the Commissariat. All clerks eat puffed rice. Should I eat it with fork and knife like a sahib?'

What you have read till now may be seen as the introduction to my story.

In the middle of World War II, I had to go to Calcutta with my elder brother, to find a cure for his asthma. By then Meshomashai had been transferred to Calcutta. Khageshda was in college. I remember I stood in a queue with him at the Aleya cinema and saw a film. Debeshda was unemployed and this irked Maashi no end. Lotikadi was waiting to get married.

When we were ready to go back to our suburb, Maashi repeatedly told my elder brother, 'Tell Didi they're developing an area called Jodhpur Park here, on land reclaimed from marshland. She can buy a plot of three kaathas at seventy-five rupees per kaatha.'

My elder brother gave Ma this message when we returned home. Ma said, Where can we find two hundred and twenty-five rupees all at one go? She wasn't far wrong in saying that. Mutton was ten annas a seer. Even I remember this — although I've forgotten the price of other things. Mustard oil was probably five annas, sugar fourteen pice.

Then one day the country was divided into two. We moved into Calcutta from our little suburb. Within a few years we found that a lot of monkeys were going off to America. A lot of men to Europe, actually to Germany. Onion and garlic to the Arab countries. Enteroquinol to Indonesia.

One day Debeshda and Khageshda went abroad. Lotikadi got married. Of course we didn't get to know about the wedding in time.

Lotikadi was what you may describe as my first dream woman ever since that day she was going back to Delhi after that summer we'd sat eating mangoes and fried fish, and her perfumed handkerchief had fallen to the platform. Just as I picked it up the train started moving. I couldn't return it to her. That handkerchief was to become the source of my dreams. It remained with me for a long time.

We heard that Debeshda went on to become a Labour Party trade union leader in the coal mines of Wales. That Khageshda became a mining engineer. That both married white women within a few years. But then we lost touch completely. Only little scraps of news would reach us. We too passed or failed our examinations. Won or lost our wars. And through those years, Lotikadi's fragrant hanky would come to mind. From time to time.

Then we got some news: Khageshda came home with his memsahib wife. Maashi rubbed mustard oil into her hair and plaited it. Put sindoor on her forehead, took her to Kalighat* and got her to wear the loha, the thin iron bangle that married women wear. Maashi fed her on shojne danta and labra made of soft ripe pumpkin, a difficult mishmash of vegetables and fish for the uninitiated. Khageshda took his wife back to England.

As for Debeshda, he never returned. He has five children, one of whom is a boxer who went to the West Indies for a prize-fight.

Meshomashai retired. He didn't give up eating puffed rice. Jodhpur Park was created as envisaged by the town planners and Maashi built her house there and rented it out. She didn't let go of the miniscule flat for which they continued to pay the old low rent. She lived there with Meshomashai. Just the two of them. Lotikadi was with her in-laws of course. Her husband is supposed to be extremely well-off.

Since then, some twenty-five, thirty years have passed. Independence has become old hat. So has life. Policemen don't wear the red turbans they used to when we were children. We meet our relatives and cousins — at somebody's funeral. It is difficult to attend all the weddings, paites,* annaprashans. There are probably around two hundred relatives if you count all the branches and leaves of the family tree. Who can you keep in touch with? Some of them have lost their teeth, many have acquired dentures. I wouldn't be able to recognize them now. Ma

---

Kalighat is on the banks of the Ganga in Calcutta where it is possible to get a quick validation of a marriage. *Paite* is the traditional thread-investing ceremony.

died. Baba too. My children got married, one by one. And before I knew it, their children started going to school. Nowadays, I don't eat potatoes, sugar, red meat, sweets or fresh salt with my food. I hear that so-and-so is no more. Rani's son is in America. Poltu's daughter is a pilot.

In the same way, news came of Maashi's death, that is, of Lotikadi's mother. But Meshomashai is alive. The tenants could not be evicted from the Jodhpur Park house. They live there in health and happiness, still paying the 1950s rent of a hundred or a hundred and fifty rupees. It's been about thirty, thirty-five years now.

I went to visit Meshomashai, he who liked to eat puffed rice and used to once work in the Delhi Commissariat. It's been a long time since he retired. The staircase rose straight up from the tram tracks. The flat was on the first floor. Two small rooms. A sitting area. Kitchen. Bath and toilet. Everything neatly in place. Having run a household in Delhi on a small budget had made Maashi a terribly organized person. Meshomashai's earnings had gradually increased. Debeshda and Khageshda sent pounds from abroad but Maashi had refused to change her ways till the end. Foreign Ovaltine tins still stood on every shelf.

Now, Meshomashai raised his head out of a foreign-looking pullover made in England to ask, 'Who is it?'

He was lying on an easy-chair. I introduced myself. He recognized me. We started talking. 'Eighty-seven,' he said proudly. 'I've been getting a pension for 32 years. Worked for 35 years. I started at 20.'

Who stays here with him?

'Nobody. It's two years since your Maashi died.'

Who looked after him?

'If there are servants, they. If there's no one, then no one,' he said. 'Servants don't stay for long these days.'

I was shocked. I looked at the hair on Meshomashai's pale white legs which was still surprisingly black.

'Who locks the door at night?'

'Some days it's locked, some days it isn't.'

What was he saying! Everything will be stolen!

'What will be, will be. What can be done about it?' he said. And, after a brief pause, 'What will I do with possessions when I'm dying myself?'

'Please . . . don't talk like this!' Meshomashai looked as if life would run out of him any minute. The innumerable veins on his neck were like the circuit board of a transistor radio.

'A letter was sent to Debesh to take us away, that is, while your Maashi was still alive. There was no reply. Instead, the two brothers doubled the amount of money they were sending.'

'How do you collect the money?'

'When do I collect it? It gets credited to my account. Every month. The pounds, the house rent, my pension. The bank sends a receipt by post. Someone comes round and gives me money at the beginning of the month and takes my signature.'

What did this mean? How much did he sign for? And how much was given to him? They might be swindling him!

Meshomashai looked as if he'd guessed what was going on in my mind. His thin lips let out shreds of laughter. 'What use is money to me today?'

'What are you saying? Money is always useful.'

Meshomashai took out two little bird's feet from under the sheet that covered him to search for his slippers. Finally he said, 'I too used to think that money is a valuable thing. That in my old age money will look after me. Money will summon the doctor, hire a nurse, give the medicine. Money will feed me. But did that happen?'

'What about your meals?'

'Where do I get them from? A boy from the tea stall downstairs comes and boils some rice. Once in a while he cooks fish.'

'How can you carry on like this, Meshomashai?'

'I know I can't. Lotu has come and seen me. She will take me to her place. And in the bank, all that money, the interest piling up like a mountain. But it's of no use. Who will cash it? Who will spend it?'

Who puts up the mosquito net? Who opens the door? After a meal, who picks up the dirty plates? Who will look after him if he falls down?

Who shuts the door? I came down the stairs, worrying. Debeshda and Khageshda didn't want to take the old man to Britain. Instead they have doubled their monthly allowance.

Before I left, Meshomashai had signalled me to look at the wall. Addresses scribbled in pencil. Debeshda was in Aberdeen. Khageshda in Hampstead Heath. Below Lotikadi's name it said Akshoy Parui Lane, Shibpur, Howrah. All those addresses whirled and danced in my mind and sitting in their midst was Meshomashai's mountain of compound interest throbbing like a tumour . . . I kept thinking that mutton costs forty rupees these days. Sugar seven. Mustard oil is twenty-four rupees in the open market. What's the world come to?

If Lotikadi doesn't take him away soon enough, Meshomashai is as good as dead. A bag of bones, his neck sticking out like a stork's. He speaks and his head shakes. He laughs and the paper-thin skin on his lips seems to rip apart. It's as if bits and pieces have been glued together to make Meshomashai.

That final day of reckoning — Rammohan Roy's song isn't enough to visualise it:

Think of that last fearful day
when others speak but you remain wordless.

That day always arrives suddenly. But we'd like to believe that as long as there is breath there is hope. For who can accept with equanimity that final day? We all want to live after all.

My own life was losing its turbulence. I lived to wake and eat, to draw money and collect the rations from the fair price shop. Most friends were gone. The few that were left . . . talking to them made me feel idiotic.

In the middle of all this, I got a one-page letter from Lotikadi. 'Baba is most eager to see you . . .'

I'd left my address with him. Good. Meshomashai has finally gone to his daughter. Thank God. At least the poor man won't have to die alone and helpless. Having got used to Delhi's dry climate, the dampness of Calcutta had taken its toll. And Maashi was no more.

I had to look around a bit before I finally located Lotikadi's house. Lotikadi was in charge. The parents-in-law were in their photographs. Lotikadi's husband had a flourishing tarpaulin and canvas business. The whole house stank of wet rubber. That dream woman of mine was now the ultimate housewife, the large studs on her ears held in place with chains of gold. The house was three-storeyed. Huge. In the courtyard a milch cow. She had married off her eldest son. The daughter-in-law covered her head with the end of her sari and touched my feet. Lotikadi's husband was at work. Lotikadi said, 'Go to the first floor . . .'

The room I found Meshomashai in could only be described as a dump. He was surrounded by blank walls on three sides while the fourth had a window that framed a fig tree. A fan hung from the ceiling, its four blades moving lazily. I was shocked to see Meshomashai. His skin was a bloodless white. He barely recognized me.

'I have high blood pressure, blood sugar . . . Lotu doesn't care. She gives me rice twice a day.'

I turned, thinking I'd go confront Lotikadi. But she must have followed me up. She was standing at the top of the stairs saying, 'All his life he saved his money and lived like a pauper. His sons send him pounds, and he doesn't even cash them. One day he'll be dead and the bank will swallow the money. As it is the tenants are feasting on the house.'

'It'll all come to you anyway. What's the hurry?'

'I'll tell you what's the hurry. If Baba dies now, we won't be able to lay our hands on either the house or the money.'

'Why?'

'You think my brothers will come from abroad to sign the papers? And without their signatures, we won't get a succession certificate. It's undivided property. All that money will just lie in the bank's belly!'

That was also true.

'Do you know what Baba says? His son's children too should get equal shares in his property. He wants to make a will. All he has is a lakh and eighty thousand rupees and a house. And he wants to divide it and then redivide it. As if they'll rush across the seas to collect their five annas and six pice worth!'

Meshomashai sat listening to all this. Then he said with a laugh, 'All right. Bring the deed to me, I'll sign on the dotted line. That'll be the end of the matter.'

Lotikadi turned and left.

I looked at Meshomashai. He looked like a stork. No flesh at all except some black hair on two pale legs; lying on an easy-chair his body folded into three pieces. He said softly, 'I'll feel destitute if I gift everything away. Who knows which will finish first — my life, or the savings?' He paused. 'If I made a will, all the dividing up would take place after I am gone. But Lotu refuses to wait.' He sat staring at the floor.

'What does your son-in-law say?'

'He's the one who has prepared the gift-deed and left it in that wooden box. He says, Since we are looking after you in your last days, we have a right to your money. My son-in-law is a practical man.'

There was no one else in the room. I asked, 'Meshomashai, do you want to go back to your old flat?'

'They gave that up, packed my bags and papers and dumped me here. Where will I go now? Death too is taking so long, my son!'

Meshomashai was saying all this sitting in his own daughter's house, in the house of Lotikadi, my first dream woman, whose handkerchief I had preserved for a long time.

She came into the room suddenly, saying, 'Baba listens to you. If you tell him, he is sure to sign the papers.'

It's between father and daughter — who am I to say anything? I gave a meaningless smile, feeling like a fool.

I didn't stay much longer that day.

I too have a household. A tooth-ache. A position in society. Liabilities that I cannot say no to. But, in the midst of it all, I shut my eyes and I can see clearly — a father turned white, lying in an easy-chair, his daughter who goes about her housework determined to possess whatever the father owns. A mansion built around a courtyard. Even a milch cow in a cowshed. Some days I felt as if Meshomashai was beckoning me, asking, 'When will you come again? Why don't you come again?'

I did go. Quite suddenly. A Saturday afternoon. In the middle of winter. When the late afternoon sky turns blue with cold.

Not seeing anyone around, I was going straight up the stairs, when I heard Meshomashai, a definite tremble in his voice. 'How can I cheat my other grandchildren while I am still in my senses?'

It was the gift-deed again.

Lotikadi's voice: 'They won't come to this country to pick up your three pice.'

There was rebuke in her words. I could imagine her standing there. Words of anger and reproach, the worry and doubt she felt sealed in her eyes. I was wondering whether I should leave when Lotikadi spotted me.

'Come. Come and see what Baba's up to!'

She sounded as if Meshomashai had got into the pond to take a dip without the customary oil massage. So commonplace. Just a laughing matter. The easy tone of Lotikadi's voice would make one believe that Meshomashai was being pushed into participating in a friendly tug-of-war in a sports day event in a local school.

He is probably 88 years old. Wearing that old familiar pullover. His neck protruding like a stork's. A lock of white hair falling on the narrow forehead; long in-growing nails on thin fingers.

Lotikadi said, 'You try telling Baba . . .'

'I'll see,' I said and entered the room. Meshomashai was lying in the easy-chair staring at the fig tree outside. I didn't say anything.

Still staring at the fig-tree, he said, 'I have known for a long time, no one matters to anyone in this world. Your Maashi went two years ago. Do we have any bond left with her? It is maya that makes us laugh and cry.'

I stayed silent.

'You know that a calf starts running as soon as it's born. But it takes a human child five years to walk firmly. We lean on our parents and so develop an inferiority complex for life. It is in revenge for this that the adult makes his parents suffer.'

'You are tired. Let it be for now.'

'No. I will say what I have to. My brain may not function later. Do you know, son, a bird can merely whistle a few notes. A human being puts the whistle to tune, makes it into a song. And do you know what is the primal pleasure of that same human being? Murder! A human being gets the greatest joy from killing another human being. This hunter's instinct is millions of years old. I'm saying all this because I may never get another chance. I probably wouldn't even remember.'

'Meshomashai, don't say that!'

'I'm right. Today, you must listen to me. Just go on listening. If you interrupt, I'll forget, my son. I'll lose the thread . . .'

I sat listening. The long infancy of Man, and from that the urge for revenge . . . Birds merely whistle . . . The human being sings . . . The primal joy of that same human being lies hidden in murder.

'To cover up all this, the infant binds us in the illusion of its glorious smile. Under this spell, we build homes, we save money. But in reality, we are nothing to each other. Nothing. I am a separate being. So are you . . .'

Meshomashai tried to sit up.

I said, 'Let it be. Don't talk any more. Lie down.'

Suddenly, Meshomashai lay back with a thump on the easy-chair, and shut his eyes.

'What happened?' I asked.

'The earth swayed,' he said.

'Open your eyes.'

'No. I can't. I'm afraid, my son.'

'What's there to be afraid of? I'm here, Meshomashai.'

His eyes still shut, he said calmly, 'I can't. I felt as if the easy-chair was sinking on one side.' Silence followed. 'The wall in front seemed to lean sideways, taking the window with it.'

'What are you saying?'

His eyes clenched shut Meshomashai said, 'It's happened before, a few times. Lotu knows. I think . . . the river waters have entered the room. I'll slip off the easy-chair. I'll fall. Son, hold me . . . hold me . . .'

Gripping the arm of the easy-chair, Meshomashai seemed to be struggling to pull past an invisible current, fighting continuously, gritting his teeth. Any moment now that invisible torrent of water might wash him away. He might fall off his easy-chair.

I sprang up and held him with both hands.

By then, Meshomashai was screaming for help: 'The water's coming, coming . . . it's come! Hold me . . . hold me firmly . . .'

From behind, Lotikadi spoke calmly. 'Let go. There's no need to hold him.'

I lost my cool. 'What if he falls? He'll crack his skull!'

His head was rolling like that of the hookah-smoking doll at a village mela, its neck held by a wire spring.

Lotikadi sounded calmer than before. 'No. He won't fall. Baba is imagining things.'

'What!'

'A doctor has seen him. The fluid in his ears dried up long ago. A valve is not working. An ENT specialist has seen him. He is given a Stugeron tablet twice a day. He'll get back his balance with the medicine.' She leant close to her father's ear and asked loudly, 'Did you have your tablets?'

Meshomashai opened his eyes. They looked dull. Unfocussed. 'What tablet?'

'Stugeron. What else?'

'I don't remember.'

'Do what you please!' she said abruptly and disappeared once more into her richly-endowed household.

Meshomashai lay flat in his easy-chair with his eyes shut. And I, not knowing what else to do, left.

What joy can one get wrestling with a sick old man just for a signature? Or even from watching such an effort? Especially when the old man is the father, and the heroine of the wrestling bout his only daughter? Who am I to say anything?

These days I find myself thinking, We don't matter to each other. My wife has been suffering from malaria. She takes Metakelfin. Once when she had taken medicine and got into bed I said, 'We do not matter to each other, do we?' Shephali's head was aching. She had had fever. She said shakily, 'I know. You don't have to spell it out. The way you behave says it all. I'm of no concern to you.'

I tried to make amends. I massaged Shephali's forehead. It wasn't any good . . . My mind wanders. It's Meshomashai's helpless face that grows large in my mind. Those expressionless eyes. That lock of hair on the pale forehead.

Next morning, I happened to be travelling from Howrah to Andul, across what was known earlier as Bangalbabur Bridge, and which today joins Salkia, Maidan and the Howrah station. The bridge stretched, flat and sticky, like a gargantuan slab of mango pulp. Then, I saw Meshomashai emerging from the gate of the station. In a wheelchair. Behind him were four coolies. Behind them Lotikadi and her younger son. And right behind them was Platform Number 6. The Kalka Mail must have just left.

I stepped off the bus.

Quite a family album. On the bridge, in slight fog, Lotikadi's husband's car.

What's going on?

Lotikadi saw me and smiled. 'Ah! It's you! Of course!' Having got this far, she said in a coy voice, 'I brought Baba to look at the trains. We got in from the far end and came out this way.'

Meshomashai is not a child that he should be shown trains. Even so, I was pleased. A gentleman who's touching ninety is being shown trains to his heart's content by his daughter. The wheelchair is hired from the railways as also the four coolies.

'Meshomashai! How do you feel?' I asked in a spurt of happiness.

Meshomashai looked up. He didn't even recognize me.

A state of great joy or overwhelming pleasure makes a man forget everything. Maybe that is what had happened to Meshomashai.

About a month later, I was reading the newspaper one morning. An advertisement from the police department on the second page made me leap off my chair. I dressed and went straight to Lotikadi's house.

What's happened? Why the advertisement?

Without glancing at the newspaper, Lotikadi said, 'That's right. We put him in the Kalka Mail. The plan was that Amritada would come and take him off the train at Delhi. It stops there for a long time on its way to Kalka.'

'Amritada? Who's Amritada?'

'Oh, you won't know him. When we were at Raisina, he knew my parents. Called them Ma and Baba. He was just like a son to them.'

'But that was ages ago!'

'Yes. It's an old relationship. Baba wanted a change. So we thought he could spend some time at Amritada's. It would make him feel better. That Baba would be so naughty as to get off at some station on the way . . .'

I felt shaken. A man who had no memory at all — you could put him on a train? Alone?

'We got a letter from Amritada . . . Baba hasn't reached. That's when we called in the police. They took a photograph we had and put in the advertisement. Missing from the Kalka Mail.'

Oh I said, and then, 'Did he sign the deed?'

'He did that long ago. Remember, you saw him in a wheelchair that morning? That was just after he'd signed the papers.'

I said Oh again.

Even today I don't know if there was somebody called Amritada. Even today I don't know whether, on the day that I saw them all at the Howrah station, they were coming out after having tried to put him on the Kalka. That senile man with his lost memory and empty eyes, is he alive or dead? This is a vast country. Who knows where he may be now? Did he get off at Jhanjha? Or at Tundla? Only I am left behind. And that fig tree.

RUKUN ADVANI

•

DEATH BY MUSIC

•

NOMINATED BY NISSIM EZEKIEL

'If suicide wasn't such a permanent thing,' said my brother, 'I'd commit it once a day. Some days maybe twice.' I wasn't surprised. He was looking at film magazines which had pictures of Elizabeth Taylor.

The cup of my brother's life brimmed over with a shallow wit. We looked quite different from each other, but he felt the same way as me; every time we saw beautiful women the injustice of life came home to us and, like Hamlet, we weighed the pros and cons of doing ourselves in. A battle between desire and death raged within us all the time.

Looking at those pictures and gauging our impossible distance from Hollywood, I agreed with my brother, though I knew that on other days, when the blues hadn't struck with their habitual ferocity, life seemed tolerably livable, occasionally even ecstatic. It was that oscillation between feeling traumatically low and excitedly high which sank me in gloom, making me sceptical about living out life with an emotional gas regulator, always checking on how much feeling to let flow, how high to keep the flame without burning other people or burning out, how much of myself to express without feeling vulnerable, exposed, misunderstood.

Of course we weren't serious about suicide, desisting out of fear of pain: my brother said Hamlet's problem with suicide wasn't that it was unaesthetic but that he didn't have an anaesthetic. It would certainly have hurt to have passed into a realm where one couldn't even savour apple tart the next day. In some vague way we felt there lay ahead of us a future pregnant with possibilities. Our palate for what it held in taste for us dampened the desire for self-slaughter, and so the native hue of resolution was sicklied o'er with the pale cast of a proven pudding. Desire won the day; death might have seemed acceptable if it didn't cut us off so dismayingly from the senses, or if it took us off painlessly to some undiscovered country from whose bourne no traveller returns.

'Hey man, put on the Emperor Concerto,' said my brother, scattering the magazines all over the bed.

For Martin and Jane — R.A.

'Okay,' I said. I opened our record box and put Beethoven's Emperor Concerto on the record-changer.

In those adolescent days, when life seemed a balancing beam between perdition at one end and orgasm at the other, music served in some ways as a ready-to-hand substitute for sex. My brother and I had immunized ourselves against the impossibilities of lust and intimations of mortality with Beethoven's Emperor Concerto, in which the melodies seemed to give sufficient form to all the feelings we had ever harboured. Earlier, I had fretted awhile over the words to choose in some stupendous literary endeavour to transform soulful torment into aesthetic torrent, but the flow of my phrases got nowhere near the tunes in the Emperor Concerto. That music set in perspective everything else in life and seemed the highest cathartic interruption within the general desirability of silence.

Not that it was possible to get away from desire. Even the act of putting on that music had a faintly sexual tinge. Our record-changer had an erect metallic obelisk wedged into the centre of a rotating disk. The record sat on this Cleopatric needle for a few seconds and then, with a subtle bit of foreplay, the needle nudged the record right down its firm length, onto the rotator. Now it was time for the record-changer to use its arm: it had a phallic arm with a gentle curve and a hard tip. For a few seconds that arm hovered in the air, as though searching an entrance, and then gently but firmly it closed in over the Emperor Concerto. As that diamond tip nestled into the opening groove and the orchestra came alive with a triumphant orgasmic crash, we felt our veins flood with the sound of salvation. We closed our eyes and felt our bodies embrace something as sweet as Elizabeth Taylor.

'Lower the volume for God's sake,' yelled Amma from her bedroom. We paid no heed and she came in storming. 'For God's sake,' she said, softening the Emperor and closing the magazines full of Liz Taylor, 'can't you boys do anything better with your lives than mooning around filmstars?'

'Elizabeth Taylor is my birthright,' said my brother with gusto, 'and I shall have her.'

Amma raised an eyebrow, angling her disdain in our general direction. In her hierarchy neither plastic film nor orchestrally manufactured sound could surpass the hum of domestic contentment. She knew the difference between illusion and reality and patted each into its proper place, smoothing their creases. She clicked mostly to the music of knitting needles, which communicated present tranquillity and future warmth. My brother and I took the sounds of domestic bliss for granted; we were in search of the exotic and the extraordinary.

'I had a dream recently,' he explained, 'a very strange one. I dreamt I was playing the lyre in Sparta, near Mount Olympus, and out of the blue who should come walking down to me but Elizabeth Taylor, arm in arm with Zeus.'

'I'm surprised,' said Amma smiling. 'Are you sure she wasn't arm in arm with you?' She walked off towards the reality of her cushions, which needed to be tidied, and the music of her whistling pressure-cooker.

My brother explained the rest of his convoluted dream to me, a happy frolicsome dream which contrived to pull together so many of the images which rotated like planets upon the disk of our minds. In his dream my brother attempted the sweet violence of the Emperor Concerto on the lower tones of his antique instrument, and the nobility of this ridiculous effort, spotted by Zeus, made the god so full of mirth that in a fit of magnanimity he offered to make Paris out of my brother as reward for his next life, when he could have Helen all to himself and sway to the rhythms of her dance in all the Hindi films that ever came out of Bombay.

But my brother, desiring his companion Elizabeth Taylor instead, was intemperately changed into a Golden Retriever by the irate god, being retrieved from a canine end only by the divine intervention of Miss Taylor, who liked Golden Retrievers. One day, with Zeus asnooze, she disguised one of her hundred husbands as Achilles, then asked him to take the kennel and fling it with all his might, dog and all, into the River Gomti, which filtered unnoticed past the obscurest town in all Asia, where Zeus would never look. She also ordained that before the kennel fell upon the river it would change its form to a basket made of bulrushes anxiously awaited by a horde of barren washerwomen, all in search of forlorn babies which might float past their river in baskets made of bulrushes. When the women had done killing themselves over this scarce resource, the only survivor among them, after drowning the rest along the prescribed rules of Indian capitalism, would find inside a musical baby with hearing so perfect he would be the envy of Ludwig van Beethoven when he was full-grown. To this full-grown inheritor of the Emperor Concerto, declared my brother, Elizabeth Taylor had made it known that she would some day return. 'And if I remember the whole dream right,' he said, 'she's going to arrive in the shape of a queen. Yes, that's right, she'll come like an empress.'

The level of anarchy in that dream somehow faded out of our bodies as we grew older, but in those days it made perfect sense to me. That dream seemed a premonition, or the articulation of an exciting pos-sibility, or at worst a sensuous alchemy of exaltation and despair which found symbolic form in that strange pairing of Emperor and empress. The incredible harmony of tempestuous impulse and quiet sadness which moved within the grooves of the Emperor Concerto seemed linked, with an eccentricity which fortified us against the inequities of life, with the always restless, always mobile, foreever beautiful form of Elizabeth Taylor.

Something of this same restless, questing, searching feeling lay in the ample bosom of Elizabeth Taylor as she stepped out of the cinema screen of the Mayfair Theatre in Lucknow, leaving Mark Antony, Octavius Caesar and a swimming pool of asses' milk to play out the rest of *Cleopatra*.

It was perhaps a fortnight after that dream. My brother and I were part of a normal, sexually-repressed crowd of fellow natives watching the late show of that film in our small city theatre, when she calmly detached herself from tinsel and celluloid, stepped into our little movie hall, walked down the four wooden steps that separated the screen from the audience, and came straight towards our seats.

There were perhaps five hundred people in the audience, all erotically hungry for Elizabeth Taylor. English movies had begun giving way to the Hindi cinema, and the crowds only paid money to watch Hollywood heroines if they knew they were getting sex in return for their investment. 'Strictly for Adults,' the tag attached to *Cleopatra*, partly betokened the censor board's antediluvian notion of sex — which was a white woman who revealed anything between her neck and her knees — but mostly it served to draw in the throngs. In our town that label usually brought in every man to leer awhile and return home cheered.

News had got around that there were juicy titbits in *Cleopatra* which involved some queen floating about in an untransparent pool of milk, so a full house watched the film eagerly, hoping the milk in Egypt was as diluted as in India, at least enough to reveal the erogenous zones of a Nubian empress. Sitting by their side were other voyeurs like my brother and me, who had one foot in Los Angeles and the other in Lucknow. It was a motley crew that lay in wait for burnished gold to barge Cleopatra into view.

We hadn't bargained for her barging into contemporary India in a debut quite as casually spectacular as this.

'Hello,' she said softly, 'd'you think I can squeeze in somewhere for a bit?'

'Sure Cleopatra,' I replied coolly in her own sort of Hollywood drawl to aid instantaneous comprehension, 'you c'n sit right here between us.' The arm-rest between my brother and me seemed to have vanished with her appearance, and she squeezed between us to watch the rest of the movie.

Naturally, we waited for the hall to erupt in pandemonium with her entry. But to our amazement the consternation which ensued from her caesura out of ancient Egypt was visible only on screen; there seemed not the slightest evidence of it in our theatre. We looked this way and that, we rubbed our eyes and adjusted our vision, but no change of focus followed. Cleopatra sat beside us, watching what would happen next in *Cleopatra*, apparently invisible to our fellow watchers.

The movie was still running, except Mark Antony and Octavius

Caesar were no longer antagonists; they had come close to each other and were looking aghast in our general direction. For some reason, which I saw as a lack of vision, they couldn't see beyond the screen which separated them from us; their world lay in illusion. Behind them we saw a slowly gathering herd of asses alongside an army of extras. The asses brayed vigorously in our direction before wandering off-screen to waste their snorts upon the desert air. The extras scratched themselves here and there, accustoming their bodies to the fact that in such sandy climes even a substantial woman might prove a mirage and just thinly vanish.

We watched the movie hypnotised, held in thrall by what was happening. Yet only my brother and I seemed to see that the woman who sat near us, all scented and Oriented, smiling at the bewilderment of her co-stars on screen, was the missing Cleopatra. Age had not withered her, nor husbands staled her infinite desirability. If it wasn't Elizabeth Taylor sitting by our side, it could only be her ideal Platonic form come straight out of the shadowy world of Hollywood.

Meanwhile the movie was running on, perplexing us with new evidence on the decline of the Roman empire. An odd fate seemed to have struck the emperors into an open-mouthed and paralyzed inertia uncharacteristic of that period of swashbuckling Roman history. Caesar, Antony, the asses, the extras, were all searching diffidently about them, and it was soon clear to our theatre audience that the missing object of their phallic gaze was Cleopatra.

'Hey Caesar,' shouted Mark Antony, 'does she know how to swim?'

Caesar looked in alarm at the pool of milk. Four little donkeys joined him and stared down too, moved by a different intention. They bent their heads and began lapping up the pool.

'Maybe she's down there somewhere,' said Caesar, now frenzied.

More donkeys crowded around the pool, and soon there was a whole circle of asses drinking up the bath. In a minute it was quite drained, but there was no African queen at the bottom. The crowd had paid good money to see Cleopatra emerge in the nude and patiently awaited her return on their investment.

But to little profit. The passionate international relationship between Rome and Egypt remained, unfortunately for the investors, material for future speculation. For, just at this crucial juncture of history, there was a blackout.

It was an electricity failure, organised specially by all state governments in India to keep citizens in mind of exactly which set of pussy-stroking political villains were currently in power. In the theatre everyone groaned in one go, for the energy required to keep the illusion alive was at least temporarily at an end. The exit lights glowed brighter and several shrill wolf-whistles — directed from the audience at the film operators to get their generator going — got no response at all. People were stirring irritably in their seats, wondering what was going on, exasperated by the emptiness of the pool and the capricious twists of history, and then by the film's frustrating cut before the empress with no clothes could reveal all. But everyone seemed oblivious of the most obvious truth, that Cleopatra had appeared and was now one of us.

'Excuse me,' said Cleopatra to us, loud and clear in the encompassing penumbra, 'could you direct me to a hotel anywhere downtown, if there's one near here, maybe?'

My brother was still adjusting his eyesight but I, though a bit obtuse, was readier with high sentence.

'Sure Liz,' I said 'we c'n show you some reel cool places downtown.' I spoke as though those words had lodged within me all my life, awaiting only the appearance of a nubile empress to shape my utterance.

'Gee thanks honey,' she said. 'Let's go then,' she said more urgently, as we shuffled out to the sound of louder wolf-whistles in the diminishing dark. I looked nervously about, certain they were directed at the two of us and Cleopatra, certain they'd stop her leaving with us and put her back on screen to get their money's worth when the generator got going. But no one closed in upon us, no one seemed to see us, and I realized like a one-eyed man that in the country of the blind people see only as much as they are allowed by the shared social vision which constitutes each man's cornea.

As we moved out of the Mayfair Theatre, I saw her ruffle her hair and put a hanky to her eyelids, which she vigorously wiped, and there lay the rub — she seemed to know she couldn't be seen. The liquefaction of her clothes, in which she flowed with us to the foyer, attracted no comment either, even though what she wore was as flamboyantly outlandish as some of the things I'd seen on many of the Anglo-Indian Sandras and Teresas who went arm in arm and cheap high heels down Lovers Lane or the Shahnajaf Road.

Outside the hall, on the M.G. Road which blackened every Indian town as memorial to Mahatma Gandhi's abbreviated life, rickshawallahs huddled meagrely on their enlarged tricycles and a paanwallah's rope burnt its slow way towards a swimming pool of betel leaf and white lime.

We made our way through faceless throngs towards the diurnal round of parked rickshaws, the skeletons on them crying out in the dark to attract our custom. My brother and I directed her with complete confidence now, caring nothing, while Cleopatra followed where we led. We would normally have walked to our house, only a mile away, but had telepathicaly decided that travel with Cleopatra would be more pleasantly tactile, at least for us, if we squeezed into a rickshaw.

There were several people about. Two pregnant men approaching labour scratched their scrotae and had developed white moustaches eating Tootie Frooties. A Bengali gent clutched the tail of his dhoti and repeatedly insulted the nearest wall with vermilion spittle. Jesus, hoist with his own petard on the church steeple opposite, felt helplessly cross carrying the weight of avian multitudes which gurgled and crowned his nest of thorns. Below him university criminals roamed in small bands, combing their hair and then the streets for passing women. A pavement loudspeaker with a sore throat, long devoid of song, screeched its undirected abuse of music alongside the local Come September Brass Band, which brayed encouragement to a three-piece groom already astride his nag. Skeletons plied aimless rickshaws and a South Indian lady, buying a flower garland, whispered to her husband, 'Do you think that was cent per cent donkey milk in which she would be taking her bath?' They all saw straight through Cleopatra, looking at us briefly but seeing nothing amiss.

We knew where to take her, naturally. Every American who ever visited our small town was on his way to a tiger, just as in Africa they were all hunting for their roots. We knew exactly where, within our little urban jungle, she might find what she was looking for.

'Excuse me Miss Cleopatra,' said my brother, 'we can drop you off at a hotel near here which is quite nice, if you like.'

'You c'n call me Liz,' she said, so we gave her our names, and fishing in her dress pocket she added: 'Sure, any place you c'n recommend should do for now, s'long as it's kinda quiet and large and if they'll take dollars.'

We were getting on quite well, I thought, and wondered at her lack of nervousness, hopping off the screen and onto a rickshaw with her first two men in a strange city. I guessed she was a traveller, like the two of us, and felt at home being always on the move. I sensed in particular the affinity between my brother and her from the air of ease they both radiated, from that capacity some people have to appear equally relaxed among schoolchildren or lawyers, golfers or historians, strangers or friends, in the most odd or unlikely circumstances. Even in that short space I had intimations that something of my brother lay in Elizabeth Taylor too, a shared impulse which drove her all that distance from pyramid and sand dune to the obscurest theatre in all Asia.

But the precise contours of a symmetry which linked her world and ours only became obscurely clear to me towards the end of her stay in Lucknow.

All the obvious questions crowded our minds as we huddled into the rickshaw and a skeleton stood on his pedals to move us towards the Carlton Hotel, where a stuffed tiger with permed coat and waxed moustaches glared out a reception from his glass case at the entrance door. How had she made her appearance? Why had she come here, of all places? Was it really true that she sat ensconced between us, being pulled on a rickshaw so soon after rolling out of a rug to a concert of emperors? What was going to happen now? Would she stay a while or return like a mirage to the screen?

There were so many questions to ask that to ask one or the other seemed futile. There were likely to be so many answers, and all so confusing to our emotions, that silence seemed the most obvious and desired conditions of being. We stayed quiet, and so did Liz, warming to each other in the solitude of that shared cold air through the slowly passing sights, the yowl of stray dogs against the temperature, the whiff of open rubbish dumps mingling with the scent of burning eucalyptus where three men crouched to hide a glow.

We were now at the tail end of a straining spine, wondering how it managed to heft three substantial people so lavishly clad. It deserved a thousand dollars, I thought, so it could get itself some warm skin from the morgue. Watching all the absent muscle as that cadaver moved us in the direction of the Carlton Hotel was like taking in an anatomy lesson. His bones were clanking and gleamed white with the oil that dropped down to keep them from rusting. But our sympathy for him was finite; we disembarked at the Carlton Hotel.

A taxidermic tiger gaped at the arrival of Elizabeth Taylor to his hotel, his incisors gleaming at her as though awaiting his dentist. Fortunately he made no other move to receive us, and while my brother haggled with our rickshawallah we waited by his flanks at the reception desk. I watched my brother bargain with some embarrassment on account of Cleopatra's obvious concern for the pedaller. Socially, we were always under great pressure never to give anything to beggars, lepers, cadavers and the poor, lest the sin of richness deny them the kingdom of heaven, and so that we could spend all we saved on Tootie Frootie and Kassata ice cream. I tried telepathy and got through. He gave the rickshawallah a thousand dollars, which was the new currency of our country, and the bones cycled away saying salaam.

There was no one behind the reception desk. We rang an electric bell which broadcast a low whine and two cockroaches. The cockroaches had their antennae out in alarm but retreated into the bell after giving some thought to our circumstances. No one else appeared. We rang and rang again, but in Lucknow it little profits a hotel rich in vermin to employ receptionists.

'Mebbe they're full up, d'you think?' said Liz finally. 'Can we try someplace else?'

My brother ran after the pedalling silhouette to re-engage his services, and we hopped on once more.

'We live just round the corner from here,' said my brother. 'With our mother,' he added, to suggest she was safe with us.

'We could go home and you could stay overnight in our mother's room, if that's okay by you.'

'Okay,' said Cleopatra with an imperial smile, 'if that's okay with your mama.'

We had no doubt that Amma, after the initial shock, wouldn't refuse a night's shelter to our stray Cleopatra at that hour of the night. But she surprised us with her perspicacity, saying she was expecting this all along, and merely scolded Cleopatra for being out so late and out of date.

'A girl your age ought to know better than to be gallivanting about at this time of night with these two,' she said. 'I knew these brats would bring you home one day, but I thought you'd be here much earlier.'

We knew she wasn't really upset, of course, recognizing the oblique-ness of her affection from the timbre of her scolding. She'd already left Cleopatra her second-best bed, and towel, soap and nightie for the nonce.

Falling asleep on my pillow I remembered asking Amma once how the emperor Babur, walking thrice around the bed of his sick son Humayun, took the disease upon himself.

'I can't tell you how,' Amma replied, adding one of her parables. 'Some things just happen and it's best to take them as they come. Edison said Let there be Light, and there was.'

I awoke the next morning as usual to the opening crescendo of the Emperor Concerto, proclaiming the triumph with which it makes sense to start the superhuman endeavours of each new day. I liked silence in the early mornings and Amma liked bed-tea, but my brother had hegemonized us both into waking up to that music. Liz was still there. She was awake too, alert and listening, which was conclusive proof for us that she hadn't been pulling the rug over our eyes.

'I need a break,' she was telling Amma through Klemperer's majestic conducting. 'I'm through with playing Cleopatra. 'Fact I'm through with playing this queen, that queen, all the time. Gimme a break I said to all those men. Men, men, men, day and night. Makes me sick. Have you noticed how there only seem to have become more and more men and then some in the world lately? Anyhow, I just need a break. I'm through with moving beds and roles and husbands, the whole lot. I need a break. I'm looking for something different, and maybe that something's brought me here.' She paused, searching for some clearer definition of her restlessness, then shrugged.

Amma was the eternal mother and understood the emotional fatigue of continuous travel. We did too, having moved restlessly from one thing to another, unsure of what we searched, certain only of the need to persist in always seeking something other than what we possessed, distrusting the immobility of comfort and accepting instead an unquenchable wanderlust which moved us towards periods of short-lived exhaustion and defined the way we were. We saw Liz as one of us and accepted her presence in our home, refusing to ask the obvious questions and taking it for granted that her visit was something both she and we wanted, or needed, or that was mysteriously but happily fated for us. Her instinctive need was to feel free to say only as much as she wished.

Two days' rest cleared some of the cobwebs in her mind. She said she had felt imprisoned for ages by men, relationships, routine, and the omniscient clamour of human beings, and one day, when it all got too much and she felt herself at the edge of suicidal despair, she thought she saw in front of her eyes a solitary grave where a tree rose out of the earth in the shape of an upturned woman, an image of overpowering beauty towards which she had taken some sort of plunge, finding herself thereafter seated in spacious comfort, and assured of movement towards an area of blissful solitude, space and silence. She couldn't recollect anything more, no more than a child recollects its plunge into the world, nor no more than does a transformed Golden Retriever when washed amnesiac down an obscure river to a new shore. It had seemed a sudden relief to shed the past, to feel free of lovers, husbands, and the stars which directed her destiny, to watch the huge and sudden gap between herself and the people who had wrenched her insides, to be distant for a short space.

All this made sense to us. It was superficially illogical, but it had an inner emotional logic beyond which questions became transgressions. The episode fitted no formula, its causes were happily unknown and beyond the tax of ascertainment. Liz Taylor had come to us because she wanted a break, because she felt some unknown pull in our direction, and because we possessed that silent state of mind by which hospitality, being unspoken, is doubly communicated. We knew her visit would last only as long as the electric current which all three of us had generated held us together, that power breakdowns were inevitable, and that she would, like every wayfarer who makes a sojourn, soon enter that undiscovered country from whose bourne no traveller returns.

A few days went happily by and we showed her all the famous historic sights, the fading palaces, the arenas of war, the residences of conquerors, the tombs where flowers disguised the conquests of death.

'Gee honey,' said Liz by way of admiration after each monument, 'that looks kinda neat.'

But she seemed in search of something else for the old restive feeling came crowding back in her, and the sound of the Emperor Concerto which caused the sun to rise each morning troubled in her an old vision, stirring within her the sight of a solitary grave in which a tree rose out of the earth in the shape of an upturned woman. With the ebb of fatigue her vision improved and she described it to us with greater clarity. 'Have either of you ever seen anything like that?' she asked. 'I'm trying to figure out what pulled me here.'

We were puzzling over this when my brother said again, in that way he always did, 'Hey man, put on the Emperor Concerto.'

'Okay,' I said. I opened our record box and put Beethoven's concerto on the slim, taut shaft of our record-changer, watching as it edged the record towards the inevitable orgasm. It was at that very moment, with the opening crash of an allegro, that we linked Liz's vision to what was commonplace in our lives, and which connected her with an unforeseen symmetry to people so distant from her world. We had seen precisely what she described. Suddenly that instant, switching on the Emperor, we knew it had switched on in Elizabeth's mind the exact location of suicidal despair, which we saw every day on our way to school.

We knew it all our lives as the grave of an unknown woman who died mysteriously during the Mutiny of 1857, leaving only a note that her remains be spared a churchyard, and that a single tree be planted by her side as protection. The tree that emerged had a double trunk which, at the appropriate height, overlapped and gave out the appearance of a woman's thighs. That grave, that tree, were almost the epicentre of our lives, lying halfway in our history, equidistant between the unspoken warmth of our mother's knitting needles and the dictations in reason we received at our school. They were for us a sight both beautiful and moving, connected through the current of our emotions and associations with the Emperor Concerto, suddenly confirmed now by the vision which linked us to Liz.

I think it may have been at this point that some suspicion of the name of the woman in that grave began to grow within us, making us wonder at the strange contours of an emotional convergence between our world and the one from which Liz had arrived.

No official history of the Indian Mutiny of 1857 records the story of an English woman who, during the siege of the Residency, gave solace to the ears of the besieged with the only piano left in Lucknow. Her music was not of sufficient consequence for history, the sound of her instrument drowned out by cannon and musket, the crowds closing in upon the precincts and leaving no room for softness or melody, leaving room only for the suicidal despair in which the woman wrote her note, asking only solitude, silence and space in the hereafter.

There was little left for us to do now, except get confirmation of what we suspected. We summoned the skeleton again and were pulled by him towards the grave where our unknown woman rested in peace, guarded by a solitary tree which grew with silent grace along the lines of her body.

Elizabeth paid him for the long haul and he left our world grinning. Elizabeth scraped the moss that obscured an epitaph.

We were right, of course, and as Elizabeth Taylor vanished from our sight we read what we had recently guessed but never bothered before to notice.

HERE LIES ELIZA TAYLOR

1827 – 1857

WHO WITH MELODY AND MUSIC LIT . . .

The gravestone broke off at that point, leaving us in the dark with further obvious questions — Who, How, What, Where, When, and Why.

Now, looking back, I attribute our feeling for the Emperor Concerto and that singular perception of Elizabeth Taylor to an uncommon Anglicization which sensitized us to the beauties of the West, until the clamour of local historians sternly warned us against being so ideologically evil as to desire white before brown. In later years we went native and adored the acceptably off-white Shabana Azmi to atone for our misguided youth, by which time the nationalist noise had given way to the feminist, dampening our desire altogether with Wills Filter evidence on the wicked lashings of power within all male sexuality.

But in those days of adolescent dreams, when we had the power to make the images of our minds come alive almost at will, the shadows of doubt cast upon us by that grave would likely have taken up the rest of our short lives to pose and answer all those profound and overwhelming questions about the visionary and the real. We could have asked those questions endlessly, then posed them again and answered them a different way: they would have yielded no satisfactory answers. That was not a time for answers. To be alive then was to revel in the illogic of our minds and feelings, to witness the inner struggle of death and desire, to dream of Elizabeth Taylor and bring her home to bed, to listen to Beethoven and connect his music with the image of a tree or the silent beauty of a grave. The happiness of our youth was no different from the ease with which our wildest dreams and desires came so intensely alive, assuming shapes with a furious, unpredictable anarchy. I remember now those wild, speculative days, when our images of passion culminated in that brief fusion of tempestuous impulse and suicidal despair which gave us, so strangely and unaccountably, the company of Elizabeth Taylor and the Emperor Concerto.*

I claim no originality in attempting a convergence of 'fact' and 'fiction' within this story. The device is commonplace; in recent times it has been used with comic brilliance in at least two works by Woody Allen: his short story 'The Kugelmass Episode,' and his film *The Purple Rose of Cairo*.

SUBRABHARATIMANIAN

•

SPACE

•

NOMINATED BY SUNDARA RAMASWAMY
TRANSLATED BY S K SHANTI

Everywhere a darkness. Yet Thangaraj's eyes sought her. If he bent a little, stretched, his hand would touch her body. But his father lay barely ten steps away. In the other corner of the room, his mother.

Mist fell softly on the sun-heated roof. It crept into the room, sent damp fingers into the kitchen that was barely enough for one person to stand and cook. The room filled with vague smells. Night noises from neighbouring houses rose only to meld into the cold. A house in the heart of the city? You've had it for four years? At two hundred and fifty rupees? People are surprised.

He had spoken that morning to Jyoti in a voice slip-sliding between eagerness and caution. Come, he had said. When the house sleeps and immediately after Gomatiyannan has come back from his four-to-midnight shift and rapped on his door, I'll clear my throat, then come, he had said. That moment had come and gone. He had cleared his throat at least twice.

Thangaraj lay staring into the dark. A habit forced on him over the last two and half years. It was only in the early hours of the morning that sleep usually bore down on a body that burned with desire for the nearness of a woman.

He was a coolie. A larger rent was beyond his reach. At the most he could look for another house with a wall standing between his parents and him. He spent long hours conjuring up visions of that happy day. Probably he'd be a mental wreck by then.

Once there was a time when, with the death of the city's voices, their one-room tenement snuggled into darkness. Jyoti moved in from where she lay. He'd feel her closeness. For just a few minutes. Dream-like. He let those moments caress him, securing himself in the belief that the old couple slept soundly.

Was Jyoti uninterested? If not, would she have stayed away today? After he had talked to her so many times? Would she allow herself to sleep so soundly? Even if she did toil in three houses and come home exhausted?

'Space' was first published in Tamil as *'Edam'* in *Manaosai*, 1990, Madras.

He rubbed his eyes and looked around. Through the many holes of the asbestos, shimmering mist leaked in to reveal a world shrouded in shadows. His parents lay unmoving in their two corners. Maybe if he reached out quietly. Grasped her hand. Jyoti would stir. But what if she starts as if in a nightmare?

Not that there haven't been nights when he has forced himself upon her. I'm worried, she has said in a firm voice. I think she is awake . . . there, I think she moved, she's restless . . . And he has often retorted, Amma has not been able to see clearly for many years now . . . His mother slept facing the wall. On those rare nights that she's slept facing him, Thangaraj has spent the night in vigil.

Jyoti knew that on the nights she didn't change places in spite of his instruction, she'd have to pay for it. Before Thangaraj left for work around eight-thirty in the morning, he'd have found some excuse or the other to slap her. Only Jyoti knew why.

Last week it had happened again. He had slapped her face saying there was no salt in his food. His mother had gently chided her daughter-in-law. 'Child, see that the food is tasty. He's a growing boy, isn't he?' She'd murmured. Jyoti could have kept quiet. She retorted sharply. 'Nothing wrong with my cooking. If I behaved during the night, there would be no beatings. But one has to think of honour and shame even in darkness . . . ' And his mother and father hung their heads in silence. Thangaraj lifted the hand he was eating with to slap Jyoti on her cheek. Again and again. His parents didn't stir from their corner. That night her closeness had made everything seem right. Yet, such things allowed a certain ugliness to grow inside him.

He sat thinking of Jyoti's house. It was some distance from town. Though four or five families lived within a single compound, their house had a spacious front verandah. As soon as Thangaraj reached there, one room would be set aside just for him. The family would sleep in the verandah. For Jyoti those days were like heaven. But they could never stay for more than a day or two. Thangaraj had his work. And the thought of his mother's tremulous hands, the weakness of the father would make Jyoti hasten back too.

His body on fire, Thangaraj thought: What if I got up now, switched on the light and walked out, slamming the door behind me? Would that wake everyone? When I can't sleep, how can they? Why should they? And that Jyoti, when I am filled with the urgency of love to a point of madness, how dare she sleep?

Anger grew and ate into him.

His friend Govindan was an angry man too. With what joy and satisfaction he had gone about picking rags. To wed Sulochana he had printed invitations and gathered the whole town together. Just after the muhurtham, Govindan saw Sundaram, the man she'd once been in love with, stand talking to her. Govindan said nothing. But goaded by his friends, he stalked up and held Sundaram by his collar. 'Why, in what way is he less than you?' Sulochana's looks had questioned and even that he could bear. But when on their wedding night she ignored him, a battle flared. They separated. 'You have the night. A wife to be with. I didn't even have a night's darkness . . .' Govindan often says to Thangaraj. It was Govindan who had taken him to the arrack shop and got him into the habit. Thangaraj thinks of the arrack shop when he is depressed. But what will remain then of his salary?

There must be many like him who have no peace in their darkness. Those who don't have even a single room. Those who sleep in the streets. This thought brought a frayed smile to his lips.

But, right now, all he wanted was to punish Jyoti for her disobedience. I'll go sit outside in the mist, catch a fever he thought. Or, should he go arouse Jyoti? Chee! How often he has asked her to come. And she has not.

He'd go mad. Then she's bound to suffer. He wanted her to suffer. He sat there imagining her acts as secret vendetta. Last week she'd shamed his parents into silence. It was as if she had stripped him naked. Then stood laughing.

For long he sat, staring into the dark. Then, raising the wick of the kerosene lamp just a little, he went close to Jyoti. She slept curled almost into a ball — her knees doubled up with the cold.

He hardened his heart. Who asked her to reject him?

Viciously, suddenly, he gripped her by the hair.

She yelped as she tried to sit up.

'Bitch!' Thangaraj slapped her hard.

'What . . . what . . . please . . .' Her voice shattered in fear.

His mother sat up in her corner. What is it? she asked.

'This bitch . . . blabbering a man's name again and again. Immersed in a secret ecstacy maybe . . . an old flame . . .'

Jyoti was wide awake now. Crying.

Thangaraj's mother stuffed the ends of her saree into her mouth with hands that quivered. His father raised the wick to a full glow.

'Muttering the names of all sorts of men,' Thangaraj said, forcing the words to sound confident.

Jyoti said, 'Aiyo!' again. Tears spilled over. 'Aiyo!' And his father sank his head into the curve made by his knees. Jyoti turned to his mother but could only say: Sleep.

People were at the door. Knocking. Gomatiyannan. Voices. They sparked off a certain panic in Thangaraj. He remembered his moment of madness. The way he held Jyoti by her hair, dragged her. All the things he'd said . . .

He sank to the ground. His trusting parents looked on with terror in their hearts as Thangaraj hit his hand against his forehead. They'd never know why.

ZAMIRUDDIN AHMAD

•

LIKE LIGHTNING
IN THE SKIES

•

NOMINATED BY GOPI CHAND NARANG
TRANSLATED BY M ASADUDDIN AND MANJU KAK

I was lying on a bed in the attic, reading a short story by Manto from *Saqi's* special issue on short fiction when I heard a tap on the window. This window, fitted in the wall between our terrace and Peshkar saheb's house, connects both establishments. Or one might say it separates them. The window is large enough for a person of ordinary height to pass through, standing.

I waited a few moments. Another tap. I tossed the magazine aside and got up. I knew who it was yet I asked, 'Who's there?'

'It's me bhaiya . . . me,' she whispered from the other side.

'He's not here.'

'I know . . . he's gone to Kannuaj for a mushaira.'

A brief silence. Then she said in a low halting voice: 'I wanted to talk to you.'

A thrill of expectation ran through me. 'Hold on,' I said and leapt onto the terrace. The courtyard below was desolate; so too was the front verandah. Abbajan had gone to the estate along with the Munshi. So there was no question of anybody being in the drawing room or in his room that was adjacent to it. Pathani would be dozing in her hut. Her husband, affectionately called Kaley mamu by everyone despite his fair complexion, would be sleeping on a charpai under the neem tree in front of the guest house. Their son, not one to miss such an opportunity, would be cooped up in a closet, poring over some pornographic novel or the other by Wahi Dhanawi. As for Ammijan and Naniamma, one could hear a faint drone filtering across the big room just below the roof in front of the attic: Ammijan would be reading to Naniamma, probably Fayyaz Ali's second novel which I had bought for her the day before. Khairatan would be pulling the punkah and Chote Mia, in deference to a parental diktat not to step out into the sun, would be staring at the durrie on the floor, restless, waiting for sun-down . . . oh no! he'd be in school.

Cautiously I closed the door at the top of the staircase leading to the courtyard, hurried back to the window and said, 'Now tell me, what can

'Like Lightning in the Skies' was first published in Urdu as *Tashna-e-Faryaad* in *Saughat*, September 1991, Bangalore.

I do for you?' I heard the sound of the latch being lifted. The window opened slightly and I saw a wrist twinkling with multicoloured Firozabadi glass bangles, a henna-smeared palm, a forefinger and thumb clutching the creased and crinkly end of a dupatta. Through the opening I glimpsed her right profile.

'Are you sure no one's around?'

'Yes. The coast is clear.' I opened wide the window. The roof on her side was lower than ours. A few steps down allowed for easy passage between the two families. She put her foot on the stair as if to come up, then hesitated.

'You come. There's no one in the house.'

It was as though the bride was leading the barat, with pomp and music, to the bridegroom's. I had a quick look around and went down to her roof. She drew her ghunghat to her face, stepped up to the window, closed it and dropped the latch. Still keeping her back to me she said, 'Please go to my room. I'm coming.' I rushed eagerly. I could see the dome of the mosque from there. So this is the room where Ruswa saheb's been having a good time! I was invited here often till she started keeping purdah before me.

There was a bed close to the rear wall. Draped in embroidered silk. Between the two doors there was a settee with a prayer rug that had been rolled up securely and a single pillow which nestled to the wall. Between the bed and the settee was a glass lamp on a round table. An armchair close by. Over the untiled floor running from wall to wall was a thick, red and blue-bordered durrie. The two doors that opened onto the inner rooms were ajar.

I was about to take the armchair but then, smiling at my folly, sat on the side of the bed. She came in and stood behind the door so I could see only one of her ankles peeping out of her poplin paijamas.

'Bhaiya, please do me a favour.'

'Not one, ten . . . and ten times over!'

'Don't tease bhaiya . . . I beg you.'

My eyes were glued to her ankle, immured in the tight paijamas. 'It's I who should beg you, bibi. But come here a moment,' I said, and made room for her beside me. 'How long will you observe this purdah? As if I have never seen you before?'

'That was different.'

'Why?'

'Then you were a mere boy.'

'And now?'

'Now, by Allah's grace . . .'

'I've become an adult?'

'Yes.'

'I admit to guilt.'

'It's not a joke bhaiya . . . I'm really very upset.'

She continued to stand behind the door. It seemed she wanted to talk about something.

'Okay, no more jokes. But you must face me or I'll go!' I got up as if to go, stretching my right foot slightly. She came to me hesitantly. Though her ghunghat was still drawn, her face could be seen.

And what a face she had! Long eyelashes shaded her eyes, the skin was smooth and tight, her lips about to part in a smile and the fullness of her breast tantalised from under the creased folds of her dupatta.

I pointed to the bed and asked her to sit. Through downcast eyes she saw my gesture, but sat on the armchair in such a way that I couldn't see her face properly.

'Fine, now tell me, what is it?'

She kept staring at her feet then said, 'Please try to persuade him.'

I waited for her to continue, but when she didn't, I said, 'About what?'

'That he should not try to see me anymore.' She rearranged the front edge of her chikan kurta on her shapely thighs and began to make tiny pleats with it, her face enveloped in a mist of confusion.

'Why? I mean what reply should I give if he asks why?' She continued making more pleats, her fingers moving furiously: 'Otherwise something terrible may happen . . . I tell you, I've been feeling very uncomfortable for the past few days.' I looked at her restless hands. Take Khamaira Marwarid, bibi; it will strengthen your nerves.

'I'll tell him if you want me to, but your reasons aren't very convincing, are they?'

She joined her palms and pressed them between her thighs: 'I'm not telling lies . . . I feel as though I'm on tenterhooks.'

'You're imagining things.'

'Could be . . . but I think Peshkar saheb has become suspicious.'

'Why?'

She tilted her head slightly to look at me blankly, then glanced down.

I said, 'What makes you think that Peshkar saheb has become suspicious? Ruswa saheb never comes to the house by the main road. Neither have you ever met him outside. So how could anyone have seen you and reported it to Peshkar saheb. He always comes and goes through our terrace and he does so only when there's no one else in your house; when Peshkar saheb is in court. And the maid is there only in the mornings and the afternoons. Have you exchanged letters? Has someone got hold of them?'

'No'

'Then?'

'For the last few days Peshkar saheb looks changed . . . his eyes seem to pierce through me.'

Indeed you're a thing to be seen, bibi! I thought, watching her downcast eyes.

'I think you're imagining things,' I reassured her.

'One thing more. Something has been weighing on my mind for the past few days. This is a decent mohalla. If it gets around I'll be utterly ruined. The neighbourhood too would get a bad name. Bhaiya, please tell him that this should end, now.'

Obligation . . . and its return! A bubble of hope arose. Yes, good for me if I could persuade Ruswa. 'But there's a problem,' I said.

She looked up at me.

'If he asks, Why do you interfere? Why doesn't she talk it over with me, then what do I say?'

'No bhaiya. He won't talk to you like that, I'm sure. You're such good friends.'

'I'll do my best. But it'd have been better if you spoke to him yourself.

Don't you think so?'

She was silent for a while, then said, 'I broached the matter yesterday . . . didn't dare tell him plainly . . . only dropped hints . . . but he flared up. Truly bhaiya, I'm scared of him.'

So this was it!

'What's there to be scared of?' I asked

'Your friend is rather short-tempered.'

'So? It's you who started it. You can end it as well.'

Her cheeks reddened. 'Don't say that! I didn't start it.'

'Then who asked for a copy of the ghazal?'

'I liked it, so I asked. But it's he who pulled my wrist as I stretched out my hand to receive it.'

'I know you peeped at him from behind the window.'

Her cheeks got redder. 'And when I went downstairs, didn't he peep slyly from the door of your attic?'

I looked at my watch. Half past three.

She got up. 'Time for the maid. You should leave now, bhaiya . . . but don't forget.'

'Oh no! I'll speak to him and tell you what he says. Is noon all right?'

'Yes. But don't tap the window. I'll talk to you myself when I get the opportunity.'

And then like a thief I unfastened the window-latch cautiously and tiptoed to my terrace, as I had seen Ruswa do many times.

The following afternoon, all through the half mile to Kamaal-ganj to see Ruswa, I continued to evaluate Majaz's *Awara* according to the principles of progressivism.

Then we sat on a culvert, Ruswa and I, against the back-drop of a radiant horizon, fields spreading far and wide, mango trees in blossom and weary peasants driving home their cattle. We listened to the birds chirping on a spreading banyan tree a little way off. A solitary bullock cart, bells jingling, rattled on the white sheet of pebbled road, and the sound of conch shells announcing the evening ritual, resounding from houses close by. A cuckoo cooed from the mango grove behind us, while a screened ikka sped by the houses, hooves clip-clopping in rhythm. The screen moved slightly and a woman's face appeared, remaining in view for a long time.

Ruswa watched appreciatively then turned.

'Yes, Yes . . . I agree,' I said.

He hummed for a while. 'Listen, a poem is born.'

'Let's hear it?'

He sang. The enveloping darkness, silence, the open air and Ruswa's melodious voice created a moment of magic. The poem spoke of the coming together of lovers; the beloved's glowing face, her bashful eyes, the lingering fragrance and the warmth of her breath, and her heartbeats as she waited expectantly in the bedroom. The refrain went:

Again, like lightning in the skies
the night has danced before my eyes.

'Wonderful, superb!' He lowered his head and lifted his hand in an adaab, gracefully acknowledging my compliment.

'On her, I suppose?' I asked.

'Yes.'

'I went to her bedroom yesterday.'

He was stung, as if a scorpion had crept from under the culvert and had bitten him.

'You did? What did you go to that room for?'

'To see her. What else would I go there for?' I thoroughly enjoyed his discomfiture. 'But I didn't go there on my own.'

'Then?'

'Was invited.'

The scorpion stung again. 'Impossible!' he said.

I put him at ease by telling him all that had transpired the day before. To add anything more was neither desirable nor necessary. Ruswa became thoughtful: 'I don't know what has got into her! Told me also the same thing the day before. Didn't say so clearly but the hints were obvious. Seems she's had her fill. You never know with such women . . . May have taken a fancy to someone else . . .' He began to search for something in his face.

I sighed amen to 'has had her fill.' But assured him firstly that I considered it wrong to think that way about my best friend's love. She hadn't had her fill of him. On the contrary she was still crazy about him. 'I feel she's telling the truth. She's got scared. What's her age? Just twenty seven or twenty eight and a novice at that!'

Ruswa forgot the sting and smiled. 'Call her a novice! Can't tell you what magic she can weave.'

'But she doesn't look . . .'

'Yes, they look like that! As though you can smell mother's milk in their breaths. But I'm not a guy who allows a prize to slip through his fingers so easily.'

Ruswa's temper did not augur well. I put in a few words of my own. 'I reassured her. I could just make her agree to another tryst so that the prize and the hunter can decide their future themselves. Apparently she wants to bring it to a close. Of course one never knows what's going to happen tomorrow . . . One thing more, she wants the tryst to take place somewhere else, not in her room.'

Ruswa's Pathan veins did not twitch this time. On our way back we decided, after a lot of thinking, where to meet and how.

She tapped the window the following day. I had come up a little while ago having reassured myself that everything was all right. Nevertheless I lifted the latch of the staircase door; also of the other staircase which descended straight down to the street — the one Ruswa normally used. Then I raced back to the window and said, 'Come in.'

She unfastened the latch on her side but didn't climb the staircase: 'No, bhaiya, you had better come this side.' This time no dupatta screened her face from my eyes, though she drew a slight ghunghat. I sat on the chair while she sat on the bed demurely.

'You've spoken to him?'

'Yes,' I said, briefly touching on those details about her skill at creating magic. Of course I substituted his dubious comments with milder ones so that even if they hurt they'd be bearable.

Her eyes moistened. 'I've ruined myself for him and he talks like this! I'd rather be dead than hear this!' With the corner of her dupatta she restrained her tears. 'There's no one in the world I can call my own — neither brother nor sister, nor anyone else. I had only my parents who tied me in marriage to him . . .' she pointed to the floor as though Peshkar saheb was there, '. . . before they left for their heavenly abode.' Once again her eyes brimmed over.

I turned in my chair to face her, then jumped up. 'Hey, what's this?' I stretched my hands towards her dupatta but she quickly wiped away her tears. 'Fact is, your Ruswa saheb loses his temper quickly and when one's angry one says all sorts of things. When I told him that you wanted to end this, he flared up . . . Well if he didn't love you why did he become so angry? You don't know, he's written a poem about you!'

Her right hand quickly went to her breast, then rose to cover her mouth. 'Hai Allah,' she whispered, blushing. 'I don't know what he's written! Sometimes he writes such embarrassing things.' The blush deepened. 'Did you read it?'

'No . . . Just told me that he'd written a passionate poem about you. When I asked him to read it, he simply said, At the mushaira.'

'Which mushaira?'

I told her that a mushaira was being held. It would be on the night of the full moon at the Parade Ground in front of the Dak Bungalow. They were to meet for the last time at Lal Diggi, only a hundred yards off the Dak Bungalow. It is surrounded by a cluster of trees and bushes so thick that even during the day one can hardly see through them. A better place for the rendezvous could not be found. 'When Ruswa saheb's turn comes, be prepared . . . He'll recite his verses and leave. Wait for a while and then come out. The ladies will sit on the corridor behind wicker screens. When you leave, don't forget to put on your burqa. I'll meet you and escort you to Lal Diggi. Then it's between you and him. I'll keep guard and let no one interrupt your tryst.'

She seemed embarrassed.

I added, 'One thing more. If I cough once, it means danger; if I cough twice, danger's imminent.'

'This Lal Diggi and the mushaira . . . Couldn't we meet here?'

'This is what he suggested.'

'But if Peshkar saheb doesn't allow me to go to the mushaira. He thinks all this frivolous!'

'Haven't you gone earlier? Just tell him that your aunt is taking you. But talk to Ammijan first.'

She talked to Ammijan that evening. Peshkar saheb came at night, after his esha namaz, the last prayer of the day, to pay his respects to Ammijan. He sat on a wicker chair in the courtyard. He was a little ill-at-ease because he had come to call after a longer time than was usual.

Standing behind the door Ammijan asked after his daughter, Haseena, married to a fellow in the footwear trade in Kanpur. Then she told him she would take his wife to the mushaira. Peshkar saheb acquiesced without demur. Sitting beside him on another wicker chair, I contemplated his dark complexion, his grizzled beard and his bulging paunch barely concealed beneath his shirt. When he left I could not resist telling Ammijan that I did not find any pocket in Peshkar saheb's pyjamas though I looked very closely. She looked up at me and said, 'What use are they if they're visible!' I laughed good-humouredly and left to give Ruswa the good news.

People flocked to the mushaira as never before. The crowd behind the wicker screens was particularly dense. Word went round that Yusuf saheb who had recently joined as the District Collector would also come.

Yusuf saheb was young and handsome and well dressed, clad in sherwani and churidars. He was seated beside the chairman.

I was going to see how the land lay around the bungalow when someone called me from behind the screens. It was Mehdi Vakil's daughter Kishwar, who had just arrived from Aligarh for the holidays.

'So you're back again!' I teased.

She implored, 'Please do me a favour, my favourite brother.'

'Go ahead.'

'Hand this chit to Yusuf saheb.'

'How do you know him?'

'I don't.'

'Why this note then? Shame! You've picked up the ways of the Aligarh girls? I'll tell Chacha Miyan!'

'Don't be silly!'

'Hey mister, read the note first before reaching conclusions,' said a girl beside her. I opened the note. 'Yusuf saheb, why don't you too recite something, please.'

'Sign this note,' I stretched my hand towards Kishwar.

'Be off. I won't talk to you.'

'Okay, don't pull a face. Fact is, Yusuf saheb doesn't write verses. A pucca I.C.S. You should've known!'

'How do you know?'

'I know, that's why I'm telling you.'

'Everyone scribbles a little now and then.'

'Well, he doesn't. Of course, if you've any other message, then . . .'

She stamped her foot. 'I'm going to tell Badiamma right away.'

I sauntered off to the back of the dak bungalow, laughing, tearing her note to shreds.

Ruswa's turn came when the mushaira was at its peak. I was scouting behind the dak bungalow. Ruswa recited his poem, waited for a few minutes, then came out and walked towards Lal Diggi. After a little while she emerged, clad in a black burqa. She looked around furtively, saw me, quickened her pace, and soon both of us were moving towards Lal Diggi. I kept looking back to see if anybody was following us.

We crossed the grove that screened Lal Diggi. A walled tank, built years ago by Englishmen, was before us when Ruswa emerged from behind a tree. I pointed him out to her. She hesitantly moved towards him. They disappeared behind the bush on the other side of the tank. I moved forward, on tiptoes, not to eavesdrop but to warn them in case of danger. I stopped about ten or twelve yards from them.

Several minutes passed. There was no sound. Then I heard their

voices. I went forward . . . but the sound ceased abruptly. Only her glass
bangles tinkled once or twice. Then I heard her saying 'no' and a
moment later, 'I swear on myself' and then Ruswa's 'It's all right,' then
the sound of someone sitting on crackling leaves and then . . . silence.
I craned my neck to peep into the bush but could see nothing. I went
further towards the bush . . . To move still further was not desirable.

They started talking again in hushed tones. One could just make out
a word here and there. Nevertheless I could follow the general drift of
the conversation. She was telling Ruswa why their meetings must come
to an end, giving the same explanation she had given me. But it was
punctuated with frequent allusions to her yearnings, her restlessness
and the fire within her. To convince him she resorted to oaths on
Ruswa's life and youth. At the same time she invoked curses on herself:
'Let me be damned! Let me rot! Let the evil hour come today rather than
tomorrow . . .' and so on. Now and then I heard my poet-friend. He was
talking of sense and circumspection, trying to reassure her, but she was
not convinced by his arguments. Then all of a sudden I heard the sound
of weeping. One hiccup, a long sigh, one 'hai' and then, 'If I knew it,
I'd not have set my house on fire.' But Ruswa was unmoved. He resorted
to another strategy: 'I can't live without you . . . I'll drown myself in the
Ganga . . . I'll take poison . . .' etc.

The sound of weeping stopped. 'May your enemies take poison!
Promise me you'll never say such things. If you do you won't see me
again. Am I dead and gone that you feel you can say such evil things?'
Then came a wordless sound that even a child would have understood!
After that, eerie silence.

Without losing time, I coughed twice in quick succession.

Ruswa emerged from the bush. 'What is it?' he asked in both fear and
irritation.

I drew closer. 'There's someone.'

'Coming this way?'

'Probably . . . I heard footsteps.' She was sitting on the strewn leaves,
looking scared. I don't know why I was relieved to see the lower part
of her burqa intact. Ruswa looked around: 'There's no one.'

'Went some other way perhaps, or could've been my fancy only.'

'What the hell!' he exclaimed and turned away.

'We should make a move now, it's getting late,' I said.

'Just a little longer.'

'No . . . I'm off. If you want to stay, suit yourself.' Before Ruswa could say anything she brushed the leaves off her burqa and got up.

'Yes, maybe we must leave now, it's quite late,' Ruswa agreed.

Standing behind a tamarind tree she took off her burqa, folded it and draped it carefully on her arm. She smoothened the creases in her dress, looked back at Ruswa who was following her, and then around, before entering the Dak Bungalow compound quickly. The mushaira was still going on in full force.

The following evening Ruswa came to my house. He said salaam to Ammijan and acknowledged her appreciation of his poem, received Naniamma's blessings and then raced up the stairs to me. He was happy. I knew why. Still I asked him. He recited a passionate ghazal which they had sung to each other inside the bower in Lal Diggi. The concluding couplet ran something like this: 'The matter has been sorted out and the poet says, everything is right with the world.' He peeped into Peshkar saheb's house but she was nowhere in sight. He chatted listlessly for a while, then left saying he would come again.

He came at noon the next day, the day after, and the day after that — for four successive days. He'd peer through the window, but was unable to see her. He would tap the window but no reply came. On the fourth day he looked for a stick. When I asked why, he replied, 'I'll unfasten the window latch.'

'For God's sake, don't do it . . . if there's anyone around all hell will break loose,' I implored.

He couldn't find a stick, kept pacing the terrace and left.

On the fifth day he didn't turn up and on that very day she chose to tap. As the window opened she stood there, her ghunghat drawn up a little. With demure, downcast eyes she looked entrancing. She held an envelope out to me: 'Please give this to him today.' I took the envelope sealed with too much glue. It had neither a name nor an address. 'Don't read it,' she implored. 'Don't worry,' I assured her. Repeating 'This very day' she closed the window.

Though tempted, I didn't open the envelope. The formidable glue was a deterrent. Besides, I thought, Ruswa would certainly tell me the gist of it.

Ruswa read the letter twice — first, impatiently and then, slowly with frequent pauses. He said she had invited him. 'Her Peshkar saheb has gone on a tour with the Collector and he will return tomorrow. He has told the maid to stay with her tonight. A daytime assignation being risky, she has called me over at night. Tonight, after eleven! By that time the maid'll be asleep. The window will be left unlatched. She writes, But first make sure that our (look at this 'our!') room is dark. You mustn't come if you find the light on. Wait till it's switched off.'

It was barely sundown when Ruswa arrived. He had dinner with us and when Ammijan, Naniamma and Chote mia went to sleep in the courtyard, he came upstairs with me. I asked Kaley mamu to close the door as Ruswa saheb would leave by the outer stairs.

We quickly peeped through the window. The light was still on in 'our' room. Ruswa sat impatiently leafing through books and magazines. Then he went out, looked through the window to the other side, then came back. 'Keep waiting, on and on, and . . . on!' he recited.

After a little while he went out again but came back disappointed. 'It's not eleven yet,' I said.

'Suppose the old hag stays awake tonight?'

I guffawed. 'Why? Is she also waiting for you?'

It was five or six minutes to eleven when he went out for the fourth time. I was with him. We looked towards her side. 'Our' room was now enveloped in darkness. Cautiously he opened one window panel, crossed over and climbed down the steps to her terrace. Keeping close to the wall, crouched like a thief, he tiptoed across the terrace, entered her room and merged with its darkness.

I pushed back the window panel, closed the staircase door and lay down . . .

When he woke me it was almost dawn.

'Close the door . . . I'm leaving,' he whispered.

I got up, bleary-eyed. He was already at the staircase door. 'Meet me in the afternoon,' he said. I nodded, shut the door after him and went to sleep.

I could not meet Ruswa that evening because I had to escort Ammijan to Mehdi Chacha's place. I tried my best to get out of it, but she was firm.

By the time Abbajan returned from the tour of the estate the following day, the PCS results were out. I had got in. Naniamma said a prayer of gratitude to Allah. Ammijan's stature had increased. Khairatan revealed she had pledged a floral sheet for the grave of Nogazey Peer. Kaley mamu had already conceived of me as a future District Collector, Chuttan had decided that he would appoint himself my orderly and finally, Pathani opined it called for the distribution of sweets. Chote Mia was at school. Had he been home, he would have wheedled at least ten bucks off me.

When Abbajan heard the news, he hugged me. 'Didn't I tell you!' he said to Ammijan. So overwhelmed was he with emotion that he kept pacing the verandah, end to end—as God's my witness!—at least thirty times. Then sweets were brought from Kalicharan halwai and dispatched to relatives, friends and acquaintances and alms were distributed to the beggars in the area.

Chachi bi arrived as soon as she got the news, along with her three daughters — Appi, Kishwar and Nahid. When she saw me she exclaimed with a gesture to ward off ill-luck, 'May God bless you and make your troubles mine!' Kishwar mimicked her mother with great gusto and everyone burst out laughing. She drew her ghunghat a little and raising a cupped hand to her chin said: 'The slave girl pays her humble respects to you, Deputy Collector saheb!' I raised my hand to slap her playfully but she jumped away crying, 'Look Badiamma!' and hid herself behind Ammijan, bringing forth another roll of laughter. I caught Ammijan glancing meaningfully at Abbajan who appeared non-committal. Chachi bi looked from Ammijan to Abbajan, reflected a moment and then renewed her blessings.

Ruswa came. He was seated in the outer drawing room. Munshiji who had accompanied Abbajan on his tour was examining the accounts there. We had no opportunity to talk of what lay uppermost in our minds. Ruswa was offered sweets. He gulped down one motichur and a piece of barfi. Appi, Kishwar and Nahid implored him to sing a ghazal. He refused. All of them, specially Appi, cried out 'Ghazal, ghazal, ghazal!' Ruswa gave in and sang one of his soulful ghazals. The applause was tumultuous.

The following day the whole town was agog with the rumour that Peshkar saheb's wife had run away with another man. No one seemed to know how it all began and who spread it. The old maid, a confidante of Peshkar saheb's former wife, came to our house at dawn to find out if she was at our place. She told Ammijan, swearing by her grey hair, that she had not told anyone so far, nor would she ever do so: 'My lips are sealed.' Abbajan had gone to Peshkar saheb's house seven years ago when his former wife died. Now, seven years later when he went once again, Peshkar saheb implored him to keep it to himself.

Yet the rumour spread.

Khairatan got to know of it from Dr. Purusuttam Das's maid, Kaley mamu heard about it at Nadir the butcher, Chuttan got to know it from Nawab the paan-seller. Pathani's friend, a maid working for Farooq Hasan, the retired judge, came trudging a long way to pass on this news to her. 'Where can she go after all? Who's there to call her own that she'd run away after a mere tiff?' said Pathani, sitting on her haunches, to Ammijan who was seated on the bedstead.

'I smelt a rat when she disappeared from the mushaira. She was gone for an hour and when she returned she was not herself,' Ammijan said. Then she turned to me as I lay beside her, asking, 'Do you know anything about this?'

'Me? . . . No!' Fortunately she couldn't see my face.

Khairatan who had been tightening the nivar of the bed stopped and said, 'Must've been carrying on with some fellow.'

'Hey girl, softly. Master's there in the drawing room,' Pathani reprimanded Khairatan though both Pathani and Ammijan seemed to agree. But Naniamma, who sat reclining on the pillow, seeing everybody from behind thick spectacles, remained silent. I got up, slipped into my sherwani and went out saying, 'I'll be back in a moment.'

I met Ruswa on the way. He had heard the news. He took me aside, 'Didn't I tell you that such women are never faithful! Must've been carrying on with some other guy too.'

'How's that possible?'

'How do I know?'

'If you don't mind, may I . . .'

'Sure'

'I thought it was you.'

He was taken aback. 'Do you think I'm crazy?'

'No! What I meant was, perhaps she had run away to you.'

'And I've hidden her somewhere?' he burst out, 'You're the limit, I must say.'

By afternoon the riddle was almost solved. No one doubted that she had run away with her lover. The only thing that remained undiscovered was his identity. 'For how long can you keep something like this a secret?' I heard Abbajan telling Akhlaq Hussain who, Ammi said, 'had appeared, as if from nowhere' and was sitting in the drawing room.

'You know, Peshkar saheb divorced the whore last night,' Khairatan remarked to Chuttan in the kitchen.

'Why?'

This Khairatan didn't know.

But Saffu, the postman knew. When he met me in the street he congratulated me, handed over a parcel, and then gave me the details of the scandal. 'She was in her room with her lover when the maid woke up. She went upstairs and saw everything with her own eyes. Peshkar saheb was on tour. When he returned the following day, the maid told him all . . . and she ran away that night.'

But when Pathani went to Farooq Hasan's haveli, she heard a different tale from his wife. Pathani told Ammijan when she came back. 'The Peshkar hadn't gone on tour at all. He had his suspicions, so he thought up a strategy. He told her that he was going on tour and asked the maid to stay with her. But he returned stealthily at night and caught them. Had it not been dark, he would've identified the fellow.' Then she looked around, put her dupatta between her lips, and said, grinning slyly: 'Everyone looks the same, undressed.' Ammijan also put her dupatta between her teeth when she saw me and demanded, 'What're you doing here?'

But all speculation ended in the afternoon when the bhishti came to draw water. He dropped the bucket in the well. Terror struck him. A body lay, floating. She had not run away with any lover after all.

After dusk Ammi climbed the roof to go to Peshkar saheb's house. She took the maid aside and coaxed her into telling her what had actually happened. From the terrace I could hear Ammi narrating the sequence to Naniamma: 'The maid admitted that she had seen the Peshkar's wife making love. She didn't raise an alarm for fear of calumny. She told the Peshkar everything when he returned from tour the following day. She'd have betrayed her master had she not done so. The Peshkar threatened to turn his wife out. To divorce her. So wanton was she that she wouldn't give out her lover's name. The next morning when she couldn't be found everyone thought she'd run away . . . The maid said that had she not been asleep, she'd have stopped her.'

Naniamma was silent.

It was about ten at night. I wanted to talk to someone and went downstairs. Abbajan and Ammi, despite the heat, were closeted in the inner drawing room talking in hushed tones. Ammi mentioned post mortem and Abbajan said only Yusuf saheb could prevent it. I broke into a cold sweat.

Naniamma was in the courtyard, on the takhat, knees folded under head bent in prayer. I went and sat close to her. Finishing, she recited a Dua which was longer than usual. Then she folded her prayer rug, leaned back on the bolster and, as was her habit, fell into deep meditation. After a long while she opened her eyes slowly, and addressing no one in particular, said: 'What an unfortunate girl, to have given up her life for *such* people.'

VIVEK SHANBHAG

·

EACH UNTO HIS OWN

·

NOMINATED BY D R NAGARAJ
TRANSLATED BY RAMACHANDRA SHARMA

Having walked around the backyard as she did every morning, picking ripe cashewnuts, straightening the trellis under the straggling creepers of the basale, gathering the clean fruit from among the purple berries that had dropped to the ground and bundling the bark-strips of the tree for the bathroom fire, Bayakka stood near the fence before entering her house. She thought she saw an old woman in a strange dress sitting on the verandah of the house two doors from hers. Must be Shankara's mother Kamalakka she thought, but what was Kamalakka wearing? Bayakka stopped a passerby coming from the direction of that house. 'Venka, it's Venka, isn't it?' she asked. 'Who's that on Shankara's verandah?' And Venka said, 'I don't know for sure. It *looked* like Kamalakka . . .'

Whatever happened to the old thing? Bayakka wondered as she turned and walked into the house. But she could barely allow herself to store the fruits and have something to eat. Her curiosity grew and grew as she recalled what she had seen and when she thought she'd burst, she pulled the door shut behind her and walked over to Shankara's house.

And there was Kamalakka, in a nightgown that was splattered all over with garish flowers. Bayakka had seen it on Lalitha before. She burst out laughing and, laughter melting into words, asked what it was all about. Kamalakka smacked her forehead as if to say, Just my fate, what else? Bayakka was standing there at a loss for words when Lalitha came out, as if on cue.

'What's this on your mother-in-law? A fancy dress?' Bayakka asked as she went up the front steps.

'She trips in a sari and I have to be there to tie it everytime. It gets wet when she goes to the bathroom. I thought she'd find a nightie more convenient . . .'

'I have no problems with the sari,' Kamalakka intervened, 'All this is just to flout my wishes. Who knows what I have to go through before I die?'

'Each Unto His Own' was first published in Kannada as *'Namma Padige Navu'* in *Lankesh Patrike* Special Issue, November 1991, Bangalore.

'Why do you force her into doing things she doesn't like?' Bayakka asked. 'So what if she has problems with the sari. Go get it. I'll help her tie it.'

Lalitha didn't like this one bit. 'There's no need for that, thank you. I wish you wouldn't interfere. Let's each mind our own business,' she said. Lalitha's voice was a little raised.

Bayakka came back home feeling depressed. As she fed the bathroom fire to make the hot water for her bath, she recalled what Lalitha had said and felt a sudden surging pity for Kamalakka. Poor Kamalakka. She had been much happier when she lived alone, constantly yearning for her son. Her troubles started as soon as her son and daughter-in-law came to live with her, with Shankara talking of looking after his mother, now that he had retired from service.

How Lalitha bullies her helpless mother-in-law! That girl has a swollen head, Bayakka thought. Others too said the same thing but when Bayakka said it they chided her, saying that she shouldn't interfere in the affairs of the village. Bayakka couldn't find any fault with herself. Was it wrong for her to point out when others erred? She certainly was not the sort to spread rumours and break up families. But these days, anyone and everyone thinks they can advise me, she thought with a short, exasperated sigh, as she broke the coconut fronds to feed the fire. Yes, that Lalitha was indeed swollen-headed, she told herself again, though inside her there grew a vague feeling that perhaps a new way of life was opening up in Heravatte and she was no longer a part of it.

She was barely fifteen when she came to Heravatte as the bride of Venkatesha, a school teacher. Venkatesha was older than her by twelve years. The family she came into had her in-laws and her father-in-law's sister, Priyagi, who had been widowed in childhood. Bayakka managed to get on with her in-laws, people who were obsessed with religion, rites and rituals, with things like puja, madi,* and saligrama.*

Madi means ceremonial purity and, *Saligrama* is a rare stone kept in homes as an object of worship.

Venkatesha was serious by nature and always went about clad in immaculate khadi. The people of Heravatte had a great regard for him. They hung on his words.

Venkatesha's love towards her pleased Bayakka. Sripathi was born three years into their marriage. But before this child who'd carry forth the family name could even lisp, Bayakka's mother-in- law died. Priyagi soon followed. And Bayakka's father-in-law who'd gone around harping on puja and madi grew senile and started roaming the streets eating out of a packet of beaten rice he bought from Babuti's hotel. Venkatesha had shown great understanding till the end and had left his father to his own ways, having advised Bayakka to do the same. Her father-in-law died one day in the precincts of the temple.

Just as Bayakka was beginning to think that she'd be setting up a family of her own, everything was suddenly over. When Sripathi was ten years old, Venkatesha, who had never been bedridden even for a day, died and left her heartbroken. Bayakka felt that the wheel of her life was turning too fast for her.

She soon resigned herself to her fate. The only thought she had was for Sripathi and his future. She felt that a great responsibility had fallen on her shoulders as she recalled the words of her father-in-law who always talked about the prestige of his family and its lineage.

'Why should you stay here with the child?' her father asked. He had suggested that she go back with him.

Bayakka remembered sad, hapless Priyagi who had returned to live with her brother when she was widowed. Bayakka said, 'For good or bad I'll stay here.'

She moved into an outhouse with her son. She had no problem making both ends meet as she was entitled to a pension, Venkatesha having died in harness. Besides, there were the coconut trees and the vegetable patch. She saw to it that she didn't smother Sripathi with her love as if she realised that death might snatch her away any time. She took care to see that her love for him didn't stand in the way of his freedom.

Sripathi took after his father. Bayakka didn't even realise that he was growing up. He went about his life as if he didn't belong there, studied hard, cycled to the college in Kumta, passed all his examinations and eventually ended up in Bombay.

Bayakka was left alone in Heravatte. Having lived there since her arrival as a bride, she made no distinction between her life and that of others. There was nothing that happened in other families that she didn't know.

She helped everyone in one way or the other. She moved heaven and earth to have Milkman Rangappa released when the police locked him up for no reason. 'Was making money the only object of your studies?' she asked Ramesh the lawyer when he refused to go with her to the court. Taunting him further she said, 'It's a shame that you are a lawyer practising in this place if you can't put in a word for a man who has been unjustly locked up.' Ramesh went with her to the court where she stood surety and had Rangappa released on bail. Later, the police found out that he was innocent and did everything to hush up the matter. Though the people thought that the old lady was a busybody who poked her nose into everything, having nothing else to do, they granted, however grudgingly, that but for her, Rangappa wouldn't have been set free so soon. She had a knack of landing up in any place where papadam was being made. She threw herself wholeheartedly into everything that happened in the village. No one can say when Heravatte would have seen a coat of tar on its roads if Bayakka wasn't there. People were amazed at her inner strength.

When it was known that Heravatte was soon to come under the jurisdiction of Kumta municipality and that there would be an election, four or five declared themselves as candidates. It was Balappa who was finally chosen as the consensus candidate. Before it happened however, Bayakka insisted that he declare his intention of getting a new road laid that would lead into Heravatte and that there would be street lights. In his enthusiasm to get elected, Bala promised the earth. People had laughingly told Bayakka that, considering everything, she would have been the best candidate.

There was no news of the new road even after six months. Not a stick had moved even though Heravatte was now officially under the municipality in Kumta. Bayakka brought up the matter with others. She thought they should get together and do something about it.

'Oh Bayakka, let things happen in their own good time . . . Why should you bother about the road, Bayakka? Where do you want to go?' they had said.

But Bayakka was not one to take things lying down. One day, she stopped Bala on the road and started a virtual fight. 'What on earth can I do, Bayakka?' He pleaded, 'I'm all alone.'

'Aren't we all there with you?' she had asked. 'Tell us what we have to do . . . Shall we take out a procession and stage a sit-in strike? If you can't do anything, resign. You talked big at the time you wanted to be chosen, didn't you?'

Poor Bala, he went to the President of the Municipality and did everything but wail loudly. Bayakka had also said while she harangued him, 'I'll throw hot water on anyone from your office who comes this way, remember that.' One does not know whether it was just an empty threat or a strategy that Bayakka had thought of. Soon rumour had it that the people of Heravatte would pour boiling water on anyone from the municipality coming there to collect tax. The President conferred with some of the elders of the place and they came to see her.

'The road will probably be laid in the near future,' they told her. 'Don't get caught in the meshes of their politics, Bayakka.'

Bayakka hit the roof with rage. 'I don't care if this is politics. Let him get out if he can't keep his word. There's only one place which I can hope to go to . . . and for that I don't need any road. It's the entire village that needs it. If he is that helpless, let him come into the open and confess. If you want to call all this politics, well then I'm in it. But tell me, doesn't any one of you think that he's in the wrong?'

Those that came to advise her had to return with a hangdog expression but the people soon started muttering that Bala had wronged them by making false promises. Eventually Heravatte did get the tar road but there was no change in Bayakka's routine.

It was only on two occasions that she left Heravatte.

The first time was when she went on a pilgrimage to Kashi which some of the people in the village had organised.

When it was suggested that everyone visiting Kashi should give up something very dear as a token of submission to God, Bayakka immediately announced that she'd give up bitter gourd for the rest of her life. Bitter gourd phodi was her favourite dish. Next was Kamalakka's turn. People around laughed at her when they heard her say that she would give up brinjal. It was a well-known fact that Kamalakka hated the very sight of brinjal. 'What do you think is the meaning of pilgrimage?' Bayakka asked her, in her usual forthright manner. 'It signifies the death of all desires.' And finally Kamalakka decided to give up bitter gourd too. Bayakka didn't talk about it again, but Kamalakka, though she continued to grow bitter gourd and give it away, even now wished that she'd given up something else.

The second occasion was when she left for Bombay, ten years after Sripathi's marriage.

His marriage had been such a problem. Sripathi had insisted on finding a girl who had a job in Bombay. Bayakka wrote innumerable letters to all and sundry and finally found a girl he accepted. Savitha, who went on to become Sripathi's wife, worked in an insurance company. Since they had never celebrated an auspicious event in the house, the wedding had to be in Heravatte she had insisted.

There was no change in Bayakka's life after the marriage of her son. It was only when her two cows died suddenly of a mysterious disease that, perhaps, the links between her and her house in Heravatte were snapped. She decided to spend some time with her son. Sripathi came all the way from Bombay to take her back with him.

But during those two months she spent in Bombay she felt her hands and feet were tied. She was bored and frustrated in spite of Rashmi, Sripathi's seven-year-old daughter. Sripathi had an apartment with just three rooms, on the third floor of a ten-storeyed building. Everything happened behind closed doors. The only time the front door was opened was when someone had to go out or come in. Her daughter-in-law got up at five in the morning to bathe, dress, fill the lunch boxes, wake up the half-asleep child, give her a bath and leave with her at seven. Rashmi waited in a friend's house near her school for Sripathi to turn up after work and bring her home. And with their return came a host of groans and grumbles about a missed morning train, the crowded evening bus. Life, tied as it was to the ticking clock, measured time in terms of noons and evenings even as it raced relentlessly against it, fitted the daily chores into hours and minutes and trains and buses missed by half a minute, and rigidly mechanised itself, like the movement of the seconds-hand.

Bayakka found Bombay dull. She had no contact with the world except for the stray smile or word exchanged with the neighbour on the landing. Once Bayakka had come out and noticed that there were locks on three of the five doors on their floor. Just then the door of the flat opposite theirs opened. Bayakka turned expectantly, but before she could open her mouth, the lady of the house had beaten a retreat and shut the door behind her.

It was during the first few days of her stay in Bombay that Bayakka had seen the children of the opposite flat waiting outside their locked door one day. She had asked them to come in and had given them something to eat. The children were soon lost in play. Their parents returned, there was a frantic search for the missing children and all hell broke loose and it was only when Sripathi came back from work that the children were discovered and shooed back to their home. One does not know what exchanges took place between him and the parents of those children, but that Sripathi shouted at Bayakka is a fact. 'Why did you have to meddle in their affairs? The children would have waited outside the door or on the road. There's no one here in Bombay who's sitting around, looking for help, remember . . . It's enough if all of us look after our affairs.'

Bayakka could never find time to sit and talk with Rashmi. Her parents would insist that she did her homework soon after she came back home with Sripathi at half past six. Sleep followed soon after dinner so that she could be up early the next morning. The only free day was Sunday, usually spent in visiting someone. Sripathi was particular about giving advance notice of their visit. What if the other family had planned something or was not there when they called? The journey would be for nothing. He would fret unless every detail had been taken care of. Bayakka was fed up. She yearned for Heravatte. No one in Bombay seemed to be interested in anything beyond his own family, the child in that family, its homework and how to spend the Sunday.

She returned to Heravatte having decided that she would never leave it again. No more did she dream of going to live with her son towards the end of her life. She bought two cows and went back to the familiar rhythm of her life.

But the changes that had taken place in Heravatte soon came sharply into focus. For instance, the division of the hereditary property in Dr. Gopal's family came to light only when the first son sold his share. Bayakka was upset that one more great family had disintegrated. She remembered how close her family was to Dr. Gopal's. She was miserable trying to understand or keep pace with the changes taking place in her village. Once Heravatte lived and thought like a single family. No more. Often she felt she was an outsider in her own village.

When she came out after lunch she saw Kamalakka on Shankara's verandah. She was waving her hand as if asking Bayakka to come over. Thinking that her friend was asking for help, Bayakka went across even though there was a slight hesitation in her as she remembered the events of the morning.

Kamalakka was retching. It seemed Shankara and Lalitha had gone to attend a wedding in Kumta.

Bayakka took her to the bathroom.

'Bayakka!' sobbed Kamalakka. 'She served me some sambar with brinjal in it, Bayakka, though she knows that I can't stand it . . . There was nothing else and so I had some of it somehow. I think I'll die vomitting, Bayakka . . . I have had enough of this life, believe me . . . And this fancy dress since yesterday . . . I was ashamed to be seen in it . . . I came out today, utterly tired of sitting inside all day . . . and I feel that every passer-by was laughing at me . . .' Her eyes were full as she narrated her tale of woe.

Lalitha was nothing but a she-devil. But what could one say of Shankara? Bayakka paused for a moment before she said, 'Come home with me, Kamalakka. I'll look after you. Come.'

Kamalakka seemed ready to go with her. 'Okay, get my two boxes. They are inside,' she said and got up.

Bayakka gathered Kamalakka's sari and other clothes and brought her home. She helped Kamalakka take off the nightgown and got her into a sari. She went back and brought the heavy boxes which Kamalakka wouldn't forget even for a minute and arranged for Ramesh, the boy next door, to care for Shankara's house till they came back.

When Shankara and Lalitha returned in the evening to find Ramesh guarding their house, they thought that Kamalakka had taken ill and Bayakka had taken her home. They rushed to Bayakka's house only to hear Bayakka say, 'She is still alive.' She gave Shankara no chance to put in a word edgewise. Straightaway she launched into attack: 'If you can't look after your mother properly, we are here to care for her. The whole village knows that she can't stand brinjal . . . Your wife must be the only one who's not aware of it . . . She forces brinjal down Kamalakka's throat and makes her throw up. Tell me, are you a son or a demon? And you dress her in a nightie-kietie at this age. Do you think she is a doll? Why don't you strangle her instead?'

Shankara stammered into an explanation. Lalitha tried to mumble something that implied that it was Kamalakka who was the problem.

Bayakka rejected the remark outright.

And all the while Kamalakka sat there without a word.

Shankara was humiliated by her silence. He didn't think that it would come to this. He tried to threaten his mother saying that he wouldn't take her back unless she went with him right away. And yet she maintained her silence.

He went home in a huff.

There were tears in Kamalakka's eyes as she attempted to say something. Bayakka shut her up saying, 'Don't say anything now.

Watch my words, your gem of a son will come back.'

He did come back just as Bayakka had predicted but he had some elders with him. It didn't take long for news to spread in Heravatte. Some came out of sheer curiosity. But the elders were silenced when Bayakka challenged them with 'What would you have done if your own children had behaved like this?' Bayakka was unyielding.

Shankara threatened to get the police.

'Go, get them. You can take your mother back if she is alive by the time the case is settled,' retorted Bayakka.

'Why should you bother? I know why you brought her over to your place. It's the gold on her. I know your great fondness for her, don't I?' Shankara mocked.

Bayakka was furious. 'You want to know why I bother about her? It's because you don't know how to look after your mother, understand? And you talk of gold . . . What does one who is going to die tomorrow care for it? If she is prepared to give it, take it all home. I haven't forced her to stay here. Ask her if you like. If she says yes, you are welcome to take her with you . . .'

And there was Kamalakka inside sobbing her heart out.

'You heard him, didn't you?' Bayakka asked. 'Say you don't want to go with him . . . I'll look after you . . . What matters to him more than you is the gold on you . . . Hand it over to him if you want. What are you scared of? You don't have to depend on him for food. Let him realise it. Let our people know what happens if one doesn't look after one's parents . . . If they don't change, drive them out of the house. The house is in your name, isn't it? Why do you sit there like that sobbing?'

Kamalakka seemed to have been overwhelmed by the crowd outside, her son's anger and Bayakka's insistence. The courage she had displayed earlier seemed to have deserted her. She sobbed as she wiped her eyes and nose and said, 'No, Bayakka. I can't take all this. Leave me alone, Bayakka . . . It's one's own flesh and blood, after all . . . It does not matter if they treat me unjustly . . . I shall survive on the gruel they may serve . . . Leave me alone Bayakka . . .'

Meanwhile the people outside waited for her to come out.

MILIND BOKIL

•

THIRSTING
FOR WATER

•

NOMINATED BY VIJAYA RAJADHYAKSHA
TRANSLATED BY ASHA DAMLE
AND ARVIND DIXIT

Rohini never really expected her mother to visit her. Not that Aai has not been planning to do so. But she knows what Rohini is doing in this remote village tucked into the mountains. Knowing that would she come? Rohini has asked herself many times. Yet, here she's been for four days and it is now time for Aai to go back home by that evening's bus.

Four days were far too short. So many people connected with the campaign had come and gone, keeping Rohini busy, and I have not given her enough time, she thought guiltily.

She turned to look at her mother as they sat, she and Aai, on the spacious mud platform around the peepal tree by the river. Aai was reading *Dnyaneshwari* as usual. She sat in her usual padmasana, the book in her right hand, her left playing with her toe-rings. The end of her nine-yard sari was as usual wrapped tightly, over both her arms. White and freshly-washed, the sari had a delicate and familiar floral print. Aai's greying hair was gathered into a low knot. And as always, she was reading to herself, her soft voice sounding like the buzz of bees.

As Rohini watched her it came to her with startling clarity that this was the image which always came to mind when she thought of Aai. Aai looked the same, whether she was at home, at the neighbours' or at a wedding. And while reading the *Dnyaneshwari*, if she came across a verse that appealed to her, she'd read it out to whoever happened to be around — her daughters Rohini or Nalini, one of their neighbours, the maid, maybe the dhobi. Once she had even been caught reading it aloud to her black cat!

A bemused smile spread across Rohini's face. She leaned against the tree and stretched her legs. The sun had come up, but the air was still cool. The river banks were strewn with big rocks — a few were four

'Thirsting for Water' was first published in Marathi as *'Udakachiya Arti'* in *Mouj*, Diwali Issue, 1991, Bombay.

The title, *'Udakachiya Arti'* is from Chapter XI.53 of *Dnyaneshwari*, a popular 13th century commentary on the *Bhagawadgeeta*. This corresponds to Chapter XI.1 of the original. In this Arjuna says, after he has listened to the upadesha of Lord Krishna: 'I have been thirsting for water, drinking all the while from Rohini.' Rohini means mirage.

metres high. The yellow-grey waters gushed through the rocks. Wet muddy land rose up to a space that allowed the fifty-odd thatched huts of the village to sprawl out languorously. Hand-patted cowdung cakes dried on mud walls. A goat here, there a bull, stood patiently tethered to door-posts, and empty carts rested on their shafts. Women could be seen walking briskly towards the river, their brass vessels gleaming in the sun. And in the temple at the entrance to the village, people bustled about importantly preparing the palanquin of the village deity for the ceremonial procession.

Rohini sat in the midst of papers. Letters had been sorted out and now lay, some on her lap, some stacked in neat piles around her, weighted down with an assortment of pebbles. Some had been answered; some were still to be opened. The discussions, the many meetings, the running around to get people together fragmented her time. They were supposed to be taking a breather before the action started again, yet how many people surrounded her day and night — activists, folks from neighbouring places, even a correspondent from an English periodical who'd been camping there for the last two days.

'What do you think — of these lines, baby?' asked Aai.

> *A drop of buttermilk metamorphoses*
> *a pot of milk into curd.*
> *Thus does Nature*
> *all things in the Universe.*

Rohini knew her question was purely rhetorical. Aai loved *Dnyaneshwari.* A little moment of respite, and she'd have picked up the book. She knew most of it by heart and could give you the essential *Dnyaneshwari* as easily as she could shell a pod to cull out fat peas that you could pop straight into your mouth. She called Dnyaneshwar Dnyanu, Dnyanba, Dnyaniya. Her daughters would often tease her. 'Is he such a close friend of yours?' Nalini would ask. Or Rohini would say, 'I'm sure if he were alive and here, you'd take him for a walk in the garden.'

The book had always been a source of strength to Aai. Rohini sometimes thought this book was more important to her mother than even her husband. After Nana died Aai's occasional talk about her life with him lapsed into a total silence — it's been a long time since she's mentioned his name — but she's never once abandoned the book, or talking about it, often urging Rohini to come to Dnyaneshwar. 'Rohini, do read this book,' she'd say. 'It will rid you of all your worries.'

But Rohini could never take to *Dnyaneshwari*. In fact, there were people who said that she enjoyed creating problems for herself and for others; they accused her of raising issues where none existed. Like the question of how many people would be displaced if the dam was built. Dams have been built before, haven't they? they asked. People have always got displaced. And there always have been villages that had to be shifted, submerged. No one has murmured. This could have happened here too. What did it matter? Didn't she know that the mere fact that she raised issues meant nothing? And didn't she know that if one were looking for issues, there were any number that you could come up with, right from whether the country needed big dams at all to discussing what is good and what is bad for the people. But what use were such speculations, such strife?

Rohini had no answers to such questions; the only thing she could murmur on such occasions was that some of these questions needed a lifetime to answer.

'Didi!'

Rohini turned to see Maniram approaching her. With him was an old man in a bright ochre turban.

'This is the Sarpanch of Gangavati village,' Maniram said. 'He has come to attend today's meeting.'

'Gangavati! Why, that's quite some distance away, isn't it?' she said in welcome, switching with ease to Hindi.

'Yes. Twenty miles or so from here.'

'I don't understand. Your village is not going to be affected, is it?'

'Our village is spared,' said Gangavati's headman. 'Yet, these people here. They are *our* people. Their battle is *our* battle. If you can be with them, we should be, too.'

'He has brought two bags of wheat for us,' Maniram said.

Rohini smiled in appreciation. 'What could be better than having you with us. It is your battle. If more people like you join us, it will definitely increase our will to fight.'

Rohini was overwhelmed by the old man's gesture. Long after they had left, she sat lost in thought.

She knew that though she was the one who was in the limelight, the real battle was being fought by the people — the tribals, the Bhils of this arduous mountain terrain; the old, the young, the men, women, and children. She was merely the catalyst. Yet, how long it had taken her to realise this. She had gone about things as if it was her own private issue till Aai had made her see, understand. 'Don't be so presumptuous!' she had said in her usual direct way. 'You can control nothing. It's the people behind you. Don't ever forget that what you are today is because of them!'

Aai always had a way of being brutally frank, but now that Rohini was older, more mature, she realised how perspicacious Aai was. She dithered; Aai never did. She was never ambiguous, thought Rohini, suddenly feeling an overwhelming desire to place her problems before Aai to seek quick solutions, as if she was incapable of shouldering her own responsibilities any longer.

Maniram was back. 'Didi, everything is ready, what do we do next?'

'What do you think we should do?' she asked.

'Let's first visit the temple and then hold the meeting.'

'All right,' said Rohini and, turning to her mother she asked, 'Ready, Aai? The procession is about to leave.'

Aai took a minute to finish the verse she was reading. She closed the book and came sat next to Rohini.

They sat companionably together again, watching people mill around them, men in crimson and ochre turbans that set off their startling white kurtas, women in their many-coloured saris, musicians, drummers, pipers, and children clinging to the saris of their mothers.

Myriad hands worked on giving the last glorious touches to the palanquin. The goddess was all dolled up and ready to go. Now only the ceremonious seating of the deity in the palanquin remained. Then she'd be taken to the temple at the top of the hill. To visit her sister.

A bus from Gosawada came puffing up, in a cloud of dust. It stopped in front of the temple, disgorging more devotees. The noise of the engine reverberated in the air. Crowds converged on the temple. Walking out of this crowd and towards them was Janaki, bringing two men with her. They had close-cropped hair and wore sandals on their feet. They carried leather bags.

'Our friends are here,' Janaki said, winking at Rohini.

'Come, come Shaukatbhai,' Rohini said, welcoming them with a smile. 'Long time since I saw you!'

'The problem, Behenji, is that a posting in this area is hard to come by,' said Shaukat before he turned to Aai, joined his palms in a namaste and asked, 'When did Mataji come?'

'Shaukatbhai, am I hearing right? You who are always so well-informed, you really want me to believe that you didn't know when my mother came here?' Rohini teased before she turned to the other man. 'Yadavji, how is your sister now?'

'Your blessings, Behenji. Your introductory note to that doctor in Bombay worked wonders. She's all right now!'

'Good!' Rohini started gathering her papers.

'What's the programme, today?' asked Shaukat.

'We go to the hill temple first, then lunch, and then the meeting. So many people have come from distant places to attend the meeting. It'll go on till late in the evening. Aai is returning home this evening.'

They sat talking of inconsequential things for a little while till Shaukat turned to Janaki and asked in a bantering voice, 'I know there won't be any tea for us, but do you think you can find me some water, maybe?'

Janaki had barely disappeared when Shaukat looked around to make sure there was no one in sight and said softly, 'I have news for you. One more batallion of the State Reserve Police is coming here. The S.R.P. may camp in the adjoining village. Keep off that place. If you must meet, meet elsewhere!'

Rohini looked grim for a second. Then she turned to him and said pleasantly, 'Thanks a lot Shaukatbhai, it was good of you to let us know.'

'Right then, we'll move on. We'll talk after you come back from your visit to the temple.'

'Rohini, who were those people?' Aai asked as soon as they left. 'They looked like goondas!'

'Don't worry, Aai. They were just plain-clothes police from the L.I.B.; Investigation Bureau people.'

'Does that mean you are under police observation?'

'No Aai, nothing of the sort! They only gather information. The poor chaps are good at heart. They help when they can.'

Aai said nothing more.

Rohini wished Aai had not known about the S.R.P. She'd keep on worrying unnecessarily now, she thought. She knows that my life is hectic and full of hazards, yet she doesn't know the extent of my risks.

Shaukat had said there was another battalion joining the police force. The government seemed to be comtemplating some action. It didn't surprise her. She'd known about this for a long time. Shaukat had warned her. A week before the action you'll be arrested and whisked away to a distant, unexpected destination, he'd said. But she didn't think it was important. It would not make a difference, anyway. The movement had gathered enough momentum.

The temple that stood at the entrance to their village was small and old. Its walls were freshly whitewashed, the mantap painted and the precincts cleaned. On seeing them arrive Maniram came forward and said, 'Mataji, I shall arrange a cane chair for you to be carried up to the hilltop temple. It is a rather steep climb.'

'Don't be stupid. I can manage.'

'Are you sure?' Rohini asked, concerned. 'It's not the height, as much as the slope. It is pretty stiff, and remember you complain of pain in the knees these days!'

'Never mind. The knees can complain if they want. I will only attend to them later. Come on, let's go. Maybe I'll reach ahead of you.'

There was no question of any further discussion.

Soon the priest gave a signal. The drum beats began to the clanging of cymbals. The trumpeteers puffed out their cheeks to bring out a strangely high-pitched note, and the mask of the temple deity was brought and placed inside the palanquin.

As the six pole bearers were about to lift the palanquin, Maniram signalled them to wait. He raised his hand high. His clear voice rang out loud and clear. 'The dam shall not be built!'

The villagers echoed his call. 'We dare you to evict us!'

And then the procession wended its way up the narrow path. Surrounded by the chattering women of the village, Aai walked behind the palanquin, feeling quite at home amongst other women who were also walking, holding onto their aching knees.

Rohini trailed far behind. The journalist from that English periodical had been busy clicking Aai and now he came to join Rohini, brushing his hair back, saying, 'I have taken more photographs of your mother than of anyone else.'

'Don't forget to send me copies. I don't have a single recent picture of hers.'

'Will do!' he quipped, then, 'Can I say something? The generation gap and other differences not withstanding, I am truly facinated by your mother. I am proud to be a friend of hers.'

Rohini smiled. She knew her mother's ability to create confidence in others and her knack of making friends. Even with cats and dogs.

Rohini had not liked this man when he had landed up a couple of days ago. His unkempt hair, his baggy jeans, the fact that he worked for an English glossy. He wanted to write an in depth article on her. He was here to observe her, he had said. And Rohini had fumed. Had he not arrived bag and baggage she would have asked him to leave. And when he'd said shyly, 'I'd wanted to spend a couple of years here, for this cause, but . . .' she had lashed out at him. 'Everyone says that when they are here. Then they get back to Bombay and out go all such noble thoughts. What you look for is spicy gossip about film stars, ministers, cricketers.'

'Each has his own problems,' he had said lamely.

'Ah, excuses!' she had sneered. 'All this talk of dedication to the Cause, etc. Nothing more than a veneer. Who wants such superficial publicity!'

Aai had sat quietly through her ranting. It was that night in bed that she asked, 'Why did you have to be so rude to that journalist?'

'Why not?'

'He was with me this afternoon. Forget the way he dresses. You must see he's quite a sincere man. When he mentioned that he had his own problems, you snubbed him. Did you know that his only son is a mentally retarded seven-year-old: a dribbling, fretful bundle of flesh. His wife's a school teacher. He had his dreams too, but now all he can do in life is look after the child.'

'Oh no! How did that happen?'

'Some drug his wife was given during the delivery. He did mention that he sued the company. Waged a single-handed war against them. Wrote articles. Till the company withdrew the drug. Things are never what they seem . . .'

Rohini had given him an extensive interview.

Now walking up to the temple with her, he said awkwardly, 'May I tell you something.'

'Mmm.'

'You know, you gave me a complete background of the andolan, all the facts and figures, why large dams should not be built. Somehow I was not really convinced. Then I was talking to your mother and she put it succinctly in one sentence. It made the whole thing crystal clear.'

'What did she say?'

'She said, It is morally wrong that many should die for the benefit of a few. That was it! I was totally convinced!'

Rohini nodded understandingly. Soon the journalist moved ahead, leaving Rohini alone with her thoughts again.

Yes, Aai never had any doubts about what was right and wrong, just and unjust. When the rift between Arun and Rohini had become serious and Rohini was not able to take any decision, it was Aai who had given her sound advice. 'If you want to survive, you'd better leave him,' she had said firmly. Through those difficult days her support was unstinting. No one could have been better. Nana was no more. But even if he'd been alive, what use could he have been? All his wonderful problem-solving capabilities stopped with the games of chess he played, day in, and day out. He was no good when it came to real life problems.

When Rohini wondered if she should join this movement, it was to Aai that she had turned. 'You're convinced, aren't you? Then go ahead and do it,' Aai had said, not a trace of doubt in her voice. Aai didn't need to be told why it was wrong to build the dam. She instantaneously grasped issues that many intellectuals had problems seeing in their entirety, thought Rohini. They think me a fool Even Nalini failed to see the point. They think I am wasting my life.

Arun had said similar things in his letter. Aai had brought it along. She had handed the rest of the mail when everyone was around but Arun's letter she'd given Rohini when they were alone. She had said, 'Read it with full control over your emotions. Probably an invitation, from what's printed on the cover. He's marrying again.'

It was a large envelope. A glossy card inside. The announcement swaggered right across the envelope: Arun Weds Supriya. The place, the date, the time, everything right there on the cover.

The wedding was over. There was no need to read the contents, yet she found herself opening it after Aai left. The invitation was in a predictable style. A picture of Ganesh at the top. The bold red English words on a snow white card trimmed with golden edge and tucked inside it a small note: Rohini, the announcement. I know, you'll feel bad, but I can't help it. I am not interested in leading a drab life — Arun.

It amused her. She told herself she wasn't surprised. She had expected it to happen one of these days. In fact she'd expected him to remarry within a couple of months . . . But what a strange note! He was sure that she'd be upset or . . . was he suggesting that she should be? I am not interested in a drab life! Ah! That was a laugh!

She had climbed quite some distance by now and it struck her that the trees were suddenly denser, the grass a sharper green, springing out exuberantly everywhere except in the deep tracks ploughed into the mud by bullock carts. The bushes snuggled into one another, they looped and laced and meshed in front of her. There was nothing she could do but walk around them. Under the spreading trees dew sparkled in secret corners, a distinct fragrance of damp earth arose to welcome her. The drum sounds seemed so distant. The procession must be far ahead.

Rohini took out Arun's letter from her shoulder bag, looked at the card and the note and then put them back in again. She'd have to disappoint Arun. She was not hurt. There was no reason to be. The moment she decided to separate, he had lost his ability to hurt her. But this was so typical of Arun, always hurting others with his sly remarks. Who'd believe he could be warm and generous, splurging on friends when they went out together. Only those close to him could see through the thin veil. His sister had warned Rohini: Do you think you know him enough to marry him? He is not what you think he is; I have known him since childhood. But Rohini loved him. And they'd gone ahead and got married. She told herself that hers was not a blind love; she knew him inside out. She admired the way he managed his small factory. He played the harmonium. He could carve wood beautifully. He was liberal in his attitudes. Look as she might there was no obnoxious side to his character. Even Aai had not found any fault with him.

Where did it go wrong then? Questions she'd firmly put behind her whirled inside her again. So many situations, so many events; awkward petty acts, misunderstandings, suspicions, nastiness, a lack of harmony! The first two years were not bad, there were tiffs but those they had resolved. Then, all of a sudden, nothing seemed to go right.

Rohini could have put up with the flamboyance which led to the mismanagement of the business; she could have even borne his accusations about her reasons for getting involved in the andolan, his doubts about her integrity, his craze for amassing wealth, his total disregard for law and ethics. But his dishonesty . . . she just couldn't stand the dishonesty. His financial dishonesty, his sleeping around, the many promises not kept.

She heaved a deep sigh as memories crowded in on her. How often she had gone through these agonizing moments since their separation. The only conclusion she kept coming to was that they were incompatible. In spite of some exceptional qualities he was a mediocre man. After her decision to separate, the way he had harassed her over minor details, over the possession of the house, his disgraceful behaviour towards Aai, the lawyer's notices . . . Her greatest mistake was marrying him. Nalini always maintained that it was a classical example of bad choice.

Memories. How she hated them. Arun's note had achieved its purpose, after all. She didn't mind his marrying again. But the note stirred acrid memories. Four precious years of her life, wasted. If it hadn't been for him, she could have got into the movement long ago. When the work on the dam had just begun. If they had managed to build up a viable opposition then, they might have licked the problem before it started. But today? So much money wasted and a government growing more obdurate by the day.

At first Arun's unrelenting debates had made her laugh. How often she had floored him with her counter-arguments. All those ifs and buts of his, based on wrong hypotheses, leading nowhere.

How was she to know that her marriage with Arun would be on the rocks? During the first two years she'd been perfectly happy. They agreed not to start a family immediately. Life was full of charm. If during those days someone had pleaded with her to lead the movement, convincing her of the injustice inflicted on the tribals, she might still not have left her home to throw herself so completely into a fight for justice. In fact, had Arun not behaved the way he did, she would have been a perfect, happy housewife.

Yes, if Arun had not . . . she stumbled on that once again. She was side-tracking once again. Was she not to be blamed at all? Was she in no way responsible for the change in Arun? Yes, he had not changed, but then, aren't all of us like that? Has she not pressurized him? Did she not mock him because he didn't know a thing about social work, about politics, because he couldn't write even a single correct line of English.

Did she not ridicule him out of the frustration of not being able to put a stop to his affairs? Was this why he was left with no other option but to retaliate the way he did?

Perturbed, Rohini walked alone, the others seeming to have understood her need to be left alone. She thought she had made a mistake. If she'd walked with them, talking, arguing, planning, she'd have been better off. She had gained nothing; all these stirrings led nowhere. They just upset her.

She quickened her steps in the direction of the drums — their rhythmic beat was soothing. She was only half-way up and it sounded as if the palanquin had already reached the temple.

When she finally reached the top, she was surprised to see her mother leaning on the dilapidated compound wall, breathing heavily, beads of perspiration on her forehead, a triumphant look on her face. 'See, I've managed!' Aai was quite excited. 'You were unnecessarily anxious.'

The hilltop temple was ancient, made of stone. The pillars of the verandah had somehow survived. The mantap seemed to have been recently repaired. The sanctum sanctorum was small, dimly-lit. Someone had lighted butter lamps and agarbattis. The place smelt good. The face-mask of the deity was of polished yellow brass; she wore a green handloom sari. The bulging eyes were lined with kohl and looked fierce; the forehead was smeared with haldi and kunku; her lips parted in a proud smile.

'She looks so much like Yamai of my parents' village.' Aai had fixed her intense gaze on the deity and was soon talking to her: 'Why have you come here? So I could meet you? Are you here because I don't come any more to my parents' place to see you? You are great. You have been so very kind to me.' She annointed the deity with haldi-kunku, touched the lobes of her ears, slapped her cheeks and rested her head at the feet of the deity in silent prayer.

Rohini agreed with Aai. The deity did look like Yamai though there had been no temple for her in Rohini's grandparents' village. The deity stood under a peepal tree where somebody had provided a small canopy.   When Rohini was young, she used to be scared of those ferocious eyes, and yet she remembered feeling a strange attraction. When Aai prayed, Rohini would stand there peeping from behind her, clutching the end of Aai's sari. We see many pictures and icons of gods but do not join our palms every time we come across one. But this deity stirred reverence. She couldn't say why.

Soon both of them came out and sat in the shade. The crowds moved in and out of the temple, holding out their prasad reverently to Aai and Rohini, placing the haldi-kunku on Aai's forehead, on Rohini's.

'I wish they'd finish quickly,' Rohini said after a while.

'Why? Let them take their time. It is only once in a year that this palanquin procession is taken out.'

'Because I'm so hungry!' Rohini said petulantly. 'You know how I miss my breakfast. People here have their early morning nyahari. I can't eat that early in the morning. We do have cups of tea several times but that doesn't fill the stomach, unfortunately.'

'How often have I told you to carry something in your bag — dates, copra, peanuts; even puffed rice if you like. You have to look after yourself, Rohini. If you don't who will?'

Rohini knew that but this was how it had always been. She was all alone. At school there had been many friends; they seemed to genuinely like her, but it was more comforting to be left alone. And now, loneliness was her companion. Except for Aai. Aai was on her own, too, yet she knew how to look after herself.

Luckily for Rohini, the deity was soon ready to go back.

The meeting was scheduled for after the meal. But when they got back, the cooks were still bustling about, the meal not ready, saying they were waiting for others to come back and help them. So, as if the spot was reserved for them, Rohini and Aai came back to sit on the mud platform around the peepal.

Aai sat cross-legged. She started massaging her feet.

'They are hurting, aren't they? I warned you!'

'What else can you expect at my age? I am past sixty,' retorted Aai.

'What's the average life-span of a person in this country — fifty? Well, I'm living on bonus time!'

Rohini had never seen it that way. Aai's presence was something she never questioned; as if she refused to understand that day by day her mother was getting older and a day would come when she'd be gone. How quickly the days pass! She complains about the pain in her legs now; but she must have lived with such pain for some days now, maybe years. Maybe there were other complications. Since Nana died, she'd been on her own. She'd visit Nalini once in a while, but she preferred to be on her own, in her own old house. Like me, thought Rohini. Like mother like daughter.

'I have seen many rivers, baby,' Aai said, emerging out of the silence, 'but this one is downright silly. Remember Krishna back home? As soon as she comes down the mountain she lingers, in no hurry to meet the sea. But this one here! The sea is a long way off, yet look at her madness! Look at those huge rocks, that drop, but she still rushes on. They're trying to build a dam against this impatience? You think she'll tolerate such nonsense?'

Rohini looked at the river and then at Aai. There was no need for comment. Aai had always grasped the real essence of things around her, like she did that of the guava tree, the black cat, or a child of a gipsy pedlar. She knew how to love. Rohini too loved this river yet it was only Aai who dared call it silly!

'You know,' said Rohini, 'I'd wanted to show you the temple of Mahadeo. It is not very far from here. It's a shame that I found no time to do it. Wish you could stay longer!'

'Next time. For now, this will do. Let me tell you, baby, I'm not that keen on temples and shrines. I have been to enough. Right from a stone icon of Maruti under a peepal tree to gold-laden ones in stately temples. I walked up with you because I didn't want to be left on my own here. Whatever be the icon, there's only one God! Why should one fuss?'

Rohini, her head resting on her knees, sat looking at Aai, silently, till Maniram announced the dinner.

They sat in the courtyard of the temple, in rows, on long stretches of folded durries and ate out of pala leaves. Rohini and Aai went and sat at one end, after Rohini had looked around to see that everyone was comfortably seated and were served the spartan diet of jawar bhakri and curried dal.

As was becoming the habit, it was time once again to remember the struggle before the meal could start. Maniram thundered out his slogan: 'Till our last breath we will fight!'

And like an echo the many voices around him rose: 'The flowing river shall flow all right!'

'I like this food,' Aai said, biting into a piece of bhakri.

'It's okay when you're here for a couple of days. But frankly, I'm fed up of this. Nothing but this every day. No vegetables. Just dal and more dal. And the occassional potato, if someone remembers to get it from the bazaar. I tell you Aai . . . you know what I like best? Your hot steaming phulkas; that cauliflower bhaji, butter in the morning. And I haven't had chocolate eclairs for ages now!'

Aai ate on for a little while before she said, 'Well, you've come far from those pleasures. Why think about that now?'

Aai was right. The pleasures of lying in bed till late in the morning; drinking cups and cups of coffee; reading without worry, without interruptions; eating bhelpuri with friends; Aai massaging and washing her hair; going to a cinema with her husband; and most of all, of holding a little baby close to her body — yes, everything was left far behind.

Once she was asked to lecture at a gathering of people concerned about the forest getting submerged. She accepted because they were offering her a fat cheque that would foot the travel expenses of the workers for six whole months. The lecture was arranged in a massive bungalow which thronged with women in rich saris, expensive perfumes. Impressed by her speech, the secretary had asked her out to dinner. He was tall, dark and handsome, straight out of a T.V. commercial. He had an elegant white imported car, and the most pleasurable manners. His speech, the warmth of male company, his rich heady perfume . . . the pleasures were within her reach. A nod away. But there were a couple of her colleagues with her. She did not dare accept the invitation.

As Maniram and others had to help with the cleaning operations after the meal, there was some time for the meeting to start. Rohini and Aai came back to the peepal tree and Aai stretched out, using her arms as a pillow. Rohini leaned against the trunk, wishing she could go lie down. Her back ached so.

'Hope Arun hasn't written anything nasty in his letter.'

'What can he write. It was just a little note.'

'I just wondered! I remember how nasty he was towards the end! Let him marry if he wants to. Do you know who the bride is?'

'No. How would I?'

'Just asked. Surprising the way he changed. You know Godawaribai? Her son worked in Arun's factory. He once told me how, when some official tried to extract a bribe, Arun had him physically thrown out. This could have meant indefinite closure of the factory but he didn't care. Get out! he yelled, Get out! Can't believe it was this same Arun who acted as if he was our arch enemy!'

'No point talking about it,' said Rohini brusquely.

'I do understand that, baby. That is your fate. Once an astrologer I met had predicted this for you. Fame and popularity this child will enjoy but the path will be rough. She'd make thousands happy but not herself, he said.'

Rohini smiled. She wanted to assure her mother that though life was difficult and she wasn't sure whether she was happy, she was definitely at peace with herself. People may accuse her of being adamant, but the experience has been good for her. She was a lot easier on herself.

She wondered whether her mother remembered the story of the star. She had gone on a picnic with her school friends. There was an old temple by the river. It was surrounded by large trees. Having lost her earring she'd stopped to look for it while her friends had gone ahead. A tall, lanky, bare-bodied brahmin had come stomping towards her and asked in a shrill voice, What are you looking for? He was soaking wet as if he had come out of the river. My earrings, she had said. And, What a thing to look for! Go look for your star, he had ordered her. When she narrated this to her mother, Aai had said, That sounds like an oracle, baby. There are many stars that we can see; many that we can't. But each one of us has her very own star that shines over us, making our lives happy. Follow that star, child.

Rohini didn't understand a thing of what her mother said, but the incident stayed in her memory. Then something else happened. After the divorce, she was working in a school for the deaf and dumb. One day, she was sent to a village to conduct a survey. This riverside village. There was an old temple of Mahadeo built in black stone. People in the village had gathered around her pouring out their woes. Their temple was to be submerged; a dam was to be built. The village, the hill behind it, the forest were all threatened. And on that hot afternoon with the sun directly overhead, the black hard stones under her feet, Rohini remembered in a flash the words of the brahmin. Her star, the star brighter than the sun!

She plunged into the movement. Nalini wryly said, A good camouflage for a failed marriage. Friends said, You always did look for trouble! and older friends passed a judgement: You're banging your head against a stone wall. But did anyone even think that she might have seen her star? That she had to follow it? She didn't try to convince anyone that this gave meaning to her life; maybe not success, but definitely satisfaction.

She knew people like Arun and Nalini were incapable of understanding such things. They banked on the rational. They thought they made things happen. Once she too believed that. But the decision she had taken that day was not her own. Someone had guided her to do so. After the survey she had gone back home only to return within a couple of days, back to this village. Why did she come? They said that when such moments come in your life, you accept them. No questions asked. The how and the why didn't matter.

The memory filled her with quiet satisfaction.

When Maniram asked her to open the meeting, she refused, saying, It is your meeting, you should speak.

She listened quietly to all of them. The andolan was indeed entering a decisive stage. The Government was being adamant, as expected. But one thing she knew: The iron hand of administration will wield its strength. The poor, the hungry, the half-naked barefoot tribals will have to face it. What mattered now was conviction. The days of strategy and manoeuvering were over. It was time for steadfastness. People who accused her of overdoing things didn't know the strength of her convictions.

As she finally rose to address them, she looked composed. In front of her ran the river, its hazy edges touching the horizon. Her eyes fixed on the river she spoke in a measured, confident tone: 'By now, you are aware of the intentions of this Government. They never do what they say. In their past there is no record whatsoever of benevolence towards the poor. It is all a question of how strongly we stick together for our land. Should we buckle under the might of the administration or do we do so to the gushing waters? The choice is ours.'

The people stood spellbound. The sun was setting. Her words flowed effortlessly. All eyes were glued on her. But Rohini's mind was full of thoughts about her own self. It was as if she saw, not the people in front of her or the rocks in the river bed, the gurgling waters, not the yellowish-grey mountain plateau, nor even the expanse of bright blue sky but only something far beyond. Like Arjun, her eyes were fixed on her target, the eye of the parrot.

When the meeting dispersed, it was late afternoon. Aai had finished her siesta and come and sat quietly beside her. Rohini didn't notice her. When Rohini had finished instructing the activists about their immediate strategy, Aai came forward to talk to her.

'I was listening to you, baby. Wonder where you learnt to speak so well! You did take part in school and college debates, but the way you spoke today, it was different. Touching. No wonder people follow the path you show them!'

With a grin, Rohini said, 'The problem is so complex, no outsider can come and help solve it. If the people concerned do not take steps, they will be doomed!'

'You are right,' Aai's appreciative voice continued. 'I have been watching you for the last four days. I must say I feel so very happy and proud of you. Maybe in the past I showed some resentment but now I have no doubts. Maybe the breakup of your marriage has done you good. You would not have been able to work as single-mindedly as you do now. What you'd have got out of your marriage was nothing different from what others get. Here you will make so many people happy — to say the least!'

The words touched a deep chord in her. Aai's appreciation — that was the best reward.

The people had dispersed and mother and daughter were left to themselves under the peepal tree.

'I couldn't give you a grand-daughter. You always wanted one.'

'True,' Aai said, 'Nalini has two sons, I didn't expect much from her anyway. If you had had a daughter that would have made me happy. Well, it is good to keep the chain going; mother-daughter-mother-daughter.

Rohini was quiet. It was getting dark. It was time for Aai to leave.

Rohini felt a wave of guilt pass over her. 'Aai, why don't you stay on?' Rohini said, hugging her tight. 'You live alone, anyway, then why not with me? We will rent a decent room somewhere. In a central place. Then you don't need to accompany me everywhere I go.'

Aai shook her head. She tightened the wrapped end of her sari around her body.

'No. My ways and yours are different. I will be a millstone around your neck. Besides, I spent forty years of my life in that house and it has grown on me. I can't leave it. You keep coming home when you can. I will come, too. We will meet more often, if you like . . . It must be time for my bus now.'

There was enough time for Janaki to collect Aai's luggage. Rohini felt sad. She'd spent the last four days happily with her mother. The weather had been pleasant. They had slept outside in the courtyard, on charpoys, in total darkness, under a canopy of stars. Aai had reminisced a lot about Rohini and Nalini and their days of growing-up; she had long-forgotten stories about her childhood also, about which Rohini had known nothing till then. After the meetings and discussions they had often joined the other women when they went to the river to fetch water. Aai could not stand the cold water, so she stayed on the bank and talked to the women who gathered round her. She had learnt their dialect. Once she even tried philosophising in Hindi, a language she was not very conversant in.

The bus arrived on time. It was already very dark. The whole village had gathered to see her off. The journalist was going by the same bus. He would accompany Aai right upto her doorstep. Such a relief for Rohini!

Rohini touched Aai's feet as she was about to board the bus.

'What blessing would you like?' Aai asked.

'Say I will be successful. You've always blessed me so.'

'So be it,' said Aai and took Rohini in her arms.

The darkness deepened. After Aai's bus left, the people scattered.

Rohini asked the volunteers to leave her alone and unknowingly her steps turned towards the river.

The river looked different under the night sky; the scattered rocks serene, peaceful. The only sound was that of water splashing against the rocks. A lone gull flew by. Leaning against a large rock Rohini stood watching the water. Aai was right. However many friends and relations one has, one is basically always alone. I have the whole village behind me; I am welcome in every house yet no one belongs to me, not in this village, not in the neighbouring ones. Not even in the city where I come from do I have a place I can call my own. But then, maybe it is best that I know the reality of my life at least now.

The river flowed past her, gurgling; the rock she leaned on was hard and rough and real, yet she felt a sudden emptiness. What was her tomorrow going to be like? The whole universe seemed to be suspended in nothingness. Where did she come from? Where was she going?

It suddenly struck her that it didn't really matter whether she had any answers or not. All that did was the fact that there would always be that star of hers shining on her from God knows where, and there'd always be this river and the people. May they lead me well.

She took Arun's letter out of her shoulder bag. Her eyes lingered on those red letters. She caressed the smooth, white, gilt-edged card, then, raised her hand and let the papers fly in the air.

Rohini stood watching as the pieces cartwheeled, landed on the water and floated away with the stream. And as she walked back, her steps were brisk, confident; only her eyelids felt slightly damp.

N S MADHAVAN

•

HIGUITA

•

NOMINATED AND TRANSLATED BY
SUJATHA DEVI

All Father Geeverghese knew about the book was its title: *The Loneliness of a Goalkeeper Waiting for the Penalty Kick.* Father Capriatti, his Italian friend, must have mentioned it a couple of times. The name was enough to make Father Geeverghese feel that he had read the German novel many times.

Betrayed by all, his powerful arms outstretched, the goalkeeper awaits the penalty kick. In the stadium, fifty thousand parched throats go silent. A lone spectator crows thrice.

In Father's mind, the goalkeeper was born and reborn, each time a different personage. But not once did he feel like reading the book. That would mean a sudden end to the Nativity plays of the goalkeeper; his lives telescoping to nothing more than just the novel's plot.

At first and invariably so, the goalkeeper was our Lord. Donning a No. 1 jersey, Jesus kicked and saved many balls. A little later, all of a sudden, the goalie became Goliath, with no person tall enough and within reach even to murmur to. He waits then, in towering solitude, for the penalty kick from a sling. Day by day, possibilities of this man of many roles multiplies.

Father Geevarghese's parish was South Delhi. A few Malayalees and some tribal girls from Bihar were all the congregation he had. Once a week he would visit the Bishop and occasionally Father Capriatti would drop in to discuss literature. For the last few weeks, as he came out after mass, a tribal girl, Lucy Marandi, would be waiting for him.

'Father, he has come again,' Lucy had said when he met her last.

'Who Lucy?'

'Didn't I tell you last week? The same person.'

'What did you say his name was?'

'Jabbar.'

'That's right. Jabbar. Yes, I remember. Why did he come?'

'For the same reason he came last week.'

Father grunted a weak assent.

'He's asked me to go with him again.'

'Higuita' (Title of the original story) was first published in Malayalam in *Mathrubhoomi Weekly*, 23 - 29 December 1990, Calicut.

Memories rushed into Father's mind like a sudden shower of falling stars.

Jabbar was a middleman who dealt in rough cotton, fowls and the intoxicating flowers of the mahua. He bought them from the tribals and sold them to outsiders. Later, in the lean months when the tribal girls dug into the parched earth for roots and trekked miles for water, he enticed them with promises of jobs in big cities, and took them with him.

That is how Lucy reached Delhi from Ranchi, leaving behind stations that reeked of mustard oil.

Jabbar kept his word and found Lucy a job with a family. Every month he arrived to see her.

At first Lucy was afraid he might ask for money. But every time he visited, he brought her a gift — sticker bindis and sandalwood talcum powder and her first proper brassiere, that too in black.

One day when Jabbar told her, 'Stop working and come with me,' Lucy walked out with him without hesitation. That evening Jabbar brought her a new, readymade salwar kameez. Turmeric yellow with red polka dots. He insisted that she go out with him, all decked up, a red nylon duppatta draping her head and her dark negroid lips painted with dark gleaming lipstick. They reached the door of a hotel room. Before entering he said, 'I am not coming in. Sethji inside is a good man. I can tell from his excitement it must be his first time. Your good luck. He'll give you seven-fifty when you enter. Send it outside. You'll get your tip when it's over. Let's see how smart you are. The tip is all yours.'

Lucy ran out, through the hotel lobby, with Jabbar in hot pursuit. At the end of the chase she was in a locked room in Jabbar's house.

'I am going to marry you.'

He applied sindoor to the parting of her hair with a burning cigarette. Then he told her she was nothing more than a kid and began tickling the soles of her feet with the same glowing butt. And right through he kept talking like some sleazy villain in a Hindi movie, Lucy said.

Father couldn't remember how Lucy escaped because by then the

galleries of his mind were full. The careless goalkeeper had stopped all
the penalty kicks, but one by one the balls slipped from his grasp. That
day the goalie was Onan, the son of Judah, who couldn't help spilling
his seed.

Lucy got another job in a South Delhi household. This time without
Jabbar's knowledge. But it took him only ten days to trace her out . . .

'And then what did you tell him?'

'That I couldn't go with him.'

'That's fine.'

'But Jabbar?'

'You could complain to the police,' Father suggested.

'I'm more afraid of the police.'

'What do you want to do then?'

'If you could come with . . .'

'Don't be afraid,' Father said, then hastily added, 'I must be going
now.'

Father reached his room. The ground was deserted and littered with
popcorn wrappers and ice cream cups, strewn like bits of memorabilia.
The goalies must be resting.

He went to bed after dinner. But he couldn't sleep. Then he
suddenly remembered the World Cup series being played
in Italy. He switched on the portable black and white TV
and sat down to watch.

On the northern wall of the school, mouldy with the piss and piddle
of generations, some boy had scribbled in charcoal — Geevarghese has
been selected for the football team only because he is the P.T. teacher's
son. But everyone in school came to know him for the corner kick that
swung a perfect rainbow arch into the Olloor High School's goal post
— flimsy bamboo poles stuck into laterite grounds stippled with spiky
grass on which they played barefoot.

After defeating Olloor High School in the first game of the District
Championship, they went to Kunnamkulam. The boys were silent in the
bus. Rappai, alias the Killer, already selected for the state team, was

Kunnamkulam's team captain. Appan alone was talking — 'As soon as the foot gets the ball, the eye must dart around to see if anyone in our team is unmarked.'

Devouring the huge bananas and masala vadas which Appan bought from the school fund, and booed by the Kunnamkulam crowd, the victorious boys returned home in a practically empty night bus. They sang, dozens of feet tapping to the rhythmic beat of their palms, 'My oh my, Kunnamkulam is out, oh my my, Rappai too is out.'

'Come on, sing, you blighter,' coaxed Appan, looking tenderly at the silent Geevarghese. 'Don't be afraid. I'm not your father now, I'm your P.T. master.'

The next game was on their home ground. When Captain Gopinath's sharp volley was chest-trapped by Geevarghese, scissor-cut, and propelled back into the goal, people started coming from Malabar in search of him. He was invited to play in the sevens* tournament, and they promised him ten or fifteen rupees for each game. Harvest over, the dry fields were thrown open to them. Here Geevarghese played sevens to the loud cheering of punters. Appan couldn't reconcile himself to this. He told him once — 'Son, football is my faith, but sevens is Antichrist.' But Geevarghese just couldn't stop himself from playing sevens. Appan stopped talking to him about football. The year Geevarghese failed his B.A. was the very year Appan passed away. Geevarghese stopped playing sevens, as a reparation to his father.

Before long he received the Call.

Now staring at the World Cup game, numerous goalies flitted through Father's mind. He was not following the game, he was just watching the goalkeepers.

Lucy came to him again one morning when he was stepping out after mass.

'Father.'

'Yes.'

Sevens is a variation of football popular in northern Kerala.

'Jabbar.'

'Jabbar?'

'He has asked me to go with him at once.'

'Don't ever go.'

'He knows when I am alone in the house. Else how does he promptly call me on the phone just then? I'm scared.'

'Everything will be all right,' Father reiterated.

Penalty kicks are the best way to understand goalkeepers, Father Geevarghese told himself as he walked back to his room. Ruminating over it, he was surprised at yet another discovery — the goalkeeper waiting for the penalty kick is not lonely. On the contrary, he is more concerned over the loss of loneliness when people crowd around.

Zipping past on his scooter, Father Geevarghese saw Lucy again. Lucy was in an autorickshaw near the INA market. She saw him too, but by the time she tapped the driver's back to stop him, Father had changed into top gear and scooted.

Columbia's goalie, Higuita, who appeared on TV was a short foot-note to Father Geevarghese's study on goalkeepers. His long curly hair spread out like the locks of Siva before his tandava; his face, dark granite; a thin moustache. Higuita was an exception among goalkeepers.

The dharma of a goalkeeper is to witness. Only rarely does he deviate, when he faces a penalty kick. This is when he gets struck with stage fright. But not Higuita. He walks nonchalantly into happenings. Like a ship's captain discovering new meridians, dribbling the ball, to the left now, now to the right, he surges forward to midfield, land hitherto uncharted by goalkeepers.

Father Geevarghese abandoned other goalies to concentrate on Higuita from the day he noticed him facing a penalty kick.

Waving his arms like a conductor, Higuita creates inaudible beats of an impossible crescendo for the audience in the crescent-shaped stadium, the player about to take the kick was merely the first violinist in the first row of his orchestra.

At last it had to happen. An opponent snatched the ball from an advancing Higuita's feet and pushed it past the vacant post, throwing Columbia out of the World Cup. Only Father Geevarghese noticed Higuita smiling quietly to himself, musing on his role even at such a turn of events.

That day as he stepped out after mass, Father saw Lucy waiting for him. Nodding to her, he strode off to his room without stopping to talk.

Father loved Higuita most when he returned from the centre after passing the ball to a team-mate. Unlike other goalkeepers who rush back to the brooding warmth of the goal post, he sauntered back calmly, without a sense of nostalgia.

'Father,' Lucy called. He stopped.

'Father, I am going to Jabbar.' Her resistance was cracking.

'Do you want to go?'

'Well . . .'

'Well?'

'If I don't reach his house by evening he said he'd throw an acid bulb in my face.'

'Do you want to go?'

'Maybe he will marry me if I go,' Lucy said without conviction.

'Do you really want to go?'

'What if he throws an acid bulb at me?'

'Stay,' Father said asking her to wait outside. He stepped into his room, took off his cassock and rosary that he wore over his shirt and trousers and strode towards his scooter with her.

'Hop on,' he said, starting the scooter.

'Where does Jabbar stay?'

'Near Shakkurpur Basti.'

He dribbled his scooter, to the left now, now to the right, through rows of cars and scooters, as he sped along.

Jabbar opened the door at the knock. He stood five and a half feet tall, with curly hair and knit brows. His scanty moustache had not yet darkened, but his hair was already beginning to grey. It was difficult to guess his age. Jabbar asked, 'You've come?'

His soft, low voice surprised Father, especially when he noticed the thick bull neck, taut with muscles.

'Come in,' Jabbar said, his voice becoming softer.

'No.' Father Geevarghese answered, but Jabbar was looking only at Lucy. His eyes refused to acknowledge Father.

'Aren't you coming in?'

'No,' repeated Father.

Jabbar still didn't look at him. In an expressionless tone he whispered to Lucy — 'Isn't it better for all of us that he leaves?'

'No,' Lucy said.

Then, in a lightning flash, Jabbar raised his hand threateningly. Lucy lurched a step back, and the crowd watching sevens in a field near Thalassery bellowed hoarsely, 'Geevarghese, oh Geevarghese.'

With memories of the P.T. master leaning against a distant arecanut palm patinated on the edges of his vision, Geevarghese hit. Taking the ball smack on his broad chest he thrust it forward. The next was a sharp raised kick. Again and again. Then a replay . . . in slow motion. Blood spurted from the prostrate Jabbar's nose. Pulling him up by the T shirt which had OKLAHOMA emblazoned on it, Father Geevarghese quietly said, 'As sure as the sun rises tomorrow, you must not be seen in Delhi.' When Father let go, Jabbar crumpled in a heap.

Dropping Lucy in front of her house, Father sauntered back to his room calmly, without a sense of nostalgia.

JAYAMOHAN

•

ETERNAL RECURRENCE

•

NOMINATED BY SUNDARA RAMASWAMY
TRANSLATED BY M VIJAYALAKSHMI

'In Switzerland flows the river Inn, and on its bank is Ingadin,' Nambudiri began. I glanced at Paramasivan who was busy munching something. It was six o'clock. The film would begin at six-thirty. And Nambudiri's words sounded ominously like the invocatory verses to an epic.

'And I suppose they cultivate potatoes there,' put in Paramu, continuing to munch. I ran a hanky over my face.

Nambudiri who had thought nothing of moving freely in the street of the Dravidars, his bare chest displaying the sacred punul, his hair tied nonchalantly into a kudumi, was the least affected by our digs. He said, '. . . The Philosopher Nietzsche used to stroll on its banks.' 'Morning walks are good for health,' Paramasivan said.

Nambudiri intoned: 'And as he stood on the rock, contemplating the river, wisdom dawned on him.'

'Aha!' said Paramasivan. 'A rock! Just like the one on which you stand to recite your nonsensical mantras to your ancestors.' This was at me. I glanced at my watch. Five past six. We'd have to leave, now! if we were to perform our Sunday evening ritual: Paramu liked the Telugu dubbed variety and I was the film society type. They were to screen *Christ Stabbed at Epoly*. An Italian film. Heard that it got the Cannes Award.

I wished I hadn't picked up this Nambudiri at the University gate. He had just been thrown out by the security guard. I was impressed with the man, the quiet manner in which he got up and patted the dust off his body. He looked as out of place as a puranic character in a modern play. As I moved towards him, he cast me an insouciant look and introduced himself. He was Melaimangalam Appan Nambudiri and could I buy him tea please. After finishing his tea, Nambudiri opened his huge leather bag, put on his reading glasses, spread out a couple of sheets on the table and peered at me through his lenses.

'Name?' he asked in impeccable English.

I answered.

'An intellectual, I presume.'

'Eternal Recurrence' was first published in Tamil as *Jagan Mithyai*'in *Subamangala*, April 1991, Madras.

I reached the pinnacle of an existential pyramid of sorts. I collected myself. 'Well, at times.'

'Great! This is philosophy, high philosophy,' he said and then, 'Shall we discuss a few things?'

It was four o'clock. Enough time. I had brought Nambudiri to my room and introduced him to Paramu.

Paramu fixed me with one of his 'special' looks, a look reserved for monkeys and other such undesirables as Nambudiri started off on a synopsis of his life history and explained to us how he had discovered the key to the understanding of this mysterious universe, the prapancha. But he and his theories had been completely ignored by those who called themselves 'scientists,' people totally devoid of brains. And the reason for this? The racial admixture that had led to the attenuation of the pure Aryan brain. Hitler had been the first to realise this and stop the trend and the world in its collective wisdom had finished him off.

In a communist regime, chipping away the trunk of a coconut palm for toddy is physics; its distillation is chemistry and the nonsense that's spoken under its influence, philosophy. Kerala has no brains today, Nambudiri said. They have all withered away. But, he has been told that a few true Aryan brains could be found in Tanjavur. Before going in their search he had gate-crashed into a science seminar and before he knew what was happening he had been summarily thrown out. So what? Not that there was any dearth of opportunities to expound a good theory, Nambudiri told us, but money was a problem. So it was left to young intellectuals like me to bridge the gulf between him and the world at large.

Nambudiri said, 'Nietzsche felt an intuition that he had seen that same river from that same spot many a time in the past. And thus did mankind come to receive the Theory of Eternal Recurrence.'

He turned to stare intently at Paramu who was staring intently out the window. The room was totally silent except for a clock that ticked away. Paramu turned to look at Nambudiri and then glanced in my direction with a sheepish smile.

Nambudiri asked in a low steady voice, 'We have met, haven't we, in this same room, with these very same questions?'

Paramu looked shaken.

'No . . . I mean I do not know.'

'Observe . . . observe your inner mind. I have said this very thing, many a time.'

Paramu's face turned ashen and his eyes suddenly looked shifty. He gave me a stricken look. Breathing heavily he murmured 'Yes.'

'But you can't sense it clearly, can you? It is like a faint shadow, your subconscious, am I right?'

'Yes . . . yes . . . just so.' Paramu now clutched my hand, calling out to me in a muffled voice. 'De, Mohan.'

Nambudiri's concentration loosened somewhat. He smiled. 'Don't be scared. This is but an ordinary thing.'

I glanced sideways at Paramu. His mouth hung open, like that of a thirsty hen.

'Nietzsche said,' Nambudiri carried on, 'that lifeless matter which we call jatam exists in this universe in a finite quantity, but not so Time or Kaalam which is endless.   In the continuum of Time, matter even of gigantic proportions is but a speck. This room, the table, these books, you,' he carried on gesturing with his arms as if to prove the point, 'our voice, language, words, their meaning — they are all manifestations of the limitless permutations and combinations within the matter.

'All happenings are but vibrations in the matter. A simple six-sided cube after all allows several lakh combinations and the universal matter with its myriad manifesatations offers myriads of combinations . . . it's beyond the pale of imagination . . .' he said with a tiny sigh. 'Yet, matter has its limits.' Now he was facing me. 'Hence the events taking places due to the linking of various pieces of this matter must also have a limit. Combinations and occurrences may run into the thousands, the crores. But these combinations will one day be played out . . . And then?'

'Aiyo!' A strangled cry emanated from a scared Paramu.

Nambudiri ignored him and went on, 'And then what? Time has no end. Therefore combinations which have occurred once have to occur again, no? Today's event, that of Appan Nambudiri talking to Jayamohan, is attributable to one of the combinations in the matter. Which means that this very combination will occur again in the future. It ought to have occurred in the past. In the eternal flow of time, it must keep recurring. This is the Theory of Eternal Recurrence. Simple, isn't it?'

Aha! Paramu turned to look at me. Here in this wide universe is a soul who will put you in place, his smug look said.

'And now for my theory,' Nambudiri carried on, completely at home now. 'It's based on the Eternal Recurrence Theory. Vibrating matter creates a million events ranging from the birth of a star to the birth of a worm. And wherein lies the difference between the one event and the other? Merely in that the larger event has a certain number of combinations and the smaller event, very many more.'

A deep palpable silence pervaded the place.

'The first point I wish to make is this: whether an event is massive or minute, the time it takes for the event to recur is the same. For instance, the time it'll take for this discourse of mine to recur in this universe is the same as the time gap between the birth of this earth and its death and rebirth. Is that clear?'

'Yes.'

'No,' said Nambudiri smiling, savouring the moment. 'It is rather complicated. We should first of all know the Mutual Relationship principle. All occurrences, every fragment of each one of these, are dependent on one another. To give an example, for our conversation today there had to be, preceding this, the evolution of the human race. This city had to come into being. This house had to be built. A million things had to happen. This earth had to be here, of course. And before it the sun. And prior to that the Milky Way. Thus, the birth of a sun and that of a worm will recur after the same time gap.' He now began to enunciate his sutra: All events in the universe keep recurring at ordained time intervals. This interval is constant.

'Friends, now let's move over to the formulae. Do pay attention.

Let C stand for combinations. And D for the events. Then it follows that
$C \propto 1/D$.'

'Yes, yes, yes.' I was in a hurry.

'That is, combinations and events are inversely related. The time
interval is a constant. Let A stand for this constant. The more numerous
the combinations, the greater the time needed. That leads us to $C \propto A$,
wherein A is constant. Hence C is also constant. Thus it follows that the
combinations do not change.'

'True,' I said.

'True? What's true?' Nambudiri was contemptuous now. 'It is wrong
to talk unthinkingly. We began on the premise that larger events have
fewer combinations and smaller events have more, right?'

'The whole formula is wrong,' said Paramu.

'Fool, it is such a simple thing.'

'So, what are you getting at?' Paramu sounded belligerent.

Nambudiri smiled.

'When I say combinations, you should not take it as the sum total of
the aspects involved. There ought to be one immutable number between C_1, by which we'll denote the larger combination, and C_2, the
smaller combination. So the immutable number is C_1/C_2. This is the
second formula. Let's combine the two now.'

Nambudiri started writing with a pencil:
1. $C \propto 1/D$
2. $C \propto A$
3. $A = C_1/C_2$

'These are the three basic formulae. And now for the calculation.' He
gave us an intense look and scribbled down more of his formulae.
'Since A is a constant, D is also a constant. Quite simple,' he finished.

I had reached the end of my tether.

'Do you mean to say that everything is an unchanging number?'

'Exactly.'

The enthusiasm was obvious.

'The drama in the universe is played out according to a rhythm. All
equilibriums are nonchanging. That is, all movements in the universe

revolve around a constant number. This we can denote by X.'

There was a let-up in the tension.

Nambudiri wiped his sweat. 'With this sutra we would be able to evaluate any event occurring in any corner of the universe without stirring from this spot, and be able to understand it. If only we are able to derive this constant, the entire secret of this universe is ours.'

'How does one achieve this?'

'That calls for special research. We have established that all the movements in the universe have a constant number. Our forefathers called this Eka or Pranavam. Could we but place the happenings on this earth according to scale . . . How fantastic even to conjecture! This constant number is what I describe as Brahma Sankhya. In fact, I call my entire finding Brahma Sankhya Sutra. The root is Sanskrit. I relate all this in English for the sake of Your Lordships.'

Paramu disappeared and soon came back with his horoscope, a fresh smear of vibhuti on his forehead. He kept the horoscope reverentially at Nambudiri's feet.

Nambudiri was genuinely taken aback.

'Swami, for quite a while now we haven't had any peace of mind, my wife and I. She is chronically ill. When will this bad spell finish? Only you can tell us, swami.'

'De Paramu! What's all this now?'

'Listen, brother. I have been talking science. I don't know anything about anything else.'

'You are a great soul. Don't abandon this lowly creature,' Paramu said in a voice brimming over with emotion.

My head throbbed.

Nambudiri gave me a beseeching look. Then as if he had already sloughed off the persistent Paramu, he turned to me and said, 'In the great expanse of Time our consciousness alone keeps coming back. Our old thoughts lie sedimented in the subconscious. With dhyana we can retrieve them. This is what happened to Nietzsche.'

I seemed to be in pitch darkness. I bashed my head against wall after wall. Then suddenly there was light. 'Nambudiri!' I screamed. 'Wait. There is one thing.'

Nambudiri was replacing his papers in the bag. He turned to me, startled.

'It's all wrong,' I said.

'What?'

'This theory is wrong.' I was vehement.

'What are you blabbering?'

'I am not. Your theory is nothing but rubbish.'

'Idiot! What's wrong with my formulae?'

'Formulae? Pooh! You took off with Nietzsche's Eternal Recurrence Theory. Didn't you?'

'Yes.'

'That itself is flawed.'

'Flawed? What's the flaw?'

'You say that matter is limited. But that's not true. Jatam, like Time, is unlimited.'

'How well you blabber!'

'Have you heard of Einstein?'

'I've heard the name.'

'Do you know what $E = MC^2$ means? It is the theory that matter and energy are one and the same. You multiply matter by the square of the speed of light then you will get the equivalent as energy.'

Nambudiri loked stunned. 'How can that be?'

'Go read, sir! When matter moves at the speed of light it is converted to energy. Energy can be converted to matter. There is no limit for energy. Hence, there is no limit for matter.'

'Einstein is wrong.'

'Yes. And you with your crazy statements are right? Go, go read up, I say!'

'Challenging me, uhn? Matter and energy are the same, uhn! I'll see that too! . . . And who are you to find fault with Brahma Sankhya? Your Einstein is about equal to this . . . this single hair of my kudumi. I'll . . . I'll . . .' he shouted, his body shaking, the eyes spewing fire. His eyes did something to my insides. He got out on the street, his strides exuding violence. He stood, shouted some more and walked away, still shouting.

'Terrific brain,' said an awe-struck Paramu. 'You needn't have been so abusive.'

'Who abused? He was wrong. That was all I said.'

'Let that be, my wayward hero. Don't I know your games. Poor Nambudiri knows no chemistry. And you picked up a formula from chemistry to fix him.'

'And who tells you it's chemistry?'

I found myself breathing heavily.

'It's in little Nana's chemistry book, this formula. Whom are you trying to fool?' He literally crowed in jubilation.

It was futile talk. 'Let it be. He's not going to come here again.'

Within a month Nambudiri was back. He walked in with a perfunctory 'May I come in?' hardly taking note of my hesitation. His countenance was cheerful.

'What a great truth, that was. I can't thank you enough. My greatest fault was that I never noticed Einstein. I have since burnt up my formulae.'

'And what are you reading now?' I was keen not to revive that old hurt.

'More of Einstein. You'll be surprised to know how compatible the two theories are. Wonder of wonders! And that great man, he is of the same ilk as us.'

'Us?'

'Me, that is.' Nambudiri said with a shy smile.

I couldn't help laughing.

'You think I exaggerate? No. Einstein is a real genius, and no doubting that.'

I am thrilled to hear it, I told him.

Nambudiri opened his bag and took out some new sheets of paper. 'Einstein's theory is about the interconvertibility of mass and energy.

This fits well into the ambit of the Eternal Recurrence Theory.' He peered at me. 'Want to know how?'

'Go on.'

'Listen. Energy becomes matter. Matter has a myriad manifestations. These mingle and produce combinations, setting the material universe in motion. When the combinations play themselves out, matter reaches the state of shakti or energy. This is one block. The next block is the next stage in Eternal Recurrence, the reason being of course, the inherent limitation in the combinations.'

This was followed by a laugh — a red, betel-stained one. Leaning forward, he continued in a companionable tone: 'The interval between the first and the second blocks is equal to two cosmic events, the reason being . . .'

That constant number, of course! Something welled up in my stomach. 'Nambudiri,' I said steadying myself with effort, 'You forgot something important.'

'What?' His eyes narrowed.

'Energy does not directly become matter.'

'Then?'

'Shakti or energy converts into neutrons, electrons and protons which are the basic components of the atom. And atoms make up the universe.'

'And which fool says so?'

'Modern science! Go read it up, man.'

Nambudiri's lips quivered. His body convulsed, as if he would sob.

'An atom with a simple electron means one type of element. This is one substance. If there are two, then it is another substance. Thus the variation in the number of electrons and neutrons create a variety of elements. This too has limitless possibilities. Hence there is no limit to the number of elements, nor an end to the number of combinations.' I paused.

Nambudiri sat as though frozen. His head shook. Then he actually sobbed. His head sank into his hands, tears racked his body. I was shaken, not quite knowing how to console him. Then, in a fit, he tore up all his sheets. The bits flew everywhere in the room. For a moment he looked at them, then ran towards the door.

I was convinced that Nambudiri's troubles were over.

But there he was, and barely a month had passed. 'Sir, you were very right. Science and philosophy are now one and the same,' he began there and then, on the street. 'I read about the atomic structure in detail. A marvel! Everything is to be found in it. And how well it integrates with the Eternal Recurrence Theory. In fact, I have been looking for you to say this.' He took out his papers in a hurry. 'The constant number of the combinations is to be found in the atomic structure.'

I don't quite recall what I did but I do remember that I pushed him away and shouted a few things — that he dare not bother me again.

But as I got home I was assailed by anguish and an unbearable sense of guilt. And I never could forget that face of his, full of shock and disappointment. Why had I behaved like that? I had gone roughshod over a man old enough to be my father. He was in a way a child, a guileless, innocent child. Could that be called a mental illness? He was not of his senses. He was immensely knowledgeable. A rakshasa brain that could digest the most complicated scientific treatise in a single day. But . . . that Constant Number. That Eternal Recurrence — how did these take possession of him? It was as though a wasp had lodged itself in his brain, determined to build its hive there, destroying him in the process. I could have been more compassionate, more understanding. But I had to be heartless. Bent on breaking him. Why?

I was assaulted by self-doubt at that instant. Did I see in him a caricature of myself . . . was it the awareness that my literary pretensions, ideals, self centric imaginings, my tireless labour could be swept aside as a mad man's rantings with just a deft deflection, as it were. Wasn't this why I imagined mine to be a meaningful existence. And wasn't it similar to Nambudiri's?

I wished I could see him just one more time, so I could be kinder to him, to make up for my rudeness.

But Nambudiri had wandered off in search of the Tanjavur brain.

I met Nambudiri again under entirely different circumstances. Our last meeting. I was visiting a Malayali poet in Thrissur where a visitor, a mutual friend, happened to mention Brahma Sankhya Nambudiri. That he was in the local charitable hospital, in the last throes of life.

The very next day I went to see him. His emaciated and aged frame was laid out on a torn mat, on the floor of a hospital ward smelling as usual of urine and medicines. His eyes were fixed on the wall.

I sat near him, bent close and called out his name. I shook him gently a couple of times. He responded, bleary eyes hardly focussing.

'Who is it?'

'Can't you recognize me?'

'No.'

I was full of remorse. Mine was one of the thousand faces which had mocked him. And now for him this bed and death like a worm's. What a waste of an existence!

I could bear it no more. Suddenly a thought emerged. He had certainly crossed that moment in his life when he could realise the foolhardiness of his theories. Why not let him die secure in the illusion that he is a great discoverer?

'I am your sishya,' I said. 'It is only now that I realise what a great master you are.'

Nambudiri did not seem to have taken in any of this.

'I have been working on the Eternal Recurrence Theory. I have proved that your findings are of great importance. Soon your name will be a household word.'

'Eternal Recurrence,' murmured Nambudiri with a vacant stare.

'Yes. The Brahma Sankhya Sutra.'

Nambudiri suddenly started weeping loudly in a way that touched me deeply. I held his shaking shrunken body. Tears poured down his wizened cheeks.

'Please . . . Saar . . . don't weep!'

Nambudiri's body shook.

'Waste . . . my life is a waste . . . '

A chill stole up my spine. No there remained nothing that I could do. I placed him down gently. His tears wet the pillow.

The old man was suddenly clutching my hands. 'I don't understand. What is the meaning of this life? I understand nothing.' His voice trembled. 'All my life I went from place to place explaining my theory. Nobody understood me. And my theory now perishes with me.' His eyes had a strange glimmer. The face wore a tortured look. 'But why should this happen? Why should a life be so wasted? Has this happened to me many times before? And am I destined to live and live again, only to be destroyed? In the endless flow of time am I destined to lead this wasted life, over and over again? No, no more of this tortured existence! But I'm helpless. This is an endless whirl . . . inescapable . . . Eshwara! Jagadishwara! Let me be . . .'

I gently released my hand from his. I got up to leave. What more was there to say?

ATULANANDA GOSWAMI

•

THE ROGUE

•

NOMINATED BY PANKAJ THAKUR
TRANSLATED BY THE AUTHOR

Word spread like wild-fire. The rogue is coming this way! Panic gripped the whole village. What should they do? What could they do?

Men gathered in someone's front yard to plan a strategy: There must be enough firewood stacked up in one place; a big fire should be lit at that end; the elephant would appear from this.

Women were everywhere, like anxious hens before a storm, as they tried to herd their young ones to the safety of their homes. The elders sat looking at the frightened women. Then they shouted. Didn't the women realise that their bamboo and thatch huts were but match boxes for a wild elephant? One nudge from him would raze these to the ground.

A wild elephant has gone mad! It is a big tusker. It was seen coming out of the sanctuary and heading westward. It has not only damaged several houses in its frenzied march but has killed some five or six people. News had already reached the village. A bride trampled to death in one village. A couple in another. A peasant has been killed on his way to the field. An old man, returning one evening from the weekly market, was kicked around like a football. Who knows how many houses have been destroyed?

The Government too is aroused. On the advice of the local authorities, they have issued a public notification declaring the elephant a rogue which must be caught and killed. They have announced an award. But the villagers are not interested in administrative details.

Has the rogue been killed?

No?

They say that it is coming this way?

Forest guards have spotted it?

The dreaded news hits every villager like a bullet. They are hysterical with fear. They forget their meals. Anyway there is nothing to eat. The women have forgotten to cook.

The elephant has gone mad, someone explains. It is all because of a

'The Rogue' was first published in Assamese as *'Bolia Haati'* in *Krantik,* 16-28 February 1991, Guwahati.

poacher. He gave it chase. The tusks were big, you see. They were too tempting for the . . .

Let it be, let it be! What use is this talk? Just tell us — Has it been killed? Can we breathe in peace now? O God, send us some kind message in this hour of crisis.

Villages to the east have organised a night watch. Drums, empty tins, even threshing pins were being sounded intermittently. Big oil torches were kept ready. Fire frightens an elephant.

This village is a lonely one. It's not far from a forest. To the north is the big river. A few hillocks to the south, mounds really. The forests provide sustenance for several households. And though it is unlawful these days, they fell trees on the sly and make charcoal. They burn the logs in a shallow pit inside the forest itself. The task is tough and demands much strength, stamina.

Gajala has been fretting for the last two days. He had prepared a full pit and set it on fire. It took him an entire day to fell the chosen tree, cut it to measured pieces, stack them in the proper way. Then he had had to cover the pit with a thick mat of grass and twigs and daub mud on the outside before he could ignite it. He left for the night deciding to come back early next morning to repair any cracks that might have appeared on the plaster.

When he reached home, everyone was talking about the rogue.

Two days have gone by. Gajala's mind is filled with thoughts of the mud plaster. If it has cracked, the pit will have burst into flames. A lesser yield. All his pains wasted. He yearns to go out there and save his charcoal, but he is not allowed to utter a word. Nor does anyone volunteer to go with him.

Fear is contagious, especially in such places. And Gajala is afraid. But the charcoal? He expects more than four hundred rupees from the pit. If the plaster gives way, the upper layer will turn to ashes. What will be left for him then?

Two days, and still no news about the rogue. Someone says the whole thing was a hoax. But still, who would dare prove him right?

Gajala was sure that the rogue, if there was one, had changed its

course. Its movements would have been known otherwise. I must go
to the charcoal pit, he decided. Today. If the fire has caught properly,
the charcoal will be done by now. Two more days for it to cool, and it
will be ready to bring home to sell. He had already asked two of his
friends to help him carry it back.

Immediately after his midday meal, Gajala left for the pit, a little over
three kilometres away. The site was at the foot of a big mound near a
small brook. If you walk along it the thin flow of water can take you
back to the village. Gajala and his friends used to picnic here sometimes.
They cooked their food in tender bamboo joints which gave the food
a rich, pleasant aroma.

Gajala had his handy knife with him. He was in a hurry now. The job
must be finished soon and he must return home in time.

He was pleased with the mud plaster. The charcoal burned to his
satisfaction. He walked around the pit, taking one last look before
turning back.

He had barely gone a hundred paces when he heard the sound.
Someone treading loose mud. Gajala stopped dead in his tracks. It must
be the elephant! But where was it? In which direction should he run for
his life? He knew the forest inside out, but now he was afraid to choose
a path. The elephant must be watching him from behind those trees. It
might rush on him any moment. He stood shivering, rooted to the spot,
straining his ears. If only he could hear the elephant's steps, he'd know
which way to run. With his heart booming in his ears, he slowly looked
around. No sound at all. And then . . . He saw the trunk of the elephant
lying on the ground, twisting like a massive python!

The sight cast a spell on him. He could not move. Then he turned
and fled. But soon he stopped.

Why was the trunk lying on the ground?

Gajala turned around. Yes, there was a trunk on the ground. The
elephant seemed to wave it as if calling him nearer.

He walked a few paces towards it.

The elephant was in pain. He was sure of that. The giant animal had
fallen into the deep hole that lay hidden under the thicket. And could

not get out.

How could there have been such a deep pit under the thicket?

Gajala walked a few more steps towards the animal. He stooped and stretched out his hand to touch the trunk. The elephant seemed to have been waiting for just such a gesture. It moved its trunk from side to side. Gajala felt bolder. He went closer. The elephant was calm and docile. Probably exhausted.

It was the rogue all right. Gajala saw the tusks. He hadn't seen any domesticated elephant with tusks such as these! He walked around the hole, examining it carefully. No. The elephant would never be able to come out of that hole on its own. It was narrow and deep. The animal filled it completely. Unless helped it would have to die there.

Impulsively, Gajala turned to run to the village for help. He'd ask some of his friends to come help the elephant out of the hole and back into the forest.

But he stopped again. Would it be wise to inform the villagers about the elephant? Would they believe him? Would they help a killer rogue? Would they not rather collect whatever weapons they could lay their hands on and rush here to massacre the animal in turn? Any talk of helping a rogue would be construed as the babbling of an idiot. Gajala looked at the large animal in distress.

No, he would not return to the village. It would mean sure death to the elephant.

He went back and inspected the pit once more. The elephant raised its trunk to touch Gajala as if imploring for help. Or so Gajala thought. The knave had submitted itself to his mercy.

Gajala gently touched the rogue's trunk. 'Wait, I'll do something.'

The elephant raised its trunk again as if in acknowledgement.

Gajala cut through the thicket to one side of the hole to reach his coal-pit. He had left some branches to dry there. They had been too soft for coal. But he had thought they would serve for firewood. Now he chose a few straight and sturdy pieces out of them. Squatting, he sharpened the ends to make a hoe of each and returned to the hole. He sank the crude hoe at one end and started digging. A sloping path would have to be cut to make a way out for the elephant.

The elephant was apparently puzzled at the young man's lone efforts but it could somehow understand that he was doing something for its benefit.

As he worked briskly, Gajala started talking with the elephant. 'But how could you have fallen into such a hole? Have you lost your senses? You are a creature of the forest, and yet . . .'

The pointed stick got blunt soon. Gajala sharpened the end again, shortening it in the process. A sloping path was yet to take shape. Gajala did not know how long it would take. He didn't know how long he had been at work. It was getting dark.

The elephant raised its trunk and rested it on Gajala's hand.

A satisfactory ramp was emerging. Gajala threw away the small stick and took another. He was sweating all over now.

The elephant guessed what the man was trying to do. It tried to heave itself up.

'Patience!' Gajala shouted, raising his stick as if to hit the elephant.

The animal flinched like a child saving itself from the wrath of its mother. The single eye that Gajala could see closed shut.

Gajala softened.

'Don't you see I am working? Have I stopped? It's for you, don't you realise, you scamp! You'll come out when I'm done. Wait a little.'

It was a difficult task. Had he gone home for a real hoe and some help, the job could have been finished by now. He felt as if he was trying to scoop out a mountain with a needle. But there was no way out. He would not let the animal be killed by a mob.

His palms turned raw and painful. Besides, it was quite dark now. He stopped the digging, overcome by fatigue. Throwing the stick aside he sat down, put his arms around his knees and rested his head on them.

'You must wait a little,' he told the elephant. 'I'm too tired. Let me get some rest.' He sank deep into sleep in that uncomfortable position.

Time slipped by. Gajala rocked and almost fell on top of the animal. The elephant nudged him gently, as if trying to push him back into his sitting position.

Gajala woke up with a start. It took him a few minutes to realise where he was. Then he saw the elephant. He grinned apologetically.

'Oh, I didn't know I had fallen asleep. Come. Let me help you out.'

He started digging again.

By the time a ramp had been finally cut, the eastern sky was lighting up.

Gajala held out his hand to the elephant.

'Come . . .'

Gajala took hold of the elephant's outstretched trunk and gave a tug. It was a painful process. The elephant shuffled from one foot to another as it slowly inched forward to level ground. It was early dawn by the time the whole operation was through.

Gajala moved his hand over the elephant's body. 'Hmm. There's mud all over you. Wait . . .'

Then something compelled him to look closely at the elephant as if it were tame.

'What is this? What happened to you?'

There was a big gash just above the right front leg of the animal. It was putrid and still oozing pus. Gajala touched the gaping wound. The elephant jerked away sharply, but did not move. It should have rushed away into the forest the moment it was out of the hole. Was it too exhausted to do so?

Gajala held one of its huge ears and pulled.

'Come, I'll wash the wound.'

The elephant walked towards the brook on Gajala's command. Gajala walked slowly, muttering to himself. 'I know. This is the job of a poacher. They are after your tusks. Don't you know that you dumb devil?'

Reaching the brook Gajala commanded the elephant to remain still while he went to get some dried grass. He took his gamocha off his shoulder and dipped it into the stream. Then he wrung it over the wound. 'Is this why you ran amuck?' Gajala asked as he gently rubbed the rot from the gash with the dried grass. It was evidently painful for the animal, for it gave a few jerks again, but did not protest further.

'These tusks are your death, do you know that? Lucky you weren't killed by that bullet. But tell me, why did you get that angry? Should you have mauled so many people? Can you guess what has befallen those families after your murderous march?'

Gajala railed at the mute animal while cleaning the wound.

It was day now. Gajala put his hand on the elephant's trunk and asked it to stand still.

'Wait right here. Let me see if I can get the plants I'm looking for. I will apply them to your wound.'

He did not get the poison fern he wanted. Instead he plucked a few wild arum leaves and stems. He crushed them on a stone and applied the pulp to the wound. The elephant jerked again.

'I know, I know it burns. But it'll help. If I could have taken you home, Elder Cheni Kaka would have healed the wound in two days flat. He knows the right herbs. But how can I take you there. The whole village would raise hell and you may do something stupid again. Wouldn't you? That's why I'm going to send you right back to the jungle. Never come near us men again, do you hear me? Never!'

The elephant gave another jerk.

'Stop! Don't you dare vex me!' Gajala snapped.

He stared at the eye he could see above him. The elephant raised its huge ear and placed its trunk on Gajala's back.

Maybe it wanted to remove his hand from the painful wound.

'Ah, calm down. It's for your own good, you dumb one. It's over, see? Now go back. Don't you kill anyone anymore. Mind you . . .'

Gajala never finished his sentence. A gunshot split the silence. The elephant trumpetted jerking its head up. A tusk hit Gajala's head. It sent him flying to the edge of the brook. He lay still, his head cracked open like a ripe bael fruit. Blood flowed to mix with the meagre water of the brook.

The elephant knelt down on its front legs. Then it rolled to one side, its trunk stretched towards Gajala, stopping only a couple of inches from his lifeless feet.

The hunter, equipped with a license to kill the rogue, had been tracking the elephant all day. He had hunted cautiously through the night. He was told in the village that a young man had come this way but had not returned. The disappearance could mean only one thing and none would utter the cursed word.

He and his gun-carrier reached the hillocks only towards dawn. They saw the elephant from the top of a mound. It was well within range of his Magnum 404.

The single hard-nosed bullet felled the elephant. Yet the hunter fired a further confirmatory shot. Then they rushed to the fallen giant in great jubilation. Reaching the spot, the hunter clapped a hand to his mouth and stared at the man lying dead behind the elephant.

'Look!' he said, pointing. 'The rogue has killed yet another man. The seventh so far, isn't it?'

The villagers too heard the shot. At the second shot, reassured that the rogue had indeed been tracked down, they set out. In search of Gajala.

MOHAN PARMAR

•

WADO : THE YARD

•

NOMINATED BY GANESH N DEVY
TRANSLATED BY ANJANA DESAI

The mongoose ran clean through the bars of the baari, the small swing-to door of the house, and into the hedge enclosing the yard. Khemo chased him, knocking his neem switch on the dung-plastered floor. The mongoose's intrusion into the house alarmed Khemo but it frightened Puni even more. She knew Khemo well and realised that he would not now give up the pursuit. As a matter of fact the mongoose often went into and out of the house but Khemo had not noticed him before. Now, noticing, he was incensed.

Puni's footfalls fell lightly on the echoing dung-plastering, over the shadow dance cast by the clouds as they drifted across the skylight. She stamped her feet as if they had gone to sleep and peeped through the baari. Khemo was running his switch in and across the hedge. Someone had made an opening in the thick hedge of goondi and other prickly bushes and sturdy creepers.

Khemo stepped back and glanced towards the baari.

Maddened by the nervous expression on Puni's face he groped blindly in the hedge. Clusters of sour goondi lay strewn all over the yard. Khemo liked to eat them, plucked straight off the hedge. But today the berries seemed riddled with confusion. A few prickly kantodas hung from a creeper and here and there a baby squash or gourd had appeared. Though the sight of these soothed his eyes his heart was bitter, haunted by the hedge.

The mongoose was not to be seen. Where could he have gone? Khemo's mind wavered, like a wind-swayed creeper. For a moment he felt like going back into the house and bolting the baari.

But there were many other ways for the mangoose to enter the house. He could climb the rear wall and slide in under the displaced rooftiles. Or, he could climb the goondi tree and from there leap onto the porch and come through the front. There were any number of ways. Khemo agonized: This doesn't look like the first time he's come. Seems to be quite at home, else he couldn't have escaped through the baari so fast, could he?

'Wado : The Yard' was first published in Gujarati as *'Wado'* in *Parishkrit Varta*, 1991, Baroda.

Khemo again started rummaging. Gripping the switch tightly he thrashed at the hedge. It was a useless exercise. Bending, he peered as far as he could, putting the hedge through a cross-examination. All he found were dry, brittle leaves. Cobwebs obstructed his view.

Why can't I see him? Khemo grumbled.

He started stirring the creepers with his switch. Something fell into his eyes. He rubbed them vigorously. He slashed a creeper bare. Leaves whirled all over the yard. He lost his balance and fell against the trunk of the mehndi tree, bruising his head against a swinging branch. Mistaking it for the mongoose, he retreated, running towards the baari.

Puni burst into laughter.

'What's so funny, you whore! It's okay as long as he's only got into the hedge. Once he gets into the house you'll forget to giggle.'

Puni clamped her lips and held back her mirth.

Khemo hacked at the branch of the mehndi until it was shorn bare. He came close to the opening and peered beyond the hedge as if looking for traces of the mongoose. His eyes searched for a while. Then he turned back. The footmarks were clearly visible, he reassured himself. There was need for such assurance; and there wasn't.

Sensing his tussle with himself Puni pulled her head back from the baari.

Khemo was seething. His mother had been ailing for a long time. The rattle of her cough heard from the lean-to sounded like dry twigs rubbing against each other. He too was drying up like a withered lime bush. He looked towards the baari with disgust and, not seeing Puni there, was mad with sudden anger: 'Just look at this woman! Is she at all scared of the mongoose? Mark my words, if that mongoose doesn't skin and gobble her up even as he blows numbingly over her!'

Khemo threw away the switch and stood, leaning against the wall. He rifled through his pockets for a bidi, and found only a matchbox. He took out a matchstick and began to dig into his ear, feeling as if he had lived through several years of a many-coloured existence. All at one go.

Gently, he turned towards the mehndi tree.

Puni ever so often ran around it, excited. At such times Khemo enviously eyed the chameleon scrambling up the goondi tree grown full three heads taller than the hedge, and tried to hit it with a brick. But as always he could never bring it down.

Regret sprang afresh in his mind as he gazed at the tree.

There was a sound of something stirring.

Khemo turned away from the tree and looked back.

Puni had entered the yard with a broom. She chose the end opposite to the one where Khemo stood.

He looked in her direction and fell to thinking: Something seems to hover around the yard in practiced bewitchment. All the flowers and trees are swaying to their own rhythm. Hoards of ants swarm the path connecting the borders of the yard.

Khemo moved away from the goondi and stood at a distance.

Puni was bent, sweeping vigorously. As she moved about her hair-pins glinted in the sun. Khemo stood looking. Puni straightened herself and rested her arm on her waist. Eyes swept around. What was within bounds and what without — the two come together in her eyes.

Khemo felt abashed. He mistook the fluttering rags on the cactus for pennants of a saint's tomb. To him the flower bushes seemed possessed. They shook so! He was perplexed. There were hollows around the trunk of the mehndi. The air was damp.

Suddenly, Khemo caught sight of the presence he'd sensed hovering around the yard, now reflected in the watered bed of the almond tree. He was about to ask, Is there something there? when there was a sudden movement outside the yard.

Khemo felt trapped as if having to unravel knots of tangled string. He fought to extricate himself. He was like a bull whose horn is caught in a web of creepers. The more he struggles to free himself, the deeper the trap. Khemo felt confused, as if the movement beyond the hedge had invaded his heart.

It must be so. Yes. It has to be so.

He glanced into the hedge and glimpsed the head. It looked peculiar. Mongooses are blue; this wasn't. Had there been a metamorphosis?

Khemo sprinted to get his switch, rushed back, and started a desperate search as if his little remaining poise had vanished.

Memories crowded his mind, hindering him.

The mongoose had vanished, nor could he get any fun out of throwing bricks at the goondi. Crows raised an uproar in that tree. Without the usual sense of enjoyment, he threw a brick viciously at them. The brick reached only halfway.

'How come you've fallen to brickbatting, Khem'bhai!' asked Bhala's wife from the other side of the hedge as she winked at Puni.

Khemo smouldered.

The atmosphere was bathed in waves of laughter.

The shape he'd sensed hovering around the yard was trying to hide behind the trees.

Khemo smiled weakly, trying to hide his vexation. And Bhala's wife, coming so close to him that even Puni could not overhear, said, 'I thought a mongoose had got into your house. Be careful! Even as he blows on you numbingly, he'll skin you and he'll gobble you up!' She smiled in a way that made Khemo's hair stand on end.

At the other end of the yard Puni was collecting the litter in a basket. The trunks of the mehndi and the goondi were so tightly bound together with cotton twine that they seemed to be copulating.

Khemo's gaze moved from Puni to this.

The water dripping from the sheet hung out to dry on the line brought a shine to the stones that paved the courtyard. Then somewhere someone muttered, Why does this stone look so dry today? and at that Khemo turned full circle.

His footfalls shook the other end of the yard.

He felt he was going through something he had experienced before. But pretending not to have seen the shape trying to hide behind the goondi Khemo started moving towards the baari.His eyes hurt as he stood pressed to the baari and watched Puni collect the litter in the basket.

'You're great! It took you an age to sweep such a small yard!'

Puni, flustered, shuffled about and started moving with her basket towards the opening in the hedge.

But Khemo's eyes were suddenly riveted on the shape trying to move out too, from behind the screen of trees.

He began to lose heart and strained to evade the eye of the intruder. Like lightning he changed places. Now he was on the porch. Now he was compelling his body, crushed against the baari, to enter the house. And, once inside, in utter bewilderment he fumbled about but could not find what he was seeking. He looked out again, through the baari, his eyes searching for his double beyond the yard. Looking intently at one spot made him dizzy. His wife Puni's photograph smiled coyly at him from the wall of the room.

A sense of self-humiliation made him feel drained and ill at ease. Was he being eaten up by the shame of not having caught the mongoose or was it the misery of not having traced the double that wouldn't let him rest — what was it?

Like a prisoner held forcibly by unseen hands he came into the lean-to.

His mother was moaning.

Khemo's eyes softened.

As if trying to make up for years of neglect he went close to her.

'Ma, shall I bring your medicine?'

'What? Yes, yes.'

The mother gazed steadily at him. A fount of affection sprang in the sunken eyes. But Khemo, keeping a hold over himself, went to fetch the medicine. When he returned with it his mother was weeping.

'Ma, what's the matter?'

'It's nothing son.'

'Tell me. You must tell me.'

'Where were you all this time?'

'Lost.'

Khemo felt like talking on and on with his mother. He sat by her on the bed and held out the pills to her, but she turned away. He pleaded and coaxed but she refused to take the medicine. He put it on the table and looked at her wasting body. Every fibre of his being seemed to break down in tears: as if it was futile to seek communion with one after having turned away from another. This pain kept welling up. Everything seemed to lie at odds. He stood up in alarm and rushed to the room at the other end. He looked through the baari.

But there wasn't a sound. Nothing stirred. Sparrows were fooling around on the hedge.

Khemo turned away. The small opening in the hedge was enlarged in his eyes. Seeing two pairs of footprints there, Khemo wrung his hands. Can't everything be swept away in one swoop?

He came back to his mother. She had turned over and was lying on her back, staring into space. Seeing Khemo she motioned him nearer.

'Your guess may be right and may not.'

'Why are you talking in riddles?'

'You've started finding all this mysterious, haven't you! Khemo, find out what made me ill.'

'That's enough, Ma. Enough!'

Khemo fled, head between hands. He ran clean through the baari as the mongoose had done.

As he entered the yard once again he saw the sparrows again, fooling around. He rapidly approached the mehndi tree and caressed its trunk. Not on the goondi alone, but everywhere, everywhere there was an uproar. His gaze got fixed on the hedge of the yard. Something rustled. He picked up the switch; poked it here and there.

Bhala's wife was smiling as she returned homewards. Seeing Khemo poking about in the hedge she could not contain her laughter. She said, 'What are you looking for, Khem'bhai, the mongoose? Even if you keep searching for ten days you won't find him. When Puni took away the basket of litter I saw him follow her.'

The switch remained suspended in Khemo's hand. He was deep into worrying about how the mongoose would blow numbingly on Puni even as he skinned her and gobbled her up alive.

RENTALA NAGESWARA RAO

•

TILADAANAMU

•

NOMINATED BY VAKATI PANDURANGA RAO
TRANSLATED BY RANI SARMA

Bhagyanagaram slept. The waters of the Moosi river shimmered in the dark of the night, like the tears of a mother whose sons have killed each other for money, or in communal violence.

It was past midnight. A figure walked stealthily, clinging to the shadows cast by the railings of Chaderghat Bridge. His clothes merged into the shadows created by dim neon lights that seemed to have been commissioned only to line the pockets of politicians. A man in his thirties, tired and hungry-looking. An unkempt beard. A hunted look in his eye. A much-used cloth bag hanging limply from his left shoulder. A loaded revolver under his shirt. A prize of fifty thousand rupees on his head. He was heading towards Islamia Bazaar. A misleading name, that. Paradoxically, the street housed not Muslims but the Brahmins and the priests of the twin cities of Hyderabad and Secunderabad.

The stranger reached a small tiled house and rapped on the door.

'Who is it?' said a feeble voice from within, between bouts of coughing.

'It's me. Raghuram.'

After what seemed like an interminable wait, he heard the sound of dragging feet, and the door creaked open. Raghuram entered the room quickly and shut the door softly behind him. The old man peered at him, putting his right hand to his eyebrow.

Even in the dim light that filtered into the room, Raghuram couldn't help noting the tejas on his father's face. The aquiline nose, the high forehead marked with vibhuti, the sharp, wide-set eyes, a rudhraksha-mala round his neck. Raghuram could see the gray stubble on the sunken face. But neither poverty nor age could dim his presence and stature.

'It's me, Raghuram. How are you, Nanna garu?'

Tiladaanamu is the gift of alms given to propitiate the malefic planet, Saturn. A Brahmin who accepts tiladaanamu is considered lowest in the heirarchy of priests and purohits.

'Tiladaanamu' (Title of the original story) was first published in Telugu in *Andhra Prabha Illustrated Weekly*, 10 April, 1991, Hyderabad.

'Is that *you*? Why have you come?' His voice was harsh. 'Won't you let me at least die in peace?'

The old man looked haggard and tired. He once was Brahmashree Vedamurthy Subrahmanya Shastri garu, one of the greatest scholars in his district. Today he was reduced to being Tiladaanam Subbiah. Tears welled in Raghuram's eyes.

'Nanna garu, has Padma delivered?' asked Raghuram anxiously.

'Yes. A boy. Born under the inauspicious Moola nakshatra. Shanti has to be performed.'

Tiladaanam Subbiah lay down on his bed, with a sigh.

Raghuram drew the sheet that partitioned the single room into two and peeped in. Padmavathi was sleeping, the baby at her breast. Raghuram knelt down and shook her gently.

'Padma!'

Padmavati woke with a start and clasped the baby to her bosom.

'Who is it?'

'It's me, Padma. Here, let me see the child.'

He took the baby into his arms. Joy and love washed over him. He smothered the child with kisses, fondling its tiny hands and feet, marvelling at the child's beauty and the wonder of it. Padma began to cry softly, unable to control herself.

'Where have you been all these days? We have been so worried. The police have been searching all over for you.'

Raghuram pulled her close to him. Her tears wet the front of his shirt.

'How long will you hide like this? What have you achieved by staying away from us? Your father says a Shanti has to be performed — the child was born at an inauspicious time. Look at him, he is running a temperature. There's not a paisa at home; if anything happens to you what is to become of us?'

'You don't understand, Padma. I'm not fighting for myself, it is for the people . . .'

'You can't take care of your own family and you want to fight for society?' sneered Subrahmanya Shastri from across the room. 'You can't provide milk for your son and you want to feed the world.'

Raghuram looked sharply at his father.

'You held your Vedic learning and knowledge sacred all your life, Nanna garu. They neither helped you nor society. People blamed you and your caste for keeping the Vedas out of their reach. How many of them are learning these now? How many are opting to become priests, purohits, to earn their livilihood? The temples at Thirupathi and Manthralaya are offering to teach the Vedas, irrespective of caste, but how many are prepared to learn them? At least I'm trying to bring about a change.'

'Oh stop deluding yourself!' Tiladaanam Subbiah turned away in disgust. 'What do you achieve by burning buses, kidnapping petty politicians and government officials? Living in the eternal dread of getting caught. Do you ever think of the affected families? How does reducing the price of liquor help the common man? Or, getting wasteland distributed to the poor change society? If you must do something, go strike at the roots of government!'

'You don't understand Nanna garu,' Raghuram said, handing over the baby to Padma who looked on helplessly. 'This is only the beginning. We have to awaken the people, educate them and popularise our ideology, then we can achieve a classless society where hunger and poverty will be wiped out.'

'As if you people really understand Marxist philosophy,' snapped Subbiah. 'Socialism of the Russian and Chinese kind are not for our country. Our people are easy to satisfy. Build choultries, give them cheap grain, distribute cheap cloth — they are happy. What ails this country is its leaders — all self-serving opportunists. You are mistaken if you think you can revolutionize society by resorting to violence.'

'Some people have to be sacrificed to achieve our ends, Nanna — at least the coming generation will be happier than us.'

He took out a wad of notes from his pocket.

'This money's for you, Nanna.'

Tiladaanam Subbiah turned his face away in disgust. 'I do not want your blood-stained money. I, who have studied the Vedas and Puranas, who can conduct the most complex rituals, I do not mind begging and accepting tiladaanam. I don't mind carrying corpses. I would rather be called Tiladaanam Subbiah than accept your . . .'

Suddenly both of them heard a police whistle from a distance. Raghuram acted swiftly. In a second he had vanished as suddenly as he had appeared, melting into the shadows from which he had come. Subbiah sank to the floor helplessly, shedding bitter tears. He did not have the courage to face his daughter-in-law. Padma stood holding her baby tightly as it sucked at her dry breast.

Kuchipudi, in the Krishna district of Andhra Pradesh, is famous not only for dance but also for its Vedic scholars. Subrahmanya Shastri was born into a family of scholars and learned men. His people were well-to-do. The agraharas and land granted them by the rulers of yore allowed them enough leisure and comfort to pursue scholastic interests. Subrahmanya Shastri studied the Vedas, the Puranas and other Vedic literature as well as English at his father's feet. He became well known as a great scholar in the entire district. Raghurama Shastri was his only son.

But with time Vedic learning lost its relevance. Patronage of society melted away and the agraharas died with them. Some scholars took to priesthood. But Subrahmanya Shastri was too proud to resort to anything as commercial as that. Selling his learning and knowledge and performing rituals for payment was abhorrent to him.

As for his son, Raghurama Shastri had never been inclined to follow the family tradition. He took to modern education which brought him in touch with the teachings of Mao and Karl Marx. After his graduation he married Padmavati. But jobs were hard to come by and soon he drifted to the twin cities in search of a job. He joined the Railways as casual labour. While colleagues forged ahead he was left behind. Disappointments in his job led to bitterness and frustration. He developed an interest in revolutionary literature, forming protest groups and organising strikes.

After his wife's death Subrahmanya Shastri joined his son in the city. He was an unhappy and broken man by now. Society and its values had changed. What he held as sacred and precious all his life had become irrelevant. Not even his son shared his sentiments.

Raghuram was barely making a living. Finally he broke away from his responsibilities to his family and joined the Movement. The government called him a Naxalite — he was hounded from place to place — he went underground, paying fleeting visits to his wife and father.

Subrahmanya Shastri was forced to support the family. His scholarship and learning were of no use in Hyderabad, nor did he care to tell people who he was or what his background was. He could not find a place among the mercenary priests who performed religious ceremonies for payment. Every ritual seemed to have a rate, depending on the capacity of the patron to pay. Subrahmanya Shastri was a misfit in that world — all he was allowed to do was accept tiladaanam and carry corpses; two jobs nobody is eager to perform. In his wisdom he knew no job done honorably was worthy of contempt. Such inequalities were the making of the man and the society he lived in.

It was eight in the morning. Brahmins of different ages and statures had lined up on the verandahs of the houses in Islamia Bazaar. All ready for work, freshly bathed, foreheads smeared with vibhuti and duly equipped with the sacred dharba and the almanac. Sporting dark glasses and chewing paan they came walking, or on cycles; some even on mopeds and scooters. They were all sishyas of Avadhani who ran an agency for priests and purohits in the twin cities.

Tiladaanam Subbiah also came after having recited his usual early morning chantings of the Gayatri japam and his Sandhya Vandanam.

He diffidently went and stood next to Kotiah Shastry who shifted his ample body to make place for him. 'Come come Subbiah, any tiladaanam today?' he sneered.

He thought Subbiah was a real joke. He himself had a prosperous business going though he quite frankly admitted to not knowing his Gayatri japam properly. As for the Sandhya Vandanam, a useless pursuit. Even without it, wasn't he capable of performing all kinds of rituals from weddings to funerals, with great ease and aplomb? He was not to be blamed if the fools, his clients, did not know the difference between the mantrams for a shubhakaryam and an abhakaryam. All you had to do was change the pronunciation and style of chanting. They trusted you and sought you — so popular and busy was he that he was able to build a house and acquire a great deal of property in town.

'I hate these shanidaanam brahmins, Krishnamurthy!' he said presently to his neighbour. 'That one should stoop so low as to take on the curse of that malevolent Saturn for a pittance . . . chee, chee!'

'I know friend, they carry Shani with them — that is the reason they look so wretched, the poor devils.'

'It's not like that, friends,' Subbiah tried to explain to them. 'You chant the Shani japam and the Sahasra Gayatri japam every day and Saturn won't dare affect you . . .'

'Who has the time to waste on such nonsensical things Tiladaanam Subbiah? Who has the time?'

Subbiah looked puzzled. How could the Gayatri be a waste of time? How could they perform pujas for others when they didn't believe in the most basic japam themselves! But it didn't help to argue. He needed Kotiah's help. He moved closer to Kotiah and asked humbly, 'Babu Kotiah, I hope you have not forgotten my request?'

'What request?'

'I told you, I'm blessed with a grandson — but he was born on Moola nakshatram. As you know, this augurs ill for his father and grandfather. Shanti has to be performed to remove the dosha and it has to be done before the day after tomorrow. You know my circumstances — I'm a poor brahmin, I want all of you to help me. Please come and accept what little I can give as Shanidaanam.'

Kotiah burst out laughing. 'Aha Subbiah, you who make a living by accepting Shanidaanam and begging, you want to perform puja to Shani and the other planetary gods? If you want to perform a Navagraha Pooja you have got to feed brahmins. *You* are not capable of feeding a single brahmin. What can you give as dhakshina? The going rate is eighty rupees for shradham, two hundred and sixteen for a Satyanarayana vratam and two thousand and sixteen for a wedding — and even more for a Shanti. Navagraha Pooja is so laborious, how can you afford to perform it?'

'Please babu, it is very important to do the Shanti, otherwise it is very dangerous . . . please help me.' Tiladaanam Subbiah was on the verge of tears.

'Nonsense, these are all superstitions, old-fashioned ideas. There's nothing like Moola nakshtram or Shanti. I can't come for your Shanti, I'm busy and anyway, you can't pay me. So forget it.'

'I don't understand,' Subbiah said, baffled. 'Don't you really believe in any japam-thapam, Kotiah? How can you then perform pujas for others?'

'How does that matter?' retorted Kotiah. 'It is the man who has the capacity to pay that should believe in them. Anyway, go and ask Avadhani if he can help you. I can't.' Kotiah turned his back to Subbiah and got busy with his snuff-box.

Avadhani was in his office. He was seated in a revolving chair behind an impressive table. There were two telephones on the side. A ceiling fan was on. He was dressed in saffron robes, had a rudhrakshamala around his neck and vibhuthi and kumkuma on his forehead. He was the leader of the purohits. He supplied priests to meet the needs of all kinds of clients. If there was business in the houses of politicians, IAS officers, industrialists or film stars, he attended to them himself; anything less important was assigned to his underlings. He had a share in everyone's dakshina.

Avadhani lifted his head from the newspaper. 'Yes Subbiah, what do you want?' he said indifferently.

Subbiah explained his predicament.

'How can you perform Shanti unless you are prepared to spend money, Subbiah? You are the only brahmin willing to accept shanidaanam for a paltry dakshina in the entire twin cities of Hyderabad and Secunderabad. Others will demand at least two hundred rupees. Can you afford to pay? Go and find some money then come back.'

'Where can I find the money?' mumbled Subbiah, 'You know my circumstances.'

'I agree that the evil star Moola is dangerous for the father or the grandfather. I heard your son has joined the Naxalites. Hasn't he sent you any money? Anyway he is sure to be killed in an encounter. Why waste your money?'

'That's exactly what I am trying to prevent. Babu Avadhani please help me. Shanti has to be performed before the star changes position. That is before the day after tomorrow. Please . . . '

'No, no, Subbiah, you have to find the money first. In any case, you have three days time — the star does not change position for three more days, here, look at this panchangam if you want.' Avadhani opened the almanac, and pointed to the astrological calculation.

'That calculation is wrong, nayana,' said Subbiah gently.

'What? The calculations are wrong? This book is written by my guru, Brahmashree Sachidananda Sidharthi garu. How dare you say the calculations are wrong! All right, we will consult another panchangam. Here, look, this also says there are three more days.'

'I'm afraid that too is wrong.'

Avadhani raised his eyebrows. 'Yes? So only you know the right calculation. Who do you think you are? A jyotish? A great scholar? You miserable brahmin, you are the poor wretch who accepts shanidaanam. Don't you know your own limitations?'

Subbiah smiled nervously. 'My calculation is accurate, Avadhani garu. Check any astronomical manual you want. The planet Guru has a loop this month, so time gets shortened. Namaskaram.'

Subbiah walked out of Avadhani's office.

Avadhani snorted with anger and sank back into his revolving chair. But he couldn't return to his newspaper. He frowned at Subbiah's retreating back, for a moment. Then picked up the telephone receiver on an impulse. He dialed a number. It was that of an astronomy lecturer in Osmania University whom he happened to know. He explained the problem to him in great detail.

As he listened his expression changed. Tiladaanam Subbiah was right! It was his renowned and experienced guru who had erred. Not one panchangam but both the books had been wrong! This Tiladaanam

Subbiah . . . He shook his head, perplexed. How could he? Was he a jyotish or . . .

Avadhani rushed out of his office and sent his sishyas to find Subbiah. 'Bring him back here as fast as you can,' he told them.

His assistants scoured Islamiah Bazaar. There was no trace of Subbiah.

Subbiah was going around Chikkadapalli, Secunderabad, Hyderabad, looking for a brahmin who would accept his daanam, someone who'd cooperate with him in performing Shanti. He found no one. They feigned bhakti and devotion and played on the weakness and sentiments of their poor patrons. Where were wisdom, honesty, generosity and humility, the real attributes of a true Brahmin? 'This is why society hates Brahmins,' he muttered to himself.

He reached home, defeated and tired. Padmavathi was waiting for him, worried. Her child continued to run high fever.

'You must take the child to the General Hospital tomorrow,' he told her as he washed his feet and came into the house.

He couldn't sleep that night. He had to perform Shanti the next day. But how? His mind reviewed all that he had learnt. He repeated all the shastras to himself. He had to find a solution, there must be a way. He tossed and turned.

Yes! He would perform a Krituvu, the greatest yagna of all to propitiate all the gods and goddesses, including the navagrahas and the ashtadikpalakas. He would please all the gods in one yagna.

The next morning by the time Padmavathi swept and cleaned the front yard Subrahmanya Shastri had seated himself on the floor in padmasana. A glow exuded from his freshly-bathed body. His eyes were like burnished coal. His forehead smeared with vibhuthi looked like that of Lord Parameshwara. He had spread sand on the floor, arranged bricks, prepared the image of the destroyer of all obstacles, Vighneshwara, with turmeric paste and placed it on the mantapam.

He started the Sthala pooja. His voice rang out loud and clear like a temple bell as he started chanting the mantrams. He laid the wood, lit the sacred fire and invoked the ashtadikpalakas, the guardians of the eight directions.

By this time people had gathered in front of his house, awestruck, unable to believe what they saw and heard. But Subrahmanya Shastri was oblivious to all that was happening around him. He saw nothing but the sacred fire and the gods he invoked. Avadhani and his shishyas had come rushing to the spot. They stood now amazed, looking on with wide-eyed wonder; no one had to tell any one of them that what they were witnessing was no ordinary ritual. This was the ultimate Krituvu itself.

Those brahmins who were learned joined Subrahmanya Shastri in the chanting only to soon drop out, unable to keep pace with him as Shastri invited the navagrahas to accept his offerings and the yagna went on with unabated solemnity.

In the space partioned by the sheet, Padmavathi held her baby close. The child's fever raged on.

And then, a boy came running out of nowhere, a letter clutched in his fist. For Padmavathi.

She ripped it open with trembling fingers.

My dear Padma,

I am confident I have chosen the right path for myself but I don't want to cause hardship to my family or leave you helpless.

Ours is an ugly society. We recognise exploitation but we don't oppose it. There is selfishness everywhere. Differences have surfaced in my organisation too. Can we fight for a cause when we are so divided amongst ourselves?

I want to make your future secure. It would be an easy way out if I robbed a bank or unearthed black money from somewhere and passed it on to you. But that is not my way. So I am selling myself.

The price on my life is fifty thousand rupees. That is the reward the government has announced. I am surrendering myself to the police through my friend Ramesh. Ramesh will collect the reward and pass it

on to you. Give a bright future to our son. Please look after Nanna garu.
He is old-fashioned and set in his ways. Have the child examined and
treated immediately.

Yours
Raghuram

Padmavathi could not give herself over completely to her grief for,
just at that moment, the baby gasped for breath in her arms. And even
as the chanting continued, not even waiting to tell her father-in-law,
Padmavathi picked up her firstborn and rushed to the hospital.

The next day's newspapers carried the news that a hardcore
terrorist had been caught. It carried Raghuram's photo. It also
announced that the reward for his capture was given to
Ramesh.

The same day the child's fever subsided and Padmavathi returned
with her son to find a huge crowd in front of her house.

Brahmins bustled around, paying homage to the mortal remains of
Brahmashree Subramanya Shastri garu, the newly-discovered scholar.
Avadhani himself stood supervising the arrangement. After all, it was
not every day that a man performing a yagna dies while still in yoga. It
was a privilege to attend to such a great man. And so Tiladaanam
Subbiah, who couldn't find a soul to accept Shanidaanam from him was
carried out on his last journey eagerly, willingly, by the Brahmins of
Bhagyanagaram.

As for Padmavathi she stands, her tearless eyes scanning the street,
waiting for Ramesh.

BHUPEN KHAKHAR

•

PAGES FROM A DIARY

•

NOMINATED AND TRANSLATED BY
GANESH N DEVY

24.9.1972

Should you happen to stop by the Ambika Mill and wish to see the boss, seek out Sundarlal first. His desk is right next to the air-conditioned cabin. Don't miss him. I specially recommend you to see him. He is a person worth meeting. You will not like his face from a distance. Ink-black complexion, inch deep hollows in both cheeks, yellow teeth, and they fall out as he laughs. Did I say Sundarlal is good looking? I said he was someone worth meeting. Sundarlal works hard in the office, and he has earned the Seth's confidence. When others leave the office at five-thirty, Sundarlal continues to sit with the Provident Fund ledgers. You would like to see the boss. The boss won't ask you to his cabin instantly. Have to wait outside for a while. There's a chair to sit on, no sofa. No old magazines to flick through to pass the time. Feel hesitant about striking up a conversation with a stranger, don't you? Sundarlal has been eyeing you for quite some time. Let your face be a little less stiff; if you look at him, he will tell you about the boss's moods — whether you should see him or not. If you get bored he will entertain you with gossip about the boss. That's why I say do meet Sundarlal when you go to the Ambika Mill. To our eyes he is not beautiful. His white cap off, specs down his nose, bending over the ledgers as he works, one gets a full view of his bushy hair. Once Arundhatiben told the boss in no uncertain words: I feel more attracted to Sundarlal's bushy hair than your porcupine hair.

Sundarlal spent the next seven days in a trance.

1.4.1985

It happened about the twentieth March.

Nights, returning from work, I carry folks up to the station on my scooter. The station is on my way home from the downtown area. At times folks get sentimental, give their addresses, give

Pages from a Diary' was first published in Gujarati as 'Dayarina Pana' in Gadyaparva No.12, 1990, Baroda.

thanks. At times, they get off and rush to the station without uttering a syllable.

I offered a lift to a man in a striped ash-coloured shirt and trousers standing near Jubilee Garden. He wanted to have a chat, so asked me to stop the scooter in Sayajigunj.

We sat on the steps of a house nearby. Ordered two cups of tea.

: People call me Kumar saheb :

: Are you headed for Bombay? :

Kumar saheb : Yah. :

: Your bag? :

: Well, I *do* have Vijay Kumar's house! :

: Where do you stay? :

: If you wish to see me in Baroda I will be at the Vijay Adarsh Lodge, every evening at six. Tonight I leave for Bombay. Have organised an important programme. Rajiv will be there. Vijay Kumar and Rajiv Gandhi . . . schoolmates in Delhi. He's given the responsibility to me. I will see Lataji and Ashaji. In fact I've just rung Laxminarayan and R.D.:

: When do you return? :

: In two days. For the time being give me five hundred rupees if you have it. I will return it to you when I come back. :

: I have just fifty. :

: Will do. See you. :

Three days later I went to Vijay Adarsh Lodge at six.

: Come, come . . . : So saying he bid me sit on the rope-khatla.

: You came back? :

Kumar saheb : What can I say? :

: Why? :

: I have to go to Bombay today. :

: Again? :

: Yes, the programme is fixed to take place in Lalbag. Since Rajiv is to be there, the stage is big enough to take twenty-five thousand. Vijay Kumar telephoned and decided it all. If Rajiv comes, all the film stars will definitely come. But Rajiv says that a portion will have to go for charity. I will make a hundred thousand or so. :

: Well, shall I push off then? :

: Want to go? What's the hurry? Let's go downstairs, have something to eat, and go sit in Jubilee Garden. My train does not leave until eleven.: We had tea — he ate. As soon as he finished eating, he made a quick exit. I paid the bill.

It was about seven when we sat down on a bench in Jubilee Garden. Taking my hand in his, he said, : you won't believe this . . . : and pressing my fingers, Kumar saheb asked, : Guess how old I am? :

: Fifty-five? :

He roared with laughter. : Got fooled, eh? Am a solid sixty-five. I have abstained from sex for the last twenty years. Three or four times my wife became very passionate. I said, bathe waist-down in cold water. I am a Shiva-bhakta. This mark between my eyes is Shiva's third eye. It was this eye with which Kamadeva was burnt to ashes. I worship Shiva every night at eleven. Twice he was pleased with me and gave me darshana of his lotus feet. :

He dropped my hand and entered the past. : In Bombay a Parsi woman was crazy about me. She asked me to conjugate. I explained the story of Bhishma Pitamaha to her, and flatly said no to sex. You see? Meet me after three days. Of course, you have to give me the money for my fare to Bombay. :

After a gap of three or four days I went to the Lodge. With him there sat a fat young man in a black checked bush-shirt, wearing thick glasses.

Kumar saheb said, : This is J.P. Patel. Owner of Shital Fans. Wants to go to Delhi. If he gets the licence his sales will be fifteen crores a year. Wants to make me his sleeping partner. The previous partner siphoned off twelve lakhs. Cheated J.P. Now the factory is closed. We have to go to Delhi. :

: When do you go? :

: We leave today. I told J.P. that as soon as Khakhar saheb comes we will get fifteen thousand. Vijay Kumar will reach there directly from Bombay. We will meet Rajiv and have Shital factory declared a sick unit. Rajiv is a friend of Vijay Kumar. He knows me too by name. :

: How come he knows you? :

: I had told Indiraji, you won't see 1985. That letter must have gone to Rajiv. Vijay Kumar has been insisting on introducing me to Rajiv. But I told him, forget it; such things are affairs of the mighty. I'm a small man. :

: I do not have fifteen thousand. Not now, not in my bank account either. :

: Get the money from your friends. Once the factory starts working there will be no problem at all. :

: Sorry, I don't think I can manage that. :

: If you give fifteen thousand today all problems can be solved. I had money in Bombay, but out of that I paid twenty-five to Lata, twenty-five to Laxmikant and fifteen to Asha. If I had not paid them J.P's job would be through by now. As soon as he gets the licence, there's the machinery waiting in Germany all ready to be despatched. It will be useful for me too to get into a partnership without investing anything. :

I stood up in order to get out of the question of giving him fifteen thousand. So, Kumar saheb quickly said, : Come, I will go downstairs with you. :

Then he turned to J.P. : Don't worry. I am there! I will fix your fifteen thousand. :

Tea, like the last time, his quick exit and the bill paid, we settled down on a bench in Jubilee Garden. Again, taking my hand in his, he said, : This whole month is the month of Shivashankar Bholenath. You know, it was forty years ago that I got married. In those days my intercourse with wife would last for half an hour. Others jump off in five minutes. From my very childhood I have been a Shiva-devotee. In the Shravan month I wouldn't even look at a female. If you don't trust me, ask your Bhabhi. She will tell you that I haven't touched her in the last twenty years. Well, once or twice I had a tremendous desire. Almost lost my head. Had thoughts of nothing but sex. Then I took cold water baths. Kept pouring water over my head for half hours, kept thinking of Shiva. Twice I have had the vision of Shiva's lotus feet. Shivaji asked me to ask for a boon. I said, : Release me from this cycle of births. : Shivaji said, : You will get to live your next life in this very life. : Khakhar saheb, do you see this bald head? Just wait till December. There will be dark hair. The body of a twenty five year old. You won't be able to recognise me. J.P. will keep waiting there and will cry. Now, no going back to the lodge tonight. Vijay Kumar will reach Delhi on the third. The meeting with Rajiv is on the fifth. Bye, Bye! See me in December. Well, now in my old age I must be of use to other people. Once Lataji's programme is over, I mean to take everybody with me to London, Paris, Moscow, New York. Khakhar saheb, I will buy your ticket too . . . See you. :

7.3.1987

When we left the Garden he was impatient to reach home. I was crossing the road slowly. Jitubhai had already crossed over, weaving his way between the rickshaws with not a worry for himself; then he waited on the other side impatiently. I was halfway to the other side and had just managed to avoid the last cyclist in my way, when he asked, : Where is the scooter? :

I said, : Next to the Acharya Book Depot. So we will have to go round the circle. :

: Come, walk a little faster. :

He was soon standing near the Acharya Book Depot. Immediately he said, : Which scooter? :

: The grey one. :

: There are three here. :

: Here, this one. :

I had to obey the authority in his commanding voice. I ripped out the scooter-key from the back pocket of my trousers and started the scooter.

: Which way? :

: The lane next to the fire-brigade station. :

Impatience, curiosity and the eagerness to arrive were Jitubhai's. That's why he had been commanding me. I too was aware that this relationship was to last no more than half an hour. Both of us would forget each other within a day. There was no joy nor excitement in my mind. There was a weariness, a monotony in the chain of happenings in such relationships.

I knew what kind of house it would be. A house with a rexine-covered sofa, a mini-swing, a ceiling fan, and the walls painted white or grey . . . Lost in thought, I reached the third floor. He had already climbed a staircase ahead of me. I saw him press the bell of room number 305. I climbed the stairs and stood behind Jitubhai. He too was breathless. The door opened three inches.

Jitubhai : Key. :

The door shut. Two minutes later a bunch of keys was held out by the fingers of a child. She wore bangles on her wrist. Jitubhai took the key.

He unlocked the house right opposite. Inside, an office table, under it a mattress gathered into a roll. Jitubhai switched on the fan. The glass window was shut. The typewriter on the table was covered. Since I wasn't certain where to sit, I pulled out the chair that was pushed into the space under the table and sat on it. The lower fringe of his shirt touched my mouth. Once in a while it flapped across my face when the wind blew.

Jitubhai : Wouldn't you like to stay here? :

I shuddered at the thought of spending the night in that room with no ventilation. I lied. : I have to catch the morning bus to Ahmedabad at six. :

: Go from here. :

: I have to collect some office papers from home. Besides, I haven't told my people at home, either. :

We both knew that this first encounter was also the last one. Jitubhai took off his cap and shirt and stood close to the chair. For the first time I looked at his face in the stark tubelight. An illness years ago had scarred it. The shining head, the sweat-drenched and pock-marked face looked ugly. Moreover, the thin lips made it look cruel too.

A hoarse voice emanated from the tall strong body.

: The building-gate closes at nine every night, so be quick. :

With this he moved the typewriter with a jerk, and sat on the table. Before my eyes now the white vest, the white dhoti and the phallus that sprang from it. I looked up. The pock-marked cheeks had been smiling. Both eyes were shut to a slit, like the eyes of a Chinese.

He said, : All well? :

I said, : Let's skip this today. :

Jitubhai, : Why? :

: Some other time. :

: You know as well as I do that . . . :

: What? :

: We shall never meet again. :

He caught my hand. Involvements, allurement, attraction had disappeared from my heart. I was thinking of paintings. A complete canvas full of the white vest, the white dhoti and the slight transparency that revealed the phallus. I tried to get up from the chair. He took my hand, made me sit and said,

: What's wrong today? :

: I'm not in the mood. :

: What happened to your mood. Did I do something? :

: No, just feeling off. :

Jitubhai : Come on, for my sake. :

I stayed there till nine for the sake of a man I would never meet again in my life.

DHRUVA SHUKLA

·

HIDE AND SEEK

·

NOMINATED BY NIRMAL VERMA
TRANSLATED BY GILLIAN WRIGHT

The girls never say where they hide . . .

Every evening they both play hide and seek. In some corner of the house one girl hides her face in her hands and begins to count up to a hundred while the other tries to hide in some other part of the house. She has to hide before the count is complete.

He returns home every day at dusk. As he knocks on the door he hears the sounds of hide and seek — the counting has just begun. The younger girl is counting. The elder girl would still be looking for a hiding place. The counting continues — the time of his return home and the time for the game of hide and seek are one.

When the counting's over his wife opens the door — the house is quiet. Goodness knows where the elder girl is hidden. The younger one can be seen heading towards the kitchen as if she were a cat. It occurs to him that even if there's nowhere to hide you can still play hide and seek.

There's nowhere to hide in the kitchen. Wheat is already hiding in the wheat bin. His wife keeps the milk hidden for fear of the cat. Turmeric, salt, red chilli, tea and cooking oil are all hidden in their own pots. The sugar is hidden in two jars. He can find one of them, and the girls can also reach it. His wife has counted up to a hundred and hidden the second jar in a place where only she can find it. The tin of ghee must be hidden in a similar place.

There's no place in the house which the members of the family don't know. But they're convinced that no one but them has ever seen where they hide their things. His wife knows what is hidden where, but sometimes she hides things so well that she can't find them even when she looks for them. Whenever she's searching for something she's hidden it seems as if she's robbing her own house. She goes to the places where she hides her things when no one's looking. She's afraid that if these secret places are revealed she won't be able to find another hiding place.

'Hide and Seek' was first published in Hindi as *'Chipne ka Khel'* in *Saptahik Hindustan*, 9-15 April 1989, New Delhi.

He knows the nooks and furthest places of his home where, amongst other things, his wife is also hidden. But he pretends not to see them, as if he's never even noticed them. Those places, and the things hidden there, themselves peep out from his wife's face.

He feels thirst — like some hidden desire wanting to escape. He asks for some water. As his wife opens the door of the fridge the cold sighs that are trapped inside rush out. He drinks a glass of water, hastily pushing his thirst back to from where it rose. He sees vegetables and fruit, shrinking and scared, hiding in the fridge for fear of rotting; the moment they are touched they will start shrivelling.

He thought to himself, how rarely we touch the objects dearest to us. We hide them for fear of touching them. Who knows what quality hands possess, that the moment they touch anything it becomes soiled, it withers. Perhaps objects fear that hands hold a hidden knife; they guess a hidden sleight of hand. The tired vegetables from the bazaar seem so anxious to hide themselves in the fridge. They want to draw a breath of relief before going on to the fire. Fruit that has been picked from the tree and hidden in separate bags must remember its own tree. Shrivelled fruit seems sunk in deep unhappiness. Fruit is accustomed to hiding itself. On the tree it hides among the leaves; it must feel that it's hidden and no one will be able to see it. But a slight gust of breeze snatches away its cover.

Suddenly there was a strong gust of wind and all the doors in the house began to bang. They opened and closed, closed and opened — as if the home was trying to save itself from becoming naked, was preventing its blueprint from flying out with the wind. But when the wind blows strongly nothing in the house can contain itself. Everything begins to tremble, to blow into the air, things start to leave their places, they flee and there are never enough hands to gather them.

Even a single fruit cannot be quite contained by a pair of hands, though the map of a whole human life, which no one can comprehend in its entirety, is concealed within them. What a great map in such little space, like the map of a tree concealed within a seed. When people shake hands it seems as though they are exchanging blueprints for life.

But hands fall quickly apart. Nothing comes to hand. Not a single line is straight. They are all as crooked as crooked, like drains full of sweat. But the lines on the hands of a man whose arms are cut off, where do those lines hide?

The younger girl has come out of the kitchen and is looking all round the sitting room. In one corner is the dining table and in another four chairs. Three of them are sitting on their own, and his wife is sitting on the fourth. The television in front of her is showing a film.

The younger girl has begun to watch the film. Perhaps she thinks that the elder girl's hiding there. She generally asks how people hide behind the screen. He never answers these questions. He himself sometimes feels scared of the television — this box in his home is like the goonda standing in the street who secretly shows a knife but doesn't stab, and brings anyone he likes under his power. No one can question the goonda, you have to accept anything he says. The younger girl is staring at the screen as if she's about to discover the elder girl in the running film and will pull her out by the hair the moment she comes in front of her.

Gunfire. He jumps. There has been a rain of bullets in the street. The town is in uproar. People are running towards their homes, trying to hide themselves in the street. For as far as they can see there is no place to hide. There are policemen, not trees. Shops have been shut, shop-keepers are hiding inside the shops.

Where do *they* hide? Where is *their* hiding place? Is it within themselves? Murder before it happens must hide itself in someone's heart; as desires hide, as jealousy and malevolence hide, revealing themselves the moment they have the chance. They don't hide and then attack all at once. They rise like the dust concealed in a whirlwind and surround you on all sides.

The younger girl has climbed on to the roof. On the small roof small small plants smile in flowerpots. They never hide their smiles; no one can hide behind them. What is she doing on the roof? Perhaps looking for a hiding place. Dissolved in the breeze, the sweet smell of flowers enters the sitting room.

He starts to think, when the wind doesn't blow for a long time you begin to feel suffocated. But flowers hold their breaths in their stems and keep smiling as if they will stay like that until their last breath. When a flower hides itself behind leaves it reminds him of shy children who can't find a hiding place and cover their faces with both hands. Sometimes they run to hide between their mother's thighs and she bends over them like a branch.

The girl is running into the study. In this room stands a large cupboard containing books. The space left by the books which come out as far as the desk remains completely empty. Books alone hide in this space. The moment one book's place is empty two books lean towards each other to fill it. It looks as if one book is sleeping with its head resting on the shoulder of the other. When he picks up any such book to read it seems as though he's woken it from a deep slumber. The moment he touches it, the pages begin to flutter, as if some classic beauty were cracking her finger joints, and stretching languorously. As he reads he begins to hide, taking cover in the book. He hides himself in such a way that he has to search for himself even in the hiding place.

He catches sight of the younger girl heading for the bedroom. Seeing her his wife smiles. Perhaps his wife knows that the elder girl is hiding in the bedroom. In this room there is a big wardrobe in which hang the girls' frocks and his wife's saris. When the girls don't manage to hide among their frocks they start to take cover among the saris.

His wife can no longer hide herself in her saris, but she keeps trying to do so every day. Whenever the girls persuaded her to play hide and seek with them she takes shelter behind the bed. When she is in bed with him they both hide in one another.

One day when his wife hid in the big trunk, she made the acquaintance of the things already hidden there. But not for long. She began to feel stifled. She had to open the lid of the trunk just enough for breath and light to be able to come in together. In all this hiding and being hidden she found an embroidery needle — when things are hidden for a long time they begin to prick. You feel like touching them and looking at them. When no one looks for things they themselves come seeking you — she must have hidden the needle herself. She had imagined it lost.

He thought, nothing is lost, it lies hidden. We ourselves keep on hiding things. But even when they're hidden they remain with us. Their forms never become clouded in our memory. Even if we do forget them, we remember them again. Only those people who don't miss the things they've lost long ago can understand their own pain and restlessness. Then again there are people who accept that what is lost is lost.

Both girls become so absorbed in their game of hide and seek that they even forget to be hungry or thirsty. As they are playing suddenly they feel their hunger and then they forget their game and begin to ask for food. After their meal, if the same game doesn't come to mind, they play another one.

The younger girl has come out of the bedroom and begun to look for something to eat. She takes out the food which has been hiding in the fridge since morning. Seeing this his wife immediately advances on her, thinking that there must definitely be something hidden in the fridge which she doesn't want the girl to have. His wife gives her the food she thinks she ought to have and hides the rest back in the fridge.

The younger girl is eating. The elder girl is still hiding somewhere. Suddenly her voice calls out — I'm hungry too.

He says — if you're hungry why don't you come here and have something to eat.

She says — I'm still hiding. I'll only come out if someone finds me.

MANJU KAK

•

BLESSED ARE MY SONS

•

NOMINATED BY NISSIM EZEKIEL

Shamim was the best butcher in Na Khas market. He was known as Laalu. Actually he wasn't Laalu; his father had been. But now the name stuck. He liked it. It brought luck. The name brought respect as well. When new customers came around inquiring after him Shamim would stroke his moustache with three fingers and nod. Though there were three more butcheries, excluding the air-conditioned Essex Farms, most people came to him. People that mattered. One could see on a particular day, Arun Chowdhry, ex-minister buying a leg of mutton. Or look, that was Dimple the TV newsreader ordering mince.

Just like ordinary people they came. After they left, bystanders would rush excitedly in and ask. Shamim felt elated but all he did was let out a bored yawn, drawling, *arre yaar, tho kya.* They would leave impressed with his nonchalance. This brought Shamim repute. The fools he thought. It's because I don't fawn that they come.

He knew exactly what to do. The less than a kilo ones to Chutka, with an incline of his head. The kilo and above to his brothers Rahim and Irfan. It was just a few regulars whom Shamim would personally serve.

It took him but a minute to assess each customer who swung in through that door. Take today. That school teacher for instance. Now she bought her 250 gms in three packets. For three days of the week, he guessed. She always looked tired and harrassed. Shamim was bored, but kind. He made Chutka serve her. She sat meekly on the hard wooden bench gazing abstractedly out of her myopic eyes. Chutka's hands expertly chopped slivers of red meat, pounded it and mixing bits of discarded fat, swiftly put it through the electric grinder. She never noticed. It never troubled Shamim. The fat would save her on ghee he shrugged.

It was another matter with Professor Hidayatullah of Jamia Millia Islamia. Shamim made his younger brother Rahim serve him. He never left without three kilos. Usually chops and finely-pounded mince.

But the stout Kashmiri matron with fat haunches and exuberant torso ending in shapeless podgy toes squeezed into and delicately balancing

on high heels, why, Shamim always served her himself! She knew her
anatomy as well as any butcher. When he tried to fool her once, the rolls
of her rippling midriff had trembled and her thighs, down to her juicy
tendons clad in copious salwars, quivered in unison with the thin nasal
voice as it shrieked, No, No, you don't!

He knew the type that went to kitty parties with lots of other fat
limousine-owning women and talked. How they talked!

Now it wasn't as if the rest of the time Shamim did nothing. He sat
throughout, a hawk's eye on all, ready to rebuke. And they obeyed.
Shamim was rightfully proud. Ever so often he would look up at his
father's gold-framed photograph, mounted on a fairly bilious shade of
green with minarets etched into the background, for approbation. He
would pause, sigh smugly, contentedly certain his Abbajan would have
been proud of him.

The success of the shop reinforced his authority over his large family,
Rahim his younger brother, Mustafa, Irfan, Irshad, Rashid, Tahir and
Sadiq his cousins and Chutka his eldest sister's son. No one dared
question him.

Shamim was large and broad, with the fine Hindu Kush features of
his forebears. Swarthy hair sprung luxuriantly from his open kurta. His
eyes were large and thick lashed, his nose straight, while his well-
groomed moustaches licked sensuous lips.

If Shamim thought well of himself, goodness, he had been brought
up to. No, no, he didn't preen in front of the mirror that framed one side
of the wall away from his father's portrait, but now and then it would
catch his eye and with a careful once over he simply approved. These
feelings gave his glance a surety which to those who didn't know him
seemed disdain. He stood out amongst his brothers. His mother always
made it clear that he looked not like some *desi galli ka luccha* but like
his forebears had been before they sullied their complexions in the
Indian plains.

It was a Saturday in August. In came Shamim's favourite customer. A
proper sahib. He smoked a pipe. Wore nice clothes. All imported. And
he bought mince but chopped coarsely on the block. He cooked himself

204   Blessed are my Sons

on Sundays, he said. Qeema with beans. He probably put in a lot of garlic and ginger and finely chopped onion. Shamim's mouth watered. He speculated. It must taste nice with rotis. Roomali rotis. Like the ones Rehana made.

Aah! Rehana could cook. She could do an aromatic kabab. Or a rich korma. Yes she had the touch. It had taken her years of practice though. Shamim was not one to be satisfied easily. He used to tell her straight off. Too little of this or too much of that. There was no point being coy. No, Shamim wasn't afraid to speak his mind. Rahim had censured him once. Said it made her go all quiet. But how would she have learnt otherwise! Anyway now it was the family that enjoyed the fruits of his training.

Rehana was fat. She'd come as thin as a reed. Her looks had gone too. As they faded the red betel stains on her teeth had darkened. Their once softness now stretched into rubbery gum-like rigidity. Born six children. All girls. Shamim spat. It was strange how her mouth kept getting wider with each daughter till with the sixth it looked like a slit envelope.

He glanced at the mirror. It shone a quicksilver lake against the gaudy pink emulsion of the wall. Shamim put his three fingers to his moustache and stroked it. He still had fine eyes. He looked further down his body as he sat cross-legged. He stroked the fine hair of his calves, then pulling his pyjamas up further he contemplated the taut muscle of his thigh.

No there was nothing wrong with him. Some men might even envy his physique. Once out of his blood and sweat stained kurta and pyjama, washed and shaved, he looked . . . well he most definitely didn't look a butcher. All in all he had nothing to be ashamed of. Only Rehana did him small. This time she had really done him small. A sixth daughter!

He caught Rahim's eye. Rahim was thin, wiry and dark. Took after their father. Shamim had always thought he was too thin. But he had two sons. And all in three years of marriage. That thin weasel of a brother had balls. Two! Shamim spat disgustedly.

A kilo? Shamim confirmed of the woman who had walked in. Turning absently, he ordered Chutka.

Who's Laalu? she asked.

Shamim's sharp eyes watched Chutka put the slivers of meat on the chopping block.

Anything else? he drawled.

Who's Laalu? she repeated sharply.

A time waster, Shamim put her down to that. Too many questions for just a kilo of meat.

I am, he told her, the famous style making its appearance.

Then you serve.

Uhn . . . gaped Shamim.

I said you chop me a kilo. I'm not having some half-wit chokra boy doing it.

Shamim regained control. It wouldn't do to lose his poise. Not in front of the others. That was how he kept them in check. Give *this* memsaab a kilo he repeated to Chutka. That would put her in place.

Manifesting boredom, he turned to the window. He saw the buxom one from B block. He loved the way her breasts bounced when she walked. They sprung out from her close-fit kameez. She was in green today. Just see how her buttocks rolled. Excellent haunches they would make. Just right for those Angrezi steaks. Pink with hot blood coursing through them. Or sliced thin into tidy little pasandas. Yes she was a juicy one.

Can't you hear. Haven't you any manners? she shouted.

Uhn, grunted Shamim embarrassed at the customer's loudness.

I buy. You serve. Understand?

Shamim was beginning to get angry. No one spoke to him that way. Not in that tone. And definitely not for a kilo.

I want it from the best carcass you have. None of this *bacche ka gosht* for me. And no mixing fat, you hear.

Look here memsa... he began ominously.

No look-here-shook-here she screeched, you give me the stuff without nonsense.

He stared at her stupidly. He opened his mouth and shut it again. No words came. It was the shock he told himself. I'll settle her. But this came to him later. Right then he didn't know why he did her bidding. Right then he stood rebuked. And he didn't like it. He barked at Rahim, What are you staring at? Take down that one.

Frowning he took the carcass from him and began slicing and chopping. He weighed in a large bone. She wanted the best raan from the best haunch of mutton, then she'd have to take it with the bone. Let her pay for her rudeness he thought.

I saw that, she shouted again.

Well if you wan . . .

I'm a reporter. I'll have you know that. Serve me right and I could put you in Delhi Diary, she added with a cunning glint in her eye.

He flushed. Embarrassed at her crudeness. She thought she had him. The chit of a woman. He glanced at her from under his lashes. A short boyish crop, a long nose-held steel wire specs, fierce eyes and a whiplash of a body. These modern women, *na mard na aurat*. But he was vaguely subdued. These reporter types were quite unpredictable.

Even a photo perhaps, she added, a hint conciliating.

Now he stared at her openly. She was really trying it on him. Didn't she know his reputation, and the kind who came to his shop. But Shamim had gotten out of the mode of haranguing. His style demanded he show he was above it all so he weighed a kilo, pretended disinterest and slapped the packet on the counter.

She looked at it suspiciously, prodding it with her finger. Shamim felt his blood slowly boil. Poise or no poise he would lose his temper in a minute. His eyes pierced through her as she fiddled in her bag and thumped down some money.

Giving her his famous sizing up-down glance he slapped down the change. That should keep her. But she seemed impervious and giving him a haughty look she left.

Watching her retreating back, he sized her rumps. Not worth even a lean steak he sniggered. These starved bony women. All their juices dried up. Any day fat Rehana. At least he had felt his hands full at night. But the memory made him sigh. Yes, that was once. Not now since the baby. Now he turned his back to her and slept.

If only she had given him a son, he wouldn't have felt so inadequate. Look at Mehrotra the chemist. Puny-sized fellow. Shorter than his wife one heard. Had three sons in a row. He couldn't stand the fellow. Mubarak, mubarak, Shamim miya, he'd whined. I hear you're blessed once more with a daughter. Ugh. What are you staring at? he barked at Chutka. Go get busy. Clean the counter. He glanced at the mirror, twirling his moustache. Then he contemplated the wiry hair growing on his arms.

Yes he was man enough. Then why this doubt. Why the unease. Why when he entered and heard them giggling and talking, his sisters-in-law, cousins and aunts, why the hush, why the sudden whisper? What is it he'd ask? But they would mumble, Nothing. Which made him doubly sure it was him they talked about. About his . . . what else could it be. Not his business acumen, not the way he ran the shop. No one had questioned him in years and now . . . did he notice a sly defiance in Chutka?

Shamim looked outside the shop. It was the day before Raksha Bandhan. There was brisk business around the little stalls that had come up. They had trays and trays of gold and silver tinsel and silk thread rakhis. He might have liked wearing one around his wrist too except he was Muslim. Tomorrow being a festival, the meat would sell out early. He might not come to the shop. He might just stay and play with the little one. She was cute. Nine months now. Fair and hazel-eyed like him. Except . . . he sighed.

But the next day Shamim came. The howling of the baby at night had kept him up. He cursed and spat. Got ready and decided to go. It was better to be sitting, watching the bazaar. So many women in the house! He looked around as he opened his shop. The rakhi vendors were putting up their stalls. It would be one last sales pitch to catch the ones who had forgotton to buy theirs. He heard another shutter being cranked. Looking up he saw Mehrotra on time as usual. That mother-sucker never missed a day!

So how is your littlest Lakshmi today he asked in his nasally sing song voice. Did he detect a latent sneer? Shamim cursed the Hindu zealot under his breath. All Allah's wish he murmured. Aah what had he done wrong, where had he erred he wondered. Well, there was no point in being rueful. There was work to be done, money to be earned. Money that all those girls would eventually spend.

The whole morning the rush continued and Chutka and Rahim were kept busy. Shamim looked around idly, picked up an Urdu daily. Now and then his glance strayed to the window. The plump one was at the vegetable stall with her basket. She was in white today. Something thin and film-like. He could see the shape of her body clearly in the bright light of the outside, the ends of her dupatta coming in the pleasurable line of his vision and those supple double dunes that swelled above a belly held tight by the knot of her salwar, gently sloping down the valley of her neck . . . aah thought Shamim . . . aaah.

But something blocked his vision. He scrutinised the obstacle and as it slowly turned to his line of view . . . it was the one-kilo reporter woman . . . that . . . that . . . but wait! She was angry, angry with the vendor, gesticulating as she talked and all of a sudden she walked off in a huff, stopped by the rakhi stall, picked one, said something and put it down. Uff, thought Shamim, that one knew how to harangue. He'd seen the type. God knows how many brothers she had, and how many rakhis she'd wanted. If she had a brother at all that is! Because the type bargained over everything, whether they wanted it or not.

Oh yes, he'd cut his teeth long enough in the business to recognise the signs. What a randi she was. Well, he'd have her strung up like one of his carcasses next time. He itched for her to enter his shop just so he could put her down. He would slowly raise his eyes to her face in a manner that would make each morsel of her educated body squirm; or better he wouldn't look at her at all. He would repeat her order to mock its smallness. It always got to these middle classes. They never could afford the prices. They hated tradespeople who guessed this and who weren't respectful. But if you said 'sahib' now and then you had them by the balls.

Rina was disgusted with the way these hawkers jacked up prices. They saw you, your clothes and woe if you spoke English to the kids and tra la la there it was, a one buck rakhee sold to you for three. Everywhere and in everything they tried to take you for a ride. But she knew their tricks and she wasn't going to be taken in.

She felt a strange prickling on the neck. The fine hair tingled. She instinctively pulled down her kurta which had ridden up. No there was no one staring at her. She looked around. Glanced at the meat shop. Met Shamim's eyes which at this instance turned to a customer. Awful creepy fellow she thought. Smooth and fair. But creepy all the same. The way his eyes bored into you. A crook too. She had seen it straight off. She picked her bag and walked away. When Shamim turned to where she'd stood she had gone and so had the B Block memsaab. So the bitch didn't want meat today, he smirked. The one-kilo memsaab he grinned.

Huh, said Chutka.

Huh what, Shamim barked. Get going, you! Decapitate the chickens and put them in the deep freeze, he commanded.

Bade miya's in a cross mood, Chutka grumbled under his breath.

Aah she's stopped in front of the fruit man. Wants mangoes. Where will she put them? Into her ulcerous stomach! Better strung up in her . . . ahem . . . so she would look more woman. Look how she throws her eyes fiercely. Shamim had the terrible urge to shake her. Shake the shrew into submission. Thin women! He hated thin women. That's what was the matter with them. His eyes went to her breasts. He saw them clearly through the thin cotton of her shirt, the fine lace of her bra distinct against the brown of her skin. So much froth and so little substance! Suddenly he caught her eye, looked away hurriedly, embarrassed like a teenaged chokra, and began setting blade to chopping board.

Two days later Rina came in through the door. A kilo it was again. She barked her order staring straight at Laalu lest he try and fob her off on the chokra.

Even as he puckered his face to set it into a polite rebuke, part of the style he was famous for, he froze. He didn't know why, but the words wouldn't come. He felt an awkward self-consciousness, a gaucheness that he had outgrown many years ago. Now all he wanted was her to be out and to let him breathe freely. She must take her order and get out.

Horrible man, Rina thought. But he gave good meat. She had asked for pasandas. It took a bit of time though. Flattening those tiny bits of steak. A bit of an ogler he was. Well she'd met many. Nothing she couldn't deal with. She settled on the bench a watchful eye on his hands lest he try and cheat her off with a stale piece of mutton.

What nimble fingers she mused. What a great amount of dexterity. It was as if she was noticing it for the first time. Her job was with words . . . how to position them. In a way it was the same. Here too he had to be sure. One stroke awry and . . . oops . . . the very thought made her blood curl. Better not to look she thought. She glanced up at his face instead. A fair flat face, a high brow and on it was superimposed another image she had seen at the museum . . . a miniature of a Persian noble, a feather in his elaborate headgear and pearls strung around his neck . . . aah now what was she thinking . . . this man was a butcher . . . but it was strange how faces transgressed times and professions.

Anything else memsaab, Shamim asked, his voice sticking in his throat. She missed it. Hastily looking at her watch, she counted out the change and left.

But the thought went with her. She discovered Alexander's legendary armies at the grocer's, the Scythian in the vegetable vendor . . . how churned up it had all become . . . oh dash it she had forgotton the bread. It was all this running off at tangents that did it. She should have made a list. But when she made a list she lost it. The bread . . . she must get the bread.

When dawn broke in the Muslim area of Bare Malan, Shamim burst into a sweat. He felt hot all over. It was a horrible clammy hotness. He turned this way and that. But no respite. Next to him his wife's body lay inert, swaddled in a shapeless maxi she had taken to wearing. He touched her, his hand felt the inner plumpness of her thigh. It was clammy too.

She squirmed. Shamim grunted. She needn't have. He didn't want her at all. What for! Another daughter! He sighed long and hard. He knew he should keep it up now and then, for he was mindful of what people said. They discussed all this in the zenana. He saw it in their eyes. They were gossips the lot of them. Hai, hai, looks are deceptive they would whisper slyly. But for months he couldn't manage.

He lay on his back staring at the ceiling. His mind strayed to his shop. Profits were good. He might go on Haj this year. Maybe then he might have a son. He would have to leave Rahim in charge. That haramzada was already giving himself airs. Let him not imagine Shamim was a spent force . . . not yet. Shamim turned on his side.

Maybe he wouldn't go anywhere at all. Just get the shop painted. He never did like the green and pink walls . . . and the benches . . . the benches made him think of the new customers, that reporter woman. Her thin face as she raised an eyebrow at him. She was a shapeles bag, but she gave herself the airs of a beauty. Her thin face peering out of parted hair looked intently as he made up her order. Why couldn't he put her in place! What a woman, he humphed. He was still clammy all over but exhausted now. He fell asleep.

It was the same scene next morning. Na Khas market slowly opening up. Shutters cranked intermittently. Ahaa, Mehrotra was late today. Shamim wondered. He usually arrived early. Could it be the child? No, the child was healthy. He'd bought it to the shop on Tuesday. Was showing him around. A plump belly with a tabiz tied around it. He remembered how the tabiz had dangled with the child's . . . ahem . . . when he peed. Shamim's eyes had been glued to that little dangle between his chubby legs. All the difference it made, all the difference. And he viciously slashed the kidneys and balls off the dangling carcasses of goat. The bloody organs of man he thought.

What are you staring at, he shouted at Chutka. Get along you and put the decapitated chickens in the deep freeze. Their cawking and crowing from their latticed bamboo cages infuriated him. Wordlessly, neck dangling between his shoulders, Chutka slunk off. Dangling! Dangled! Oh damn the dangle.

The buxom matron was at the government vegetable co-operative.
She was early today. Must be having guests to dinner? It was a pink
ensemble she had on. Lacy and baby pink. Again that tight fitting
kameez that threw the points of her breasts at right angles to her body,
the lines swelling again to encompass her tight rotund belly. You could
balance a glass on them, thought Shamim. Wonder if she has children.
Sons. How they must've loved to suckle.

Shamim sighed. He stared vacantly waiting for the first customer to
show up. It was the Christian gent. Shamim gave him scraps for his dog.
Innards with a bone or two. The family were old customers from his
father's time. Chutka remarked scraps too now cost something, sahib.
Shamim scolded. That Chutka would amount to nothing. It was his
father's side in him.

Again Shamim sighed. He'd begun sighing early in the mornings
these days. Maybe it was the August humidity that was getting him
down. His older Pathan genes playing up.

Perhaps he should take a week off. Let Rahim handle it. I suppose
I'll have to get used to him taking over anyway. Peering at the mirror he
noticed the grey creeping gently into the black. Yes he would grow old
without a son to take over. Without a son he could call Laalu.

As Shamim turned his eyes wearily they fell on the reporter woman
again. Why wasn't she in office he wondered. She was hectoring the
fruit vendor. Someone should slap the insolence out of her. Look at her!
A wisp of a thing, her hair cropped short, the nobbly bone of her spine
standing clear out of the round neck of her kurta. The shameless hussy
wore no dupatta. Her kurta clung to the flat of her stomach transparent
with sweat, her boy's breasts small and rounded like a teenage girl's. A
whiplash, fiery and strong. Yes . . . strong.

Shamim went early to his room that night. He smoothed the checked
cotton sheet on the double bed. He looked disgustedly at its pink
laminated headboard. It had been Rehana's choice. He never interfered
in household matters. For a while he lay on one side listlessly watching
a trail of ants carrying one of their dead in silent procession. They were
orderly. No wailing and ranting. No highs and lows of human emotion.

He didn't know what was wrong with him. It was unlike him to introspect. The dismal sounds of the late night film the women were watching wafted up. They lulled him to sleep. He never heard Rehana come in.

Late that night he went clammy again. He got up turned the regulator of the fan faster and lay down. But sweat drenched the sheet. It made him limp. Then slowly an excruciating longing came over him. One he hadn't experienced in worlds. It surprised him. He put his hand on the limp mass of his wife. He touched her waist, felt its pulpy softness, but it was not the pulpy softness he felt. His hand was smoothing over a body as strong as reed. He reached for her neck slipped his hand below, but the knobbly bone of her nape lay buried in pampered flesh. He shifted his weight on her and his hand roamed over her opulent breasts. But it was small taut ones he encountered. And as his longing reached crescendo, he drove into his sluggish wife screeching, Take it you *haramzadi reporter ki bacchhi*.

When he lay exhausted it came to him in unshakeable belief. That this time it had been different. This time it had been urgent. This time round it had to be a boy.

ॐ

ASHA BAGE

•

TOOFAN

•

NOMINATED BY VIJAYA RAJADHYAKSHA
TRANSLATED BY ARVIND DIXIT

Having spent most of the winter afternoon indolently in bed, Mrs Sharangpani gets up, goes to the front verandah of the little bungalow and sits in an armchair, watching the top floor of the building opposite. Almost at once doors on that floor close and Mrs Sharangpani feels deprived of her favourite pastime. She sits there thinking lovingly of a cup of strong filter coffee — slightly bitter, smoothly black. But she's here for a couple of months for treatment of her asthma under a well-known ayurvedic specialist and coffee is strictly forbidden.

Mrs Sharangpani has come leaving behind her home and her husband, her daughter who has just entered the second year at college, and her son, a BSc-final student who is hardly ever found at home — all in the charge of her ageing mother-in-law. And now she's begun to like this place. She does feel homesick at times, lonely, but then, as she tells herself, it was not as if she didn't feel lonely at home. Mrs Sharangpani tries to be happy. Home is not all that far away. Her advocate husband and children come to visit her often. And she has Bayja the cook, a maid and Ganesh for company; that three-storeyed building across the road from her and, hiding behind it, the Engineering College.

The open space in front of that building and its topmost floor are always bustling with college boys. They've rented rooms on that floor. It is always noisy there. Mrs. Sharangpani would not have minded this had her afternoons and midnights not been spoilt by scooters whizzing in and out. Once disturbed she can't go back to sleep. She hasn't complained about this to anyone; only to herself sometimes.

On the second floor of that building live Mrs Ghodvaidya and her retired husband; their grown-up children work elsewhere. Mrs Ghodvaidya is a born landlady, shrewd and seasoned. Mrs Sharangpani is not her tenant and probably that is why they get along pretty cordially.

On the ground floor is a nursery school and also a tailor's shop. It is

'Toofan' was first published in Marathi as *Toofan'* in *Shree Vatsa*, Diwali Issue, 1991, Bombay.

always crowded with young women. A ladies custom tailor, he is said to stitch clothes that fit perfectly. People say that his hands touch all over you when he takes the measurements yet, Mrs Sharangpani wants to try him out. She is sure his blouses will enhance her figure, her fair complexion. How Mrs Sharangpani wished that her daughter Anita would dress well too. But Anita who reads ponderous tomes and argues intelligently in debates and things, wears no bangles, bracelets, ear-rings or chain and walks around in drab salwar kameezes, lifeless saris. This is why Mrs Sharangpani feels a bit awkward getting perfect-fit blouses for herself.

Bayja brings in the tea and a shawl. 'A bit chilly today,' he says. Mrs Sharangpani drapes the shawl over her shoulders. Sips her tea. It is strong and very sweet. Terrible. But she does like Bayja's cooking.

'Any bajra in the house? Well then Bayja. Let's have your bajra rotis with some of that sharp piquant pitla in plenty of hot garlic-oil . . .' Mrs Sharangpani's mouth waters at the mere thought. There is a heti tree in the compound and Mrs Sharangpani loves its flowers in the curry and other fried foods. But she's not supposed to take too much oil. Bayja will surely cook as asked but will conveniently forget the 'plenty of oil' part. He'd better. Or else Vakilsaheb will be terribly annoyed.

Every evening the roar of scooters fills the air. The students park all over the road, some not even bothering to switch off the engines and they begin their usual chatter. Today a young girl in salwar kameez is among them. She is as passionately articulate as the boys. She's not wearing a chunni. Mrs. Sharangpani earnestly wishes she had. It would have at least covered her shoulders. The boys are tall, strong and full-grown. One of them could well be the father of a couple of kids. Some wear dark glasses. Mrs Sharangpani is afraid the eyes behind them are staring at the girl's breasts. She wants to tell the girl to cover herself properly. She nervously readjusts the sari that sits primly on her shoulder. These boys. No innocence on their faces. But that girl, she's different. She could be Anita or Ajay.

In a while the boys storm upstairs. Then the usual shouts and songs, laughter and music blaring out of their cassette recorders. The sun sets.

It begins to get dark and that girl is still there and that burly boy in sunglasses. Mrs Sharangpani feels desperate and unsafe.

'Shall I go and get the medicines?' asks Ganesh.

Mrs Sharangpani is distracted. Her physician prescibes for two days at a time and Ganesh knows there is enough for the day. It's his usual excuse to go out.

'What shall I tell the doctor?'

'Tell him I have no appetite,' says Mrs Sharangpani. In fact what she wants to tell the doctor is that she takes meals not because she feels hungry but because it's a habit.

Ganesh will not return till well past nine. The maid's a local. And soon she's asking, Shall I go? Mrs Sharangpani asks in a bored routine voice, 'Have you finished all the work for the day?' It is pretty dark now. That girl is still upstairs and that is what is uppermost on Mrs Sharangpani's mind. As if it is her own Anita who's up there. 'Ask Bayja before leaving,' she tells the maid.

Bayja now comes to tell her that it is cold out here and Mrs Sharangpani nods. But she cannot leave her post. The Ladies Tailor is active as usual but Mrs Ghodvaidya is getting ready to go somewhere. That means soon there will be no one on the second floor and that girl is still there. And . . .

And Mrs Sharangpani's husband's car arrives. With him are the Mudholkars, the owners of this bungalow, and the driver. Mrs Sharangpani steps out to receive them.

'Ganesh!' calls out Vakilsaheb.

'He has gone out.'

'At this time?'

'Yes, for a walk.' I need not have mentioned it, she realises and adds, 'I mean, to get the medicine.'

'Not keeping well?'

'I'm all right,' she murmurs and, as she goes in to tell Bayja to get some tea her eyes dart to the top floor. She wishes fervently that the girl's left that place by now.

'When will Ganesh return?' Vakilsaheb asks as he sips his tea.

'I haven't particularly asked him to rush back.'

'You may not have but, leaving you here like this. All by yourself. It is . . .' Vakilsaheb grumbles as he walks into the house to change.

Mrs Sharangpani follows him.

'Your visit. So unexpected . . .'

'Mudholkar wanted to come. He wants to sell this bungalow.'

'Why?'

'He can't come here often enough to look after it.'

Sell this house? Mrs Sharangpani feels sad. 'Shall we buy it ourselves?' she asks. And Vakilsaheb just grins. What a stupid idea! the grin seems to say. He places a bottle of White Horse on the table and mumbles something about needing ice and chicken for dinner. 'You should not have sent that Ganesh away,' he says.

That makes her nervous. She dispatches Bayja to get one of the boys from the opposite building. She gives him money, a bag and a flask for the ice. She thanks him profusely. The boy doesn't think he is doing anything extraordinary. Mrs. Sharangpani is touched. And as she turns she sees that girl come down the stairs and take the pillion seat. Ah! The boy seems to be taking her home finally.

'Who was it?'

'One of those students. I asked him to . . .'

'Asking strangers.' There's distinct disapproval in Vakilsaheb's voice.

'I know them!' she says impulsively. She feels buoyant now that the girl is safe and on her way home. She engages Mrs Mudholkar in pleasantries. Goes to the kitchen to help Bayja who has everything under control. The men's drinking session will go on late into the night and she and Mrs Mudholkar don't think they should wait for them to join them and since Mrs Mudholkar is vegetarian it's easy to stick to her earlier plan of bajra rotis. After the meals some chit-chat and then, bed. For the men the evening is still young. But Ganesh is there to attend to them.

At about half past one, she wakes up suddenly to the sound of scooters, the thumping of feet on stairs, shouts. They splinter the silence of the night. This goes on for half an hour or so. Mrs Sharangpani tosses

and turns. Vakilsaheb is on the other bed snoring as usual. The Mudholkars are in the adjoining room. Bayja is in the kitchen; Ganesh and
the driver in the servants' room. No one is even slightly disturbed. Only
Mrs Sharangpani is. And when she wakes up in the morning, the nursery
school is in session and Vakilsaheb is getting ready to leave.

'Are you leaving? I thought you would . . .'

'I have to appear in the High Court. The Mudholkars will be here for
the day.' Vakilsaheb looks sharply at her. 'Anything wrong?'

'Nothing. Must be the disturbed sleep.'

'Disturbed? Why?'

'Those boys. Their scooters.'

'Why don't you tell them so?'

'I will,' she mumbles.

'Are you happy with the treatment?'

'Of course. Without it I would have been bedridden in this kind of
weather.'

When Vakilsaheb leaves Mrs Sharangpani feels lonely.

Why hadn't he come alone? Every time he brings along someone or
the other, feasts and drinks, then goes away in the morning. No privacy,
no intimacy, ever. She does not like to complain openly about anything
to anyone. When it was proposed that she should stay here for the
treatment, she had expected that he would visit her often and that she'd
have some time with him, some togetherness, maybe tenderness. Back
home, the day sprints away like a hound-chased fox. Tea at five-thirty
in the morning followed by a morning walk. Vakilsaheb prefers to go
alone, though he insists that she should take long morning walks. She
did try to go with him once or twice but throughout the long walk not
a word was exchanged. He kept to himself; probably rehearsing his
court arguments. So she doesn't go walking with him. But otherwise he
must always have her around. A light breakfast of milk and toast, then
tea with waiting clients: not all, only those of status. Meals at ten sharp.
Mrs Sharangpani anxiously enquires a dozen times if the driver has
reported. Once he does, she feels relaxed and once Vakilsaheb leaves
for the court, the whole afternoon simply evanesces, like camphor. She

flips through a magazine or two then gets down to putting the house in order. Vakilsahib wants the house to always be spick and span, everything in its exact place. She has it so before he returns. On his return, a cup of tea. Some tasty snacks. A presentable wife. He doesn't like her in crumpled, messed-up saris. Ever. (Anita often tells her that she's merely leading a second-hand life. But Mrs Sharangpani has no complaints.) Then more clients and the juniors who come mornings and evenings. Dinner at eight sharp. The eight-forty news: no one's allowed to utter a word during the newscast. His bed — spotless, well-ironed sheets, the mosquito net, two pillows. In winter, a quilt and its freshly-laundered case. And Mrs Sharangpani. When he so desires.

All this is her own life. No one can help that. She has no complaints. But there are some things she honestly cannot understand.

Like, what difference would it make if someone spoke during the newscast. There is hardly anything new in the news anyway. Her son plays the music so loudly that it booms off the walls. She likes the music that fills everything around her, the rhythm getting into her. Vakilsaheb doesn't. Vakilsaheb wanted his son to study law and take over his practice or at least be an engineer. Ajay is interested in painting. He has got into a college to please his father, but his room is full of paintings. Anita is an arts student. This hurts Vakilsaheb. She has read Anita's poems. Though she does not understand them or Ajay's paintings she likes the way he gets lost in them, the concentration in his eyes, the cups of tea he forgets to drink when he paints. All this she likes. Vakilsaheb's plans for their children were blown to pieces. Even this Mrs Sharangpani likes in a way and Vakilsaheb holds her responsible for that. She does not understand why. This makes her feel she understands nothing. When Mudholkar suggested that Mrs Sharangpani should come to this place and stay here for a couple of months for the treatment of her asthma she had expected Vakilsaheb to dismiss the whole thing — the ideal climate, the renowned asthma specialist — as rubbish. But Vakilsaheb had agreed readily. This had pleased her in a way but she did ask him that night, 'Do I really go there? For two whole months?'

'Of course.'

'Can you manage?'

'Aai's here to take care of us.'

'Can she?'

'Everything is possible. The children are grown-up now.'

Mrs Sharangpani was disappointed. He could have said, It is for your health that I must let you go; much against my wishes.

And now his departure in this manner!

Many buyers come to meet Mudholkar. A deal is struck. Only some formalities for completing the sales-deed remain. The Mudholkars are very happy. They get some sweets for lunch. The menu's just what she would have enjoyed any other day. But when they are about to leave for the bus station she asks them, 'Aren't you sort of sad selling this off like this?'

'Why on earth? We don't stay here and our children don't care for it. We were keen to sell it off if we got a good price.'

For the first time ever Mrs Sharangpani feels so terribly uneasy about a matter not directly connected with her. When they leave, she goes over to Mrs. Ghodvaidya.

Mrs. Ghodvaidya is surprised. She fusses around, extending courtesies and civilities to this honoured guest. Mrs Sharangpani is not expecting all this. She has come for a chat. A plain and simple gossip session, about anything — children, husbands, the weather. She was in a mood to sit there on the steps without any inhibitions, watching the changing hues of the sky, just chatting. But Mrs Ghodvaidya cannot even think of such a thing. She is not prepared to listen to Sharangpani's pieas. 'It must be a fitting reception to an honourable guest like you,' she says.

Mrs. Sharangpani just doesn't understand how she happens to be honourable. That little bungalow she has begun to fall in love with is being sold and she cannot do anything about it and how can she be anywhere near being honourable? She stays on just enough to match Mrs Ghodvaidya's hospitality, returns to her bungalow, tells Bayja that she would have nothing for dinner and prepares to go to bed.

And then the music starts. The same music. The very same rhythm. A music that drowns everything around her. The music rising slowly. To her knees. To her waist. Her neck. The volume shakes everything it touches. It sweeps everything on its way with its uncontrollable momentum. Mrs Sharangpani recognises that speed. It is the speed of Ajay's scooter, of the lightning articulation of Anita's arguments. The heady music gets to her, into her. This she cannot explicitly express at home, but here she's free. Here she can afford to let herself go, allow herself to like that music.

And she slowly falls asleep.

At around an hour past midnight she's awakened by the roar of scooters approaching, stopping, the riders talking and laughing, and the smell of cigarettes.

'If need be we'll bring her here to our rooms.'

'Those people will not let us off so easily.'

'Look Sudesh, if we must, we must. Why be afraid of how deep the water is?'

'Why buy trouble? That's what I say.'

Even without knowing what they are talking about, she understands.

'Hell! Must have some tea.'

'The restaurants must be closed by now. There's no milk in the room either.'

'Shhhhhit! Let's have tea without the milk, then.'

Laughter again. The gossip continues as if the day has just begun. Mrs Sharangpani closes her eyes tight and tries to sleep. It's impossible. Some more scooters arrive. More voices.

Mrs Sharangpani frets about her health. She gets out of bed. It's pretty cold outside. She'd gone to bed early and has had her full quota of sleep and she's fully awake now. She goes to the kitchen. Ganesh is asleep and so is Bayja. Mrs Sharangpani makes a good cup of coffee for herself. She thinks of the boys. They wanted tea. Should she call them over? No. The boys may be a bit too noisy, though she must admit the noise is good company in this untimely wakefulness. Soon the sounds die down, some scooters leave and the other boys tramp up to their rooms and Mrs Sharangpani decides to sit in the verandah. She is swathed in all sorts of woollens. The chill slowly gets into her yet she sits there, defiant, the same defiance with which she made herself a cup of coffee against the the doctor's orders. The trees in the compound appear livelier and fresher than they do early mornings. A twig swinging with the breeze looks so very friendly.

But she has to pay for her defiance. She gets up in the morning with a heavy head and a mild attack of asthma. Ganesh gives her her medicines and asks if he should inform Vakilsaheb. She says No. She's behaved stupidly, she reminds herself.

'Why didn't you wake me up?' asks Bayja. He doesn't say what he wants to — '. . . If you wanted a cup of coffee?'

Mrs Sharangpani suffers the whole day.

That evening the building opposite is rather quiet. It is a weekly off for the Ladies Tailor. Mrs. Ghodvaidya has gone to a movie. Bayja's in the kitchen. Ganesh has gone to the bazaar.

Mrs Sharangpani is in bed with a heavy head when someone calls. It is that girl. The girl from that group of boys. She wears a midi. Mrs Sharangpani doesn't like the way it exposes her legs; that salwar kameez even without the chunni was better. The girl does not look more attractive either.

'What is it?'

'May I . . . ?'

She is allowed in. Why this formality? Mrs Sharangpani wants to ask but orders tea instead.

Why this formality of offering tea? the girl wants to ask but says, 'There is no one upstairs.I don't know when they'll return. They have not left the key with anyone.'

Mrs Sharangpani is shocked at the girl's openness. Are the boys releated to her? Conversations of the previous night come to mind.

The girl simply smiles, shrugs her shoulders.

'We are just friends.'

'What is your name?' And when it is told Mrs. Sharangpani feels a sudden happiness as if she now knows a whole lot about her.

The girl says she's from Nandurbar. She has come here to study Microbiology and stays with her mother's friend. Most of the boys upstairs are from the Engineering College. Mrs Sharangpani wants to tell her that the way she behaves, the way she spends her late night hours in those rooms is not at all desirable and when the girl leaves, Mrs. Sharangpani wonders why people who are supposed to be her guardians don't guide her properly. I would not have allowed this kind of freedom.

Mrs. Ghodvaidya returns from the movie and comes over to collect the milk the milkman had delivered.

'How was the film?'

'Not particularly good. I don't like films anyway but my husband does. He always insists on my accompanying him.'

Mrs. Sharangpani tries to recollect how long ago it was that she and Vakilsaheb had gone to the theatre together. Vakilsaheb doesn't like movies and the children now prefer to bring in video cassettes.

'You don't seem to be particularly well!'

'I'm all right. You know these boys. They come and go at such unearthly hours and they're so noisy, they keep talking and talking and they disturb me. You know how it is once your sleep is disturbed. One of these days, I'm going to warn them.'

'That would be of no use. They are out to tear the sky. They are a veritable storm, a toofan! I'm also fed up.'

Did she mean what she said? The words appealed to Mrs Sharangpani. They were so very apt. Out to tear the sky. A toofan. It occurs to her that her children too belong to that clan.

That night. Mrs. Sharangpani is in bed but still awake. There is an unusually large number of scooters, mopeds and bicycles out front and a motley crowd of boys. They are talking in a tone that announces to the whole world that they wield power over everything they see.

'Is Rashmi there?' someone asks.

Mrs Sharangpani sits up in bed. Yes. Rashmi. That was the name. The one who had come in the evening. But that of course was some days ago. Once or twice after that one has seen her going up those stairs to the boys rooms. She smiles when their eyes meet and now it is that very same name which is being mentioned. At this hour of the night. Who's looking for her? Is she missing? Did those boys by any chance . . . ?

Mrs Sharangpani switches on the light. There were some boys standing in the verandah. Some with thick batons in their hands. Mrs. Sharangpani is scared. She asks Ganesh to go and see what the matter is. Mrs Ghodvaidya too comes out of her room.

Ganesh comes back. Says it was some row over a girl. That girl they say often visits a certain boy up there and both of them are planning to run away and get married. Her local guardian came to know of this and he brought those baton-wielding goondas to teach them a lesson. There are rival groups in the college also because of that girl.

This shocks Mrs Sharangpani. The girl didn't seem to be that type. Did she? Maybe her dress was a bit too flashy. In fact it was. Yes. It exposed her legs, but that didn't mean . . . Her eyes definitely looked like Anita's. Like Ajay's.

In spite of that disturbance Mrs Sharangpani does doze off at last only to be woken up again. Those boys again. She tries hard not to listen to them. She closes her eyes determinedly. Tries to forget the noises. Then she gets up, picks up her shawl, comes out, walks to the gate, and stands there looking at the boys. She waits for someone to notice her.

Nobody does. The boys are lost in their own affairs.

'Please!' she begins, but her Please hasn't registered on anybody. Smoke gets into her throat. She coughs and tries again. 'Please!'

The cigarette butts are put out of sight. 'Yes?' a boy asks. 'What is it?' asks another.

'I live here in this bungalow. I am an asthma patient. I must sleep well. And I just cannot do that with this noise. Is it possible for you to talk a bit . . . softly? I mean . . . and also try to make a little less noise when you bring in those scooters?'

'Sorry!' They are sincerely apologetic and she returns. On her way back she faintly hears a voice.

'Quite a thing she is.'

'Don't talk rot!'

Peels of laughter follow that make Mrs Sharangpani perspire profusely. Her breathing is heavy. Palms moist. Her heart beats louder. She
spreads herself on the bed somehow and after a while falls fast asleep.

One Sunday afternoon Anita and Ajay arrive on their scooter
and instead of joy and pleasure at seeing them, she asks,
'Why did you come on a scooter Ajay?'
He hugs her and jostles her lovingly.
'Should we have come on foot?'
'Isn't there a bus?'
'You're scared of my driving, no? Accidents can happen to a bus also.'
'Enough!' She is truly annoyed and tries to disengage his hands to
show the displeasure.
'This roof can fall and we . . .'
'Enough I said. Today's Sunday. Why didn't Daddy come? You could
have come with him.'
'We asked him to come later, on his own. With him around we cannot
enjoy ourselves here.'
Anita goes for a wash and on the way back asks Bayja for some tea.
'I shall make tea for you,' says Mrs Sharangpani beginning to feel much
better now that the children are here. The nursery school and the Ladies
Tailor are closed. There isn't much noise from the boys' rooms either,
being Sunday.
Anita says 'We have brought some fish. Do you mind if Bayja cooks
it for us?'
There's no question of her minding. There never had been. But they
remember she doesn't touch non-vegetarian food, don't they?
'Why not, Mummy? You used to like non-vegetarian food. You've
said so.'
What can she say? Vakilsaheb's mother did not approve of these
things and Mrs Sharangpani had decided not to go against her mother-
in-law's wishes. But now Anita insists, she says, 'No point giving up
something you like for the sake of others.' As if the mother of your
husband can be an Other.

Anita goes for her bath and Ajay brings out a cassette recorder. The same earbursting sound. Like that which pours day in and day out from the top floor, the one she has begun to like. Anita flounces out of the bathroom and switches tapes, puts on an old Lata Mangeshkar hit. The melody takes Mrs Sharangpani back to her college days. Another old hit follows and she begins to hum with it. It is Ajay who now switches off the music and a quarrel ensues. As a compromise, no more music. But the honeyed voice of Lata stays with Mrs Sharangpani. She continues to hum.

'Sing on Ma. You sing so beautifully.'

'I can't sing. Only hum. Maybe.'

'Hum then.'

'Oh no. I can't even recollect the proper words.' And to change the topic she says, 'That tailor's shop is closed today, otherwise you could have got something made up.'

'I don't like that kind of fit.'

'You should try it once,' coaxes Mrs Sharangpani. 'You dress so shabbily.'

The children enjoy their lunch. Especially the fish. Ajay goes and hires a VCR and an English movie cassette and some boys from upstairs come and join in. If it were a Hindi movie now, Mrs Sharangpani could have watched for a while. But after the movie Anita makes tea and the boys stay on and Mrs Sharangpani joins them. The boys have come here to study in the Engineering College, from all sorts of places like Kashmir, Yamunanagar, Hoshiarpur, the South. They have paid fat donations and capitation fees. They all had scored good marks, yet they were denied admissions in their home states and that makes them sound pessimistic. Sour. They want to crush the system. They want to spit at the whole world. And probably that is what is behind their unkempt hair, the lost tenderness, the total defiance. They are being unfairly disqualified even before the commencement of the race. The thought brings that music back to Mrs Sharangpani: its volume, its tempo, its rhythm, the crescendo. And when they leave, she asks, 'Anita, was what they said true?'

'Every word of it.'

'Is there no solution to this?'

'A total boycott, I suppose.'

Mrs Sharangpani is terribly sad. It is not that she hasn't experienced sorrow, disappointment, frustration in her lifetime; dejection on being rejected by a lover, sorrow at the loss of her mother and a sister in a needless accident, at the loss of her first child. What had made things worse was the fact that there was no one around to share the grief. But never before has she felt so wounded as today, listening to those boys. She gets terribly concerned about her own children.

Anita and Ajay laze around in bed. They sleep. Ganesh and Bayja are also in a mood to relax but Mrs Sharangpani just cannot. She pulls out a notebook of poems from Anita's handbag and begins to read. She cannot understand them at all but she can sense the spirit: feelings similar to what those boys had felt. Mrs Sharangpani's old friend Maloo Aravat also used to write poetry. It used to be soft and smooth, of love and tenderness, of him and her, of flowers and trees, but Anita's poems were different. There were trees but the flowers on them glowed like cinders. Mrs Sharangpani had never indulged in introspection. But today, she feels an enormous upheaval inside her. This much she knows.

It is at around eight that the children get up. With all those tensions of life how can these children sleep so! Have they learnt to live with them already?

'It is so late. Must you go now?' Mrs Sharangpani wants to say but she stops herself in time. They come here not to see her but to enjoy themselves is her usual complaint but she says nothing now. She doesn't tell them to tend the potted plants, to be nice to their Dadima, about seeing to their father's morning tea. Nothing. The children are planning a long scooter ride in this cold weather and she doesn't utter a word of caution. She covers herself with a shawl and stands at the gate.

'Any message for Daddy?'

She smiles faintly.

It is mid-December. The winter is at its peak. Mrs Sharangpani has had no wheezing so far. She has a feeling that there is something beyond the medicine which makes the difference. It is a new me, alienated from self, from illness. Her asthma is now an alien. Is she acquainted with it? Yes. Is it known? Yes. But it's not part of her any more and this is a new perspective.

A couple of weeks and then it'll be time to return. Vakilsaheb and the children have planned a New Year's eve party. They would be here the day before to pack up and leave. It would not be possible to see this bungalow again. Nor these surroundings. An uneasy hankering over-takes her.

Then one day Mr Ghodvaidya feels suddenly faint and falls to the ground. Before help can come he is dead.

Mrs Sharangpani doesn't know how to react. Life is like the thick wall of fog which had been around since morning. You encounter nothing beforehand. Yesterday there was this man going with his wife for a walk, bringing in the milk and today he is no more. It is not that she hasn't known death in all her fifty years but today she has no strength to face it. Every death unravels a different meaning.

That top-floor toofan too is becalmed by this death. The music is off. The scooter noises are missing. The boys walk ever so silently, behave so responsibly. They contact Mrs Ghodvaidya's sons, receive the guests, arrange for everything. As if the death had ocurred in their own family.

Mrs Ghodvaidya's children come and take their mother away. They have no time to stay on till the mourning period is over. They do not want to perform any religious rites. Father did not believe in them anyway, they say. Mrs Sharangpani goes over to their house when they are leaving. She does not ask any meaningless questions like when Mrs Ghodvaidya plans to return. She had come to know that the children had already decided to sell the place. But when Vakilsaheb comes the following Sunday and asks, 'Why not pack up now and go home? It is only another fifteen days treatment left anyway?' she says No. She wants to tell him a lot more, all that she has begun to feel from within, but she cannot, because she has never tried to express herself openly. Not through words. Not through the language of touch.

It does not take the boys long to return to their noisy normalcy. The nursery school, the Ladies Tailor, everything soon returns to normal except that Mrs Ghodvaidya's portion of the house is now locked. It seems as if more and more boys are visiting the place. Mrs Sharangpani senses something unusual. Something fishy. That girl Rashmi who was not to be seen during the period of mourning resumes her regular visits. And one more night the lathi-wielding strongmen storm the place.

Mrs Sharangpani's keen to know what's happening. Whom should she ask? Ganesh has the habit of blowing everything out of proportion. Bayja's the same. Mrs Sharangpani would like to ask one of the boys directly, but whom?

One evening she sees the girl going up to the boy's rooms but she does not return. The next day Rashmi is at her door.

Mrs Sharangpani is in bed.

'I need just a minute.'

Mrs Sharangpani sits up in bed. 'Do come in. Sit.'

She comes in but doesn't sit down.

'Are you not well?'

'I'm all right. It is the weather'

She waits for Rashmi to say something but Rashmi is nervous, probably scared of something. 'What is it, Rashmi?'

Rashmi picks up courage on hearing Mrs Sharangpani call her by name. 'Can we . . . I mean, I need a little help.'

She avoids looking into Mrs Sharangpani's eyes.

'What sort of help?'.

'Will it be okay if I stay with you for a night?'

'Every day if you please. Today?'

'Not that way. I mean, Sudesh and I want to get married.'

'Sudesh Bharadwaj?'

'If I can stay here the night we can leave early in the morning.'

'I see. Your people agree?'

'No. I have not told them.'

'You should have.'

'Ma says no.'

'Why?'

'Sudesh is a Punjabi, still a student, and not yet of marriageable age.'

Why can't this girl see sense?

'Do his parents approve?'

'They are even more orthodox.'

'Where will you go then?'

'We haven't decided. The most important thing right now is to get married. All the opposition will automatically crumble. I could have as well stayed with Sudesh but if my people come to know they'll come here and create a scene. Also there's an anti-Sudesh lobby in the college. They too will take advantage. So . . . With you . . . if . . . But again . . .'

'Is this all?' Mrs Sharangpani stops at that.

Shall I have this girl in for the night? Without confiding in any one? Not even Ajay or Anita? If I shelter her will it not be like silent approval? If it were my children doing such things behind my back . . . ! Mrs Sharangpani cannot decide. She knows she is not capable of doing so. Rashmi reads all this on Mrs Sharangpani's face. She moves towards the door. Mrs Sharangpani wants to stop her. Have I not shattered her hopes? What a poor impression I must have made on this girl?

Ajay and Anita come again the following Sunday with their friends. Mrs Sharangpani wants to ask them if she did the right thing. But the children are always surrounded by their friends. There is no opportunity for a confidential whisper. She does not want to make this affair public. She is annoyed with herself. Always it is her husband who takes all the decisions. Even the unimportant ones. For the first time in her life she is totally frustrated with her own helplessness.

The last day of the year. The weather is not only chilly but there is that piercing wind and a thick wall of fog separates her from everything. The nursery school is closed, probably due to the weather.

She feels uneasy. It is uncomfortable in her room and even more uncomfortable in the verandah. Mrs Sharangpani has put on all her warm clothing, the socks, a shawl, a muffler, the woollen blouse and all. The Ladies Tailor opens at ten as usual but there are no customers. There's an occasional sound of a scooter. That's all. Mrs Ghodvaidya's flat is still closed. Everything, especially the top-floor toofan, has opened up a whole new world for her. This she feels most intensely.

In the evening Ganesh asks if he could visit his friends. 'I will be back early morning,' he promises.

No harm she thinks because Bayja is anyway there to give her company. Mrs Sharangpani gets into bed but she cannot sleep at all. At around midnight she senses some movement outside. A bunch of boys. No scooters though. They seem to be moving around taking the utmost care not to awaken anyone. Mrs Sharangpani switches on the lights and notices Rashmi there. They dart forward and hide in the shadow of the stairs.

Mrs Sharangpani is now concerned. The boys are climbing the stairs. There is not enough light there, but she can see a pool of torchlight moving up. She becomes restless. There is definitely something wrong somewhere. Why should they enter their own rooms like this? Why is Rashmi with them at this unearthly hour? Granted she's going to get married to that boy. But still . . . She visualises Anita in Rashmi's place. This upsets her even more. She begins to pace up and down, finally makes up her mind, goes to the window and looks out. The top floor lights are not on.

That is it. She doesn't care that she has removed all her woollens before going to bed and now is wearing only a thin half sleeved sweater. She picks up her shawl, flops out in her bathroom slippers and deter-mindly steps out of the room, unlocks the garden gate and walks to the staircase. She doesn't know where the light switch is, but doesn't bother to find out. She gropes for the wall and begins to climb. With every step she feels she is becoming bolder. It is the first time ever that she experiences this. She reaches the top. It is terribly cold there. The doors are closed shut but she can hear whispered conversation behind them. She taps a door. No response. Knocks. No response. More knocks.

Rashmi must be helped. It could be Anita in her place tomorrow! I did want to help the girl when she came to ask for a night's shelter.

'Who is it?'

'It's me.'

'Who is me?'

'Mrs Sharangpani from the house opposite.'

'What do you want?'

'First the door.'

The door opens. Lights are switched on. There are two or three boys in the room but not that girl. Mrs Sharangpani virtually forces herself in.

'What is it?'

'There is a girl in this room.'

'So? There is no girl.'

'I have seen her come.'

'Do you see her now?'

'I have.'

'Go. Get lost. Don't disturb us.'

'I will not. Not until I have seen her safe. I will take her with me.'

She is more determined than ever. She must save Rashmi. At any cost. The doors of the adjoining rooms open.

'What's the matter?' A boy growls.

'There is a girl in here.'

'Look here! It is none of your business.'

'Don't push your dirty nose around here. Go.'

'I will not unless I have seen her safe.'

There is a strength of conviction in her voice. It could be Anita next!

'Do you know the consequences, madam?'

Mrs Sharangpani looks in the direction of the voice. The face doesn't look any different from Ajay's. She hates his arrogance.

It is cold and windy but Mrs Sharangpani does not feel the cold at all. As she stands there defying the violent and uncontrollable storm she becomes a toofan herself. She has freed herself of all her shackles.

'I have seen the girl coming here and I am not going to let her stay here at night.'

This woman! Suspecting our intentions? Such distrust?

Before she knows what is happening, that boy with Ajay's face pounces on her. The others too are mad with anger. Her shawl is snatched, her sari pulled. She tries to cling on to its end, but her sweater is ripped off, the blouse torn to pieces, she holds on to her petticoat with all her strength but it tears open at the seam. In this frenzy, nobody remains an individual. Each one is mad. Mad. Mad. Mrs Sharangpani is trembling with fear and cold. She looks at them in disbelief and shock. Shameful. Disgusting. The toofan has uprooted her. She gasps for air.

Rashmi rushes in. She looks aghast at the terrible sight. The fury of her incensed friends. Mrs Sharangpani tries to cover her shame. Rashmi goes to her, holds her by the hand, picks up the shawl and puts it around the nude Mrs Sharangpani.

'Prashant! Stop it! Stop it, I say!' she shouts. 'What the devil! What's happened to you?'

The boys step back, their eyes still burning.

Rage! That is what Mrs Sharangpani sees on their faces. Rage. But not lust. No.

Rashmi turns to the boy she's going to marry.

'You too Sudesh!'

'Tell her we are not what she thinks we are. We have not kidnapped anyone.'

'Stop it Prashant.'

Rashmi gathers the tattered clothes, somehow wraps the sari around Mrs Sharangpani and slowly leads her to the door. Sudesh comes in the way but she pushes him away.

Rashmi leaves Mrs Sharangpani at the gate and asks, 'May I?' She wants to say a world of things but does not.

'Yes.' says Mrs Sharangpani feebly. She too wants to say much more.

Rashmi does not return to the boys' rooms. Would she be going to her local guardians at this time of the night? All alone?

Mrs Sharangpani wants to ask her to stay but Rashmi is gone. Mrs Sharangpani somehow staggers to her room. Bayja is fast asleep, and so are the rows of houses beyond. The wheezing of the public water tap at a distance can be heard. They are all unaware of the horrific experience of the toofan.

Mrs Sharangpani loses her confidence. The chill gets to her. Goes to her bones. She begins to shiver. Feels feverish. She wants to shake Bayja awake. She reaches for the medicine chest, grabs a bottle of brandy. Rubs some on feet, on palms, tosses off a peg and still in her torn petticoat and rucked-up sari she throws herself on the bed. And even in that half unconscious state she remembers those eyes and finds in them nothing but uncontrollable anger. Just the anger. None of those eyes stick to any part of her stripped body.

In a few hours Vakilsaheb and the children will be here to take her home.

VAIDEHI

•

A DAY SCARRED BY
A KINSMAN

•

NOMINATED BY D R NAGARAJ
TRANSLATED BY PADMA SHARMA

Shrouded in a cold. An irresistable urge to pluck the nose off and plop it somewhere. A fever coming on . . . There's a knock on the door.

When opened, there stood a man anyone could have described, eyes closed, as someone who had retired many years ago. Flat face, dry wilted body, a blanched umbrella rolled up and shoved under his arm, he stood as if rooted to the earth under his feet.

As soon as he saw her he stepped right in with an extravagantly broad smile, saying 'I searched and searched and, look at me, I went right past. This *was* the house after all. And look at me, I just went on and on walking.' The searching, the asking around, the coming back eventually to reach this house — he narrated just this in as many ways as he could, then asked her as she stood wondering who he was, 'Is he there?'

'No. And you . . . ?'

'Me? I know your husband. He often comes to my son's shop . . . his name's Gopinath.'

She had heard her husband mention the name Gopinath once or twice. 'Gopinath's father,' she said, in a flat voice.

That was all. The man seemed to think that she was filled with the joy of recognising an old friend. 'There, you see! Now you know,' he said with a shrug. 'When is he coming back? I came this way on work. Thought I'd drop in,' he said, sitting down, wiping his sweat.

What shall I do? Shall I just go in?

But he sat looking at her expectantly.

'No, I'm afraid I can't say when he'll be back. One o'clock, half past one. Sometimes it's even two. Any message? I can tell him.'

'Che che, nothing much. I'd come this side. So I thought I'd . . . visit him.' The same old refrain.

'I know your husband very well.' He sat glued to the chair. 'Don't bother about coffee-goffee. Buttermilk? Not at all! I shall catch a cold.' She caught the hint. Went in to make coffee. As she served it she thought

'A Day Scarred by a Kinsman' was first published in Kannada as *'Hagalu Geechida Nenta'* in *Lankesh Patrike*, 24 February 1991, Bangalore.

she'd go in, letting him wait by himself but the strange manner in which he laughed without her joining in, the way he chattered without any encouragement, carrying on as if he were an intimate, much-needed friend (probably he was ignored wherever he went) made her just sit there, facing him.

Smiling as if he were indeed a member of this her house, he asked again in a light, easy voice, 'When did you say he'd be back?'

'Around one.'

The old man looked at his watch. As if it wasn't enough, he looked at the wall clock. 'Oh, my watch is a little slow,' he said, setting it right, pretending to be absorbed, buying time as it were, saying, 'That means . . . it is half past twelve now. Half past twelve, quarter to one, one o'clock! Should be here in half an hour.' He spoke as if half an hour would fly in a snap of one's fingers.

'Yes, half an hour.' She sighed. 'Anyway, why should you wait till then? Probably, he'll be delayed. If there's something . . .'

Even before she could stop, he stiffened, gathering himself together in suspicion that she might be hinting he needn't stay. 'No, no. I won't stay for long. I'll just see him, have a word and be off. After having come this far, to go away without seeing him . . .'

There he went repeating himself again. However did her husband come to know him? Good God!

She sat for a while out of courtesy, thinking she should go in but then his discomfiture, his repeated attempts to get rid of it, the old faded coat, covered with dust and worn to conceal his fragility, and the ceaseless effort he made to be still, to focus his unwilling eyes on one object . . . She watched the way he shrank into himself, the way he straightened his back over and over again to sit with his head up and 'No please stay on,' she said. 'It doesn't matter. If you really must speak to him.'

The man, ready to look for rubies in words, found many to gather in what she said. 'There's no must about it. Just a chat. This and that, ha, ha, ha!' Yes, a nice day and casual conversation.

She would usually finish cooking and sit by herself, a queen, before her husband came home for lunch. Now she sat in front of this man as if time had been pledged to a sense of duty. She had never understood Einstein's Theory of Relativity before but now she was beginning to. The hands on the clock weren't moving at all!

As if it was impossible to sit without the prop of conversation the man looked around and asked, 'This house . . . rented?'

'Yes.'

'How much?'

She told him.

'Children?'

She let him know.

'Boys? Girls?'

She answered.

'A nice house. A house like this might fetch . . .' He went on and she kept sitting, apparently listening to what he said.

'Even my house is rented. We have lived in it for thirty, thirty-five years. How big do you suppose it is? Three rooms, built on a mere two cents of land. There is a little space at the back. Nothing worth mentioning. The rent isn't high. Like old times. Thirty-five rupees. The landlord wants to increase it.' The old man appeared to have twisted a turban of words about his head. 'Why should we give it up? Can he evict us? Does he think we'd vacate the house? And since we can't be made to leave, why should we pay more?' A dry fibrous man with a dry, fibrous voice. She was compelled to ask in a teasing voice: 'What if he sells it?'

'If he sells it to us we'll buy it.' He rested both arms on the chair, stretched out his legs and looked up, a king on a throne. A man might rid himself of all desires but never from the dream of owning a house. He spoke again with an air of prosperity. 'We'll buy it.' When a man tries to act big at the end of his life, after having spent it slaving for others, it doesn't become him. He appears ridiculous.

As she watched him, she forgot that she intended to sit there only till politeness demanded it. His whole frame was a negation of all he said. Wanting to find out just how far he'd go, she asked, 'But then . . . it's all so expensive nowadays.'

'So what? I'm an old tenant. I could get it cheap. Has he ever repaired anything? Just pockets the rent every month. That's all. Wasn't I the one who painted the ceiling of two rooms?' With what righteous pride he said this! It's not the landlord who sleeps under it she wanted to retort but held back, thinking her words might skip towards other nuances. She looked at the clock. Dear God! The hands weren't moving at all! There should be clocks that move according to one's inclination.

'What do you think?'

Must he be told? Where on earth did he come from?

Sneezes in a row. In between them, she could hear him talking about his job, his office, the officers. Stopping every now and then. She thought: A girl has slept under the same roof even with this man who looks like a faded photograph with eyes like holes of darkness.

She felt like asking about his wife. But somehow it didn't look as if she'd be alive. Impulsively she asked, 'Do you have daughters?'

Ah! Here was a question that could be answered in great detail. He started off enthusiastically. 'Five children. Two boys and three girls. The boys are in some kind of business. Recently they have found moneyed partners and are looking after the management . . .' He shook his head from side to side, as if to say management was too big a word for what they did.

'Management is such a hassle.'

'What does it matter, anyway? They don't come home because they are dead scared of the girls. Have you heard of anything like this?'

'Why? The girls . . .'

'I married one off when I was still in service.' There was a noise outside. He bent over to look, squeaking 'Who could that be?' as if he were the host responding to every sound at the door and she herself the stranger. No, it wasn't her husband. Somebody or the other kept coming in and out of flats in their tenement. There were always noises.

The old man carried on as if tightening the turban which had become loose. '. . . What was I telling you? Ah, yes. I got her married. A boy in a government job. He was a clerk then. I paid a dowry of five thousand rupees. Now he is an officer in Shimoga.' He straightened his collar.

'Today one has to pay twenty-five thousand for the same alliance,' he added with the same thrill he'd show if comparing the cost of a wooden cot bought long ago, to what it would fetch now.

'There are two more. For the older one, something came up when she was twenty-four. Everything seemed settled but it fell through. Once you lose a chance you lose it. It takes a long time before anything else turns up. A year went. When I thought of getting the younger one married, the older one threatened to kill herself. Anyway, how could I marry off the younger unless a suitable alliance came up? You just can't marry a girl off to anyone that comes along.'

He was using cliches to shield himself from the fact that his daughters were still unmarried. He appeared to be used to it, perhaps he even enjoyed going around saying such things.

She continued to sit quietly. 'Now something has come up. They are asking for a dowry of thirty thousand. That's not much if the boy and the girl say yes,' he said. His words, the lines on his face, the drawl of his voice — none of these made it possible for her to ask, 'For whom? The older girl or the younger one?' The words seemed to have exploded out of him, to stand separated. She was amazed.

'. . . No. I'm not saying this because they're my children. They are not qualified to do anything but cook and eat — at times not even that. But talk of marriage and their ears prick up. Maybe that's why they never got married . . .' The same thin smile. A fly settled on his face. He made no effort to brush it away. As when a fly sits on a corpse. It crawled this way and that, then flew off. Perhaps he became conscious of it. 'I told them to get an education. They didn't. Now they are whiling away their time at home. I told you the brothers don't come around at all. Everything falls on me.' His eyes demanded sympathy. White unseeing eyes.

'I don't give them much leeway. If I do they'll run away with someone today. Won't wait till tomorrow. They're like that. Right now I've locked them up and come. Else they'd have flown away before I return. Whom can I possibly find for them? Others are young too, aren't they?'

She felt her fever rise. A look at the clock showed no movement of the hand. He had shifted to the edge of the chair as he talked and talked, sitting with his palms seemingly sewn together between his knees. He started suddenly, waking up, kept his hands on the arms of the chair, then leant back again, crossing his legs.

What now? He appeared to be deep in thought about something else to talk about. The crackling heat of the afternoon sucked away the ticking of the clock.

'He hasn't returned yet. Please go ahead and have your lunch. I'll wait for him.'

'No, I eat only when he gets back.' She didn't budge from where she sat. Didn't even tell him to leave. Instead, she said, 'He told me he had to go somewhere and may be quite late coming back . . .'

'What's the time now? Nearly two . . . aren't you going to eat? Then I shall make a move.' He made no effort to rise from his chair.

She could not ask him to stay. He had waited long enough. He could have had lunch. She couldn't even find a reason for not asking him. Why do you feel like this when you meet some people? she wondered, getting enmeshed in her own confusion. This was an old man, hungry, in a torn jacket. It was lunchtime. Even then . . . Her fever seemed to burn.

'May I have some water. Then I'll leave.'

As he lifted the tumbler to his mouth, she worried about the distance he would have to walk in the sun.

'Where do you live?'

Even as he gulped down the water he gurgled, 'Quite a distance. You know Shambhavi Talkies? Past it. I'll make it easy . . . you know the house where the two half-witted girls live? Just opposite that.'

How easily he said it! As if idiots and half-wits were a common ocurrence in every town. She shivered with rising fever.

'Half-witted girls?'

'Why? Don't you know? They are well known. There's no one who doesn't know them. All through the evening they don't budge from their gate. You haven't come over there? Then you wouldn't know.'

She found she was listening to him intently.

He stirred. Cleared his throat. 'What can I say? You won't believe it. They solicit so many. But who will come? Demons?' He laughed. Good Heavens! Only a devil could laugh like that . . . in broad daylight, in the burning sun, with those white unseeing eyes . . .

'Sometimes it's me. Really! An old man like me! As soon as I step out, they call me. Imagine! Quite disgusting. Brazen girls. You'd say they should be locked up. But for how long? How long? And you know what? When the men walk past them, ignoring them, they start attracting the attention of girls. Girls, mind you! Frustration, what else? Have you heard of anything like it? Anywhere?'

Her scream remained stifled.

He put down the glass of water. 'Imagine. Calling me of all people . . . really!' He stood up, having twisted, cut, braided the same thing over and over again. 'I'm leaving. Please have your lunch. Do tell your husband I called. I know him but he doesn't know me. I came over just to get acquainted.' She said nothing.

The old man grumbled to himself, putting on his slippers. 'Have to go now . . . a long way. Who knows whether there'll be lunch . . . maybe they're far too busy powdering themselves, standing at the window watching the road. The sluts.' But still there was no invitation from her.

White sunlight, forked tongues stretching out to devour. He went walking slowly, opening wide his white eyes under his blanched umbrella. Not a trace of colour.

She remained seated. The fever had raced to her head. Eyes filled with dread . . . drowning girls, hands flailing, endlessly beckoning, sucked in until only the fingertips showed . . . mouths open yet unable to call . . . eyes, dying behind window bars . . .

She got up slowly. Then in one sudden spurt of fluid motion, she pulled off the loose cover that draped the back of the chair he had sat on, floated towards the bathroom, flung them into the bucket of water, and pushed the bucket into a corner with trembling feet. She finally stood, holding on to the door.

As if she had not heard the clock strike two. Loudly.

BIMAL KAR

·

SATYADAS

·

NOMINATED BY SARAT KUMAR MUKHOPADHYAY
TRANSLATED BY ENAKSHI CHATTERJEE

There was a glint of soft light at the crack of dawn. Then the clouds took over and it poured as if it were the height of the rainy season and not the month of Poush, with winter just round the corner. Even the nights were wet and soggy.

The brief glow at dawn had made Raghunath think that maybe the untimely rainy spell would be over now, after five long days, and everything would grow nice and dry again under the winter sun, the trees wearing the colours the north wind had brought them. But the rains started again. Business was dull at Raghunath's grocery shop. Who would venture out unless he had to?

Raghunath sold rice, pulses, salt and cooking oil. He also stocked muri, batasa, potatoes and onion. Even bidis. But try as he might, his business had stayed modest over the last seven, eight years.

He can't possibly compare his outfit with that of Haladhar babu's. His family has been running it for two generations, the oldest and the largest store in the locality. They stocked anything one could possibly want. Apart from groceries there were dry cell batteries, tinned powdered milk, aqua-ptychotis, oil cloth for babies, umbrellas, mosquito nets. The babu had nice manners too. He always offered bidis and matches to old customers.

No, even in his wildest dreams Raghunath could never think of becoming another Haladhar babu. But he could have become like Gadai Kundu, Neelu Ghati or Prasad. They were doing well, each in his own way. Gadai has been in business longer. But look at Prasad. His business has flourished in just five years. Now he holds Kali Puja every year with great pomp.

Raghunath sometimes feels sorry for himself. What has he achieved? Perhaps the mistake was to set up his shop at the far end of town where the Nishipur siding railway tracks end.

Raghunath was not a bad man. He treated his customers well. He was not greedy. He never sold things at double the price, nor palmed off stale stuff. But he has to earn a living. Like everyone else he wants

'Satyadas' (Title of the original story) was first published in Bangla in *Desh Weekly*, 8 December 1991, Calcutta.

to make money. He has to maintain his wife and Bishu, the odd-jobs boy. Bishu was a little lame and Raghunath had him to help in the store and whenever possible, Yamuna at home. He did not stay with them. Bishu came in the morning, went home in the evening, but he had his two meals with them.

When it rained, Raghunath saw more showers than customers. Sometimes it poured, sometimes it was a mere drizzle, and sometimes the skies scattered drops of rain, large and soft, like flakes of cotton. Raghunath would sit watching the rain, the thick darkness of the sky turning translucent, then darkening again like magic, for the flash of lightning and the rumbling clouds. He'd observe the trees and shrubs, the jarul, the bakul, the many creepers, the stunted palm and the wild thorny bushes. He'd contemplate the crows trying to shield themselves from the rain, cawing, but most of the time sitting huddled on branches.

How long could one sit still, doing nothing? He sold pulses or cooking oil to an occasional customer; a stray buyer asked for salt, pepper and spices; another came for potatoes, onions, bidis. He tries to make conversation: Foul weather isn't it, Nagen? Not a ray of sunshine! Things are changing, even the weather. But soon, left to himself he gets tired of watching the wet foliage, the shrubs, the water-logged lane, the endless shower. He tries to kill time by picking up soiled potatoes from the sack. Patches of fungus grow on damp potatoes and onions — he tries to keep the bad ones in a separate basket. They sell at a cheaper rate. He asks Bishu to clean out the canisters. There are about seven for pulses, chira, muri and the rest. He has changed the polythene covers to keep them fresh, but it doesn't help much. He makes a few trips inside, to ask for a cup of tea, to talk to Yamuna about the state of business, asking her if she's feeling better — she's been complaining of fever lately. So the days go. After sunset he pulls down the shutter, changes, does his puja. He has his tea with some muri and sits down with his *Ramayana* or *Mahabharata*. Stooping by the lantern he reads the epic in a sing-song voice. In another part of the room Yamuna does some stitching or just lies down. By the time they finish dinner it is late.

Today something out of the ordinary is to happen.
The rain started early afternoon with all the appearance of a real good Sravana shower. It stopped after a while. It grew dark quickly. He called Bishu to say, You better get home early. It does not look too good. Don't get wet. Cover your head.

Wrapping himself in a torn polythene sheet Bishu left.

A short while later when Raghunath was lighting the agarbatti before the picture of goddess Laksmi, a man materialised through the drizzle. Raghunath looked at him. Anyone he knew? He most certainly did not belong to the neighbourhood, or any part of Panchpukuria for that matter.

The stranger was perhaps the same age as Raghunath though he looked somewhat older. He had a week's stubble on his chin, his hair was dishevelled. He carried a faded black umbrella in one hand and a small wooden box in the other, its lid held in place with a piece of rope. From his right shoulder hung a bundle. He wore a soiled dhoti and a shirt over which he had a black coat with some buttons missing. There were patches on his coat. His slippers too looked weather worn.

'What do you want?' asked Raghunath.

Putting down his box the stranger asked, 'Can I get some puffed rice here, babu?'

Raghunath nodded, 'But it won't be good, I can tell you that. Muri tends to get soggy in this weather.'

'Well then, some chira would do. Do you have gur?'

'Yes.'

'That'll be fine.'

The man deposited his belongings one by one on the ramshackled old bench.

'Where are you from if I may ask?'

'You could say from Dharmapur.'

Raghunath did not know of any such place in the vicinity. But then in a radius of about ten miles there were all sorts of places — villages, towns, coal mines, settlements. And names by the dozen — Ratibati, Manasatala, Sripur, Badam Bagan.

'Babu, I would like to wash my hands. Can I have some water in a lota?'

One lota would hardly be enough to wash off all the mud that stuck to his feet. Yet Raghunath was wary of taking a stranger inside. Murmuring a Let me see, Raghunath went in and returned soon after with a bucket of water and a tin mug. He put the bucket outside his premises. 'Go on, wash yourself. It's water from my well.'

Embarrassed, the man said, 'Why babu, a small lota of water would have done.'

'You are muddy all over. Go ahead. Wash yourself.'

The man moved a little away and cleaned himself.

'And your good name?'

'You can call me Satyadas.'

'Caste?'

'Good enough for you to accept water from me. But a poor man's caste. What is it worth after all?'

He finished washing his feet, rinsed his mouth, then observed, 'Nice water you have here, babu; tastes good.'

Raghunath tried to assess him. The man seemed to be simple. He had a gentle way of talking.

'Where are you off to in this rain?' he asked.

Satyadas, his washing over, answered, 'Can't say for sure. I just set out, wherever the wheels stuck to my legs take me . . .'

Raghunath smiled. 'But you must need some place for the night.'

'Well yes. But then, any shade will do,' Satyadas said, giving back the bucket and mug.

'Just a minute,' Raghunath put in. 'Where will you soak your chira and gur?'

'I have a small bowl.'

Satyadas was about to untie his bundle.

'Please don't bother. I'll get you one,' said Raghunath.

Satyadas had taken out a gamcha from his bundle to wipe his hands and legs by the time Raghunath came back with an enamelled dish and

water in a lota. 'Here. Soak the stuff in this. You can wash it after you
have had your meal.'

The chira looked limp but the dampness did not really matter; after
all it had to be soaked. But, Raghunath wondered: How much would
he eat? The man seemed to be really hungry.

'What do you do for a living Satyadas?'

A smile flitted across Satyadas's face. 'I roam about, babu, selling
herbal cures. Roots and things.'

'Roots and things?'

'I have about a dozen different kinds. Herbs to cure scorpion bites,
snake bites, old wounds, indigestion, rheumatic pain . . .' He recited
slowly, not in the tone of a professional peddler but as though these
herbal drugs were honest cures.

Raghunath was amused, curious. Perhaps he had something for
infertility as well? Raghunath and Yamuna were childless. For the last
eleven years Yamuna had tried all possible methods — amulets, charms,
herbal medicines — roots included. But nothing worked. Now she had
given up, at least outwardly.

Satyadas was gobbling down his food, as if he were starving.
Raghunath sat looking at him; he didn't know how to come to the point
directly. Instead he said in a casual tone. 'Well, Satyadas how good are
these roots of yours for snake-bite? I have seen a few cases. The roots
are no good.'

Satyadas spoke as he continued to eat. 'To tell you the truth babu,
snake poisons are of different kinds. These herbal remedies can't do a
thing if the snake is really venomous, but they are good for the minor
ones.'

'You said something about rheumatic pain.'

'Yes I have something for that, not for old pain though. What I have
is good for recent attacks, like those which flare up during the rains.'

'My wife suffers from them — that is why I ask.'

Satyadas drank some water.

'What else do you have?'

'Cures for vertigo, contraceptives . . .'

'You are the great god Dhanwantri himself!' laughed Raghunath. 'So you have contraceptives. How about something for conception?'

Satyadas shook his head. 'None, babu.'

His meal over Satyadas had another drink of water. He belched contentedly. Then he went out and washed the utensils. The dish and the lota were put back in place.

'Want a bidi?'

'Wouldn't mind one.'

Raghunath gave him a bidi and a box of matches. 'Who waits for you at home?'

Lighting the bidi Satyadas said, 'Not a soul. I am a wanderer. God is with me.' He smiled to himself.

Raghunath eyed him. What a peculiar man. No attachment anywhere, a perfect vagabond.

The rain started again. It was growing dark too. Time to pull down the shutters. Time for Raghunath to go inside, change and sit for his puja. But where would Satyadas go? One couldn't possibly ask him to leave in the rain just because it was time to close the shop.

With his eyes half closed Satyadas seemed to be enjoying his smoke. He had had a long trudge. At the end of a long day the chira gur seemed to have satisfied his hunger. The smoke, after such a full meal, was making him sleepy.

Raghunath did not know what to do. He could neither drive him out nor keep him company till the rain stopped.

'Let me suggest something Satyadas. It is raining again. You can't leave. You better wait here. Let me go in, it's time for my evening puja. Let me get it over with.'

All at once Satyadas seemed to wake up. 'Oh no, no. I am keeping you from your puja. I'm sorry. Let me go . . .'

'Are you mad? Where would you go in this rain? Sit down. Leave after the rain stops. I'll be inside. Call out before you go.'

'But you will be doing your puja.'

'That hardly matters. I'll know.'

'Then let me pay you, babu.'

Raghunath felt a little ashamed of himself. Accept money from this penniless vagabond and for such a small thing? He seemed to be a simple man. Raghunath almost felt warm towards him. After all what did he possess? Some herbal roots. God knows if he had any business at all. No, he could not accept money from him. The poor man had strayed here in bad weather, had had some chira, worth not more than a rupee perhaps. Raghunath would not be poorer for the loss of a rupee.

'Forget it. You don't have to pay.'

Satyadas stared at him. 'No babu, I can't allow that.'

'Why?'

'I may be illiterate but you have read the Shastras. It is against dharma not to pay says the Shastra. Even the goddess Annapurna paid with gold . . .'

'Enough of your dharma!' Raghunath said but soon, smiling briefly, 'All right. You win. Give me fifty paisa.'

'That is not the right price, babu.'

'I'll follow my dharma. You keep yours.'

Satyadas fumbled in his pocket first. Then he thought of something and began untying the rope which held his box together.

'Pay me later. There is no hurry.'

'No babu, please.'

Satyadas untied the knot and opened the box, revealing a strange assortment of objects — small paper packets, glass bowls, a pair of tumblers, small black balls large as jamuns, a stick, some coloured handkerchiefs. At last he pulled out a pouch made of black cloth.

Raghunath stood watching this strange treasure box. When Satyadas opened the pouch something dropped from it. Satyadas didn't notice it. But Raghunath did. He was flabbergasted to find a gold coin in the bag of this poor peddler.

'Here you are babu.' Satyadas offered the money. 'You could have taken a rupee at least.'

Raghunath who was still in a daze, merely said, 'No, fifty paisa will do.'

He took the money, looked at the box and said in as casual a voice as possible, 'Quite a collection you have here!'

'Well, this happens to be my magic box as well.'

'Magic box?'

'I wander around babu, as I told you. I have to sit to sell my wares. In order to attract customers I show some tricks — card tricks, sleight of hand, some juggling; I change the colour of water. You have to do all sorts of things to earn a living.'

'So you are a magician too!' Raghunath laughed. 'You are a man of many talents, Satyadas.'

Satyadas looked embarrassed. 'Oh no sir, I am a poor man, a nobody, hardly worthy of your compliments.'

'If you say so. You stay right here. I'm going in. Do let me know before you go.'

Raghunath pulled the shutters down a little before going in.

The rain had stopped. When Raghunath came out after his evening puja he saw Satyadas huddled on the bench, a torn sheet thrown over him. The half-open sling bag from which the sheet had been taken out and the box lay on the ground. The man was shivering.

'Satyadas. . . do you hear me?'

Pushing the covering sheet off his ear, Satyadas said, 'Yes babu.'

'What is wrong?'

'Fever.'

'Malaria?'

'Remittent fever. I've been suffering with it for the last three years. It comes and goes. Don't you worry sir. I'll be all right soon. I'll leave as soon as the fever goes. Don't you worry.'

A little hurt, Raghunath said, 'Who is asking you to leave? It is the fever I'm worried about. You are shivering so.'

'It comes from all this walking in the rain, babu. But it'll go.'

'Let us hope so. You know what I think? Even if the fever goes, stay here tonight. You can sleep in the shop.'

'But that's impossible! A sick man in your house?'

'Do as I say. I'm going in now. I'll come back later.'

Raghunath pulled the shutter down a little more and moved the small lantern to one corner.

In the light of the lantern Raghunath sat in his room reciting the *Ramayana* while Yamuna stiched a kantha, an order from Ishani, the youngest daughter in-law of the Dutta family. She was very friendly with Yamuna. In fact Yamuna had built up quite a reputation for embroidery and often had to oblige people. But Yamunu was not in a mood to listen today.

There was a sound from the shop.

She said, 'He must be up.'

Raghunath looked at his wife but said nothing. He was not able to concentrate either.

'Why don't you go and take a look?'

'Okay. But you know I've asked him to stay on.'

'To stay on!'

'How could I ask him to go out in the rain and on such a dark night. Besides he is sick.' Raghunath stood up. 'The man is funny though. Earns his living by selling roots and things. Where did he get that gold from?'

'Could be brass for all you know.'

'No. It is gold'

'May be gold-plated.'

'Oh no. I can recognise gold. Don't forget my father used to work in a goldsmith's shop. I have seen plenty of gold. Quite a lot, in fact. Then I saw you and forgot all about gold. What do you say to that my little Yamuna?' He smiled affectionately.

'Fat lot of good this gold has done you. Did it bring you luck? From one room we have moved on to two. The same bad state of affairs. Yours is the luck of tin; not gold, not even brass.'

'It's my luck. You have nothing to do with it. Did not King Harish Chandra serve as a low caste . . . Anyway, forget that. What I can't understand is how that beggar came by the gold coin.'

'Perhaps he inherited it.'

'But he has nobody.'

'Ask him.'

'How can I? He would think me a mean crook. Took no time to spot the gold, he'd think.'

'I hope he is not a thief.'

'Oh come on. He seems to be a good man. Besides he is our guest. One should not speak ill of a guest.'

'All right. But why don't you go and see?'

Putting aside his *Ramayana* he went up to the shop to find Satyadas up, wiping the sweat from his forehead and neck. He smiled.

'The temperature is down, babu, this is what happens. It does not last for more than half a day.'

'Stay the night,' Raghunath said. He pointed to the shutter. 'Shall I close it fully? We'll have to shut the back door. Is that all right with you?'

Satyadas nodded. 'Perfect.'

But Raghunath knew it was far from perfect. The bench for one was not spacious enough to stretch one's legs.

Suddenly Satyadas blurted out. 'You are a very kind man, babu. Nobody allows a stranger to come in. You've given me shelter. The All-Seeing One does not miss anything. Isn't that right?'

Raghunath shrugged. 'He does too. That's why I'm in such a wretched state. I sold my land and set up shop here. With time everything grows, even desire. But in my case nothing has. I started with a single shed. In seven years it has grown to two — that's all. The All-Seeing One has seen nothing. He seems to have a stiff neck. If he is looking eastward he can't turn west.'

Satyadas watched his host with unblinking eyes. Then a strange smile lit his face.

'Why do you smile?'

'Forgive me babu. I am a stupid fool. I say whatever comes to mind.'

Unwilling to continue the conversation Raghunath said, 'You can have some chapati and vegetables if you feel like. We'll see what can be done in the morning.'

Satyadas nodded. He sat still, unmoving.

Next morning the sun came out through a curtain of mist. The sky was clear. Soon bright sunshine flooded the earth.

Back from the field Satyadas washed himself by the well. He made a polite namaste to Yamuna who was sweeping the yard and went in to tie his bundle and pack his box. He was about to leave when Raghunath stopped him. 'You can't leave on an empty stomach. Tea's coming.'

'That's a good idea, now that you say so. I'm rather addicted to tea.'

'Where do you go now?'

'Wherever my legs take me.'

Yamuna brought the tea. Satyadas put on his coat. 'Here, take this. Let me get a biscuit,' Raghunath said, handing him the cup, then fetching some home-made biscuits. 'They won't taste much.' Raghunath was apologetic. Kept in one of the plastic jars, they had lost their crispness in the humidity.

'It is a nice day, babu. The Sun God is up, the earth looks all spruced up.'

To Raghunath also the day seemed to bring good tidings. The crows were up and about, sparrows chirped, a dog was loitering by the bush in front of the shop.

Satyadas washed his cup and handed it back. 'I have got to go, babu.'

'So long then.'

'The mind is satisfied babu. I am a crazy beggar but you were kind enough to give me shelter and food. Nobody does it these days. May God bless you.'

'When will you pass this way?'

'Who can tell? Maybe in a week, maybe in a couple of months.'

'Don't forget to look me up if you do come this way.'

'Most certainly babu.' He lifted his hands in a namaste and was off.

Raghunath watched him go, box in one hand, bag slung on his shoulder, umbrella under his arm, the sun shining on his black coat.

Soon the day started off in right earnest. Bishu came. Raghunath lit his morning bidi and strode in and out the shop, shooting instructions.

Bishu knew his daily chores. He had to sweep the shop floor after which his master would sprinkle a little water, light the agarbatti, bow to the picture of Lakshmi with great devotion. He would then put some rice and turmeric on a plate and begin his daily transactions.

As Bishu swept the floor Raghunath stood outside listening to the siren of the colliery far away. Somewhere a crow cawed. Someone was sawing wood.

Suddenly Bishu called out. 'Look at this, babu.'

He picked up something from the floor which Raghunath instantly recognised. It was the dirty cloth pouch tied in a knot from which Satyadas had taken out the money.

It felt quite heavy. How could Satyadas forget the most precious thing? Why did he take it out of the box in the first place? How could he forget to put it back? How absentminded can one get? That man did not carry much money with him; he'd be in trouble. He'd have to come back.

Raghunath paused. He had seen a gold coin fall from this pouch. Satyadas must've discovered it. It must now be in the box. Unless . . .

Reluctantly he started loosening the knot. Then, all of a sudden he felt difficulty in breathing. Was it a dream or was he going mad? He opened the pouch further and dipped his hand in gingerly. Of course it was gold. Gold coins. He glanced at Bishu. But the boy was busy. Raghunath picked up a gold coin, fear and conflict tearing him apart. He could not be making a mistake in the clear light of the morning. And he *was* the son of a goldsmith. He knew. They were gold coins all right, fairly old — perhaps of the Queen's time.

He turned around and went in.

'Yamuna? Can you come here a minute?'

Yamuna was by the well, hanging out the washing. In this prolonged wet spell the clothes had piled up. Like everything else in the house they were damp. Yamuna was taking her time enjoying the sunshine and didn't immediately answer her husband's urgent summons. When she did come in, Raghunath was still standing staring into his palm.

'What is it?'

Raghunath held out his hand. 'Gold. Left behind by that man.'

'Gold?' Yamuna froze. She then crept closer to have a better look at the coins and two gold rings held out by her husband. Yamuna had never seen a gold coin before. Brought up at her uncle's house where her mother had gone to live after she was widowed, Yamuna had always been poor. 'Let me have a look.'

Raghunath gave her one. 'I don't understand. This is very strange. How could he leave the pouch behind? How could he possess gold coins?'

Yamuna turned the coin in her hand. She may not have seen one but she knew gold when she saw it. 'Are you sure these are genuine?'

'Of course I'm sure. I am the son of a goldsmith.'

'Why would anyone leave them?'

'Unless he's mad — and six of them!'

'Six?'

'Six gold coins and two rings.'

Yamuna stared at her husband. Her gaze shifted to his hand.

'Will you close the door? Bishu may come any minute.'

Raghunath moved away from the window. Although it was open ground beyond he thought it safer to avoid the open window.

'These are old coins, embossed with the Queen's head. I just don't understand. How could he leave them? By mistake? And a destitute like him who makes a living selling roots and things. How did he get six gold coins?'

'What are the stones in the rings?'

'I don't know about stones. They look like precious stones.'

'Diamond?'

Raghunath picked up one ring and turned it around. 'Could be.' He examined it against the light.

'Diamond or glass?'

'It is not glass.'

'The other one?'

Raghunath showed her the other ring which had a dark stone. 'I don't know . . . could be sapphire.'

'Sapphire?'

'No idea.' Raghunath gave her the two rings. She had never seen any real stones except coral and pearl. Ishani had two small pearls in her earrings.

Raghunath put everything back in the pouch. 'What kind of a man is this Satyadas? He certainly didn't look as if he could own these things. In fact he did not even have five rupees on him — how does one explain six gold coins and two rings.'

'There is no other money in the pouch?'

'Nothing.'

'You said last night that a gold coin dropped from his pouch when he was paying you.'

Raghunath nodded.

'Then how is it that today there is nothing but gold coins.'

That was puzzling. It was a mystery, a great mystery. Somehow he felt foolish. 'Perhaps this is a secret pouch he used to keep hidden.'

'And he left *that* secret pouch behind? Not very likely.'

'That's right. But . . .'

'Perhaps he stole it. Then lost his nerve and fled.'

Satyadas did not look like a thief. He looked more like a salesman of cheap amulets. One who had to show tricks to attract customers.

'Satyadas is a magician you know, he told me so.'

'So that is what it is. His bag of tricks. Imitation gold and diamond.'

But Raghunath was not convinced the gold was fake. He was not sure about the stones though. 'I don't know.'

'What are you going to do now?'

'Let me see. He will come back surely. He will remember. After all it's not a couple of rupees. He'll come.'

'Did he say he'd come back?'

'Not in that many words. When I asked him he said he'd look us up when he next passed this way. But it may be a week, a month, or four months.'

Bishu was calling them. Yamuna said, 'So what do we do now?'

'Put it in your trunk. Don't tell a soul. But be careful. The times are not good.'

'The key is under the bed. Why don't you put it in the trunk yourself.'

But Satyadas did not return the next day or the day after. A week passed. Raghunath expected him every minute of the day, even in the dead of night. While weighing out the groceries to his customers he never took his eyes off the road, expecting him to appear through the jarul trees and dhudul shrubs — bag slung over shoulder, box in one hand, legs covered with dust.

Weeks passed into months. The winter breeze shook the leaves off the trees and turned the grass brown. Came the colder month of Magh. Eventually Phalgun came. Raghunath was losing his patience. How thoughtless could a person be — leaving his wealth like that and forgetting about it completely.

Was he dead then? Had he been arrested? It is so difficult to judge a man from his outward appearance. Perhaps he was a deep one. Leaving behind the gold coins was part of a plan. The coins were perhaps stolen. But somehow Satyadas did not look like a crook.

He grew irritated. After all how long could one go on brooding on Satyadas. 'Do you think he is dead?' He asked his wife.

'Possibly. Anyone can die . . . but, he's not coming back, that's for sure.'

Raghunath waited through the months of Phalgun and Chaitra. He had a faint hope that perhaps Satyadas might come to attend the Vaishakhi fair which drew all sorts of people. But Vaishakhi came and went with no sign of that man.

One afternoon he was reciting his *Ramayana* when his wife interrupted him. 'Are you asleep?'

'No. Why?'

'You've been repeating the same lines.'

Raghunath looked at the open page. 'I don't seem to remember anything.'

'That's what's wrong with you. You are so distracted these days. What are you worried about?'

Raghunath said after a pause. 'It is that blessed Satyadas. He's driving me crazy. Can't even concentrate on my *Ramayana*.'

'Don't think of him — how many times do I have to tell you that.'

'But the gold coins — the stones.'

'I think they are fake. You may insist but I have my doubts. Would he leave them if they were real? You are making a mistake.'

'Mmm. I don't think so.'

'Have them evaluated, then. But I still say that man is not coming back.'

Before the month of Jaishtha was over Raghunath made up his mind. He might be wrong. The last time he saw genuine gold was in his father's time. There was also the possibility that these were unreal products of magic. He hoped so. Then his worry would be over. Let me go to town, he told his wife. I'll go to Chandu babu's shop. He is a good soul. I'll take just one coin to avoid suspicion.

He went to town that afternoon and came back late.

'I told you. It's real gold. No fake.'

Yamuna was too overwhelmed to speak.

The monsoons came around again. No Satyadas. Obviously he was not coming back. So what was the use of waiting! At long last Raghunath could renovate his shop. Now he was in a position to expand his trade. The house too was in bad shape. He went to town and sold one coin. Gold fetched an excellent price these days. With the money he bought a sari for Yamuna and some household items.

That night they had a long discussion about what should be taken up first — the house or the shop. They decided to begin with the shop, to buy more provisions. So that people would know Raghunath's grocery shop was well stocked. Things should be displayed better. As for the house, they'd just change the tin sheet which served as the kitchen roof and the bathroom divider.

As expected the money did not last long. His wife suggested they sell another coin.

'But I can't go to Chandu babu again. I lied to him. How can poor people like us fish out one gold coin after another. He might get ideas.'

'What are you going to do?'

'You know what? I know the going rate now. Nobody can cheat me. I better go to Burdwan. I'll take the morning train and be back by evening.'

He came back looking cheerful. 'I got thirty more. The price of gold keeps going up.'

Before the Pujas he spent three of the coins. He was enjoying himself. His shop had a new look. He changed his old tar-coated shutter, the wretched looking platform, the rickety bench. Now he had proper tin chairs, better shutters, better stock. His home wore a new look too. People looked in wonder at Raghunath the grocer. He explained that the money had come from an uncle of Yamuna's who died recently leaving everything to his niece.

Gadai Kundu, Neelu Ghati, Prasad and others were a little envious perhaps of his new found prosperity.

Yamuna said, 'I don't want that broken fence. Haru will make a new one. I have to save the saplings.'

And so it came to be. Raghunath still recited the *Ramayana* every day. He quoted lines which described women as great seductresses, always out to mislead men. Yamuna took exception to that. But Raghunath merely laughed. For the first time Raghunath was enjoying his *Ramayana*.

'Look,' he told her one day. 'I'll be going to Calcutta to buy a real big lamp, a petromax.'

'But why Calcutta?'

'I'll look around. Some of Haladhar babu's goods are supplied from Calcutta. I'll stock the same if I can.'

'Where is the money?'

'We have some left.'

'And finish it all?'

'Once we have started let us go all the way. Remember how people used to look down on me . . . Look at them now. Haladhar babu's eldest son Sasadhar came the other day to invite me to their Puja. You must come, he said. Father has asked you. This is the only festival we celebrate at home. We have been doing it for the last fifty years.'

Yamuna understood. So they were on equal footing now. 'You are right,' she said. 'Water stored in a pitcher will dry up sooner or later. Go to Calcutta. It was a gift out of the blue. No harm in spending it all. At least we are having a good life.'

She was right. Raghunath at last forgot about the owner of the coins. He had waited long enough. Satyadas had not come. Raghunath was no thief. He had not stolen the pouch. If it came his way it was his luck — he could not blame himself for that.

His dreams were coming true one by one. Whatever was in the pouch was now his. Satyadas was dead.

The Puja was over. The month of Agrahayan drew to a close. The shop was in real good shape now. There was one more boy working there. Business was brisk throughout the day. The petromax gave a steady light in the evening. Friends dropped in for a chat — Phatik Chand, Kartik Ray, Mathur. They sat and gossiped: the new jatra play, the accident in the Natuhat colliery, the marriage negotiations of Kartik's daughter.

Yamuna had most of the things she had always wanted. The rooms were repaired, the verandah was covered, her kitchen and store sparkled. She had a proper bathroom too. Moreover they could afford a domestic help.

Raghunath was a happy man.

Winter seemed to come early that year. It was only the beginning of Poush. A generous monsoon was bound to bring a severe winter in its wake.

That day Phatik and party had left. The shop boys too were gone. Raghunath had just put out the light in his shop. There was only a lantern burning there now. He was about to pull down the shutters when somebody stepped in.

'Who is it?' he asked.

'Babu, it's me.'

The voice startled him. He waited till the man came up to him and he could see him properly.

'Satyadas?'

'Right babu. Namaskar.'

He had the same weather-weary look, an untidy growth of beard, the same sling bag and wooden box, the same umbrella, the same black coat. The only extra possession was a muffler of some coarse material.

Satyadas put his bag and box down.

'How have you been babu?'

Raghunath felt as though somebody was slipping a noose around his neck. He could hardly speak. He merely stared. Was it really Satyadas or an illusion?

'I was passing this way. I had promised to look you up.'

With great effort Raghunath found his voice. 'Where are you from this time?'

'I have no definite route, babu. I move around.'

'From where are you coming now?'

'Hridyapur . . . How are you? and my dear Ma Janani?'

Raghunath nodded.

Satyadas was gazing at the shop. He seemed amused. 'I had come last year in pouring rain.'

Raghunath stared at him. Why was he here? What business did he have to come back from the dead?

Satyadas coughed a couple of times, then cleared his throat. 'Got a sore throat. The chill. Can I have some tea? I still remember that tea Ma Janani gave me last time.'

Raghunath raised the wick of the lantern. 'Have a seat.'

In their room Yamuna was attending to her chafed feet, massaging in a mixture of cream and coconut oil. Seeing Raghunath, she put her legs down. In her handloom sari, coloured blouse, freshly-done hair she looked quite nice these days. Even her complexion had improved.

'He is here.'

'Who?'

'Satyadas.'

'Satyadas? Here?'

'Yes. Walked in just now.'

She stood up, staring at her husband. 'What made him come all of a sudden? He is alive?'

'So it seems.'

'Did he ask for anything?'

'Not yet. He just came in. Wants some tea. Has a cold, a sore throat.' Raghunath made a feeble attempt to smile. 'Says he has not forgotten the tea made by his Ma Janani.'

Yamuna grimaced. 'Ma Janani indeed. Now what do we do with him?'

'Let me see. Give him some tea first. Let him talk.'

'Don't tell him anything. Will he stay the night or clear out?'

Raghunath shook his head. 'Where can he go on such a night. He intends to spend the night here. Perhaps he'll leave tomorrow.'

'Be careful you don't say anything. If he asks, deny everything.'

She went in to make tea.

Satyadas sipped his tea with relish stopping only to cough once in a while. Raghunath sat a couple of feet away. Satyadas began, 'The heart has become a weak cage babu, it gets affected easily.'

'How about that fit of fever?'

'It persists. Won't leave me.'

'And your herbals?'

'Same as before. Went all the way to Panchkot you know, for some special roots. But do you ever get what you want? There is one particular kind I'd wanted. It helps mothers during child-birth — an old cure. I managed to get one, about this size.' He pointed to his little finger.

Raghunath looked distracted. 'So you spent the whole year roaming?'

'That is my fate. I am the horse of the Ashwamedh, babu. Who can escape his destiny? Can I have a bidi please?'

Raghunath gave him a cheap cigarette.

'But you have a cough — should you smoke?'

'Just a few puffs,' Satyadas examined the cigarette, 'then I'll have a wash. I'll spend the night here. I had a very comfortable stay last time.

You are so kind and Ma Janani is the image of Lakshmi herself.'

Satyadas's presence filled Raghunath with fear and irritation. With great effort he said in as normal a voice as he could, 'Since you have come to stay the night, you must. But you have to excuse me, I have to say my prayers . . .'

'Yes of course babu.'

'Go in and wash. Let me get on with my work.'

But Raghunath was in no mood to say his prayers. The *Ramayana* remained unopened. He sat on the bed, smoking, while Yamuna stood close.

'You must keep your mouth shut. Don't fall into a trap,' Yamuna advised him. 'It is not your fault. It isn't as though you snatched it from him. If people leave things about it is not your responsibility, is it?'

'Well, I did wait. Month after month. What can I do if he doesn't turn up? After all I am made of flesh and blood too. How long could I let that gold rot there? Tell me.'

Yamuna agreed. If Satyadas had left something behind then that was his fault. He did not come back to recover it, neither did he leave any address or name of a relation. Such a vagabond. It was no fault of her husband's. Lost property belongs to the one who finds it.

Raghunath shook his head. 'No, I am not saying anything.'

'I wish he had died. Why did he appear again?'

'It is all our bad luck.'

'I wish I could poison him. The devil. Why did he come now? He could have come earlier. The scoundrel. The crook!'

Satyadas was all alone in the shop. 'Get him something to eat quickly. I don't want to go and talk to him,' he said. 'Let him leave first thing in the morning.'

His meal over, Satyadas was getting ready to sleep when Raghunath went in again. 'Your shop looks real nice,' Satyadas said by way of conversation.

Stung to the quick Raghunath looked at him. But he was busy rummaging in his bag for a sheet, his face hidden from view.

'You have a lot of stuff here like any other big store. Very nice. I like it babu.'

Raghunath mumbled some feeble excuse. He was afraid the question of finance would come up next.

But Satyadas only said, 'Your house has been done up nicely. You have done the right thing babu. Ma Janani won't have to suffer now. She has such grace. If she is happy, everything'll be fine. I am a poor illiterate man babu but, if I may say so, look at Ramchandra. Never had a moment's peace because of Sita's bad luck.'

Raghunath felt the ground slipping from under his feet. He did not dare to stand before that man. He was uncomfortable, scared.

'Have to go. Had a hard day at the shop.' He yawned. 'Got to go and eat. I feel so sleepy.'

'I am sorry babu, I should have realised. Please go ahead.'

'Are you sure you have everything here?'

'Of course. Nice place, very comfortable.'

'Good night then. Are you . . .'

'Yes early morning tomorrow. There's a place I want to reach tomorrow. But I sleep like a log. Would you please wake me up?'

'Yes, definitely.'

Yamuna switched off the light and came to bed. 'You mean to say he never mentioned it?'

'No.' Raghunath was staring in the dark.

'That's strange.'

Raghunath did not reply.

'Then it does not belong to him.'

'Whose is it then?' Raghunath sounded irritated.

Yamuna had no answer. Then, 'You know what? He must be thinking he has lost them. If he knew he had left them here he would have asked, at least once. Good for us, don't you think? He doesn't suspect us, thank God,' she said.

After a pause her husband said, 'But he's seen everything.'

'Let him. Seeing is not everything.'

He said nothing.

It was getting late and the nights were turning colder. Yamuna had dozed off. But Raghunath could not sleep.

It was Raghunath who woke him up early. Satyadas packed, washed and was ready to start. Raghunath said, 'There is a mist outside. The sun hasn't come up yet. Why don't you wait for a cup of tea. It must be ready.'

'Oh no babu, I can't. Give my regards to Ma Janani.' He wrapped the muffler about his head in such a way that much of his face was not visible. 'Let me go, babu,' he said, his hands coming together in a namaskar.

Raghunath followed him outside. The morning mist spread over the fields. The grass was wet. Satyadas paused, then, stepped forth briskly before Raghunath called out to him urgently.

'Satyadas!'

With great effort Raghunath blurted out, 'Did you leave anything here? The last time you came?'

Smiling a strange smile Satyadas asked, 'Why, babu?'

'Did you?'

Satyadas looked up at the sky. 'Only he can tell.'

'He? You mean God?'

'The sun. He brings the day with him. When he sets it is dark all around. Then comes night. Night and day — light and darkness — their union has been going on since eternity — that is what the Shastras say. One is bright with light, the other is black with darkness. They too have eyes, you know!'

Raghunath gave a start as he thought of the two rings — one white the other dark. Both were valuable. He had sold them. Terror seized him. He was going to say, You also left six gold coins behind.

As if reading his mind, Satyadas, wiping the dew from his face began, 'You know babu, day and night constantly meet in an eternal union. And six seasons keep dancing around our earth. There is hardly anything which escapes their notice — greed, sin, vice, everything. They watch over everything, only we are oblivious of them. They notice all our lapses and misdeeds . . . But I am a poor illiterate man. It does not behove me to talk of morals,' he said with a namaste. 'But I sympathise with you. I understand. Good bye.' And Satyadas of Dharmapur disappeared into the mist.

Raghunath stood as if turned to stone, his eyes slowly filling with tears.

OUR CONTRIBUTORS

ANJANA DESAI is a scholar and critic, her area of specialisation being Shakespeare and 17th century literature. She has a Ph.D from Cornell University, U.S.A., and teaches English at the University of South Gujarat, Surat. She enjoys translating fiction from and into Gujarati and English.

ARVIND DIXIT has written several short stories and plays in Marathi, and a novel, *Odh,* which won the Yashwantrao Chavan Sahitya Puraskar, instituted by the Marathi Sahitya Sanskriti Mandal. His other interests include producing plays in Marathi for the Delhi stage, reviewing Marathi theatre for *The Hindustan Times,* and running marathons. He presently serves as a Senior Technical Officer in the Plant Molecular Biology Department of the University of Delhi.

M. ASADUDDIN teaches English at the Jamia Millia Islamia University, New Delhi. He translates frequently from and to Bangla, Urdu, Hindi and English.

ASHA BAGE is an established writer in Marathi with three short story collections and two novels to her credit, *Marwa* and *Attar* being two of her important collections of stories and *Jhumbar* a novel that came in for critical acclaim. Three of these five books have won awards from the State of Maharastra. Many of her stories have been translated into English and the other major Indian languages. She lives in Nagpur and is a connoisseur of classical Indian music.

ASHA DAMLE has published two collections of short stories. Her first major foray into translation was S.J. Joshi's fictionalised story of Dr Anandibai Joshi (the first woman to receive a medical degree from an American University in the 19th century). She has translated extensively from Marathi, including Dalit literature. She lives in Bombay.

ATULANANDA GOSWAMI is a writer with four collections of short stories to his credit. His novel *Namgharia* won the Assam Sahitya Sabha

Award and has been serialised both by Doordarshan and by All India Radio. He has translated extensively from English, Oriya and Bengali into Assamese; and from Assamese into English. He has been closely associated with the Kamarupa Anusandhana Samiti, the oldest research institute of the North-east, and is now its Secretary. He serves as Senior Superintendent of Taxes with the Government of Assam and lives in Guwahati, Assam.

BHUPEN KHAKHAR is known primarily as a painter. He has participated in various exhibitions, the most recent being the Documenta Exhibition held at Kassel in June 1992. Howard Hodgkin showed his work at Tate Gallery, London, in 1982 and an English team has just completed a film on his life and work. Known for tackling controversial themes, his *Maujila Manilal* has become a classic of modern Gujarati drama. He is an occasional writer of fiction in Gujarati. He works part-time as a chartered accountant in Baroda, Gujarat.

BIMAL KAR is acknowledged as a leading Bangla writer. A journalist by profession, he retired from *Desh Weekly* as Associate Editor in 1982 and presently edits a short story magazine from Calcutta. Among his many honours are the Sahitya Akademi Award, and an award from the Calcutta University. 'Satyadas' was one of the five allegorical stories recently published in book form as *Upakhyanamala*, and received the Ananda Puroshkar in 1992.

DHRUVA SHUKLA is a poet and novelist who writes for children and adults. His works include two novels, *Usi Shahar Mein* (1988) and *Amar Talkies,* (1991); a collection of poems, *Khojo To Beti Papa Kahan Hain,* (1989); and a collection of short stories entitled *Hichkee,* (1990). He was the assitant editor of *Poorvagraha,* the literary journal in Hindi, brought out by Bharat Bhavan, Bhopal. He lives in Bhopal, Madhya Pradesh.

ENAKSHI CHATTERJEE is a writer, translator and media critic. She has translated a wide range of Bangla novels and has written over 30 books on science and science fiction for adults and children. *Paramanu Jignasa,* a book on atomic science, written jointly with her husband, won her the 1983 Rabindra Puroshkar from the Government of West

Bengal. She is actively associated with All India Radio and Doordarshan as script-writer, performer and as a member of various advisory committees. She lives in Calcutta.

GANESH N DEVY is Professor of English at the Maharaja Sayajirao University at Baroda. He translates from Marathi and Gujarati into English and was editor of a journal of translation in Gujarati and English called SETU. He's currently Visiting Professor at Yale University, U.S.A.

GEETA DHARMARAJAN is a writer for children and adults. Her books have been published by Rupa & Co., National Book Trust and Affiliated East-West Press, Ltd; five have been translated into Bangla. A Children's Book Trust (CBT) prize-winning book and a collection of stories by Indian women, edited by her, are slated for publication Winter, 1992. She edits a health and activity magazine for children called *Tamasha!* and is the executive director of Katha.

GILLIAN WRIGHT studied Urdu, Hindi, Politics and History at London University. She has translated Shrilal Shukla's classic novel, *Raag Darbari*, (Penguin, 1992) and is currently working on a translation of the late Rahi Masoom Reza's *Adha Gaon*. Among her travel writings is *An Introduction to the Hill Stations of India*. She has also worked with the BBC's Mark Tully on his three books on India. She lives in Delhi.

GOPI CHAND NARANG is a respected scholar, linguist and critic. He has published more than 30 books in Urdu, Hindi and English. He is a Professor of Urdu at the University of Delhi. He received the Padma Shri in 1990. He has also received the President of Pakistan's Special Gold Medal (1978), the Ghalib Award (1985), the Khusrau Award (1987), and the Delhi Urdu Academy Award (1991) among other honours.

GOPINATH MOHANTY was a distinguished Oriya novelist and short story writer with more than twenty-two novels, eight short story collections, three plays, two books on tribal culture and seven works of translation to his credit. He received the Sahitya Akademi Award for his novel, *Amruta Santana,* in 1955, and the Jnanpith Award in 1977. In 1981 he was awarded the Padma Bhushan. He spent the major part of his professional life as an administrator when he undertook extensive research into the life and culture of the tribals of Orissa. He has served as Adjunct Professor of Anthropology at the San Jose State University, California, U.S.A. He died in 1992.

JAYAMOHAN published his first story and his first poem in 1978 when he was 16 years old. His first novel, *Rubber* won the Akilon Memorial Prize for 1990. *Tarkala Malayala Kavidaigal,* a collection of poems edited by him was published in 1991. He lives and works in Dharmapuri, Tamil Nadu.

D KRISHNA AYYAR was a government servant and retired as Chairman, State Public Service Commission, Manipur. He lives in Madras and has an all abiding interest in books, ranging from fiction to science and politics to religion and philosophy.

N S MADHAVAN started his career as a short story writer with 'Sishu,' a story which won the first prize in a competition held in 1971 by the literary journal, *Mathrubhumi*. In the next two years he published ten stories which were later brought out as *Choolaimethile Savangal,* in 1981. After a silence of more than a decade, he published 'Higuita' (1990), which has been chosen in a literary survey conducted by *Malayala Manorama* as one of the ten best stories written in Malayalam in the last century. He presently lives and works in Gaya, Bihar.

MANJU KAK is a freelance journalist and writer living in Delhi. Amongst other things, she has worked several years as a teacher and broadcaster. She also designs and paints and is interested in film-production.

MILIND BOKIL is a sociologist with a Ph.D in social anthropology. He has done several socio-economic studies of development projects and voluntary agencies. An activist, he has worked in tribal and economically backward areas. The first collection of his short stories is slated for release this year. Born in 1960, he is presently with an organization in Pune which provides support to nongovernmental organizations.

MOHAN PARMAR writes in Gujarati. His latest collection of short fiction is *Naklank,* (1991) while *Neliyu,* (1992), is his latest novel. He is presently doing his Ph.D in Gujarati Sahitya on the renowned writer, Suresh Joshi. He lives in Ahmedabad, Gujarat.

D R NAGARAJ is a noted writer and critic who teaches at the Centre for Kannada Studies, Bangalore University. He has published two books of critical essays (1983 and 1987) and has co-edited a book of Urdu literature (1991). He received the Vardhamana Award for Literature in 1988 for his *Amrutha Mattu Garuda.* His other interests are rural development work and people's movements. He is presently putting together a collection of modern Kannada plays for Katha.

NIRMAL VERMA is the acclaimed author of four novels, five collections of short stories and numerous essays and travelogues. One of the leading writers of the Nai Kahani Movement of the 1950s, he received the Sahitya Academi Award in 1986 for his collection of short stories. The film *Maya Darpan* was based on one of his stories. Readers International, London, and Penguin India have published collections of his stories in English translation.

NISSIM EZEKIEL is well-known as a poet. He has written plays, edited literary texts and published several hundred book reviews. His *Collected Poems, 1952 - 1988* was published by the Oxford University Press in 1989. He received the Sahitya Academi Award in 1983 for his *Latter-Day Psalms,* and the Padma Shri in 1988. He is editor of the quarterly journal, The Indian PEN and lives in Bombay.

PADMA SHARMA is a teacher by profession. She has worked in Ethiopia, England, Zambia and Malawi and now lives and teaches in Bangalore. She translates regularly from Kannada into English. Her translation of K.P. Purnachandra Tejaswi's classic, *Carvallo,* was published in 1990, and her co-translation of Masti Venkatesha Iyengar's Jnanpith Award winning novel *Chikaveera Rajendra,* in 1992, both by Penguin India.

PANKAJ THAKUR writes in Assamese and is known mainly as a satirist. His collection of short stories, *Apuni Kiba Koboneki* has been translated into Hindi. He has edited works on developmental studies and has translated Ibsen, Strindberg, Sartre and Wole Soyinka from English to Assamese. He is presently editing a collection of Assamese short stories in English translation. Editor of *Ajir Asom,* a popular monthly, he also serves as honorary editor of *Paryatak,* a magazine on culture and tourism. He lives in Guwahati.

RAJI SUBRAMANIAM is a freelance journalist. Her articles have appeared in *Malayala Manorama.*

RAMACHANDRA SHARMA is regarded as one of the pioneers of the Navya School of writing which breathed freshness into Kannada poetry and fiction. An established poet, he has published some 25 books in Kannada — poetry, short stories, plays and criticism, including *One Hundred English Poems of This Century* in Kannada. Many of his poems and stories have been translated into several languages. He has co-translated Masti's novel *Chikaveera Rajendra,* (Penguin India, 1992) and is presently engaged in translating a collection of stories by Masti for Katha. With a Ph.D in psychology from the University of London, he has served as an educational psychology expert for the UNESCO. He lives in Bangalore, Karnataka.

RANI SARMA has an M.Phil in Ancient Indian History from Osmania University, Hyderabad and teaches in Springdales School, New Delhi. Her interests include carnatic music, interior decoration and gardening.

RENTALA NAGESWARA RAO has written 10 books, both fiction and nonfiction (popular science), many of which have received awards from leading Telegu magazines. 'Tiladaanamu' won the second prize in the Ugadi Short Story Competition conducted by *The Andhra Prabha Illustrated Weekly.* A post-graduate in psychology and para-psychology from Andhra University, he serves as a non-medical assistant in the National Leprosy Eradication Programme at Piduguralla, in Guntur District, Andhra Pradesh.

RUKUN ADVANI has written seven stories till now, three of which were included in *First Fiction*, published by Faber and Faber in 1992. He has a Ph. D on E.M. Forster from Cambridge University, U.K. and presently works in the editorial department of the Oxford University Press, New Delhi.

S K SHANTI describes herself as an avid reader of both English and Tamil. This is her first attempt at translation.

SACHIDANANDA MOHANTY teaches in the Department of English, University of Hyderabad. He was a British Council scholar (1990), and a Fulbright post-doctoral fellow (1990 - 91). His book on D.H. Lawrence was published recently and a second one is forthcoming. His essays have appeared in some of the leading journals in India and abroad. He is currently involved in a Sahitya Academi project of translating medieval Oriya literature into English.

SARAT KUMAR MUKHOPADHYAY is a major poet, critic and fiction writer. A chartered accountant by profession, he gave it up in 1983 to become a full time writer. He acts as a counsellor in the Creative Writing Programme of the Indira Gandhi National Open University in Calcutta where he lives. His latest publications are, a collection of poetry, *Shrestha Kavita* (1985), a collection of short stories, *Shreshtha Galpa* (1991) and a travelogue on Europe (1992). He lives in Calcutta.

SHAMPA BANERJEE is an editor by profession who started her career with Oxford University Press, Delhi. She has worked with Seagull Books, Calcutta, for whom she produced a number of post-production scripts of films by well-known Indian filmmakers such as Satyajit Ray, Adoor Gopalakrishnan and Ketan Mehta. A Delhi-based freelance editor for many years now, she has written and produced publications on development issues for UNICEF and DANIDA. Her two special interests are designing publications and translating from the Bengali language.

SHYAMAL GANGOPADHYAY is a respected Bangla writer and editor. His latest work is a two-volume historical novel, *Shahzada Darashuko*. His interest in history stems from his experiences which include the

Partition, the Famine and the War. In a career spanning more than forty years, he has worked with an open hearth furnace for three years, organised and run a co-operative farm for landless labourers, and been on the editorial staff of *Jugantar* and *Anand Bazaar Partika*. He has also served as editc. of the Bangla literary weekly, *Amrita*. Among the many honours for writing he has received are the Bibhutibhusan Award (1992) and the Siromani Award (1992). He lives in Calcutta and is deeply interested in vintage motor cars and classical Indian music.

SUBRABHARATIMANIAN was born in 1956 in Coimbatore District, Tamilnadu and lives in Secunderabad, Andhra Pradesh. He has published three collections of short stories, *Maruthadam, Naveenam* and *Appa;* and *Naluperu* consisting of a novella and 15 stories.

SUDHAKAR MARATHE teaches in the Department of English at the University of Hyderabad. He has been a British Council scholar. He has written extensively on poetry and fiction, including a book, *T.S. Eliot's Shakespeare*. He is the editor of *Narrative: Forms and Transformations*. He has been translating poetry, fiction and critical works from Marathi to English for the past 12 years and is currently engaged in translating poems from mediaval Marathi for the Sahitya Akademi and in editing a collection of stories by Vyankatesh Madgulkar for Katha. His other interests are environmental conservation and theatre.

SUJATHA DEVI teaches English and writes poetry and articles in Malayalam. She is a commited environmentalist.

SUNDARA RAMASWAMY is a doyen amongst writers in Tamil. He is best known for his novel, *Oru Puliamarathin Kathai*. He is also a poet and has received many literary awards. He lives in Nagercoil, Tamilnadu and edits a small literary journal called *Kaalachuvadu*.

VAIDEHI is the pen-name of Janaki Srinivasa Murthy. She is the author of four collections of short stories, one novel, a collection of poems. Her latest collection of stories was *Samaja Shastragneya Tippanige,* brought out in 1992 by Akshara prakashana, Sagara. A collection of her plays for children is slated for release this year. Many of her stories have been translated into English, Hindi, Malayalam, Marathi, Tamil and Telugu. She lives in Udipi, Karnataka.

VAKATI PANDURANGA RAO is an information professional with multimedia experience. He is the author of about 25 books, four of which are collections of short stories. His stories have been translated into many languages, including Russian. At home in Tamil, Telugu, Hindi and English, he has translated widely from and into these languages and has edited books for the National Book Trust and the Sahitya Akademi. He is presently Deputy Editor of the *Andhra Prabha Illustrated Weekly,* and lives in Hyderabad, Andhra Pradesh.

VIJAYA RAJADHYAKSHA is an eminent writer and critic in Marathi. She has published 15 collections of stories, the latest being *Anamik, (1990),* and a collection of her best stories, *Vijaya Rajadhyaksha Yancha Nivadak Katha* (1990). Many of her stories have been translated widely and have been adapted for the stage and television. As a critic, her special areas are modern poetry and the contemporary short story. Her two-volume work on the poetry of B.S.Mardhekar won her the prestigious Kothavale Award as the Best Book for 1991. She is currently Head of the Post-Graduate Department of Marathi at the SNDT Women's University in Bombay.

M VIJAYALAKSHMI serves as Librarian at the Sahitya Akademi, Delhi. She has translated poems from Tamil for *Indian Literature,* and the journal of the Authors' Guild of India, *Indian Author.* She is presently engaged in translating and editing a collection of stories by Na. Muthuswamy for Katha.

VIVEK SHANBHAG is an engineer by profession and works for Brooke Bond. He has published 2 collections of short stories, the latest of which is *Languru,* published in 1992 by Akshara Prakashana, Sagara. He lives in Bangalore.

M T VASUDEVAN NAIR is acknowledged as one of the outstanding living writers of India. His publications include 17 volumes of short stories, eight novels, a play, and nine other books which consist of critical writings, stories for children and travelogues. He has received all the prestigious awards for fiction in Malayalam, among them, the Kerala Sahitya Academy Award in 1959 for his novel, *Nalukettu*, in 1978 for his play *Gopuranadayil*, and again in 1981 for his short story collection, *Swargam Thurakkunna Samayam*. He won the Central Sahitya Akademi Award in 1970 for *Kaalam*, and the President's Gold Medal in 1973 for the film *Nirmalyam*, written, produced and directed by him. He joined the Malayalam journal, *Mathrubhoomi* in 1956, and is presently its editor. He lives in Calicut.

ZAMIRUDDIN AHMAD is considered a front-ranking short story writer in Urdu, though his published corpus consists of just two slender collections, *Pahli Maut*, and *Sookhe Sawan;* the latter was published posthumously from Karachi in 1992. His other published works include critical essays, plays and TV serials. A journalist by profession, he migrated from India to Pakistan in 1947 and then to England in 1971. He has served as broadcaster for the BBC, the Voice of America, Radio Pakistan and Pakistan Television. He died in 1990.

A SELECT LIST OF REGIONAL MAGAZINES

ASSAMESE

Ajir Ahom Prantik, Silpukhuri, Guwahati 780003
Ajir Asom, G.S. Road, Guwahati 780005
Assam Bani (Special Issue), Tribune Building, Guwahati.
Dainik Asam, (Puja Special), Gopinath Nagar, Guwahati 780016
Prakash, (Special Issue), Publication Board of Assam, Guwahati.
Prantik, Navagiri Road, Silpukhuri, Guwahati 781003
Pratiwandi, Gopinath Nagar, Guwahati 780016
Sadin, Sarania Road, Guwahati 780003
Sutradhar, Manjeera House, Motilal Nehru Road, Guwahati 780001

BANGLA

Aaj Kaal, 96 Raja Rammohan Sarani, Calcutta 700009
Ananda Bazar Patrika, 6 Prafulla Sarkar Street,
  Calcutta 700001
Bartaman, 76A, Acharya J.C.Bose Road, Calcutta 700014
Bibhab, 6 Circus Market Place, Calcutta 700017
Desh (Weekly) , Prafulla Sarkar Street, Calcutta 700001
Ekshan, 73, Mahatma Gandhi Road, Calcutta 700009
Jugantar, 41A, Acharya J.C.Bose Road, Calcutta 700017
Khela (Puja Supplement), 96 Raja Rammohan Sarani,
  Calcutta 700009
Parichay, 89, Mahatma Gandhi Road, Calcutta 700009
Pratikshana, 7 Jawahar Lal Nehru Road, Calcutta 100013
Proma, 57/2E College Street, Calcutta 700073

GUJARATI

Gadyaparva, 12A Chetan Apts., Baroda
India Today (Gujarati Edition), F-14/15, Connaught Place,
  New Delhi 110001
Kankavati, Nani Chipwad, Ambaji Road, Surat.
Kumar, Kumar Kaviyalal, 1454 Raipur, Ahmedabad.

Milap, District Court Road, Bhavanagar.
Navchetan, Narayanagar, Sarkhej Road, Ahmedabad.
Parishkrit Varta, Madh Pole, Sultanpura, Baroda.
Sanskar, Dadakar Wada, Dandia Bazar, Baroda.
Sanskriti, Sandesh Building, Gheekanta, Ahmedabad.
Vi, Madh Pole, Sultanpura, Baroda.

HINDI

Dastavej, Visvanath Tiwari, Bethia Hatha, Gorakhpur, U.P.
Hans, 2/36 Ansari Road, Daryaganj, New Delhi 110002
India Today (Hindi Edition), F-14/15, Connaught Place,
    New Delhi 110001.
Indraprastha Bharati, Hindi Akademi, A-26/23 Sunlight Insurance
    Building, Asaf Ali Road, New Delhi 110002
Kathya Roop, 224, Tularam Bagh, Allahabad 211006
Madhumati, Rajasthan Sahitya Akademi, Udaipur
Pahal, 763 Agarwal Colony, Jabalpur, M.P.
Pratipaksh, 6/105, Kaushalya Park, Hauz Khas, New Delhi 110016
Purugrah, Bharat Bhawan, Bhopal, M.P.
Samkaleen Bharatiya Sahitya, Sahitya Akademi, Rabindra Bhavan,
    Copernicus Marg, New Delhi 110 001.
Sapthahik Hindustan, Hindustan Times House, Kasturba Gandhi Marg,
    New Delhi 110 002
Sukshatkar, Madhya Pradesh Sahitya Kala Parishad, Professors' Colony,
    Bhopal, M.P.

KANNADA

Granthaloka, 92, Rangaswamy Temple Street, Bangalore 560002
Lankesh Patrike, Bangalore, Karnataka 560002
Mayura, 16 Mahatma Gandhi Road, P.O. Box 331,
    Bangalore 560001
Nanda Deep, CTS No 504/B, Club Road, Hubli
Sudha, Bangalore, Karnataka
Shankramana, Dharwar, Karnataka 580001
Tushara, Manipal, Karnataka 576119

MALAYALAM

Bhasha Poshini, Malayala Manorama Co. Ltd., Kottayam 686001.
India Today (Malayalam Edition), A1/A2 Second Floor Gemini Parsn
   Commercial Complex, Kodambakkam High Road, Madras 600006.
Janayugam Janayugam Publications Ltd., Kodappakada, Kollam 1.
Kairalisudha, Thrissur.
Kalakaumudi, Kalakaumudi Publications Pvt. Ltd., Pettah,
   Thiruvananthapuram 695024
Katha, Kaumudi Building, Pettah, Thiruvananthapuram 695024
Kerala Kaumudi, Post Box 77, Trivandrum
Kumkumam, Lakshminada, Kollam 691001.
Malayalaya Manorama, Malayala Manorama Co. Ltd., P.B. 26,
   Kottayam 1.
Manorajyam, Manorajyam Press, T.B. Junction, Kottayam 686001.
Mathrubhoomi, Cherootty Road, Calicut 673001

MARATI

Anushtubh, Maharastra Sahitya Parishad, Tilak Road, Pune 411030.
Gulmohar, S.K. Belwalkar Punlishing Co., 1347 Sadashivpet, Kamalabai
   Bhat Marg, Pune 411030.
Mouj, Khatanwadi, Girgaon, Bombay 400004.
Sreekar, Shewalkar Estate, Gandhi Nagar, N, Ambazari Road,
   Nagpur 440010.
Stree Vatsa, Media Pvt. Ltd., Nagpur Business Centre, 8 Vardha Rd.,
   Nagpur 12

ORIYA

Arya, Sudha Aparajita Mohapatra, Tulsipur, Cuttack 8
Asana, Institute of Oriya Studies, Saraswat Nilanj, Cuttack 10
Konarak, Orissa Sahitya Academi, Museum Building, Bhuvaneshwar 14
Orissa Review, Information and Public Relations Department,
   Goverrment of Orissa, Bhuvaneshwar 1
Shatadru, Qr. No 9/3D, Unit 9 Flats, Bhuvaneshwar 5.
Sucharita, address not known

TAMIL

Amudha Surabhi, 123 Angappa Naicken St. Madras 600001.
Ananda Vikatan, Visan Publications Pvt. Ltd., 151, Mount Road, Madras 600002.
Dinamani Kadir, Express Estate, Mount Road, Madras 600002.
India Today (Tamil Edition), A1/A2 Second Floor Gemini Parsn Commercial Complex, Kodambakkam High Road, Madras 600006.
Kalaimagal, 1, Sanskrit College Street, Madras 60004
Kalki, Barastham Publications, 84/1-6, Race Course Road, Guindy, Madras 2.
Kanaiyazhi, 149, Bells Road, Madras 600024.
Kumudam, 83, Purasawakkam High Road, Madras 600010.
Ponmagal, 6-A, Karnekar Street, Vadapalani, Madras 600026.
Subhamangala, 10 Dr Appadurai Street, Seethammal Colony, Madras 600018

TELUGU

Andhra Jyothi Sachitra Vara Patrika, Chetla Bazar, Vijayawada 520002.
Andhra Patrika, 14/4/21, Mallikarjunar Street, Gandhinagar, Vijayawada 2.
Andhra Prabha Illustrated Weekly, Andhraprabha Pvt. Ltd., Express Centre Domal Guda, Hyderabad 500029.
India Today (Telugu Edition), A1/A2 Second FloorGemini Parsn Commercial Complex, Kodambakkam High Road, Madras 600006.
Pragathi Sachitra Vara Patrika, Visalandhra Buildings, Machavaram Post, Vijayawada 520001.
Racchabanda, Jammikunta, Tg. Huzurabad, Dist. Karimnagar 505001.
Swati, Prakasam Road, Governorpet, Vijayawada 520001.

URDU

Aaj, B-140, Section 11 B, North Karachi Township, Karachi, Pakistan.
Aajkal, Publication Division, Patiala House, New Delhi.
Asri Adab, D-7 Model Town, Delhi 110009
Kitab Numa, Maktaba Jamia Ltd., Jamia Nagar, New Delhi 110025.

Naya Daur, Post Box No. 146, Lucknow.
Saughat, 84 III Main Road, Defence Colony, Indira Nagar,
Bangalore 560038.
Shabkhoon, 313 Rani Mandi, Allahabad.
Shair, Muktaba Qasr-ul-Adab, Bombay Central Post Office,
Post Box No. 4526, Bombay 400008
Zehn-e-Jadeed, Post Box No. 7042, New Delhi 110002

N.B. This is by no means an exhaustive list of all the contemporary journals, periodicals, newspapers little magazines and anthologies which give space to the short story. For the most part, these names represent the range of publications consulted by the nominating editors in their respective languages. However, since the compilation of a far more detailed list of publications is one of KATHA VILASAM's objectives, we would welcome any additional information on the subject, particularly with respect to languages not covered in this volume.

KATHA VILASAM, a story research and resource centre is a wing of KATHA, a registered nonprofit socity devoted to creative communication. We are interested in fostering and applauding short fiction being written in the various Indian languages, and translations from one Indian language into another. Katha Vilasam also strives to develop the skills of translation. In a limited way, Katha Vilasam acts as literay agents for good translations. Katha Vilasam works in the area of literacy, believing that the best that is being written in the country should be available for the neoliterate also. A range of books for neoliterates which are versions of quality stories from the various Indian languages, retold in Hindi, are available from us. We also publish, *Katha Vachak,* a Hindi monthly story tabloid for the neoliterate.

Our address: KATHA, P.O. Box 326, G.P.O. New Delhi 110001.

The Activity MAgazine for Spreading Health Awareness!
is brought out every quarter in English and Hindi by Katha,
a registered, non-profit society devoted to creative communication.

Children love TAMASHA! because it is filled with —

- FUN Stories   • EXCITING Facts!
- INNOVATIVE Games and Puzzles

'. . . From general knowledge to games, ecology to
education and health, every subject is treated with the
right balance of information and diversion . . .'
    — Sakuntala Narasimhan in *Sunday Herald*

'. . . with extremely attractive pictures, *Tamasha!* is sure
to make an impact on the child reader . . . Definitely a
must for those who are in the field of rural
communication . . .' — Vijaya Ghose in *Book Review*

'. . . very educative, creative.'
    — W A F Hopper, The Church of South India Coun-
cil for Education

'An excellent publication: imaginative, attractive and
useful.' — J Peter Greaves, UNICEF, New York, USA.

For more information, write to the Editor, *Tamasha!* Post
Box No. 326, GPO, New Delhi - 110001

Annual Subscription — Rs. 40/-
(inclusive of postage)

SUBSCRIBE NOW !